SUSAN ABULHAWA was born to refugees of the Six Day War of 1967, when her family's land was seized and Israel captured what remained of Palestine, including Jerusalem. She moved to the USA as a teenager, graduated in biomedical science and established a career in medical science. In July 2001, Susan Abulhawa founded Playgrounds for Palestine, a children's organisation dedicated to upholding the Right to Play for Palestinian children. *Mornings in Jenin* is her first novel and is being published in nineteen countries. She lives in Pennsylvania with her daughter.

MORNINGS IN JENIN

SUSAN ABULHAWA

BLOOMSBURY

LONDON · BERLIN · NEW YORK · SYDNEY

First published in Great Britain 2010
This paperback edition published 2011

This novel was published, in a different form, by Journey Publications in 2006, under the title *The Scar of David*. The text of *Mornings in Jenin* has been fully revised and edited.

Copyright © 2010 by Susan Abulhawa

The moral right of the author has been asserted

Bloomsbury Publishing, London, Berlin, New York and Sydney

50 Bedford Square, London WC1B 3DP

A CIP catalogue record for this book is available from the British Library

ISBN 978 1 4088 0948 8
Export ISBN 978 1 4088 1355 3

10 9 8 7

Typeset by Hewer Text UK Ltd, Edinburgh
Printed in Great Britain by Clays Ltd, St Ives plc

www.bloomsbury.com/susanabulhawa

For Natalie,

and for Seif

CONTENTS

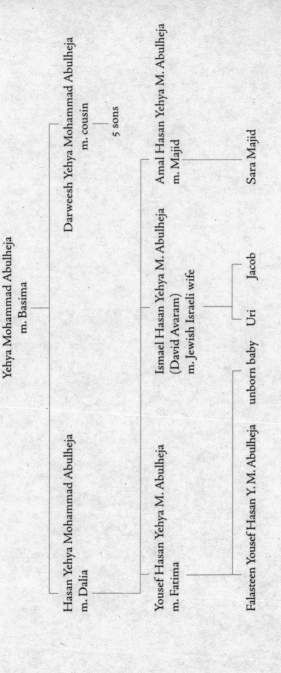

Yehya Mohammad Abulheja
m. Basima

Darweesh Yehya Mohammad Abulheja
m. cousin

5 sons

Amal Hasan Yehya M. Abulheja
m. Majid

Sara Majid

Hasan Yehya Mohammad Abulheja
m. Dalia

Yousef Hasan Yehya M. Abulheja
m. Fatima

Ismael Hasan Yehya M. Abulheja
(David Avaram)
m. Jewish Israeli wife

Uri   Jacob

Falasteen Yousef Hasan Y. M. Abulheja

unborn baby

AMAL WANTED A CLOSER look into the soldier's eyes, but the muzzle of his automatic rifle, pressed against her forehead, would not allow it. Still, she was close enough to see that he wore contacts. She imagined the soldier leaning into a mirror to insert the lenses in his eyes before getting dressed to kill. *Strange*, she thought, *the things you think about in the district between life and death.*

She wondered if officials might express regret for the "accidental" killing of her, an American citizen. Or if her life would merely culminate in the dander of "collateral damage."

A lone bead of sweat traveled from the soldier's brow down the side of his face. He blinked hard. Her stare made him uneasy. He had killed before, but never while looking his victim in the eyes. Amal saw that, and she felt his troubled soul amid the carnage around them.

Strange, again, *I am unafraid of death.* Perhaps because she knew, from the soldier's blink, that she would live.

She closed her eyes, reborn, the cold steel still pushing against her forehead. The petitions of memory pulled her back, and still back, to a home she had never known.

I.

EL NAKBA
(the catastrophe)

ONE

The Harvest
1941

I N A DISTANT TIME, before history marched over the hills and shattered present and future, before wind grabbed the land at one corner and shook it of its name and character, before Amal was born, a small village east of Haifa lived quietly on figs and olives, open frontiers and sunshine.

It was still dark, only the babies sleeping, when the villagers of Ein Hod prepared to perform the morning salat, the first of five daily prayers. The moon hung low, like a buckle fastening earth and sky, just a sliver of promise shy of being full. Waking limbs stretched, water splashed away sleep, hopeful eyes widened. Wudu, the ritual cleansing before salat, sent murmurs of the shehadeh into the morning fog, as hundreds of whispers proclaimed the oneness of Allah and service to his prophet Mohammad. Today they prayed outdoors and with particular reverence because it was the start of the olive harvest. Best to climb the rocky hills with a clean conscience on such an important occasion.

Thus and so, by the predawn orchestra of small lives, crickets and stirring birds—and soon, roosters—the villagers cast moon shadows from their prayer rugs. Most simply asked for forgiveness of their sins, some prayed an extra rukaa. In one way or another, each said, "My Lord Allah, let Your will be done on this day. My submission and gratitude is Yours," before setting off westward toward the groves, stepping high to avoid the snags of cactus.

Every November, the harvest week brought renewed vigor to Ein Hod, and Yehya, Abu Hasan, could feel it in his bones. He left the house early with his boys, coaxing them with his annual hope of getting a head start on the neighbors. But the neighbors had similar ideas and the harvest always began around five A.M.

Yehya turned sheepishly to his wife, Basima, who balanced the basket of tarps and blankets on her head, and whispered, "Um Hasan, next year, let's get up before them. I just want to get an hour start over Salem, that toothless old bugger. Just one hour."

Basima rolled her eyes. Her husband revived that brilliant idea every year.

As the dark sky gave way to light, the sounds of reaping that noble fruit rose from the sun-bleached hills of Palestine. The thumps of farmers' sticks striking branches, the shuddering of the leaves, the plop of fruit falling onto the old tarps and blankets that had been laid beneath the trees. As they toiled, women sang the ballads of centuries past and small children played and were chided by their mothers when they got in the way.

Yehya paused to massage a crick in his neck. *It's nearly noon*, he thought, noting the sun's approach to zenith. Sweat-drenched, Yehya stood on his land, a sturdy man with a black and white kaffiyeh swathing his head, the hem of his robe tucked in his waist sash in the way of the fellaheen. He surveyed the splendor around him. Mossy green grass cascaded down those hills, over the rocks, around and up the trees. The sanasil barriers, some of which he had helped his grandfather repair, spiraled up the hills. Yehya turned to watch Hasan and Darweesh, their chest muscles heaving beneath their robes with every swing of their sticks to knock the olives loose. *My boys!* Pride swelled Yehya's heart. *Hasan is growing strong despite his difficult lungs. Thanks be to Allah.*

The sons worked on opposite sides of each tree as their mother trailed them, hauling away blankets of fresh olives to be pressed later that day. Yehya could see Salem harvesting his yield in the adjacent grove. *Toothless old bugger.* Yehya smiled, though Salem was younger than he. In truth, his neighbor had always a quality of wisdom and a grandfatherly patience that gave of itself from a face mapped by many years of carving olive wood outdoors. He had become Haj Salem after his pilgrimage to Mecca, and the new title bestowed him with age beyond that of Yehya. By evening, the two friends would be smoking hookahs together, arguing over who had worked hardest and whose sons were strongest. "You're going to hell for lying like that, old man," Yehya would say, bringing the pipe to his lips.

"Old man? You're older than me, you geezer," Salem would say.

"At least I still have all my teeth."

"Okay. Get out the board so I can prove once again who's better."

"You're on, you lyin', toothless, feeble son of your father."

Games of backgammon over bubbling hookahs would settle this annual argument and they would stubbornly play until their wives had sent for them several times.

Satisfied by the morning's pace, Yehya performed the thohr salat and sat on the blanket where Basima had arranged the lentils and makloobeh with lamb and yogurt sauce. Nearby, she set another meal for the migrant helpers, who gratefully accepted the offering.

"Lunch!" she called to Hasan and Darweesh, who had just completed their second salat of the day.

Seated around the steaming tray of rice and smaller plates of sauces and pickles, the family waited for Yehya to break the bread in the name of Allah. "Bismillah arrahman arraheem," he began, and the boys followed, hungrily reaching for the rice to ball it into bites with yogurt.

"Yumma, nobody is as good a cook as you!" Darweesh the flatterer knew how to assure Basima's favor.

"Allah bless you, son." She grinned and moved a tender piece of meat to his side of the rice tray.

"What about me?" Hasan protested.

Darweesh leaned to his older brother's ear, teasing, "You aren't as good with the ladies."

"Here you are, darling." Basima tore off another piece of good meat for Hasan.

The meal was over quickly without the usual lingering over halaw and coffee. There was more work to be done. Basima had been filling her large baskets, which the helpers would carry to the olive press. Each of her boys had to press his share of olives the day of their harvest or else the oil might have a rancid taste.

But before heading back, a prayer was offered.

"First, let us give thanks for Allah's bounty." Yehya issued his command, pulling an old Quran from the pocket of his dishdashe. The holy Book had belonged to his grandfather, who had nurtured these groves before him. Although Yehya could not read, he liked to look at the pretty calligraphy while he recited surahs from memory. The boys bowed, impatiently listening to their father sing Quranic verses, then raced down the hill when granted their father's permission to head for the press.

Basima hoisted a basket of olives onto her head, lifted in each hand a woven bag full of dishes and leftover food, and proceeded down the hill with other women who balanced urns and belongings on their heads in plumb uprightness. "Allah be with you, Um Hasan," Yehya called to his wife.

"And you, Abu Hasan," she called back. "Don't be long."

Alone now, Yehya leaned into the breeze, blew gently into the mouthpiece of his nye, and felt the music emerge from the tiny holes beneath his fingertips. His grandfather had taught him to play that ancient flute and its melodies gave Yehya a sense of his ancestors, the countless harvests, the land, the sun, time, love, and all that was good. As always, at the first note, Yehya raised his brows over closed eyelids, as if perpetually surprised by what majesty his simple hand-carved nye could make from his breath.

Several weeks after the harvest, Yehya's old truck was loaded. There was some oil, but mostly almonds, figs, a variety of citrus, and vegetables. Hasan put the grapes on top so they would not be crushed.

"You know I'd rather you not go all the way to Jerusalem," Yehya said to Hasan. "Tulkarem is only a few kilometers away and gasoline is expensive. Even Haifa is closer, and their markets are just as good. And you never know what son-of-a-dog Zionist is hiding in the bushes or what British bastard is going to stop you. Why make the trip?" But the father already knew why. "You taking this long ride to meet up with Ari?"

"Yaba, I gave him my word that I was coming," Hasan answered his father, somewhat pleadingly.

"Well, you're a man now. Watch yourself on the road. Be sure to give your aunt whatever she needs from your cart and tell her we want her to visit soon," Yehya said, then called to the driver, who was well known to everyone and whose features asserted their common lineage. "Drive in the protection of Allah, son."

"Allah give you long life, Ammo Yehya."

Hasan kissed his father's hand, then his forehead, reverent gestures that filled Yehya with love and pride.

"Allah smile on you and protect you for all your days, son," he said as Hasan clambered into the back of the truck.

As they drove away, Darweesh cantered alongside on Ganoosh, his beloved Arabian steed. "Let's race. I'll give you an hour head start since the truck is weighed down," he challenged Hasan.

"Go race the wind, Darweesh. That's more up to your speed than this old clunker. Go on, I'll meet you in Jerusalem at Amto Salma's house."

Hasan watched his younger brother fly away bareback, the hatta tight around his head, its loose ends grabbing at the wind behind him. Darweesh was the best rider for miles around, maybe the best in the country, and Ganoosh was the fastest horse Hasan had ever seen.

Along the dusty road, the land rose in sylvan silence, charmed with the scents of citrus blooms and wild camphires. Hasan opened the pouch that his mother filled each day, pinched off a glob of her sticky concoction, and raised it to his nose. He breathed it in as deeply as his asthmatic lungs would allow. Oxygen diffused through his veins as he opened one of the secret books Mrs. Perlstein, Ari's mother, had instructed him to study.

TWO

Ari Perlstein

1941

ARI WAS WAITING BY the Damascus Gate, where the boys had first met four years earlier. He was the son of a German professor who had fled Nazism early and settled in Jerusalem, where his family rented a small home from a prominent Palestinian.

The two boys had become friends in 1937 behind the pushcarts of fresh fruits, vegetables, and dented cans of oil in Babel Amond market, where Hasan had sat reading a book of Arabic poems. The small Jewish boy with large eyes and an unsure smile had started toward Hasan. He moved with a limp, the legacy of a badly healed leg and the Brown Shirt who had broken it. He had bought a large red tomato, pulled out a pocketknife, and cut it, keeping half and offering the rest to Hasan.

"Ana ismi Ari. Ari Perlstein," the boy had said.

Intrigued, Hasan had taken the tomato.

"Goo day sa! Shalom!" Hasan had tried the only non-Arabic words he knew and motioned for the boy to sit.

Though Ari could improvise some Arabic, neither spoke the other's language. But they quickly found commonality in their mutual sense of inadequacy.

"Ana ismi Hasan. Hasan Yehya Abulheja."

"Salam alaykom," Ari had replied. "What book are you reading?" he had asked in German, pointing.

"Book." *English.* "Dis, book."

"Yes." *English.* "Kitab." *Book, Arabic.* "Yes." They had laughed and eaten more tomato.

Thus a friendship had been born in the shadow of Nazism in Europe and in the growing divide between Arab and Jew at home, and it had been consolidated in the innocence of their twelve years, the poetic solitude of books, and their disinterest in politics.

Decades after war had divided the two friends, Hasan told his youngest child, a little girl named Amal, about his boyhood friend. "He was like a brother," Hasan said, closing a book that had been given to him by Ari in the autumn of their boyhood.

Though Hasan would experience a colossal physical growth, at twelve he was a sickly boy whose lungs hissed with every breath. The labor of his breathing pushed him to the sidelines of the strict confederacies of boys and their rough play. Likewise, Ari's limp invited the relentless mockery of his classmates. Both possessed an air of recoil that recognized itself in the other, and each, at a young age and in his own world and language, had found refuge in the pages of poets, essayists, and philosophers.

What had been a bothersome occasional travel to Jerusalem became a welcome weekly trip, for Hasan would find Ari waiting there and they would pass the hours teaching each other the words in Arabic, German, and English for "apple," "orange," "olive." "The onions are one piaster the pound, ma'am," they practiced. From behind the cart's rows of fruit and vegetables, they privately poked fun at the Arab city boys, with their affected speech and fancy clothes that were little more than displays of servile admiration for the British.

Ari even began to wear traditional Arab garb on weekends and often returned to Ein Hod with Hasan. Immersed in the melodies of Arabic speech and song and the flavors of Arabic food and drink, Ari gained a respectable command of his friend's language and culture, which in no small measure would contribute to his tenured professorship at Hebrew University decades later. Similarly, Hasan learned to speak German, to read haltingly some of the English volumes in Dr. Perlstein's library, and to appreciate the traditions of Judaism.

Mrs. Perlstein loved Hasan and was grateful for his friendship with her son, and Basima received Ari with similar motherly enthusiasm. Although they never met face-to-face, the two women came to know one another through their sons and each would send the other's boy home loaded with food and special treats, a ritual that Hasan and Ari grudgingly endured.

At thirteen, a year before Hasan's formal schooling was to end, he asked his father's permission to study with Ari in Jerusalem. Fearful that further education would take his son away from the land he was destined to inherit and farm, Yehya forbade it.

"Books will do nothing but come between you and the land. There will be no school with Ari and that is all I will say on the matter." Yehya was certain he made the right decision. But years later, Yehya would reproach himself with deep consternation and regret for denying what Hasan had dearly wanted. For this decision, one day Yehya would beg his son's forgiveness as they all camped at the mercy of the weather, not far from the home to which they could never return. Yehya, a withering refugee in the unfamiliar dilapidation of exile, would weep on Hasan's forgiving shoulders. "Forgive me, son. I cannot forgive myself," Yehya would cry. And it was for the same decision and subsequent regret and heartbreak that Hasan would resolve, with determined hard labor and its pittance pay, that his children would receive an education. For this decision, Hasan would tell his little girl, Amal, many years later, "Habibti, we have nothing but education now. Promise me you'll take it with all the force you have." And his little girl would promise the father she adored.

Although Hasan was denied the privilege of formal schooling beyond eighth grade, he received superior tutoring from Mrs. Perlstein, who sent her eager young student home every week loaded with books, lessons, and homework. The private lessons started as a scheme between Basima and Mrs. Perlstein to lift Hasan from his dejection in the months after Yehya issued his final word on the matter of education.

"Hey, brother!" The young men embraced, locked hands, and kissed each other on each cheek, the Arab way. They unloaded the truck, setting the driver up with other street vendors. Weaving through narrow cobblestone paths of the Old City, the friends headed for their usual treat before walking to Ari's house. From Babel Amoud, they walked toward el Qiyameh. The aromas of earthen jars, molasses, and assorted oils drifted from shops as sidewalk vendors called to passersby to stop and sample. They turned on Khan el Zeit, their heads brushing against leathers and silks hanging from store walls. A few more steps and they entered el Mahfouz café.

"Two heads of honey apple," Hasan called to the attendant.

"This can't be good for your lungs, Hasan," Ari warned him. "Does Uncle Yehya know you smoke?"

"Of course not!"

At the Perlsteins', Hasan delivered the two trays of halaw and knafe.

"The usual from Mother," he said in German.

"Thank you," Mrs. Perlstein said, taking the sweets.

She was a reserved, long-limbed woman and Hasan thought her appearance gave no hint of her expansive kindness. His instinct, when he saw her, was to look for her family heirloom, pinned on her chest, always. *One, two, three, four . . . eighteen.* He developed a habit of counting the small pearls of her brooch while she inspected his homework.

Over the years, Hasan proved himself an assiduous pupil and quick study. The mentorship with Mrs. Perlstein continued until he "graduated" with Ari in 1943, the year when the two young men drifted apart for a while, as Ari developed a small group of friends at his school and Hasan became smitten with a young Bedouin girl named Dalia, who had stolen Ganoosh, his brother's horse.

THREE
The No-Good Bedouin Girl
1940–1948

UNLIKE MARRIAGES OF THEIR time, arranged at birth and kept within the family clan, Hasan's union with Dalia was born of forbidden love. He was a descendant of the original founders of Ein Hod and heir to great stretches of cultivated land, orchards, and five impressive olive groves. Dalia, on the other hand, was the daughter of a Bedouin whose tribe came to work in the village every year during the harvest and eventually settled there.

The youngest of twelve sisters, Dalia was willful and paid little mind to convention. Despite living at the pitiless end of her father's belt, she did not always remember to wear the traditional coverings of hijab and let the wind roam her hair. Unlike proper girls, she'd hike up her dress to chase a lizard, soiling the bright Bedouin designs of her thobe with mud stains and cactus thorns. Often, she would forget to empty her pouch of strange new bugs and beetles collected that day, for which her mother would beat her. But the force of nature within her compelled her back to her curious ways. She relished her time with her six- and eight-legged little secrets until she had a four-legged one, a horse named Ganoosh.

Its young master, a boy whom she knew to be Darweesh, son of Yehya Abulheja, offered her a ride when he happened to see her walking the hills. She couldn't accept a ride with a boy. She'd be beaten if her father learned of it.

"No." She was as emphatic as an eleven-year-old can be, but as soon as she answered, her face relaxed into "maybe." Darweesh spoke softly, "I am happy just to walk in front and I swear on my honor I will not look back at you on the horse." He seemed trustworthy and there was no one around for miles among the hills. She looked around at the quiet expanse of rolling land. Her heart was pure. "How do I get on?"

"Watch me first, then try it when I turn my back," Darweesh said. Ganoosh allowed the petite figure to mount his back and then he walked slowly on. Suddenly she was overcome with fear of being caught with a boy and his horse. She demanded to stop, and as soon as she had dismounted she ran off.

Weeks later she returned to the spot to wait for her magnificent four-legged secret, until it arrived with Darweesh and she experienced the magic again. The secret lasted more than two years and in that time, Dalia learned to ride alone. Darweesh would have done anything she asked, if only she had asked. In all that time, they never exchanged a word except on that first day. When Darweesh saw her coming, he would avert his eyes to show no disrespect, turn his back to her, and hold Ganoosh steady while she hitched up her thobe, pants underneath, mounted, and rode away. Darweesh would wait until she returned and go through the same ritual of modesty in reverse.

To the villagers, Dalia was like a wild gypsy, born of Bedouin poetry and colors instead of flesh and blood. Some thought the child had an aspect of the devil and convinced Dalia's mother to bring a sheikh to read Quranic verses over her. Most assumed the girl would simply grow out of her ways. Eventually, folks agreed that Dalia ought to be "broken." Almost fourteen now, she needed to be disabused of her childish carelessness.

"Break her, beat her, teach her a lesson," another Bedouin woman told her mother. "Look at her eat that orange! What shame on her family. All the boys are staring at her." Such was the village scorn of Dalia. The jingle of her ankle bracelets bothered the women. More, they hated Dalia's immunity to their acrimony. The unapologetic force that shone from her skin and floated off her hair reminded them of an irretrievable old bliss that they had willingly discarded. Dalia's vulgar carelessness was sexual, more so because she didn't know it.

Basima, Um Hasan, thought Dalia a godless thief with no shame, after Dalia had "stolen" her son Darweesh's horse for a covert respite from the backbreaking monotony of the olive harvest. No one would have been the wiser had Dalia not fallen and broken her ankle, sparking a scandal that caught the attention of Hasan. The whole village was abuzz. Darweesh thought of ways to defend Dalia, but he knew his involvement would bring a far greater punishment to bear on her.

Disgraced, Dalia's father vowed to crush his youngest daughter's insolence once and for all. To restore his honor, he tied Dalia to a chair in the center of town and put a hot iron to the hand she was forced to admit had been the one that had stolen the horse.

"This one? Put it out where I can burn it good," the father said, seething, as Dalia offered her right palm. "And if you scream, I'll burn the other hand," he added, turning to the crowd of onlookers for approval.

Dalia made no sound as the burning metal seared the skin of her right palm. The crowd gasped. "How cruel the Bedouins are," said a woman, and some people implored Dalia's father to stop in the name of Allah, to have mercy because Allah is Merciful. *Al Rahma.* But a man must be the ruler of his home. "My honor shall have no blemish. Step back, this is my right," the Bedouin demanded. It was his right. *La hawla wala quwatta ella billah.*

Dalia pulled the pain inward, the mean odor of burned flesh scorching the life at her core. Her complicity with nature, the intimacy of her hair with the wind, the jangling of her coin ankle bracelets, the sweet aroma of her sweat when she toiled, the gypsy colors of her—all of it that day became an ash heap in the center of town beneath the deep blue sky. Had she screamed, perhaps the fire would not have reached so deeply into her. But she did not. She spied a rabbit and transfixed them both in an impossible stare. She gripped the torture in her hand and held it there with a clench of her jaw as tears streaked her face. For the rest of her life, Dalia would have the unconscious habit of rubbing the tips of the fingers of her right hand back and forth on their palm while she gritted her teeth, giving the impression that she held something in her grip that was living and trying to get out.

* * *

Basima was unnerved by the Bedouin girl's stoicism and she wanted no part of "that family," for she was not unaware of Hasan's watchful eyes that followed the young Dalia as she worked at her daily chores in the village and in the fields.

To Basima, Dalia was a "no-good Bedouin" who would bring all manner of trouble to their peaceful village. Indeed, her worst fears were confirmed when her son, the young Hasan Yehya Abulheja, was unable to resist the audacity of Dalia's beauty and the wildness of her spirit and resolved to marry her.

With the determination that would characterize Hasan all his life, and with the reluctant blessing of his father, Hasan faced his mother with his decision.

"Yumma, marriage is not a sin," Hasan said, trying a conciliatory approach.

"No, no, no, no, no!" Basima was wild. In the drama of scandal, she flailed her arms, tugged at her thobe with pleas to Allah, beat her chest, and slapped her own face. She bemoaned the humiliation and rued the day "that Bedouin" ever stepped foot in Ein Hod. Her embarrassment would ripen to shame when she would be obliged to deliver the news of her son's rebellion and his refusal of his own cousin, who was already betrothed to him.

"Ya Abu Hasan, what will people say of us?" she pleaded with her husband.

Yehya tried to reason with his wife. "Um Hasan, let it be. He's a man now. We cannot force him."

But she went on as if her husband had not spoken. "That our word is not honorable? That we promise a girl marriage to our son, then allow him to disobey us? What fault has my innocent niece committed to be rejected for a filthy Bedouin thief?"

"This is Allah's will. Let it be, woman! The country is being turned upside down by Zionists and you're in a bad temper because your son wants to marry a pretty girl you don't like.

Don't you hear the news every day? Zionists killing British and Palestinians every cursed day? They're getting rid of the British so they can get rid of us and everybody's too stupid to see it or do anything about it." Yehya grabbed his cane in one hand, his nye in the other, and walked outside in disgust of his fears, which had been intensifying with the near daily BBC reports of terrorism by the increasingly militarized Zionist gangs.

On the marble steps of their home, Yehya exhaled through his precious nye, moved his fingers, and raised his brow at the first sound. He played for his trees, to resurrect simplicity and peace.

"Stop that!" Basima marched onto the portico Yehya had designed and tiled himself. She was furious.

"One of these days I'm going to break that thing," Basima growled softly, so the neighbors wouldn't hear, and stomped away, fearful that she had crossed a line. She was still muttering her displeasure as she walked across the Persian rugs of her foyer, through the tiled grand arches, into the family room, where she struggled onto her knees to sit briefly on the floor cushion. Years earlier, Yehya had wanted to buy sofas, like the British had, but Basima had refused; and now she thought sofas might be better. Restless, she unfolded her prayer mat to submit to Allah. After she had prayed two rukaas, she pulled herself up, walking over more Persian rugs scattered over the marble floor into the kitchen, where she looked around at Yehya's blue and green tile design. *He's stubborn, but he sure is an artist*, she thought. *Ya, Yehya, how can you agree to this marriage!*

No amount of Basima's pleading or cursing could dissuade her son. Only Darweesh understood the resolve with which Hasan defied their mother, for he too loved Dalia. And when the family went to ask for Dalia's hand in marriage, Darweesh wept in the company of his beloved Ganoosh and Fatooma, his other Arabian horse and Ganoosh's mate that had a distinctive white streak between her eyes.

Dalia's father accepted with a great sense of relief from the burden of his youngest daughter, and two days later, as was the custom, he received her dowry. On that day, Dalia watched through the little holes in the privacy mesh of her window as a convoy of men brought money and gold to her father. She was less moved by the impressive dowry than by the sight of Darweesh walking among those men.

She had no say in the matter, though the idea of becoming an aroosa appealed to her, in the way dressing up like an adult appeals to little girls—but she wished it had been for Darweesh.

On the day of Dalia's wedding her female relatives—mother, aunts, married sisters and cousins—scrubbed and buffed every inch of her body. Aeeda was repeatedly smeared on and snatched off her legs, thighs, arms, belly, and buttocks. Dalia stretched her neck each time to survey the tiny forests of black hair extracted with every yank that seemed to send electric currents through her skin. The tender flesh between her legs was most painful. "It's okay, daughter," the mother said as she spread her daughter's legs wide. *Bismillah arrahman arraheem.* With the confidence and dexterity of a midwife, Dalia's mother drew away all of her daughter's recent pubic hair (of which Dalia had been so proud) in a single swipe of the aeeda that made Dalia spring to her feet with pain. The women laughed goodheartedly. "Come, daughter. Come back to the world of women." And when an aunt noticed the moisture on Dalia's thighs, she exclaimed to her sister, "Looks like your daughter will make a fine wife." They laughed again as Dalia was an obedient spectator to her own transformation.

She watched in the mirror as lines of kohl shaped her eyes with seduction and sketched on her face the age and maturity that she lacked. She was an aroosa, the pretty center of her culture, and all the little girls watched her as she had watched brides before her being prepared for marriage.

Heavy with glowing gifts hung around her neck and across her brow and dangling from her wrists, ankles, and ears, fourteen-year-old Dalia married Hasan Yehya Abulheja in a grand ceremony. It was a celebration befitting the vindication of Dalia's father, the virulent bitterness of Basima, and the melancholy heart of Darweesh.

Bejeweled with half her weight in gold, the small bride inhabited her wedding quietly, rubbing her hand unceasingly, her jaw motionless on tight hinges, even when kissed by well-wishers.

Before joining the women, the men celebrated separately, sacrificing a lamb, dancing, and making joy with song and music. With a wounded heart, Darweesh led a dabke for his brother and toasted the groom with love, a secret sadness, and acceptance of Allah's will.

"Inshalla, you're next, brother," Hasan said sincerely, hugging Darweesh.

"Inshalla." God willing.

Within ten months of the wedding, Dalia ingratiated herself with the village by bearing a son, whom she named Yousef. Thenceforth, from the age of fifteen, Dalia was respectfully called "Um Yousef" and Hasan "Abu Yousef."

Even before Yousef was born, Basima had softened toward Dalia. She could not help being impressed by the tenacity with which Dalia tackled her chores, the skill with which she helped her own mother deliver babies in the village, or the delight of her new husband in her company. Furthermore, the families had agreed that Darweesh would marry the niece who had been abandoned by Hasan, and thus Basima's pride was saved.

Dalia's inexperience compelled the maternal instincts of her mother-in-law to induct her Bedouin daughter into the world of motherhood, teaching her the rhythms of breastfeeding and the treatments for colic. She instructed her in the secrets to regain the body's firmness and in tricks to keep the interest of her husband after childbirth.

"It all goes eventually—the breasts, thighs, they just fall," Basima said. "But olive oil is the trick." Basima's narrowing eyes glimmered with conspiracy as she moved closer and began describing the beauty concoctions she had discovered herself. "These are a woman's secrets that I'll only pass to you and, inshalla, Darweesh's wife, since it wasn't in Allah's plan for me to bear daughters."

Basima led Dalia through her herb garden, revealing the uses of various plants. She was giddy, excited to have a female heir to her empire of enchanted herbs. She had already taught Dalia how to prepare Hasan's chest medicine. "However, for beauty, olive oil is the main ingredient," she whispered. "Crush mint and basil in the oil and rub it over your body to keep the skin firm, and on your scalp to put a shine in your hair."

During times like these, Basima and Dalia learned to love each other, and slowly they became bound in a maternal allegiance and affection the likes of which neither had known before.

Ten months after Yousef was born, Dalia gave birth to a stillborn child, for which she suffered a feverish grief, cloistering herself in lockjawed solitude. An ungenerous village woman, wanting to curry favor with Basima, took the opportunity of that tragedy to tout Dalia's misfortune as proof of her unworthiness. "I'm not surprised. Bedouins are known to have their hands in black magic. How else could a girl like Dalia have gotten a man like Hasan to marry her?"

"Out of my house!" Basima threw the woman to the ground and went to Dalia. "No more mourning, my Dalia. Let's breed new roses, for a new beginning," she said, coaxing her daughter-in-law from the clench of her own jaw and ending that episode of grief.

Three years later, when the olive trees were shedding their silver-green color, a bomb exploded in the near distance. "Damn Zionists! What the hell do they want from us?" Basima screamed toward the rising smoke, her husband's fears as much hers now. Basima's anxiety knotted in her chest, in her heart, and made her head spin, legs weaken, until she fell amid her rosebushes, clutching her right shoulder. She was still alive when Dalia ran to her, just in time to hear her last words: "Binti, binti." *My daughter, my daughter*.

Following Basima's death, Dalia became the custodian of her beloved roses. She crossed them for fragrance and color as Basima had taught her, expanded the garden, and planted a gravesite bed of the white-streaked red roses, Basima's most prized. She took Yousef with her every week to the cemetery to tend to that bed of roses. And months later, when Dalia's second son, Ismael, was born, she toted him along as well in a back harness.

But as the danger of Zionist incursions intensified, she went to the cemetery alone, leaving her boys to the care of relatives and the protection of the village for a brief while each week. It was on one such occasion that an accident occurred, an injury that would mark Ismael's face forever.

Everyone in the family had his or her own grotesque version of the injury. Yousef, the only witness to the event, never spoke of it, not even when asked.

Yousef was four years old at the time, the state of Israel was not yet born, and Ismael was almost six months. He was fussy that day, crying in the same crib that was once used to sleep his father. Though it was old and worn, Basima had insisted that

Dalia use it for her children, for it had been blessed by a Syrian Sheikh, known to heal the sick and perform miracles.

When Dalia became pregnant with Ismael, Basima had taken it upon herself to reinforce the crib rails with cedarwood that she nailed herself. And she bought new lining and padding and nailed that, too, in place. As Ismael lay there crying and Dalia was making her way home from Basima's grave, Yousef gathered the baby from the fluff of the embroidered white blankets, which Basima had sewn but had not completed before she died. With the unexpected weight of the crying, kicking baby, Yousef dropped Ismael. The baby's face caught a nail on the crib as he fell and Ismael's skin was torn in a line from his cheek up around his right eye.

The physical remnant of that day was a distinctive scar that would mark Ismael's face forever, and eventually lead him to his truth.

FOUR

As They Left

1947–1948

ARI PERLSTEIN LEFT TO begin his medical studies shortly after attending Hasan and Dalia's wedding, but although each had gone his own way, the two friends did not completely lose touch with each other. When Basima died, Ari took a leave from school to mourn her passing with Hasan in Ein Hod.

The weather was clear and crisp on the afternoon when Hasan and Ari left the formalities of mourning that would go on for forty days. The hypnotic recitation of the Quran sounded from Yehya Abulheja's home and became fainter as Hasan and Ari walked farther away toward the olive groves.

"It's very bad, Hasan," Ari said. "Zionists have hordes of guns.

They've recruited an army from shiploads of Jews arriving every day. You don't know all of it, Hasan. They have armored cars and planes, even."

Hasan looked about him at the farmland he would one day inherit. *It looks like we'll have good crops this year.* The sound of a nye swirled over the trees and Hasan instinctively turned toward the cemetery, squinting to see if his father was there. No one. Just a melody, its center carved out and filled with silence, as if the nye were crying.

"Hasan, they're going to take land. They've launched a campaign across the world calling Palestine 'a land without a people.' They're going to make it a Jewish homeland."

"Father has been saying for years that this was going to happen, but it seemed so far-fetched," Hasan said.

"It's real, Hasan. You know the UN is meeting in November and everyone believes they're going to partition the land. They are very well organized and you know the British disarmed the Arabs after the revolt years ago. Some of the orthodox Jews in the city have organized an anti-Zionist campaign. They say creating a physical state of Israel is sacrilege. But powerful men in America have waged a relentless campaign to persuade Truman to recognize and support a Jewish state here." Ari was clearly shaken.

"How do you feel about it? I mean, making a Jewish state here," Hasan asked, squeezing an olive between his fingers to gauge the harvest they might have in November. *The harvest will lessen Father's despondency.*

"I don't know, Hasan." Ari lowered his eyes, sat down on a stone, and began to toy with his fingers in the dirt. "I'm a Jew. I mean, I think it's wrong. But you don't know what it was like before." Ari's voice began to tremble. "It killed us, what happened, even though we escaped. Have you ever noticed how empty my mother's eyes are? She's dead inside. Father, too. Hasan, you don't know what it was like. And now we aren't sure if we'll be safe. Father is emphatic that what they're doing is wrong and he wants no part in it. But it isn't safe for us anymore. There's talk the British are going to pull out. Then it's inevitable. They're determined that this land will become a Jewish state. But I think if the Arabs just accept it, it'll all be fine and we can live together."

Hasan sat on the ground beside Ari. "But you just said they want a 'Jewish' state."

"Yes. But I think they'll let the Arabs stay." The words came out before Ari could stop them.

"So these immigrants will let me stay on my own land?" Hasan's voice rose.

"Hasan, that isn't what I meant. You're like a brother to me. I'd do anything for you or your family. But what happened in Europe . . ." Ari's words faded into the awful images they'd both seen of death camps.

Hasan squeezed another olive, as if trying to pinch Ari's words from the air where they hung like a betrayal.

"Exactly, Ari. What Europe did. Not the Arabs. Jews have always lived here. That's why so many more are here now, isn't it? While we believed they were simply seeking refuge, poor souls just wanting to live, they've been amassing weapons to drive us from our homes." Hasan was not as angry as he sounded because he understood Ari's pain. He had read about the gas chambers, the camps, the horrors. And it was true: Mrs. Perlstein's eyes looked as if life had packed up and left them long ago. *One, two, three . . . eighteen pretty pearls.*

Anticipating the conflict that lay ahead, Hasan said, "If the Arabs get the upper hand in the Old City, go to my aunt Salma's house. You know where it is. She has a big house and you can hide there."

The Irgun, Haganah, and Stern Gang. The British called them terrorists. The Arabs called them Yahood, Jews, Zionists, Dogs,

Sons of Whores, Filth. The recent Jewish population called them Freedom Fighters, Soldiers of God, Saviors, Fathers, Brothers. By whatever name, they were heavily armed, well organized, and well trained. They set about getting rid of the non-Jewish population—first the British, through lynchings and bombings, then the Arabs, through massacres, terror, and expulsion. Their numbers were not large, but the fear they provoked made the year 1947 quake with menace, injecting it with warnings of the coming history. They came at least four times in 1947 and 1948 to Ein Hod while Palestine was still a British mandate.

The first attack occurred on the Jewish holiday of Hanukkah, December 12, 1947. An explosion rocked the air and Dalia ran screaming from the cemetery. Hasan hurried home when he heard the blast. Not finding his wife, he raced toward the cemetery and met Dalia along the way. She threw herself into his arms, crying. "The Jews are coming! The Jews are coming!"

Hasan led Dalia toward their home as plumes of smoke rose from the adjacent village, al-Tira, and the curious and frightened residents of Ein Hod gathered in the square to watch. Hasan made his way into their house and gingerly laid his wife on their bed, wiping blood from her feet.

"What happened to you?" he asked, inspecting her bleeding leg.

"I was tending to the roses over Basima," Dalia panted. "Then I heard the blast and a hand reached from hell to grab my leg. But I just kept running and they left."

Yehya came in with an anxious young Yousef in his arms. "Is everyone here? Darweesh went to check on the horses and his wife has Ismael. Where did that blood come from?"

Few things frightened little Yousef more than blood. "Mama! Mama!" he began to cry.

Dalia took her son into her arms and kissed his head. "It's just a small cut, my hero."

"I'm going to see what the hell happened," Yehya roared on his way out.

"Your ankle bracelet is gone!" Yousef exclaimed to his mother.

"Yes. I lost it."

"You won't jingle anymore! How will I know when you're coming?"

"I still have the other one"—Dalia wiggled her leg—"see?"

Yehya stormed back in. "God curse the Jews! A gang of them firebombed a house in al-Tira and fled to a truck waiting in the olive groves above the cemetery. They must have seen Dalia at the gravesite. We're lucky they didn't get her. Allah knows what they could have done."

Yehya's anger and frustration grew, his gesturing hands speaking as loudly as his voice while he paced the room. "We need some damn weapons! Where are the Arab armies while these dogs kill one town after the other? What the hell did we ever do to these sons of whores? What do they want from us?" He threw up his hands, then pushed himself down into a chair, into the defeat of waiting, leaning back, eyes to God.

"We'll put it in the wise hands of Allah," Yehya said, and rose to leave. "Hisbiya Allah wa niaamal wakeel," he whispered repeatedly to himself to ward away evil as he left.

But he did not go to help those in al-Tira. *Hisbi Allah wa niaamal wakeel.* Like the Arab countries he cursed, Yehya did not come to the aid of his fallen brethren. Secretly, he thought Ein Hod would be spared if the villagers did not get involved. He thought the sincere offering of peace with the Jews would ensure the continuity of their lives.

"Baba, are the Jews going to bomb us too?" Yousef's question pierced his father's heart.

"Allah will protect us, son. And I will protect you and your mother and brother, especially," Hasan reassured his son, looking at Dalia as he spoke. His eyes held an ocean of love for her, and that day, five years into their marriage, as Hasan held her feet in his hands and made a promise to their son, Dalia realized how deeply she loved her husband.

Less than two weeks after the incident at al-Tira, Palestinians were massacred in the nearby village of Balad-al-Shaykh. The pestilent winds of that attack blew through Ein Hod with unambiguous warning. As news of more atrocities reached Ein Hod, the villagers were gripped with dread of what was advancing their way. Anticipating more attacks, the women of Ein Hod prematurely picked the figs and grapes, drying them to make raisins and syrup, and they pickled vegetables to sustain their families through a prolonged siege by the hidden snipers.

In May 1948, the British left Palestine and Jewish refugees who had been pouring in proclaimed themselves a Jewish state, changing the name of the land from Palestine to Israel. But Ein Hod was adjacent to three villages that formed an unconquered triangle inside the new state, so the fate of Ein Hod's people was joined with that of some twenty thousand other Palestinians who still clung to their homes. They repulsed attacks and called for a truce, wanting only to live on their land as they always had. For they had endured many masters—Romans, Byzantines, Crusaders, Ottomans, British—and nationalism was inconsequential. Attachment to God, land, and family was the core of their being and that is what they defended and sought to keep.

Finally, a truce was reached and Ein Hod sighed with relief. "We will prepare a feast as a gesture of friendship and our intention to live side by side with them," Yehya decreed to the villagers on behalf of the council of elders. He gripped Haj Salem's hand with that hopeful and somber decision, an understood prayer between old friends.

* * *

Officers of the new state came in their identical tan uniforms, an impenetrable cold contradiction to the heat of July. Baking winds rustled the peppers strung up to dry, and hanging pots clanged as rifle-toting Israeli soldiers, fresh from the glory of victory, moved through the village. The sun clawed at everything it touched while the sumptuous smell of lamb and cumin struggled to seep through the anxiety.

Yousef, almost five years old now, clung to his mother's thobe, peeking from behind Dalia's hips at the feasting light-skinned foreigners in helmets. Among the soldiers was a man named Moshe, who believed himself to be on a mission from God. He ate, watching Dalia move with Ismael at her bosom and Yousef at her legs as she served the food. His eyes kept returning to her and his thoughts filtered all sound extraneous to the clinking of her remaining ankle bracelet.

After the feast, the soldiers departed in the chilling silence with which they ate, leaving behind a trail of contempt. In the shiver of that omen, the people of Ein Hod, individually and collectively, prayed for the rest of the day, putting their fate in the hands of Allah before laying down to sleeplessness. The next morning, July 24, Israel launched a massive artillery and aerial bombardment of the villages. The Associated Press reported that Israeli planes and infantry had violated the Palestinian truce by the unprovoked attack, and bombs rained as Dalia ran from shelter to shelter with terror-stricken Yousef and a screaming baby Ismael.

The village was laid to ruin and Dalia lost all but two sisters that day. The father who had burned her hand lay charred in the same town square. It had taken only hours for the world to turn upside down and for Ismael to cry himself to exhaustion. Dalia kept him clutched to her chest, afraid to lay him down despite the heavy load. Like her, other survivors roamed in a wordless haze. It was a rotten quietude, devoid of fury, love, despair, or even fear. Dalia surveyed the land, burnt, lifeless. She was aware of an itch just behind her left knee, and she concentrated on it but could not will herself to reach for it.

Hasan had been in the stables when the bombing began and ran to collect his family as soon as he could. He found Dalia frozen in the awesome silence of the aftermath. Her rigid posture, unblinking eyes, and tight clutch around Ismael frightened him. "Dalia!" he called, running to her. She didn't move.

Closer now, Hasan's heart pulled him to his knees, where Yousef's little legs trembled violently and his little hands gripped tightly to Dalia's thobe.

"Baba!" Yousef cried with relief at the sight of his father. His voice in the silence made Dalia blink.

"Come here, habibi." Hasan lifted his son, rising in fear because Dalia still had not moved. Yousef's desperate grip found its way around his father's neck, and Hasan saw that his son's pants were muddied with feces and urine.

"Darweesh! Yaba!" Hasan called out to his brother and Yehya for help, but Haj Salem arrived first. "Hisbi Allah wa niaamal wakeel, God curse them for this. God curse the Jews to hell," Haj Salem could only whisper upon seeing Dalia in her state. "She's going to break her teeth clenching them that way. Hasan, give me the boy and you carry your wife."

But Yousef wouldn't let go. Wouldn't open his eyes. His arms, legs, fear, and soiled pants were securely fastened to Hasan—his refuge. Just then Darweesh arrived and Hasan called to him, "Brother, carry Dalia. The east wing of the house is still intact." Darweesh lifted Dalia, Ismael still at her chest. She was blinking now, absorbing her view of a flawless blue sky—*How pretty and clear*—until Darweesh carried her inside and all she could see was the plastered ceiling of her home. *My Ismael is safe in my arms. And there is Yousef, safe in his father's. A bad dream, was it?*

*   *   *

Less than a day passed before Israeli soldiers reentered the village. The same men who had received the offering of food now marched through, pointing guns at the people who had fed them. Hasan, Darweesh, and other men were ordered to dig a mass grave for thirty fresh corpses. The village men were able to identify all but two of them. Hasan somberly wrote the names of his fallen friends and countrymen on the sleeve of his dishdashe as he hollowed the earth in such shock that he was unable to grieve. Al Fatiha. Dust to dust . . .

Stunned—*is this a dream?*—their nerves cracking, children crying, the villagers were tractable.

"Gather the valuables. Assemble by the eastern water well. Move! This is only temporary. Go to the well," ordered a voice from a loudspeaker like a hidden god, distributing destinies. The sky still infinite. The sun unforgiving. Dalia put the gold in the chest pocket of her thobe and gathered the valuables as told, Ismael on the left hip, Yousef in the right hand.

"Mama, I want Baba to carry me," Yousef pleaded.

"Go, habibi. Allah be with us all." Dalia released his little hand and the boy jumped on his father. *Allah be with us all.*

The area around the well teemed with faces, all creased and twisted with alarm. But for the fright, Yehya thought they could have been gathered to prepare for the harvest. *The harvest,* he thought.

"Now what?" Haj Salem wondered.

Darweesh and his pregnant wife were the last to arrive. He approached stooped, one foot after the other, leading his heartbroken mare, Fatooma. Ganoosh, Darweesh's delight and Fatooma's lifelong companion, the horse that once had broken Dalia's ankle, had been killed in the fighting and it had taken much persuasion to pull Fatooma away from the massive carcass of her mate.

Now what?

At the well, soldiers whipped their batons, herding the terrified crowd down the hill. A cart, weighed down with the belongings of several families, wobbled, churning up dirt. An old woman fell and someone picked her up. "Go, go!" yelled the loudspeaker god. Terror flew from people's hearts and circled above like birds. *Chirp. Chirp.*

Dalia held Ismael to her chest and Hasan carried Yousef in one arm, a sack of hastily packed belongings in the other. Yehya lugged a basket of food on his back and, without water, the villagers stumbled toward the hills beneath a parched sky.

"Stop here," said the loudspeaker god. "Bags here. Tomorrow you come collect them. Leave everything, jewelry and money. I shoot. Understand?"

Go. Stop. Understand? Return. Tomorrow. Safe. Yehya could hold on to some words. Yousef held onto his father. Dalia on to Ismael, whose scar was still red but healing. Perhaps there was hope. So they dropped their belongings—the golden jewelry that had weighed Dalia down on her wedding day, food, clothes, and blankets. Basima's pruning shears. *Why did I bring those?* Dalia wondered.

Darweesh stripped Fatooma of the sacks saddled on her back and laid their contents next to the gold and other valuables. "The horse! Leave the horse," a soldier ordered. Not the loudspeaker god, but his disciple, surely.

"Please!" Darweesh had no pride left.

Fatooma was worth begging for, but the begging irritated the soldier. "Shut up!"

"Please!"

"Shut up!"

"Please."

The soldier fired his pistol twice. One shot between Fatooma's eyes, on her white streak. She fell instantly dead. The other through Darweesh's chest. His pregnant wife, Basima's niece who had been betrothed to Hasan, shrieked, screaming by her bleeding husband as people gathered to carry Darweesh a distance away, where someone produced a jar of honey to prevent infection and bandaged him with strips of his own clothing. The bullet lodged in Darweesh's spine, condemning him to motionlessness, to a life plagued by unsightly bedsores, a life tormented by the burden of his wife's cheerless fate, bound to a husband who lived only from the chest up. And even from the chest up, he lived on memories of horses and wind.

Panic rose from the shots and the birds of terror were supplanted by clouds that made Yehya hope for rain. It wasn't the season yet, but his trees needed water. At times rain had been everything in Ein Hod, other times it was merely precious. Then he saw his son Darweesh and nothing had meaning. Rain be damned. Yehya dropped the basket from his back and began to cry for that strong boy of his, that impressive rider and beloved son.

Dalia still hadn't caught up. The panicked throngs had separated her from Hasan, but she could still see the top of his kaffiyeh ahead of her. He was taller than most men; she'd always liked that. *God, what is happening?* The clouds passed as suddenly as they came. The sun stung like a scorpion. Dust was high, cactus low, and Dalia thought of water.

In an instant.

One instant, six-month-old Ismael was at her chest, in her motherly arms. In the next, Ismael was gone.

An instant can crush a brain and change the course of life, the course of history. It was an infinitesimal flash of time that Dalia would revisit in her mind, over and over for many years, searching for some clue, some hint of what might have happened to her son. Even after she became lost in an eclipsed reality, she would search the fleeing crowd in her mind for Ismael.

"Ibni! Ibni!" My son, my son, Dalia screamed, her eyes bulging in search of her son. Dust at her face, cactus at her feet. "Ibni! Ibni!" She scanned the ground, looked up, and Hasan's tall figure was not there. "Ibni! Ibni!" Some people tried to help her but gunshots tolled and Dalia was shoved along. *Is this a dream?* Nothing seemed real because it was unbelievable. She looked at her arms again to be sure. *Maybe he's crawled into my thobe.* She felt her chest. *No Ismael.* Her son was gone.

Dalia stopped and so did time. She screamed like she hadn't when her father burned her hand. A loud, penetrating, consuming, unworldly scream from a mother's deepest agony. From the most profound desire to reverse time, just a few minutes. If there is a God, he heard Dalia's wail. Hasan ran to her and searched the crowd as desperately as Dalia had. Afraid for his older child, Hasan held Yousef close as he looked for Ismael. Yousef squeezed his father tighter, afraid to speak, and the three of them at last made it to safety on Hasan's strength and will, but without Ismael.

The villagers sat on the ground in the valley. The land was as beautiful and peaceful as it had always been. Trees and sky and hills and stone were unchanged and the villagers were dazed and quiet, except Dalia. She was mad with anguish, questioning people and uncovering other women's babies in hope of revealing a boy with a scar down his right cheek, around his eye. She searched with frenzied foreboding, even though Yehya tried to reassure her that surely someone had picked up the child and surely it was only a matter of time before they would be reunited. *Surely,* Yehya knew, *you can't hold on to words*.

Dalia spent the last of her energy on tears, replaying that instant, over and over and over. Little Yousef, not comprehending the sudden hell that had befallen the whole village, agreed to let go of his father and sat in his jiddo Yehya's arms, both of them dazed and teary.

Hasan shuffled restlessly between his wounded brother, Darweesh; his inconsolable wife; his terrified son; and his bewildered father, until finally he succumbed to exhaustion and slept on the ground among merciless mosquitoes, a stone to rest his head. But not even sleep could assuage the inadequacy he felt. He had failed to protect his family. He could not provide assurance, nor could he bring Ismael back.

"Jiddo, can we go home now?" Yousef asked his grandfather.

Yehya could not lie, nor could he tell the truth. He kissed his grandson, pulled him closer, tighter, to his chest, and said, "Get some rest, ya ibni, get some rest now, ya habibi." *My son, my beloved*.

They tried to go back the next day, but the guns behind them forbade a return home. For three days and two nights, they made their way up and down unforgiving hills, under the sun's glare and the unseen but sure watch of snipers. A diabetic boy and his grandmother fell and died. One woman miscarried and the dehydrated bodies of two babies went limp in their mothers' arms. Jenin was as far as they could go, and they rested wherever there was space among the flood of refugees converging from other villages. Residents of those towns helped them as much as they could, giving away their food, blankets, and water and fitting as many as possible into their homes in that time of crisis. Soon Jordan, Iraq, and Syria gave out a few tents, and a refugee camp sprang up in Jenin, where the villagers of Ein Hod could stand on the hills and look back at the homes to which they could never return.

So it was that eight centuries after its founding by a general of Saladin's army in 1189 A.D., Ein Hod was cleared of its Palestinian children. Yehya tried to calculate the number of generations who had lived and died in that village and he came up with forty. It was a task made simple by the way Arabs name their children to tell the story of their genealogy, conferring five or six names from the child's direct lineage, in proper order.

Thus Yehya tallied forty generations of living, now stolen. Forty generations of childbirth and funerals, weddings and dance, prayer and scraped knees. Forty generations of sin and charity, of cooking, toiling, and idling, of friendships and animosities and pacts, of rain and lovemaking. Forty generations with their imprinted memories, secrets, and scandals. All carried away by the notion of entitlement of another people, who would settle in the vacancy and proclaim it all—all that was left in the way of architecture, orchards, wells, flowers, and charm—as the heritage of Jewish foreigners arriving from Europe, Russia, the United States, and other corners of the globe.

In the sorrow of a history buried alive, the year 1948 in Palestine fell from the calendar into exile, ceasing to reckon the marching count of days, months, and years, instead becoming an infinite mist of one moment in history. The twelve months of that year rearranged themselves and swirled aimlessly in the heart of Palestine. The old folks of Ein Hod would die refugees in the camp, bequeathing to their heirs the large iron keys to their ancestral homes, the crumbling land registers issued by the Ottomans, the deeds from the British mandate, their memories and love of the land, and the dauntless will not to leave the spirit of forty generations trapped beneath the subversion of thieves.

FIVE

"Ibni! Ibni!"
1948

IN THE DAYS BEFORE the attack, in late July 1948, the hot winds of el Naqab swept toward Jerusalem as Israeli soldiers came to the village to consolidate the truce. September was only weeks away, and it always arrived with dry southern winds and baskets of rain.

Rain, just a hint of its coming, was a reminder of hope. *And the feast of the truce,* thought the villagers, *will mark a peaceful beginning.*

As soldiers of this Israel ate, the one named Moshe watched an Arab woman. At her legs, a small boy clung to her caftan. In one arm, an infant nestled to her chest and with her free hand, the Arab woman served lamb to Moshe and his comrades. In his soldier's tan uniform, he thought how unfair it was that this Arab peasant should have the gift of children while his poor Jolanta, who had suffered the horrors of genocide, could not bear a child. It made him weep inside.

Moshe wanted Jolanta to be happy. Jolanta wanted a child. But Jolanta's body had been ravaged by Nazis who had forced her to spend her late teens serving the physical appetites of the SS. That nightmare had saved her life but had left her barren. Having lost every member of her family in death camps, Jolanta had sailed alone to Palestine at the end of the Second World War. She knew nothing of Palestine or Palestinians, following only the lure of Zionism and the lush promises of milk and honey. She wanted refuge. She wanted to escape the memories of sweaty German men polluting her body, memories of depravity and memories of hunger. She wanted to escape the howls of death in her dreams, the extinguished songs of her mother and father, brother and sisters, the unending screams of dying Jews.

Moshe understood her pain. He saw it in the eyes of orphaned, widowed, devastated Jews arriving by the hundreds each day on the shores of Palestine. But Jolanta was special. So fragile and pretty. He fell in love with her and the two married within months of her arrival.

"Jolanta, you are safe now," Moshe comforted his wife on their first night together.

"How can you be sure, Moshe?" she cried in his arms.

"We will live to see the land between the Mediterranean and the Jordan River with nothing but Jews." He held her tighter. "Palestine will be ours. You will see. Together, we will raise a family. We are starting a new life. Go to sleep now. Dream of the children we will have, my darling. We will never be persecuted again."

Moshe held Jolanta close and considered their plans to oust the British.

First the British, he thought, *then the Arabs.*

He was right. Zionists succeeded in getting rid of the British and most of the Arabs. He and Jolanta saw the birth of Israel. Indeed, Moshe helped deliver the new state, a Jewish state rising from Europe's ashes. Still, they could not conceive a child of their own.

Moshe left Ein Hod with his comrades, the image of the Arab woman and her children lingering in his mind. Jolanta had suffered so much; how could God deny her the elemental gift of motherhood while granting so many healthy children to Arabs, who were already so numerous? The injustice of it all solidified in him a resolve to take—by force if necessary—whatever was needed.

After the bombing the following day, in the crowd of fleeing villagers, he saw that Arab woman, her baby held tight to her chest, her defiant ankle bracelet as pretty as she.

Moshe made his way toward the crowd, coming up behind the Arab woman. Before he reached her, the throbbing crowd jostled the baby from her arms, into that fateful instant. In a flash, Moshe snatched the child, tucked it in his army sack, and kept moving without looking back. He heard the woman yell, "Ibni! Ibni!" and that made him believe that she had seen him take her baby.

But she had not. The crowd pushed on, more gunshots rang out, and the woman was shoved along.

The baby cried. Moshe could feel little kicks inside his sack as he made for the jeep, away from the eyes of his comrades. The Arabs had already moved on from the center of town. He had the idea to pacify the child with alcohol the soldiers had stashed to celebrate their imminent victory that evening in Ein Hod. Dripping gin into the baby's mouth, Moshe noticed the scar on his face. It was still red and his eye was still swollen.

"The Arabs are gone!" shouted a soldier.

The inhabitants of Ein Hod were removed from the land. It was now time to celebrate and that was Moshe's opportunity to get the baby out of sight.

"I left the liquor. I'll be back," Moshe yelled.

He secured the intoxicated child in the sack rustling about in the backseat of an army jeep as he sped toward the kibbutz where Jolanta was likely sleeping. Moshe thought she slept too much. Ate too little. Rarely smiled anymore.

Young life to care for will bring her back.

The young life was Ismael, son of Dalia and Hasan, fellaheen from the Palestinian village of Ein Hod. Moshe did not know their names, nor would he or Jolanta, ever. The Arab woman's face, and her scream of "Ibni, ibni," would haunt Moshe's years and the awful things he had done would give him no peace until the end. But for now, Moshe was propelled by love to steal a child. To chase people from their homes, he had been commissioned by an omnipotent edict. *A land without a people, for a people without a land.* He said it until he could have believed it, but for that Arab woman.

But for Dalia.

Jolanta's face opened like a spring blossom. Her nurturing instincts overtook her depression, her ghosts, her misery. She held the precious child, half-drugged, dirty, and maimed. She enfolded him with her deepest yearnings, caring not that he was an Arab. That day she learned the first thing she ever knew about Arabs: that they circumcise their boys.

Jolanta fell in love. "He's beautiful, Moshe." She trembled with delight.

"He . . . the baby . . . his parents . . ." Moshe was not sure what he was starting to say and was grateful when Jolanta interrupted him.

"Stop. I don't want to know anything. Just tell me, is he our son, Moshe?"

"Yes, my love. He needs a mother."

"Then his name is David, in memory of my father," Jolanta decided, and Moshe returned to Ein Hod with the liquor, happy. He felt complete.

First the British, then the Arabs.

And now Jolanta had a child.

As the people of Ein Hod were marched into dispossession, Moshe and his comrades guarded and looted the newly emptied village. While Dalia lay heartbroken, delirious with the loss of Ismael, Jolanta rocked David to sleep. While Hasan tended to his family's survival, Moshe sang in drunken revelry with his fellow soldiers. And while Yehya and the others moved in anguished steps away from their land, the usurpers sang "Hatikva" and shouted, "Long live Israel!"

SIX

Yehya's Return

1948–1953

WHILE A FOREIGN MINORITY went about building a new state in 1948, expelling Palestinians and looting their homes and banks, the five major powers—the Soviet

Union, France, Great Britain, China, and the United States—appointed a UN mediator to recommend a solution to the conflict.

"He's Swedish," Yehya said to a group of men who gathered each morning near his tent for the latest news. "Who is Swedish?" asked a passerby. "Shut up. Hasan is reading the newspaper to us," someone snapped. Yehya nodded to Hasan. "Continue, son." Hasan read:

> Serving his commission, the Swedish UN mediator, Count Folke Bernadotte, stated, "It would be an offense against the principles of elemental justice if these innocent victims of the conflict were denied the right to return to their homes, while Jewish immigrants flow into Palestine, and, indeed, at least offer the threat of permanent replacement of the Arab refugees who had been rooted in the land for centuries."

There was a pause filled with the persistent hope of return before someone spoke again.

"It's about time someone spoke up against this foulness."

"I just hope the Jews didn't mess up my house too bad."

"I don't care. I'll fix my house. I just want to go home."

"Let me go tell the family. Um Khaleel will be so happy. She's been so worried about her lemon and almond trees."

But just as the men began to disperse, a small, five-year-old voice stopped them. "Jiddo"—little Yousef looked at Yehya—"can we go home now?"

It was the assumption they all had made, but being confronted with the question, now they were unsure of the answer. So they turned to Yehya and Haj Salem sitting next to him. Yehya looked at Hasan, then turned to his grandson and said, "The truth is, Yousef, we just don't know yet. We have to wait, ya habibi." *My beloved.*

*   *   *

Gathering for the news became a morning ritual in the refugee camp. Women had their own groups, as did children. But to the men, it was the most important event of the day. It was a time and place where the hope of returning home could be renewed. Even when those hopes were perpetually dashed. Even when the old began to die off. And even when hopes grew fainter, they continued to gather in this routine of the Right of Return.

A few days after they heard of the Swedish mediator, they listened to another news item.

Hasan read:

The Swedish UN mediator, Count Folke Bernadotte, was assassinated by Jewish terrorists.

Israel would not allow the return, and the family waited captive in that interminable year, with its surreal twist of fate and tentative conclusion, stretching on and on, renewed each morning with the news.

Yehya aged tremendously in those confused months that stretched into years, until one day in 1953, when he realized that his miserable tent in Jenin had turned into clay. The symbolic permanence of the shelter was too much to bear. He would rather have stayed in the cloth dwelling, its leaky top and muddy floor confirming only a temporary exile.

In the years of waiting in the tent city, Yehya would awake at the adan and idle through the day, playing the music of his nye between rationed meals and five daily prayers. He found some comfort in the love of his family and daily games of backgammon with Haj Salem and Jack O'Malley, the UN director of operations in Jenin. The three men were inseparable from midafternoon until eight or later in the evening, depending on how well the game was going, or how well-prepared the hookas were that day.

But in more than sixty years of life, Yehya had become accustomed to the daily activities of agrarian self-sufficiency. The aimlessness of captive dispossession warped his mood and bent his posture. The string of broken promises and UN resolutions, not worth the paper on which they set down demands of return, wore at his spirit and made him taciturn, and he shuffled about with the qualities of a man defeated by the wait. Defeated by the quiet nag of his hands wanting things to do.

Something in the clay of his new shelter, the way it solidified him, stirred him from his resignation. One early November morning in 1953, he handed some clothes to Dalia.

"Ya binti," Yehya said, "will you make these as white as they can be?"

Dalia took the clothes and pushed them in the soapy water. Leaning into the wash bucket to scrub, she lifted her head, a few strands of hair escaping from her scarf, and watched her father-in-law walk away. *He's in better spirits, thanks be to Allah.*

On a rock outside his clay shelter, Yehya sat in his long white underpants and a white undershirt, and leaned into the wind. He took in a premeditated breath, closed his eyes, and exhaled into the nye at his lips, playing a new tune. It was not the sad music of waiting. Nor was it a melody of his heritage. It was a call to the earth. To Allah. To the country within him. It caught the attention of passersby, touched their hearts and made them bow their heads inexplicably. He played his nye all morning, rarely opening his eyes, brow raised. When he was finished, he went inside his tent and returned with his grooming tools—a blade, a leather strap, and a piece of broken mirror. He sat upright, anchoring his callused old feet in the dirt, breathing deeply.

The olives are ready.

He shaved. He twisted his mustache into two perfect upward-turning curls and fixed them in place with gum arabic sap.

The grapes and figs have surely fallen by now and are rotting on the land.

One garment at a time, he dressed himself in vintage dignity, putting on his best dishdashe, a jacket that was too big for his frame, and a red-checkered kaffiyeh held on his head with a twisted black egal.

October's rains have surely loosened the ground.

And he walked out of his tent a proud man.

Realizing what Yehya was up to, Haj Salem begged him to find prudence. He pleaded, "Ya Abu Hasan, I know what you're doing. It's November and we're all feeling it. But it's too dangerous. Don't be foolish, my friend. Wahhid Allah!"

"La ellaha ella Allah," Yehya answered the call to proclaim Allah's Oneness, but he would listen no more. Jack O'Malley knew better than to think Yehya could be stopped. He put his pudgy white hand on Yehya's shoulder and in his Irish accent said, "Be careful, brother. Your chair and hooka will be waiting for you at Beit Jawad's coffeehouse, so don't be gone long."

When Hasan tried to stop him—"Yaba, please. They'll kill you"—Yehya gazed at his son with an Arab patriarch's unquestionable final authority. Then he turned and walked as he once had, with purpose and pride—if with a cane—up the sloping alleyway to the edge of the camp, past its boundaries, outside the limit of that eternal 1948, beyond the border into what had become Israel—into a landscape he knew better than the lines on his hands—until he finally arrived at his destination.

Sixteen days later, Yehya returned ragged and dirty with a tangled beard and a radiant spirit. The kaffiyeh that he had worn on his head when he left now formed a bundle flung over his shoulder as he walked with a merry hunch under its weight. Yeyha had made his way back to Ein Hod, undetected by soldiers. "That terrain is in my blood!" he proclaimed. "I know every tree and every bird. The soldiers do not."

For days he had roamed his fields, greeting his carob and fig trees with the excitement of a man reuniting with his family. He had slept contentedly in their shade, as he had done at afternoon siesta all his life. The old well where the soldier had shot Darweesh and Fatooma was still there, and Yehya had devised a makeshift bucket tied to vines of honeysuckle areej to fetch water. He had visited his wife's grave, where the white-streaked red roses had come back despite the destruction. He had read the Fatiha for Basima's soul and—he swore—had spoken to her apparition.

Almost thirty years later, and with the same curled mustache as his grandfather, Yousef would recall the yellow clay across Yehya's teeth on the day he came back from his sixteen days in the paradise of realized nostalgia. Yehya had left the camp with stubborn solemnity, wearing his most dignified clothes, and he returned looking like a jolly beggar with as much fruit and as many olives as he could carry in his kaffiyeh, his pockets, and his hands. Despite his vagabond appearance, he came invested with euphoria and the people lifted him to heights of esteem befitting the only man among them who had outwitted a ruthless military and had done what five great nations could not effectuate. He had returned. However brief and uncertain his return may have been, he had done it.

Yehya's audacity injected life into the refugees, who had become weary of the promises of the United Nations and lethargic with the humiliation of 1948, that year without end. For Yousef, not yet ten, his jiddo's exploit was a seed that planted itself in his memories of the terrible eviction, and it would germinate at his core a character of defiance. In the happiest days of his life, some thirty years after Yehya made his daring journey, Yousef would tell his sister Amal about their grandfather, whom she had never known.

"It was a splendid sight," Yousef would say. "He was so happy. He just unwrapped a bundle of figs, lemons, grapes, carobs, and olives in the middle of town as though he were bringing a million gold dinars. He couldn't get rid of that smile. Our jiddo was a great man."

"Like Baba," Amal would add.

"Yes. Like our father."

The patriarchs and matriarchs in the camp kept a festive vigil on the night Yehya came back from his Return. They divvied the goods and ate them with ceremonial savor, letting the olives roll in a dance with their tongues before taking the sacrament. Those fruits of forty generations of toil went down like the elixir of Palestine, like the nectar of her centuries.

"Taste my land, Jack! Taste it! This pile is special for you and the haj!" Yehya was effusive, his generosity animated by Return.

The villagers ate, laughed, wept, danced, and sang the sad and happy ballads of old, comparing their memories to Yehya's description of the new state of affairs. The homes on the east and west wings of Ein Hod were still standing but abandoned, and the jars of pickles and jams, which had been there since the villagers left five years earlier, could still be found in pantries. Yehya had helped himself. "Better I eat them than leave them to the Jews." Yes, yes. And he had seen clothes in the homes. Some toys here and there. The village mosque, in the very center of the town, had been turned into a brothel, he told them, at which point the women muttered curses and the men shook their heads in disgust. And, oh yes, Haje Magida, mercy on her soul, who had been known for her obsessive disgust for ants— her house had been overtaken by the critters. "If she could only see that!" They all laughed.

"Mercy on her soul." Yes, mercy on her soul. No one was using the olive press, except to hang paintings. It had become an art gallery. And the big oak that had grown out of nowhere in the late 1800s was still there. "Well, of course it's there." All the olives were still there, too, but they were in need of care from people who knew how to care for them.

"Those people don't know a damn thing about olives. They're lily-skinned foreigners with no attachment to the land. If they had a sense of the land then the land would compel in them a love for the olives," Yehya said, staring at the palms that had caressed those majestic, beloved trees only hours earlier. Age-dappled and rough, his farmer's hands were infused with the melanin truths of those hills. The truth that an olive branch flowers only once and if it isn't pruned back it will produce buds that become new slender sprigs by winter. The truth that an olive's worst biological enemy is a small lacy-winged fly and that sheep are good to keep around because they supply the soil with needed nitrogen. Yehya's hands knew those facts from a lifetime devoted to trees and their earth.

"Damn those people," a woman shouted in the crowd, "they didn't need to kick us out of our homes. We let so many of them settle on our land. And we gave them olives from our harvest." Everyone sighed and the women muttered curses and the men shook their heads in disgust as they continued to eat figs with meticulous relish. Then Yehya pulled out his nye and began to play the sounds of time, and women swayed and sang sad ballads until someone shouted, "None of that! Play us 'Dal'Ouna!'" He did, and the spirited tempo lifted their arthritic bodies onto their feet as they danced a clumsy dabke around the bonfire and someone improvised a tabla, adding percussion to the nye.

Yousef, the only child who had the privilege of their company until then and who struggled to remain awake, was suddenly energized by the unfolding festivities. In Beiruit decades later, with his sister Amal, Yousef would recall the evening's toothless smiles, the laughter that shook tired old bodies, the giggles that sounded like those of mischievous children instead of grandparents, and the spiraling smoke of honey apple tobacco from the hookas and Hasan's pipe.

The air filled with carousing sounds and people were drunk on the fruits of trees that had continued in time and penetrated the cloud of exile. Others joined as the gaiety wove into the night. Some women came out in their plebian finest and children, ecstatic at the prospect of a late-night vigil, gathered around Yousef and had their own celebration by the shadowy glow of the fire.

In the days that followed, the cheery spontaneity of that evening fizzled into the oppressive business of waiting and the offenses of temporary life. But for Yehya it was an intolerable anticlimax. So, two weeks later, once more he asked Dalia to make his whites sparkle.

Yehya shaved. He dressed himself, going through the quiet ritual he had employed weeks earlier. But this time, he performed the rites of the forbidden Return with the deliberate strokes of experience. Yousef sat by his side in the sunshine, watching the slow motions of the razor along his grandfather's jawline, dazzled by the sun's dance along the blade. He observed the dirty white foam in the rinse cup, the spots on Yehya's hands, and the dirt beneath his nails. And he committed to memory the precision with which Yehya trimmed his salty black mustache and waxed its tips to perfect curve and symmetry. The mantle of a patriarch.

No one knew exactly when Yehya died. But by the time the Red Crescent was able to retrieve his corpse from the Israeli authorities, Dalia had miscarried again. Everyone in the camp agreed that Yehya had known that when he again set foot outside the boundaries of that eternal 1948, he would be gone forever. Haj Salem was sure that Yehya had gone back to die where he was supposed to die, and when people spoke of Yehya's passing, they said he had died from the malady of a broken heart.

The actual cause of death was a gunshot wound. Ein Hod was being settled by Jewish artists from France and was gaining a reputation as a secluded paradise. Yehya had been spotted on his first trip by one of the Jewish settlers, and when he returned, waiting soldiers had shot him for trespassing.

When the family cleaned Yehya's body for burial, they found three olives in his hand and some figs in his pockets. In death, Yehya's face wore a smile, and that was proof to everyone that he had gone happily to the heaven of martyrs. So, from their tears, the people of Jenin's shanty camp mourned Yehya's death with a celebration of his life and his final bravery and love of the land. Jack O'Malley gave his staff the day off and they all joined the funeral procession.

In that somber celebratory crowd of mourners, Hasan walked in silence, carrying the shrouded body of his father at one corner while his brother Darweesh wheeled himself alongside in his chair. No one noticed the trauma in Yousef's young face during the funeral, and no one could sleep that night. Yehya's death unveiled a truth that seized the night and made it heave with restlessness. How was it that a man could not walk onto his own property, visit the grave of his wife, eat the fruits of forty generations of his ancestors' toil, without mortal consequence? Somehow that raw question had not previously penetrated the consciousness of the refugees who had become confused in the rank eternity of waiting, pining at abstract international resolutions, resistance, and struggle. But that basic axiom of their condition sprang to the surface as they lowered Yehya's body into the ground, and night brought them no sleep.

The next morning, the refugees rose from their agitation to the realization that they were slowly being erased from the world, from its history and from its future. The men and women held separate councils, from which a fledgling command began to emerge. In nearly every matter, Hasan was sought out because he was the most learned among them, and the tasks of writing letters and negotiating with UN officials for basic necessities were assigned to his capable hands.

Even their Palestinian countrymen, in the yet-unconquered West Bank towns, looked down on them as "refugees."

"If we must be refugees, we will not live like dogs," it was declared.

That straightening of their spines is what Yehya's death brought to the camp. A fever of pride enveloped Jenin and a campaign was organized to institutionalize education, especially the girls' school. Within one year, the community of refugees built another mosque and three schools, and Hasan played a central but unobtrusive role in it all, keeping to the periphery of day-to-day life but still busily drafting letters and documents. He would rise before the sun, pray the first salat, and read, his free hand alternating between a cup of coffee and his pipe packed with honey apple tobacco. Then he would leave for his job before his family awoke, and from there, he would go to the hills with his books, returning after his family was already sleeping. He was too ashamed of the pittance pay he brought home. Ashamed to return daily without Ismael. Some days he put his books aside to work on cars, an interest imparted to him by Ari Perlstein and a hobby that turned into a garage business, eventually earning enough money to send Yousef to college.

For Yousef, the sudden gone-forever of his grandfather made his heart curl around itself in sadness. From a distance, he watched the subdued games of backgammon between Haj Salem and Jack O'Malley, his jiddo's empty chair between them.

"Mama—" Yousef said, trying to hold back tears because Dalia insisted on strength. He was sitting at her feet, toying with her remaining ankle bracelet. *Mama jingles when she walks.*

"—I want Jiddo back."

He hadn't known what he was going to say until he said it. Dalia put her hand on her son's head. She could hardly believe how much he had grown. Counting the coins on her ankle bracelet, Yousef liked the way it moved between his fingers. *One, two, three, four . . . eighteen gold coins.* Dalia knew she had neglected Yousef since Ismael had disappeared. *I'm doing the best I can, I'm trying, God, I am. Ismael would have been five years old by now. I wonder what he would look like.*

As Dalia caressed Yousef's hair away from his forehead, he wondered if she was going to speak. Or if he had disappointed her by being so silly as to want someone to return from the dead.

I'm going to learn to play the nye, Yousef decided, and left, wordlessly.

SEVEN

Amal Is Born

1955

FOUR YEARS AFTER THE UN funded the adobe box that Hasan built for his family, a UN-sponsored school for boys was established in Jenin. Jack O'Malley offered him a teaching post, but Hasan refused.

"There are others who have official credentials to teach. It would not be right for me to have the job over them," Hasan insisted. Instead, he went to work there as a janitor.

On the occasion of his first pay, Hasan presented Dalia with gifts, which she accepted with new delight, splintering the rigidity of her mourning. And nine months later, their third child, Amal, was born into the heat of July 1955.

Until this birth, Dalia still wore a cloak of bereavement for Ismael, sheathing herself in black grief that reached to her wrists and ankles. With the good riddance of the damp tent, her husband's new job, and the bathroom and kitchen that were being built to replace the buckets and wash pans, the waiting for things to go back to normal became a tolerable interim fate for Dalia. She traded her tired black scarf for the vibrant new white one made of real silk. The birth of a new child was said even to have restored a glimpse, however brief, of the spirited gypsy she had once been. Though Dalia's spirit had long since been smothered, she could see its reincarnation in little Amal, like a whirlwind of life taking form in her daughter.

Soon Dalia recognized the quick curiosity in her growing child, whose remote black eyes seemed to have no bottom. The girl had an aspect of sorcery, as if she had materialized from the charms of alchemy and Bedouin poetry. She behaved as if the world belonged to her, and once Dalia observed her naughty daughter pushing other small children into a shadowed alley, yelling, "That's my father's sun, get away!"

It was not long before the child was compelled to create imaginary friends who could tolerate her wild nature—until, that is, she found another friendless soul, named Huda.

So passive and yielding was Huda's nature that it awakened an instinct of compassion in little Amal. They were an odd pair. But they were friends, and few in the camp ever saw one without the other.

Well into her elementary school days, Amal remained stubborn and capricious except with her father, whom she rarely saw because of the long hours he spent at work. He seemed to her like a god. When she approached him, she did so with worshipful eyes that reached to her father's depths. And when Hasan held his little girl, he did so with profound tenderness. Often, before the child took possession of her father, she would turn devilish eyes toward her mother, for Dalia was competition for Hasan's affection.

Dalia could not find the will to discipline this child physically, as she had Yousef. She left Amal to her own untamed whims, watching her daughter as if surveying a burning sensibility that had left her years ago and returned tenfold in her child. Fate had been perverse to do such a thing, for Dalia had no defenses against raw vitality.

Dalia learned to be a stoic mother, communicating the demands and tenders of motherhood with the various tempers of silence. Against this quiet detachment, the girl offered fits and petulance, mixed with bursts of kisses and feverish need meant to provoke her mother. Dalia's love found its expression during the child's sleep. Then she stroked her daughter's hair, loved her endlessly with the kisses she withheld during the child's waking hours.

II.

El Naksa
(the disaster)

EIGHT

As Big as the Ocean and All Its Fishes
1960–1963

I SPENT MUCH TIME IN my youth trying to imagine Mama as Dalia, the Bedouin who once stole a horse, who bred roses and whose steps jingled. The mother I knew was a stout woman, imposing and severe, who soldiered all day at cleaning, cooking, baking, and embroidering thobes. Several times each week, she was called to deliver a baby. As with everything else she did, she performed midwifery with cool efficiency and detached nerve.

I was eight years old when Mama first let me help her deliver a baby.

"This is a very important job. You must be very serious, Amal," she said, and proceeded with her cleansing ritual before leaving.

"Wudu and salat. Do it with me," she instructed.

We passed the homemade soap between us. I watched her, imitating every detail, every motion. The splashing of the face with water, the rinsing of the hands, elbows, feet. Mumbled affirmations of faith in Allah. I moved as her mirror image. We washed and prayed, then she braided my hair. Before we left she held her special scissors over the babboor's open flame and wrapped it in cloth "in the name of Allah, most Merciful and Forgiving."

At the expectant woman's home, I was as Mama was, deliberate and grave. I handed her the towels, stood by with the scissors, and held my nerves (and the food in my stomach) because she warned me, "Don't be weak and don't get sick." Stern as steel. "Whatever you feel, keep it inside."

I remember that day well. The slow strokes of the comb traveling in Mama's hand from the top of my head to the tips of my long black hair. Approval in her face when I anticipated a need for more towels before her cue. Imparting skills and forestalling weakness were the ways Dalia loved. Everything else, the hugs and kisses I so craved, she held with the clench of her jaw and the grip that rubbed itself in her right palm. *Whatever you feel, keep it inside.*

That evening she let me and Huda, my best friend, sleep on the flat rooftop.

"Thank you, Mama." "Thank you, Um Yousef," we said excitedly.

She didn't answer us, just pulled the shades over her heart and went on with her evening cleaning. From the roof that night, Huda and I watched Mama wait for Baba to return from the garage. She walked around with a broom in her hand, Um Kalthoom singing from the radio, and she swept the dust at the threshold until there was nothing but moonlight to sweep.

Mama never danced at weddings and rarely visited friends. Once, I awoke far into the night and found her tenderly stroking my hair. She kissed me then, one of a few precious kisses perched in my mind, and said, "Go back to sleep, ya binti."

My early years in Jenin's refugee camp are metered by such discoveries. Like the time when I was four and I saw Yousef's penis. He was getting dressed and didn't notice me watching. For days, I thought about it, inspecting myself, looking at Mama in the bath, and worrying that something terrible was wrong with my brother. Naturally, I caused a stir when I grabbed Yousef's crotch, unmindful of the neighbors, and my brother hit me hard. Everyone who witnessed the cause of my hysterical screaming agreed that Yousef had done the right thing. Except Mama.

A neighbor woman said to her, "Dalia, a girl just can't do that, even if she is four. Best break her of the devil's habits early."

Break her. Beat her. Teach her a lesson. Another said, "You can bet she won't do that again." Still another: "He's her older brother and he has every right to hit his sister if she misbehaves."

But Mama took my side, reprimanding Yousef. "Don't ever hit your sister. Ever," Mama said, and I waxed triumphant, ready to be received into my mother's arms. But she would have none of that either.

"Stop crying, Amal," she ordered, not angry, mean, or even firm. Matter-of-fact, efficient, tough.

On a morning in April, the month of flowers, I discovered a side of my father I had never seen before. So ceaselessly did he work and so infrequently did I see him that I had only adored him from afar until that day. I was five years old. I awoke before dawn in a panic to wet clothes, and I rushed to sort out my predicament in the only room that offered privacy. To my horror and shame, Baba was waiting for me as I emerged from the toilet. More than punishment, I feared his disappointment.

That day is one of my clearest childhood memories. Without words, Baba helped me into clean pajamas and I levitated off the ground in his enormous arms. He carried me a few steps, my small head buried in his neck, and sat me in his lap on the terrace, a four-by-three-meter patch of stone and tile covered with a canopy of grape vines—Mama's stubborn attempt to duplicate the glory of her gardens in Ein Hod. It was still dark, but I recall the shadowy landscape of the countryside's blossoming fruit trees. Peach, pomegranate, and olive were in bloom when, by the light of a wax candle, my father read to me for the first time.

For a long time after, my senses could conjure from memory the sweet scents of spring that had bewitched the air. My father's olive-wood pipe had protruded from the side of his mouth and the smoke of honey apple tobacco also had marked that special morning.

"Listen to the words I read. They're magical," he said. And I tried very hard to understand the classical Arabic prose, but to my young mind it seemed another language. Still, the cadence was mesmerizing, and Baba's voice was a lullaby. I dozed in his arms.

I told no one of the incident and I lived through the day in anticipation of night, the darkness just before dawn, hoping to once again have a special place in Baba's morning.

I fit perfectly into Baba's lap. His arms circled and held me there, my head resting in the hollow of his shoulder. He read to me again.

> Stop, oh my friends, let us pause to weep
>   over the remembrance of my beloved.
> Here was her abode on the edge of the sandy desert
>   between Dakhool and Howmal.
>
> The traces of her encampment
>   are not wholly obliterated even now.
> For when the south wind blows the sand over them
>   the north wind sweeps it away.
>
> The courtyards and enclosures
>   of the old home have become desolate;
> The dung of the wild deer lies there
>   thick as the seeds of pepper.
>
> On the morning of our separation
>   it was as if I stood in the gardens of our tribe,
> Amid the acacia-shrubs where my eyes
>   were blinded with tears by the smart
>   from the bursting pods of colocynth.

I could hear the turbulence inside Baba's chest, the protests of his lungs against each inhalation of honey apple tobacco.

"Baba, who do you love more, me or Yousef?"

"Habibti," he began. I couldn't help but smile when he called me that. "I love you both the same," he said.

"How big do you love me?"

"I love you as big as the ocean and all its fishes. As big as the sky and all its birds. As big as the earth and all her trees."

"What about the universe and all its planets? You forgot that part."

"I was getting to it. Be patient," he said, puffing on his pipe. He exhaled, "And I love you *bigger* than the universe and all its planets."

"Do you love Yousef that much?"

"Yes. As big as the ocean . . . but without all the fishes."

My heart grew with all the fishes, the idea that Baba loved me just a little more. "What about the sky and earth? Do you love him that big but without all the birds and trees?"

"Yes. But don't tell anyone."

"I won't, Baba, I swear." My heart swelled with birds now. "What about the universe part?"

"Don't be greedy." He winked at me. "I have to get to work, habibti. Tomorrow."

Habibti. Tomorrow.

It was difficult to wake up so early and I would nod back to sleep in Baba's arms. Eventually I became accustomed to rising before the sun, a habit that has long endured. Every dawn, while Baba read on the terrace of our small adobe home, he and I witnessed the sun pour itself over the land, drenching everything it touched with life.

Many a night has let down its curtains
　　around me amid deep grief,
It has whelmed me as a wave
　　of the sea to try me with sorrow.

Then I said to the night,
　　as slowly his huge bulk passed over me,
As his breast, his loins, his buttocks weighed on me
　　and then passed afar,

"Oh long night, dawn will come,
　　but will be no brighter without my love.
You are a wonder, with stars held up
　　as by ropes of hemp to a solid rock."

At other times, I have filled a leather water-bag
　　of my people and entered the desert,
And trod its empty wastes while the wolf howled
　　like a gambler whose family starves.

Baba said, "The land and everything on it can be taken away, but
no one can take away your knowledge or the degrees you earn."
I was six then and high marks in school became the currency
I gave for Baba's approval, which I craved now more than ever.
I became the best student in all of Jenin and memorized the
poems my father so loved. Even when my body grew too big for
his lap, the sun always found us cuddled together with a book.

My life before the war returns to me now in memories bracketed
by Baba's arms and scented with the tobacco of his olive-wood
pipe. We had meager possessions and scarce necessities. I never
knew a playground nor swam in the ocean, but my childhood
was magical, enchanted by poetry and the dawn. I have never

known a place as safe as his embrace, my head nestled in the arch of his neck and stalwart shoulders. I have never known a more tender time than the dawn, coming with the smell of honey apple tobacco and the dazzling words of Abu-Hayyan, Khalil Gibran, al-Maarri, Rumi. I did not always understand what they wrote, but their verses were hypnotic and lyrical. Through them, I felt my father's passions, his losses, his heartaches, and his loves. He passed all of that to me. This great gift from Baba was something no one could take away. And decades later, in the bleak early hours of a Pennsylvania February, the words of Gibran's haunting rhythms and the memory of Baba's soft baritone would be my only thread of solace.

NINE

June in the Kitchen Hole
1967

THEN CAME JUNE OF 1967. The hot month of pretty things and no school. I was meandering in the abandon of childhood, one month before my twelfth birthday.

Not to be outdone by Lamya, our friend with a monkey's capacity for cartwheels and flips, Huda and I had resolved to execute the perfect somersault. We were practicing in the soft clearing near the peach orchard, west of Jenin.

"You call that a cartwheel?"

"Let's see you try, Amal!"

I did and landed flat on my back.

"Pathetic," Huda snickered.

"Oh God!" I moaned. "My leg! I'm really hurt."

"Get up . . . come on. I know you're pretending." Huda's voice spiked with concern. "Amal. Amal. Oh, my God!"

I erupted with laughter and Huda's alarm turned to irritation.

"That's not funny, Amal!" she yelled. "Anyway, you still can't even do a cartwheel, much less a somersault." She knew how to make me stop laughing.

"Neither can you!"

"I'm not the one trying to outdo Lamya."

It was true. Huda just liked to play, but with me, everything was a competition.

"Want to practice again later?" I asked.

"Yeah. Let's go climb Old Lady."

Old Lady was a fifteen-hundred-year-old olive tree with serpentine arms that twisted into the air like Samson's locks bursting from the center of a grazing pasture. Fruit dangled from hundreds of knobby little twigs on an enormous misshapen trunk, which was also a resting spot for local shepherds.

Baba once told me that no one owned Old Lady. "This old girl was here long before any of us, and she'll be here long after we're gone. How can you own that, habibti?"

I loved it when my father called me habibti, my beloved.

"No one can own a tree," he continued. "It can belong to you, as you can belong to it. We come from the land, give our love and labor to her, and she nurtures us in return. When we die, we return to the land. In a way, she owns us. Palestine owns us and we belong to her."

I asked Huda what she thought Baba meant.

"Your baba always says strange stuff. Haj Salem says he reads too much. Yesterday I heard Haj Salem tell your brother to go pull your father's nose out of his books and drag him to the Beit Jawad coffeehouse to smoke a hooka with him and Ammo Jack O'Malley."

Ammo Jack was a heavyset man with a cluttered laugh that seemed to rumble from untuned bass chords in his big heart. He had a full head of white hair, usually rumpled and unbarbered. His equally thick facial hair was yellow-stained by a long liaison with Lucky Strikes and occasional hooka pipes. His UN job was to administer the schools and clinics and he rarely visited his office, choosing instead the hooka-puffing company of Haj Salem at Beit Jawad's.

We climbed Old Lady's back, swung and dangled from her limbs, balanced on her neck, and finally rested on her belly, where her trunk split into three main branches.

"Is there anything left of the nail polish?" Huda asked, inspecting the chipped red paint on her nails.

Someone had given the polish to Mama as a gift a week earlier, but she was beyond such indulgences and had given it to me. At least ten of us girls had gathered to share it, painting one another's nails, imagining that we looked like the Egyptian actresses in magazines.

"There's a little left," I said.

She perked up. "Let's paint our fingers and toes again, but without all the other girls."

"Okay. But first let's have a spit contest."

"Haven't we had enough contests today?" Huda complained, but quickly relented.

A *spit-dangle contest. That's what we were doing when we were summoned.*

"Your spit will go farther if you suck snot from your head." I demonstrated, making hacking sounds. "Just regular spit breaks off. That's how come you always lose this game."

"That's gross," Huda complained.

"Amaaaal! . . . Huuuuuudaaaaaaa!"

Baba was calling us home to the camp, where we all lived in the shade of international charity.

"Your father's calling." Huda stated the obvious, as was her annoying habit. "Why isn't he at work today?"

"I don't know. Let's go."

We ran. I turned it into a race, but I stopped before we reached the camp's first row of concrete shacks.

Something was happening. Too many people were on the streets.

Instinctively, Huda and I reached for each other's hand and we walked slowly toward the commotion. Anxious throngs were chanting in the streets and alleyways. In their embroidered Palestinian thobes, women hurried about, balancing baskets of provisions on their heads. Uncertainty shivered in the air. Some people were crying. Some displayed their joy with the trilling of zaghareet. Israel had just attacked Egypt. A loud radio announced, "The Arab armies are mobilizing to defend against Zionist aggression."

Baba came toward us and gathered Huda and me in his outstretched arms. "Habibti, something has happened. The two of you must go directly to the house." He was calm and serious. "Now go, girls," and we went.

At our house, men were waiting for my father, who had gone off to telephone my brother in Bethlehem, where Yousef worked.

Mama hurried toward us when she saw Huda and me approaching. She surprised me with a tight embrace and mumbled into the air, "Praise and thanks to You, Allah, for my child." Mama kissed me as she rarely did. If I could, I'd not have let her go. Her sudden display of affection made me grateful for Israel's attack.

"Allaho akbar!" someone shouted. "Soon we're going home to Palestine!"

With Mama's new warmth lingering, I was hopeful. I conjured all the places of the home that had been built up in my young mind, one tree, one rosebush, one story at a time. I thought of the water and sandy beaches of the Mediterranean—"The Bride of Palestine," Baba called it—which I had visited only in my dreams. A delicious anticipation bore visions of the old life, the one I had never known. My rightful life, disinherited but finally to be regained, in the back terrace of Jiddo Yehya's and Teta Basima's mansion, with its succulent grapes dangling from their vines, Mama's rose garden, the Arabian horses Ammo Darweesh raised, Baba's library, and our family's farm, which had sustained half the village.

I comforted Huda, who seemed frightened, with a reminder that we would have our own room once we returned, and money enough for dolls. In my naïve confidence, I pointed to the disorganized and untrained men. "Just look at them," I told her, impressed with the would-be fighters who walked among us. "Just look . . ."

Baba had long been hiding rifles in a hole dug in the kitchen floor, under the sink. He was back now, talking to the men. I knew the time had come to use those weapons.

For years, I had heard Baba complain that King Hussein ibn Talal of Jordan was disarming the Palestinians, leaving us defenseless against Zionists who were amassing more and more weapons with the help of the West. So whenever he could get his hands on a weapon, Baba hid it in the hole in the kitchen floor. He had covered the hole with a sheet of tile and declared it off-limits to children. I dared not disobey.

That day I watched Baba open the secret hiding place and empty it of more than twenty rifles. He distributed the weapons to the fighters, whom I had until then only known as fathers, brothers, uncles, and husbands.

I stepped away. From afar, I fixed my eyes on the gentle soul who was my father as something fierce inside him forced its way to the surface. His face became hard and the smile that lived in Baba's eyes disappeared. He spoke to the men with an unfamiliar voice that bore no hint of the intellectual, solitary man who spent his time with books or in communion with the land. I had not the fortitude then, nor the capacity, to comprehend the urgent change in my father, or indeed that in the other adults—all of whom had already lived through one dreadful war and heartbreaking eviction.

"Amal." Mama grabbed my arm. "Don't wander off. You and Huda stay where I can find you."

A clap like thunder boomed in the distance. It made me jump and put greater urgency in Mama's voice. She looked at me with her bottomless black eyes, the ones I had inherited, and repeated the lesson she wanted me to learn most of all: "Be strong like I've taught you to be, no matter what happens."

My momentary conviction that better times were at hand sank into fear as Mama moved Huda and me, like game pieces, into a corner.

"Stay here and don't leave my sight," she ordered us.

None of the adults would tell us what was going on, so we pieced together snatches of their conversations as best we could.

The hurried tempo, long sighs, intense looks, and solidifying wills pushed Huda and me closer together, the two of us clinging to the wall, wide-eyed and confused. An announcement came that the women and children should stay put while the men were to hunker into defensive positions—"Until the Arab armies come," someone said. Huda and I locked arms. Fear crawled through our bodies and made our muscles twitch and contract involuntarily.

"I love you, Amal," Huda cried.

"Me too. You're my best friend, Huda."

"You're my best friend, too."

"We'll be safe. My baba has weapons and he'll protect us."

"Let's stay together."

"No matter what."

"Swear?"

"I swear by Allah."

We hugged to seal our promise.

The men waited for the enemy, but no enemy soldiers appeared.

Time after that ran as a continuous stream, unmarked by day or night. We could not see the enemy's face, but we heard them: airplanes, so many, flew close to the earth and dropped bombs. Mama hurried Huda and me into the hole in the kitchen, now devoid of firearms.

The hole was as deep as I was tall, and wide enough that Huda and I could crouch at its bottom. I looked up from that position and saw Mama's face, bottom-up. How strong her jaws looked that way. As she was closing us in, I caught sight of a brightly painted bowl on the kitchen counter, a Mother's Day craft I had made in kindergarten. I recalled how Mama's face had opened when I gave it to her, and how it had closed when I told her I wished I had a better mother to give it to; I was five then and I had just wanted to see if I could make her clench her teeth and bulge her jaw muscles.

The lid covered us in and the Mother's Day bowl disappeared on the other side. It was dark in that kitchen hole.

"Huda," I whispered, still holding on to her as tightly as she held on to me.

"Yes." She was trembling.

"I'm sorry I always yell at you." Huda had been my only true friend. Other girls had no tolerance for my endless competitions, which I had to win. I was bossy and rude. Now I thought I was going to die.

A long time passed before Mama suddenly pulled off the tile cover and handed us a baby. It was Khalto Sameeha's little girl, my three-month-old cousin, Aisha.

"Take Aisha. I'll be back soon," Mama said, her voice hoarse.

A month earlier, Khalto Sameeha had pierced the baby's ears, and Aisha was still wearing the darling little studs with blue stones that her father had chosen to repel the evil eye. We didn't know it yet, but Khalto Sameeha, her husband, and my six-year-old cousin Musa had not survived the attack. Only Aisha had. Wrapped in a blanket that Mama had knitted for her when she was born, Aisha lay alongside the road to the East Bank, not far from where her family lay dead on the ground. A woman hurrying from Jenin recognized the blanket and knew that Mama was still at the camp, having refused to flee with the others. She sent Aisha back to Mama with a young Jordanian soldier who was separated from his retreating battalion, which had been sent by the Hashemite Kingdom to defend against Israel's invasion.

Huda, Aisha, and I remained in the hole for what seemed like an eternity of ghostly quiet. Then Mama returned with a loaf of bread and milk for the baby. She was disheveled and dirty, her eyes darting side to side.

"Amal, Huda, are you okay?" Mama asked, reaching her arm inside to feel for us.

"Yes, Mama, but—"

"Stay put, girls. Jordan, Syria, and Iraq are fighting alongside Egypt. This will all be over soon. Everything will be all right."

"Mama, we have to poop and the baby has messed her diaper," I pleaded, but she was already gone.

Without words, Huda and I removed the diaper and buried it beneath our feet. We took turns relieving ourselves and covered the mess with dirt we scraped off the sides of the hole. Mama had left the tile cover slightly off for air and light to seep in, but the only air was a cloud of dust and no light came. We heard explosions and panic above, but we dared not remove the tiled cover or move at all.

Days passed, I think. The baby was inconsolable at times. Huda and I joined her, the two of us sobbing in terror with the child. The baby screamed until she could cry no more. We heard other screams. Beyond the tiled cover, children wailed uncomprehendingly. Women, as helpless as their children, cried and prayed loudly, as if trying to catch God's attention through the chaos. We heard destruction and blasts of fire. We heard chants. The odor of burning flesh, fermenting garbage, and scorched foliage mixed with the smell of our own excrement in the dust.

"Huda, I think this is Judgment Day. It's just like it says in the Quran."

"Oh God. Let's say the Shehadeh and pray for forgiveness."

"Ashhado an la ellaha ella Allah." We recited the words that would get us into heaven.

We cried. Our faces blackened and our bellies empty, we begged for God's mercy.

"Please forgive me, Lord, for splashing mud on Lamya's new dress. Forgive me for . . ." My prayers went on and mixed with Huda's.

"Please, Lord," Huda prayed, "forgive my father."

A loud explosion blew off the tile cover. Suddenly there was light and we were covered with dust and debris. My ears rang with the blast. I was screaming and crying, but I could not hear myself. The two of us were crouched over the baby, our arms covering our heads. I peeked at Huda and saw her suspended in mid-scream, a mute screech of absolute terror. Her hair was matted, white with dust and wet with blood, and her face was covered with filth. Blood dripped down her temple. My heart thrashed with such potency that I could hear it. *Ba-boom, ba-boom.* The blast closed my ears to all sounds except the rhythm of my heart's vigor and the gurgle of terror. It was a dense consuming silence, like the calm at the center of a hurricane or the hush of sound underwater.

I looked down at Aisha. She was sleeping. Her face was calm. Seraphic. Her sweet little rosy lips were slightly parted, almost in a smile. I did not understand. My tears landed on her face, streaking the filth on her cheek. Her abdomen was a gaping hole cradling a small piece of shrapnel. The whole world squeezed itself into my heartbeat as I took the bloodied metal in my hand. So small and light, how could it have cut her open like that? How could it have taken a life with such ease?

I rose to my feet still holding my dead baby cousin and the scrap of metal. The kitchen floor had been at the level of my eyes, but the kitchen was gone and I could see sky where the roof had been. Before me were heaps of rubble, some of it smoldering still. A man I recognized as our neighbor, Abu Sameeh, was digging frantically through a heap of rubble with his bloodied hands. He disappeared in a plume of smoke, then emerged with a small child in his arms and pierced my trance with a frightful howl of condensed irrevocability.

There, on the rubble where his refugee's shack had stood and where his family was buried alive, he stood on the threshold of an abyss and cried, his face deformed with agony and his voice charged with despair. Clutching his limp child in his arms, he arched his neck toward the heavens and released a hair-raising wail, a guttural surrender to his fate.

Abu Sameeh was a refugee who had started life over after 1948. That Israeli campaign had taken the lives of his father and four brothers. He had married in the refugee camp, raised children, and supported his two widowed sisters. Like the rest of us, he looked forward to the return, when we would all go home. But in the end, the original injustice came to him again and took his entire family once more. There could be no starting over a third time. Nothing more of life was left to live.

Children, some of whom I recognized, wandered aimlessly. Some were crying, some stared vacantly. I looked down and saw Huda still in the hole, stooped in a fetal position, rocking back and forth. She had stopped screaming, but I could hear her reciting the Fatiha, the first verse of the Holy Quran.

In the name of Allah, the Merciful, the Compassionate. Praise be to the God of the worlds, the Merciful, the Compassionate, Lord of the Day of Judgment. You do we worship and to You do we turn for help. Guide us to the true path, the path of those whom You have favored. Not those who have incurred Your wrath. Nor those who have strayed. Amen.

Then she'd start over. *In the name of Allah, the Merciful . . .*

I felt frozen, unable to lift my feet, as if they had been cemented. I turned my eyes, absorbing it all, and I saw Mama. She was sitting on the ground, her eyes distant and uninhabited. She seemed not to notice when soldiers pulled up in their trucks.

I ducked back into our hole, cowering under whatever I could pull over us for cover, shreds of corrugated metal and a mangled bicycle. I motioned to Huda with the "shhh" sign as our eyes bulged through a new fear.

I stood again, careful to peek without being seen. All I could see of the soldiers were their legs. They wore big boots that seemed to stomp my body as they walked about. They had bombed and burned, killed and maimed, plundered and looted. Now they had come to claim the land.

We ducked low in the hole when we heard shouts and conversations in a language we did not understand. Then, a single gunshot. When I dared to peek out again, I saw Abu Sameeh lying on the ground, a gun in his hand and his dead son in the other arm. The soldiers had shot him. He lay there, eyes wide, forever gazing, disbelieving. His life drained from his body onto the earth, and I watched from the kitchen hole as the pool of blood widened beneath him like a whisper of unsung endings.

Abu Sameeh had mustered what strength remained in him

and tried to fire on the enemy he had been searching for but could not find. His gun failed, and the soldiers executed him. It was a merciful thing.

Huda and I remained where we were, too frightened to move. After the soldiers left, we dug a small shelf in the earth with our fingers and laid the baby there, in the wall of the hole in what had been our kitchen.

We fell asleep, wrapped around each other like twins in a womb, until a hand reached into the hole and woke us. Startled but weak, we looked up and saw a nun. She was yelling in broken Arabic: "Stretchers, quick! Two little girls! They're breathing. Over here!"

Dumb with fear and hunger, Huda and I tightened our bodies around each other in an unspoken demand, which the nun understood. We would not be separated!

Huda remained curled like a fetus as we were carried to a makeshift hospital set up by international relief agencies. I was prostrate, taking it all in, my teeth grinding the dirt that coated my mouth no matter how hard I labored to spit it out. That was when I saw the torn corpse of Huda's father pass in a wheelbarrow. She did not see him, as her eyes were shut.

Where is Baba? *Please God please*, I repeated endlessly, *bring him to me now*.

"We named you Amal with a long vowel because the short vowel means just one hope, one wish," my father had once said. "You're so much more than that. We put all of our hopes into you. Amal, with the long vowel, means hopes, dreams, lots of them." Only six years old then, I grew with the belief that I alone held my father's dreams, all of them.

I had just one wish now: to see Baba again.

The good nun—Sister Marianne, she called herself—walked

next to us with Aisha covered in her arms. Before we got to the hospital tent we were by stopped a soldier—the first Israeli soldier I had ever seen up close. He was very tall. The sun screwed my eyes shut when I tried to see him all the way to the top of his helmet.

"You cannot take the child there," the soldier said in thick, broken Arabic.

"Why not?"

"Reporters."

"You're afraid the world might see what you do to children?"

"Shut up. I will shoot you here, if you like," he warned, raising his rifle, but also, strangely, smiling.

Unperturbed, she replied, "Do it. You are no different from Nazis who stood in my way when I cared for Jews in the Second World War." She narrowed her eyes around her recognition of his accent and spoke to him in a language they both knew. His eyes expanded with surprise, then he responded in the same language and finally nodded his head with permission for us to proceed.

"Take the girls to Station Three," Sister Marianne ordered the volunteer workers. As we passed the soldier, I looked up from the stretcher and glimpsed his eyes. Blue like the sky.

Huda and I were treated for minor cuts. She received a few stitches in her head. Probably the cut was from falling debris. I saw Mama in the treatment tent and rushed toward her, aching for another embrace. She sat motionless in a corner, just as I had seen her sitting on the ground when I had stood up in the kitchen hole. I stopped. Her spacious empty eyes did not see me standing before her. She seemed to see nothing.

"Mama." I touched her lightly, but she did not respond. I put my face in front of hers, but her eyes looked through me.

Sister Marianne approached me, putting her arms around me—how good that felt.

"Do you know this woman?"

"Is she dead?"

"No, dear. She's in shock. Do you know her?" Sister Marianne asked again.

Just then, a beseeching resentment filled me. I hated Mama for being in shock, whatever that was, for not being the one to put her arms around me, for always having been different from the other mothers.

"No," I lied. "I don't know her."

I shrank behind my disgraceful lie to remain in the protection of Sister Marianne, and Huda followed my lead. She was confused and frightened, wanting only to stay with me.

I recognized many other faces in the makeshift hospital and tried to recall the last time I had seen them before all this. Basima lay sleeping on a cot with a bloody bandage around her head and a splint on her leg. I had last seen her breastfeeding her baby at Khalto Sameeha's house, the day baby Aisha had had her ears pierced. Ammo Muneer was awake and bloody in a chair. My last image of him had been at Beit Jawad's coffeehouse, where he had sat reading and cursing Arab leaders who were quoted in the newspaper.

But still no Baba.

I closed my eyes and kept them that way as long as I could, opening them just enough to dispel the images from my own head.

Later that day, Sister Marianne took Huda and me with her in a Red Crescent truck on a long ride to Bethlehem. She made us hide inside food crates when we arrived at a checkpoint. Luckily, the soldiers just opened the door, took a quick look, and closed it back. When the truck stopped again, we were at a familiar church. Baba had once pointed it out to me as the Church of the Nativity, during one of the Christian celebrations we had often traveled to watch. "They say that's where Master Esa was born," he had said to me, patiently answering my endless questions.

Bethlehem looked just like Jenin, crumbled, torched, and strewn with death. The church where Master Esa was born had been shelled and still smelled of fire. Inside, hundreds of children, most of them orphaned by the war, sat on the floor. No one spoke much, as if to speak was to affirm reality. To remain silent was to accommodate the possibility that it all was merely a nightmare. The silence reached up to the cathedral ceiling and cluttered there, echoing sadness and unseen mayhem, as if too many souls were rising at once. We were existing somewhere between life and death, with neither accepting us fully.

Sister Marianne arrived, carrying an urn of water.

"Follow me, dears. You'll need to bathe together to save water," she instructed us as Huda and I walked behind her to the washroom. The good nun poured the water and left us. We were so bewildered that we got into the metal tub with our filthy garments. The warm water traveled over my body like a loving embrace, whispering a promise of safety.

Huda and I disrobed in the tub and sat across from one another. Browned water separated us, but our legs rested together. Face to face, we stared at one another's thoughts, seeing each other's terror and knowing that we had crossed some unmarked boundary beyond which there could be no return. The world we knew was gone. Somehow we knew that. We cried silently and moved into each other's small arms.

We lay that way, in the quiet of a foreboding for which we knew no words. I looked at my toes protruding from the water. Chipped red polish. It had been only one week since we had passed around the nail polish, giddy over something that had made us feel older. Now, in that bathtub inside the church where Master Esa was born, Huda's nails and mine still bore the chipped red remnants of that day. I calculated one week as the distance between girlish vanity and hell.

Slowly, I let my body slide, pulling my head beneath the water. There, in that silent world, like the stillness I had heard after the blast that had torn the kitchen and killed Aisha, I had an odd desire to be a fish.

I could live inside water's soothing world, where screams and gunfire were not heard and death was not smelled.

TEN

Forty Days Later
1967

LOOKING OUT THE BROKEN window in our devastated camp, the sun was still hidden from view, but the sky was already ablaze with the purples and oranges that announce its coming. Amazingly, the cocks had survived, keeping to their regimen of crowing, unaware of the portentous shadow that hung over us. As always, I was up before dawn. Sunrise belonged to Baba and me, when he would read to me as the world around us slept. It had been forty days since the war had ended and Sister Marianne had returned us to Jenin and I had found Mama with a broken mind. Baba and my brother Yousef were still missing.

Soon, the melody of the adan came through the air, into our makeshift homes, to call the faithful to prayer. Decades later, after a life in exile, that unmistakable cadence of the Arab soul would summon a calm certainty in my heart that I had made the right decision to return to Jenin.

Although it was still dangerous to venture outside, little Samer, our five-year-old neighbor, was running through the refugee camp yelling incoherently, his high-pitched voice slashing the stillness of "curfew," which was now a fact of our lives.

I guessed that the poor child was reliving the terror of recent events. It would not have been surprising, for lately most of the young ones wailed in their sleep.

"They're naked," Samer panted, struggling to order his thoughts. "They need clothes. They told me."

Little Samer sounded hysterical and people began to stir. Exhausted and bewildered eyes peered from windows. Old women cracked their improvised doors for a look.

"What's going on?" called a voice down the alleyway.

"Are we at war again?" asked another. In these moments of confusion, despair, and anticipation, the rumor pulsed like a wave of hope through the living dead.

People began to shout, "Allaho akbar!"

Faces appeared at the windows of every shack and more cries were heard as excitement surged through the camp. From a window opening blackened by fire came a euphoric note: "The Arab armies are coming to liberate us!" But the people remained hesitant, for we could see Israeli soldiers perched on their lookout posts. Arrogant conquerors, they. Murderers and thieves. I hated them as much as I hated the sea of white cloth fluttering over our homes—signs of our humiliating surrender.

But as quickly as the euphoria rose, so it fell when Samer began to make sense.

"Enough! There is no more war. The boy says our sons are alive," came a man's voice, quieting the war songs. It was Haj Salem. *He survived!* I wondered where he had taken refuge.

Haj Salem had seen it all. That's what he used to tell us youngsters. It took many seasons to learn his story because he gave it in pieces. "I've seen it all," he would say. "I worked faithfully for those yellow-haired, colored-eyed men, and in return they brought us foreign Jews who stole my furniture." Always just pieces to the puzzle of his existence, offered up one at a time. "I've seen it all. All the wars. They kicked us off the land and they took all the furniture I had made." Then he would walk away, leaving us to the naggings of curiosity. But in our camp, his story was everyone's story, a single tale of dispossession, of being stripped to the bones of one's humanity, of being dumped like rubbish into refugee camps unfit for rats. Of being left without rights, home, or nation while the world turned its back to watch or cheer the jubilation of the usurpers proclaiming a new state they called Israel. Haj Salem was a sagacious man with light-hearted humor who morphed wood into ornate furniture and delicate trinkets. Once, he claimed, a high-ranking British officer had bought one of his olive-wood carvings of the Virgin Mary to give to the queen of the yellow-haired, colored-eyed men, provoking in me a fantastical notion that Haj Salem knew a queen.

He was the most animated and lively character of my youth, and it was he who passed history on to the camp's children. My treasure of Palestinian folklore and proverbs came from him. It was he who gave me the names and stories of people I would encounter as miscellaneous victims of war in the history texts that I would read decades later.

We loved to trap him, tugging at him with pleas for a story about the old days. We would beg, ten or twenty snot-nosed, barefoot urchins promising not to bother him again, until he would relent, knowing well that we would return the next day, or the next hour.

We would gather around him on the ground and position our attention to absorb the great gifts he told. Then, he would weave dynamic accounts of life and past events with such intricate clarity that Palestine and all her villages, many long since razed by Israel, would come alive in my mind as if I had lived there myself. His raspy voice, scratched by years of smoking muaasal on the hooka, would spiritedly rise and fall, prodding our imaginations to live among our forefathers, watching past events unfold as if that very moment.

To our young eyes, Haj Salem seemed inconceivably old. "At least ninety," Lamya ventured to guess on one occasion. Only as an adult would I realize that he was merely in his early sixties during those times before the 1967 war. He was nearly bald, with thinning white hair patched over enormous ears. His brown skin bore a great deal of hair, covering a tall frame of bones that protruded at his shoulders like a clothes hanger under the traditional dishdashe. Like most Palestinian men, he wore the checkered black and white kaffiyeh, loosely swathed around his head. He had an unkempt mustache that often betrayed the foods he ate. It was a massive, jet-black thing that never aged—even when he was well into his nineties—an odd relic of youth on a withered old face. Best of all, he had no teeth. He had lost them, he said, "in a battle with scurvy." Naturally, all of us children hated "scurvy," which we assumed to be an Israeli monster. When we indulged in juvenile name-calling, invariably "scurvy" was invoked as an insult. "You're wicked like scurvy" was part of my own arsenal of vulgarity. By the time I was nine, someone had set me straight and I never used it again.

I remember well that toothless grin. As children, my cousins, friends, and I had often tried to make him laugh. We would lampoon Israeli leaders, ridiculing the self-important character of Menachem Begin, whose features we imitated by squishing our faces, or mocking the gnarly disorder of Golda Meir, the "Old Hag," as the Egyptians called her. Finally, when he could take no more, his pink gums would split his brown head in hearty laughter, squeezing his eyes shut into two long wrinkles that were indistinguishable from the other lines that took their place in that wonderful laugh. Having provoked what we thought was a hilarious sight, we would join him with our giggles.

I never knew from where he came, which town or village, because he knew so much about nearly every part of Palestine. Mama never told me and Yousef wasn't sure. It was said that his family was killed in the Nakbe of 1948—although he never told us that story. He lived alone, no wife, no children, no brothers or sisters. This was quite remarkable since Arab society revolves around the extended family. No one had "no family." But Palestinians, who became scattered and dispossessed following the Nakbe, proved so many exceptions to Arab society. He had been friends with Jiddo Yehya. That much I knew from Baba.

Haj Salem was also the first person to tell me about my brother Ismael, who had disappeared as an infant in the fateful mayhem of 1948. "The baby just vanished," he said in one of his narrated exhumations of history. "Your mother was never the same after that."

The day when little Samer ran yelling through the camp and I learned that Haj Salem had survived the war of June 1967 would mark the end of life as I had known it and the beginning of a military occupation that would rule our lives. It had been forty days since Israeli soldiers had gone from shelter to shelter, rounding up all the men who remained in the camp. For forty days, we were under curfew, and during those long hours Huda and I remained inseparable, even going to the bathroom together. Our house had been destroyed, so we took refuge in Khalto Sameeha's house, where we tried not to look at Aisha's crib. Mama was already there when we arrived, praying. She didn't say anything to me, just produced an old loaf of bread and cheese for us and went back to her prayer mat. I had followed her, and standing behind her, I wrapped my arms around her. I felt ashamed, wondering if she had been aware when I left her. Mama didn't say anything and neither did I. She just patted my hand softly, maybe lovingly. Then I left her, again. Huda and I found a deck of cards in the pantry and invented games with improvised rules. Sometimes we sat silently in a corner, hypnotized by the rhythm of Mama's murmur and the slow swaying of her body as she prayed on the floor for hours on end. We combed and braided one another's hair and started to talk about what we had lived through. Eventually, we cried.

Little Samer banged on the metal door. My head was already hanging out the window, and our neighbor, Samirah, hung her head from the window next to mine.

"Amal," Samer called to me, "Yousef is alive!"

Samirah, her hair wild and eyes still full of sleep, asked about her brother. "What about Farook?"

But Samer had already moved on, his little legs sprinting. By then other children from the camp had joined him, and they ran in a growing pack, like stampeding little banshees. I pulled my head inside to wake Mama, but she was already coming toward me.

"What's happening?"

"Samer Haitham says Yousef is naked."

"What?"

"Yousef is alive."

"Allaho akbar! Where is my son?"

"I think the peach orchard."

"Is he with your father?" She asked the question foremost in my mind.

Mama and I were outside in no time. Her favorite scarf was tightly wrapped on her head, its hems pouring down her shoulders. That scarf had been a present from Baba years ago when he got his first pay as a janitor at the UNRWA school for refugee boys in our camp. Now yellowed by time, it had been white with ornate stitching along its border. When Mama's body finally caught up to her mind, which had departed the world soon after the 1967 war, I kept that scarf, and I still have it, tucked safely in a small box that holds what remains to me from my family.

But on that fortieth day, all I wanted was to see Baba. Nothing else mattered. Nothing less would heal my wound but to lie in the safety of his embrace and hear him whisper that everything was going to be fine.

By the time a small crowd of people started to form, it was clear that, indeed, some of the men were returning to the camp. Women started their ululating zaghareet and chanted, "Allaho akbar." I knew Yousef was among them, but there was no mention of Baba.

I waited in the chaotic anxiety of those endless moments before the men arrived. The longer I could not make out Baba's figure in the distance, the greater my heart's fear of the unbearable. With fatiguing will, I held back an urge to cry and climbed onto the flat roof of an intact building for a clear view.

Looking out at the new landscape of hastily built Israeli watchtowers, I felt years crammed into weeks, a terrible dream with no end. The earthen taste of demise pervaded, and those days entrenched themselves in my memory as particles of bloodied dust and the putridly sweet scent of rotting life and scorched soil. We moved but went nowhere. We looked, but reality blurred our vision. We inhaled and exhaled the dust of carnage, but we were not breathing. As the crowd grew larger, I watched from the roof in the silence of my private upheaval. We were refugees, all of us. Those who had fled had become refugees once again, in another human junkyard dotting Israel's brief history. And those of us who had remained became prisoners in Jenin.

Now our waiting was for freedom. The original hopes to return home became pleas for elemental rights. Before, we had longed to see Haifa, Yaffa, Lod. Now it was a mortal risk to step into the fresh air. Gone were the days of family trips to Tulkarem and Ramallah. Jerusalem, too, was gone. "They burned Jerusalem; may God burn them, too," came a woman's voice in a context that I no longer recall.

Huda climbed next to me on the roof, where I stood searching the distance for Baba.

Our terror in the kitchen hole had only strengthened the bond between Huda and me. She possessed a tenderness and loyalty that yielded to me in our friendship. Although adversity in the decades ahead would reveal a natural poise and a quiet strength, in our youth her timidity and solitary temperament made many think her odd, especially the adults.

The old women in the camp loved to survey Huda's eyes. "There's that strange little girl. Come over here, darling," they would say. And while she stood obediently without protest against their prodding fingers and stale breath, they would behold what they proclaimed to be the "touch of the divine" in her eyes, which were an unusual mélange of gray and bronze.

Huda had lived with us for three years before the 1967 war. Those were likely the happiest times of my childhood. Each day, fourth through sixth grades, she and I walked hand in hand to and from school. We found trees to climb where no one could see us girls behaving like boys. We collected bugs and played make-believe in a playhouse we constructed. Our friendship was hallowed with "Warda," a one-armed doll that we rescued from a garbage pile near the village of Taybeh. Our playhouse was a home we built for Warda. It had four walls of piled stone and sat beneath the third olive tree, behind the twin cedars on the footpath to nearby Bartaa. We went there nearly every day to care for Warda, and word got around among other girls in the camp that Huda and I were the proud parents of a handicapped baby whose arm had been shot off by an Israeli and who soiled her diapers and cried real tears. It was not long before bands of curious little girls flocked from Jenin to visit at the "Warda house" near Bartaa. And, to keep with custom, they brought sweets. Sometimes the sky would darken over our tea and pastry parties, where Warda was passed among the cooing of so many mothers.

Huda's father was the reason she came to live with us. He was a dreadful man who beat her and when she was eight, *It* happened. He did *It* to her. It would be an unforgivable betrayal to utter the word. After *It* happened the first and only time, she confessed to me as if *It* were her disgrace, and she allowed me to tell Baba. Alarm had concentrated in Baba's eyes when I relayed the heavy secret, which I did not fully understand. With firm caution, Baba ordered me to honor Huda's confidence with discretion. If people knew, it would have been a fadeeha. Such a scandal involving a girl's virginity was of serious consequence in our culture. Not wanting to scandalize Huda's pain, my father convened with Ammo Darweesh and Haj Salem in a sober conspiracy to dislodge Huda's father. Baba did not disclose his cause to either my uncle or the haj, nor did they demand explanation. For my father had a natural authority that inspired loyalty from those who knew him. The three men went first to Faris, Huda's older brother. Humiliated, Faris turned his outrage on the weakest target, his sister Huda. But Baba managed to have Huda come live with us. And she and I could not have been happier.

We did not see Huda's father after that. It was rumored that he was crossing into Israel, supplying information about anyone in Jenin trying to organize opposition to Israel. Perhaps that was true for a time, but not after the war. I would not have recognized him in that wheelbarrow but for his four-fingered hand that dangled over the side. I never divulged that sight to Huda.

"Is your brother one of them?" Huda asked as she searched the crowd below.

"Yes. Is Faris?"

"Yes. He's naked."

"Yousef is naked, too."

"Why are they naked?" The question burned between us.

"I think their clothes were stolen," I finally said.

In the crowd below, I saw the top of Mama's head next to Um Abdallah, the woman who lived in the shack above ours. She was Samirah's, Farook's, and Abdallah's mother, a widow who was also Mama's closest friend. They spent much time together, cooking and knitting. Now they waited together for their sons.

"There's your mother." Huda's annoying habit of accentuating the obvious.

"I know."

"She's wearing her silk scarf."

"I know."

"She's with Um Abdallah."

I wanted to yell at her, but I knew such callousness, after all she had lived through, was too cruel. In the stupidity of my youth, I did not have the bearings to appreciate Huda's sensitivity and allowed it, instead, to exasperate me. I wish I had been as good a friend to her as she was to me.

Still standing on the roof, Huda asked, "Is Farook coming too?"

I did not answer. I could not find Baba among the approaching men.

"Do you think he's naked, too?" She looked at her feet, then at the sky, and answered herself: "Probably. They're all naked."

Lamya, the girl whose somersaults I envied and a regular guest at the Warda house, climbed up next to us. "Why are they naked?" she asked.

Huda answered, "The Jews stole their clothes . . ."

I felt crowded. The sun was full in the sky now. Another

dawn without Baba made the air sink with a dreadful reality, and I found it difficult to breathe. Baba's absence since the war had grown as big as the ocean and all its fishes. As big as the sky and earth and all their birds and trees. The hurt in my heart was as big as the universe and all its planets.

The war changed us, Mama most of all. It withered Mama. Her essential fiber unraveled, leaving her body a mere shell that often filled with hallucination. Following the occupation and the disappearance of my brother and father, Mama hardly left her prayer mat. She had no desire for food and refused even the paltry rations that arrived on the charity truck. The cotton of her gown grew dark with the stench of her unbathed body, and her breath soured. She smelled of fermented misery. Her lips hardened into a web of cracks and her body shrank, while she prayed. And prayed. And while her body lost mass, I watched her eyes grow more vacant, betraying a mind that would henceforth slowly forfeit its charge of reality.

Mama's bravery during the war would later be invoked as the essence of a fellaha's fortitude. She refused to flee. She had been pushed off her land once when Ismael was lost, and she had resolved not to let it happen again. Everyone agreed that when it mattered, she showed herself to be truly courageous. "A lot of us just talked big, but we ran for our lives while Um Yousef was true to her word. She said she would not let the Jews take away the only home her daughter knew," is what people said about Mama after the war.

Mama had stayed for me. And I had left her alone to go off with Sister Marianne. I have never forgiven myself for that.

The day Yousef came back was a day when I recall having great affection for Mama. She still had moments of lucidity then, though with a softer disposition, her austerity perhaps conquered by delirium. I saw her that day in the fullness of motherhood, with all the wounds of her shattered life and broken mind momentarily healed. I saw her as the woman who had risked her life to protect me from what she had once endured. Her movements were sincere, as were her tears. But it was fleeting, as she had already begun to lose her mind. I'd have grabbed those tender moments with my bare hands if I could and stored them in a safe place.

"Allaho akbar!" she cried when I told her that Yousef was alive. Rare tears streaked her face as she joined Um Abdallah in the crowd pushing at the edges of the camp, needing to get as close to the approaching boys and men as possible. We were still under military rule, forbidden from stepping outside whatever structure we knew as refuge. But people were overcome with the news that the men were returning, and they poured into the alleyways, perhaps finding safety in large numbers, or perhaps forgetting that there were risks. I think the soldiers were just not sure what to do.

"Allaho akbar," over and over. Tens of them, hundreds. A cacophony of "Allaho akbars" merging into one powerful chant as people converged. There were few males in the crowd. Only the very old or very young had been spared. A sea of scarved heads was visible from where I stood. Mothers, sisters, daughters, and wives crying and chanting together, waiting to see what fate, after forty days, was bringing to them.

By the time Yousef made it to the edge of Jenin, the entire camp, thousands of souls, was jumping and shouting, "Allaho akbar." He carried with him a bundle, apparently extra clothing delivered to the boys along the way by people who had learned that they had been stripped bare.

Soldiers rode up in their trucks and started shooting into the air. The boys from our neighborhood, five of them, hit the ground and the crowd dispersed, with most tucking themselves in the alleyways around our quarters. Lamya and the other girls had already left by then, and when the shooting started, Huda and I both jumped through the window, over the ledge, and into an empty dwelling that was partly bombed out.

I could see Yousef in the distance. He was wearing brown pants that were too small and a ruffled green shirt, the first thing someone had handed to him to cover his nakedness. Baba was not among the men and I cried despite myself, there in the window of the partly bombed-out house with Huda next to me, both of us in a fetal position as we'd been in the kitchen hole, both of us looking out over hundreds of souls jammed into the alley beneath us, all of them confused.

The initial euphoria chilled beneath the July sun when the boys were close enough for us to see the scars and fresh markings on their bodies, nature's brazen testimony of regular beatings.

Yousef had only been gone forty days, but he looked ten years older. His body had become slight, and seeing him like that put an awful pain in my heart.

Baba was gone forever. My mother kept waiting for him until the day she died, just as she waited to return home, just as she searched her mind for Ismael.

I needed to believe Baba was dead. I could not bear the thought of him suffering away from us and I chose to know he was in heaven wearing his dishdashe and kaffiyeh proudly, the tip of his pipe at his lips, a cup of coffee at his fingers, and a beloved book in his hands. I struggled all my life to keep that image of him—a strong, proud, and loving father. But inevitably the image of Abu Sameeh dead with his gun in his hand near the rubble of his home overtook me, his face eventually becoming Baba's face.

As the boys approached, I searched for Ammo Darweesh and my cousins. None were in the crowd and I thought they too had not survived. But I would learn later that they had all found refuge in the mountain caves, returning to Jenin months after the war.

Yousef and the five other boys came inside, and people converged to welcome their safe return and to inquire about their own missing loved ones.

Farook, Ameen, Taha, Omar, Mahmoud, and Yousef sat close together, passing a loaf of bread among themselves. They were overwhelmed, exhausted, beaten, and broken. Some onlookers urged the others to give them space and let them collect their wits. Farook's mother, Um Abdallah, stood over her son, holding his shoulders and kissing his head with a sad smile. Her eldest son, Abdallah, had been killed, but she refused condolences. "I swear by Allah, I will accept only congratulations for my son's martyrdom," she insisted.

With eyes that narrated the debilitation of sleepless and tearful nights, Um Jamal, our neighbor in the camp, kept asking the boys: "Do you know anything about Jamal, Yousef? Tell me, Mahmoud, son? Taha? Please, Omar, do you know anything about my Jamal? Please, son? Have you seen him? Is he okay?" Her head followed Yousef's averted eyes from side to side trying to find a hint of her son's fate in my brother's expression.

"Jamal and I were separated. That is all I know," Yousef lied.

I learned later that Jamal's life had ended as an "example." Soldiers executed him in front of my brother and fifty others. Jamal was blindfolded, hands bound and kneeling, when an Israeli soldier put one bullet into the head of the boy who frequented our house daily, who played soccer in the dirt fields, and who used to call me ammoora—adorable—and ride with us on trips to Jerusalem, the Jordan River, Bethlehem, or Jericho. He was sixteen years old when he became an example.

Yousef was impassive and wanted little to do with food or talk. His eyes, nearly all pupil, seemed to see something eerie.

The crowd thinned. Ameen, Farook, and Mahmoud remained with us. Mama and Um Abdallah sat on the kitchen floor holding hands, praising God and marveling at their boys, half-dead but still among the living, as if they were seeing them for the first time. I prepared kahwe and Huda served it dutifully on a tray to each person. Yousef stood up when he noticed me watching and pulled me into his arms, the lacy ruffle on his green shirt scratching my face. His embrace almost made me believe that it had all been just a bad dream.

But Baba still hadn't returned.

Later, while Mahmoud and Farook slept, I overheard my brother talking to Ameen. By then, Yousef had acquired a deliberate manner of speech and the war had consolidated an intensity to his character, which would one day take him deep into love and into history.

"It was him!" Yousef said. "I saw the scar! He's alive and he's a Yahoodi they call David!"

My brother had seen a Jewish soldier with a scar identical to the one that had marked the face of our brother Ismael, who had vanished seven years before I was born.

III.

THE SCAR OF DAVID

ELEVEN

A Secret, Like a Butterfly
1967

WATCHING DAVID, HIS BROAD shoulders bent over the dinner table, Jolanta could scarcely comprehend how much time had passed since the first day Moshe had brought him to her, a frightened, wounded little bundle.

She thought of that beautiful creature, now a man kissing her cheek and saying, "I love you, too, Ma!" He was so small in her arms then; she would hold him to suckle at her dry breasts when no one was around.

She had doted and fussed over him. Made him dress in too many clothes in the winter, something he had tolerated until the age of seven, when he had realized he could refuse to wear what she picked for him. She had adored even his defiance and could barely conceal a smile when he would assert his independence.

She always worried and he always said, "Don't worry, Ma, I'll be fine." When he had his first sleepover at the age of eight, she worried that he would feel homesick and she made him promise to call no matter what time of night. During his first weekend camping trip when he was ten, the list of her worries had been so long that even she couldn't remember it now. She worried that he had not eaten enough breakfast before school, that he would hurt himself playing football, that a girl would break his heart. She worried when he went to his first party, where she knew there would be alcohol. And when everything seemed fine she worried that there was something he was keeping from her that she should be worrying about.

She worried that someday he would find out that he was not really her son. Jolanta worried most of all the year David turned eighteen.

She did not want her boy to join the army. But she had no choice, nor did her son. Israel was a tiny haven for Jews in a world that had built death camps for them in other places. Every Jew had a national and moral duty to serve. So in June 1967, when his country went to war, David already had served in the Israeli army for one year.

The army sent him north to the Golan. He was strong, ready to serve his country. Ready to fight.

He was part of the battalion that was supposed to provoke the Syrians into retaliation so Israel could take the Golan Heights. General Moshe Dayan instructed them to send tractors to plow in an area of little use, in a demilitarized zone, knowing ahead of time that the Syrians would shoot. If they didn't start shooting, David's unit was told to advance the tractors until the Syrians were provoked into shooting. They used artillery and later the air force became involved. But on the last day, when Israel attacked the USS *Liberty*, in the Mediterranean Sea, David was sent home because of an injury to his hand.

He had been wounded by friendly fire that had burned his right palm. Jolanta's heart sank when she learned that her son had been injured, and she could find no peace until David returned home.

She threw her arms around him. "My boy! Let me see your hand."

"It's okay, Ma. They fixed it all up."

She inspected him to be sure, unable to thank God enough for her son's safety. "Are you hungry?" Jolanta was delighted to watch David eat the kreplach she had made. The kugel and blintze. *My heart won't survive if anything happens to him.* Somewhere in the corner of her love, the secret lay in wait. She had not intended to keep the truth from David. Since the day he arrived in July 1948, everything she was or had been had converged to make her simply David's mother. How he had come to be her son remained unsaid, a harmless butterfly in a field of love.

Now, seeing his bandaged hand, she could not bear the possibility of losing her son. Jolanta had no control over his serving in the army, but she could keep the truth hidden. *He's my son, that's the only truth he needs*, she decided, caging the butterfly.

TWELVE

Yousef, the Son
1967

A YOUNG MAN, A STUDENT at the University of Bethlehem, bursts through the doors of my classroom in the middle of my lecture on polar and parametric curves. Under normal circumstances, I might welcome the interruption. But not this day. Not for this explosion of news in the middle of my lecture.

"The Jews are bombing Egypt! There is war!" he yells, and leaves, running down the hall.

War. The word detonates a baggage of dread, which I have lugged on my back since I was five years old. Since 1948, when war and I were formally introduced.

It makes my blood run cold.

By the time I regain my bearings, my students have cleared out of the classroom in a frenzy, rushing beneath a sound banner of "Allaho akbar."

I must get back to Jenin.

Throngs are already filling the hallways and streets of Bethlehem. I run, pushing and shoving my way toward the dormitory where I rent a small room run by the Omar Bin al Khattab Mosque.

Haje Um Naseem opens the peep flap of the ancient wooden doors and closes it quickly when she sees me. In a moment, preceded by the clang of unlocking bolts, the heavy door swings open, slowly. Haje Um Naseem's tiny frame is dwarfed by the immense door as she waves me in.

"Yousef, ya Wliedi!" she says nervously. "Have you heard the news?"

This is the first time I hear her utter my name. In my two years of living in Bethlehem, she has always called me "Wliedi." Son. She brings me leftover food daily when I return from work. "Here, ya Wliedi. Eat, eat," she says kindly.

There is charity in everything Haje Um Naseem does or says. Perfectly erect, she is no more than four foot eight. She swims in her oversized thobe and today she drowns in worry.

"I have to get back to Jenin, haje," I say, moving quickly past her.

She follows me, extending her neck forward to monitor the floor so her hidden legs, keeping double time, do not trip on her thobe.

"Ya Wliedi! It is too dangerous to go now. The trip is too long and who knows what could happen in the next hour. They say Jordan and Syria are already on the move to defend Egypt, and Iraq is coming too," she says.

"My family needs me," I say, packing a small bag while Haje Um Naseem watches me from the doorway.

"I'll call for Abu Maher to take you. You will never find a taxi in this mess," she says, turning on her hidden legs. She is right. Most vehicles are already fleeing to Jordan.

Haje Um Naseem reappears in the doorway as I am leaving. She looks serious and authoritative. "Abu Maher will have the car ready in five minutes. For any reason, if he is unable to return tonight to Bethlehem, you will make sure he remains with your family in Jenin. Here," she says, shoving a wad of dinars into my shirt pocket.

I need the money. I have less than twenty fils in my pocket

and no way to pay for gasoline. But my pride moves my hand to return the money.

"Wliedi! I'll not have you disobey me. Anyway, it is the unused portion of your rent, which you may repay when you come back. Go, Abu Maher is waiting. Allah protect you both."

I kiss the top of her head, on her hijab, and leave.

THIRTEEN

Moshe's Beautiful Demon
1967

D AVID HAD BEEN HOME less than an hour when Yarel, a high school buddy, came with reports of a particular Arab prisoner.

"The son of a whore should be dead from the beatings. He's tough . . . ," Yarel said, beginning what sounded like a long irrelevant story.

"Why are you telling me? I don't care," David interrupted.

"Well, I made the boys leave off beating him . . . ," Yarel started again.

"I don't care. Here, have some kugel. Ma made it."

Yarel's serious tone did not waver. "David, you need to come see this Arab. It's like . . . he's your twin."

"Oh yeah?" David was amused. "You saying I look like a goy, shithead?"

"I think you should come with me tomorrow." He leaned closer. "Take away the scar, and your faces are . . . the same."

David swallowed, searching his friend's face for some hint of a practical joke. "Okay. Pick me up tomorrow."

In a cell with fifteen others, Yousef crouched naked on the precipice of life, his hands tied behind his back, his face hooded, as David and Yarel signed in at the Ramle prison, overcrowded now with detainees rounded up at random after the war.

"That's him, the one with the red paint on his arm. I marked him so we could find him," Yarel said, pulling the hood off Yousef's head.

David looked down at a man, black and blue, gashed and clotted. His eyes were buried in bloated flesh and his groin was swollen.

"What the fuck, Yarel! You made me come all the way out here for this?" David fumed. He had only a limited leave from the army and Yarel had dragged him on an hour-long ride to the prison for nothing.

"Fuck you, David. He wasn't so swollen yesterday. Believe me, I'd rather be home with my girlfriend on my day off instead of here." Yarel was convincing. "Do what you want. But I think you should come back. I have a few friends here. I'll see if they can transfer this one to the clinic. In a few days he should be fine."

That evening at the dinner table, David recounted his day with Yarel at the prison in Ramle. Moshe was home, eating with the family as he rarely did, and Jolanta was busy at the kitchen counter, as she usually was.

"Yarel said the Arab and I look like twins," David said, biting off a piece of bread.

A plate crashed to the floor in the kitchen. David turned to the sound and saw Jolanta stiffen.

"Are you okay, Ma?"

"I don't want you to go back to that prison."

"I wasn't planning on going back. But I don't understand why you're upset . . ."

Moshe looked down at his plate, slammed his fork to it, and stood, pushing his chair back. "Let him go, Jolanta. He has to go sometime." With that Moshe left. He walked heavily down the stairs, let the gate slam as he left their courtyard, turned the corner, strode three blocks farther, entered his refuge, and called out to the bartender, "Ben, pour me the usual. On the rocks."

Moshe had wanted David to know what had happened all those years ago. His gift to Jolanta in 1948 had grown into a secret too heavy to carry. That truth was not a butterfly but a demon—a demon with the beautiful face of an Arab woman who had served him lamb. Whose sons, one at her chest and the other at her legs, had moved with her, and who still cried, "Ibni, ibni!" inside Moshe's head.

He had not wanted all this. He had wanted wholeness: a homeland, a wife, a family. He had fought to save the Jewish people. But at his heels now were the awful evictions, the killings, the rapes. Moshe could not face all those faces, their voices. He found so little rest in his life. What repose his heart could extract was in the solace of drink. So he walked every day around the corner, then three blocks farther, and entered his refuge to silence the demons and himself.

David left with Yarel a few days later and signed in at the Ramle prison early that morning. The tight sound of their army boots echoed off the dingy walls as they walked toward the clinic. In a moment, David stood over Yousef's bed. His swelling had lessened and an IV bag dripped fluid into his arm, still marked with the red paint. Less than six inches separated their bodies, and in that space fit nearly twenty years, a war, two religions, a holocaust, the Nakbe, two mothers, two fathers, a scar, and a secret with wings flapping in the slow butterfly way.

David felt the Arab's wrist. "He has a pulse."

Swollen eyelids opened slowly and David's scar parted the haze of physical pain. They beheld each other for nearly twenty seconds. Twenty eternities, wherein David lingered, dangling by the hooks of too many wrong questions. *Is it possible they captured a Jew by mistake? A Jew who is related to me? A Jew who came to Palestine without knowing his relatives had also survived?* He searched his mind for answers, opening and closing the doors of memories for a clue to who, or what—if anything— this prisoner might be to him.

A tear slid from the corner of the Arab's eye. *Ismael!* He reached his hand toward the soldier and fell unconscious again, his arm dropping to the side of the bed.

FOURTEEN

Yousef, the Man
1967

I CHANGE.

My world changes, beginning with the day Haje Um Naseem calls me by my name. I go back to Jenin and have to push my way through the crowd into our home. My sister is stiff with fear against the wall. She cannot see me and I want to go to her. I want to speak to her, to pull her in to absorb the fear away, but I am pulled away by my father. He hands a weapon to me from his small cache in the kitchen hole to defend against the fury closing in on the earth. For the first time in my life, I hold a gun.

I need to find Fatima. You cannot go, my mother says. Mama, an experienced victim of war, is gathering supplies and mapping out hiding places with other women. She tells me that Fatima has gone with her mother and sisters to her uncle's house in Ramallah. Then she adds, she'll be safe there.

In the days that follow, I am once again surrounded by fire and fleeing souls. By fear coiled around rage. I fire my weapon, but in the moment of truth, when the test of my courage looks me in the eyes, I cannot take the life of another. I am afraid of violating life. Afraid of losing mine. So I walk with the others, my arms high in surrender. One of the Jewish soldiers pulls my face, searching it with amazement. I am puzzled then by the disbelief in his eyes. But now I understand it was recognition.

In that week I see how familiar words can break like glass and reassemble into goblins that waylay the mind with their claws. "Example" was but a pebble. I had heard and said it countless times before: "for example." Such an insignificant and mediocre word invades the happy days of my youth and steals the memory of playing soccer with young Jamal, whom the Jews make an "example" right before my eyes. I watch life trickle from the bullet wound of a sixteen-year-old "example" and marvel how things weak, even words, will turn vicious and merciless to gain power, despite reason or history.

Yousef, the Prisoner
1967

HERE IN THIS DANK place, I live on the love of Fatima and memories of our future. These are the threads onto which I cling for breath. My body is stunned by the dialects of torture. I have passed the threshold of pain into numbness. I cannot see, for my eyes are swollen shut. I lie here, bound to myself with rope, and I think something or everything is broken. I think I will die. I think of Fatima, my love, and I can smell the jasmine in her hair. I can see her lashes float through the air when she glides her eyes, mischievously, sinfully, toward me in the crowded market. An urn is perfectly balanced on her head and it does not fall when she seductively pulls her embroidered scarf to cover her lips before looking away. Suddenly, she turns her head back, to be sure I am watching. I am thrilled and my breath goes dry in an open mouth. She is walking for me. The urn on her head saunters with her and I am struck by the symmetry of her posture. I imagine her dancing with the urn balanced on her head as her hips and belly curve into each other in a private performance for me. I read her letters again, scribbled with ribbons in my memory:

My love, my mother and sisters are going to Jerusalem on Wednesday evening until Friday. Meet me on Thursday before the dawn prayers in our usual place. I miss you unbearably. It has been two weeks!

I hear sounds around me. Soldiers are feeling for a pulse in my neck. Water is thrown on me and I am sober now. No matter; I return to Fatima, the link that holds my body to its breath.

I see her in the peach orchard beneath the clear sky of the Orient, beneath my body, which I fear will explode with desire. She whispers into my lips, "When we are married, Yousef. Not now." But she lets me taste her softness, leading me into the hot paradise of her mystery. I take her breasts into my hands, keeping pace with the thrash of her heart's beating. She moves her body in a web of inexperience, passion, and the fear of guilt and sin. Her body exhales into mine a declaration of love and it calms my fever. I rise over her, absorbing her nakedness, her sacrifice of culture for love, her submission to me. I taste her breasts, gingerly, and feel the earth's spin in my heart. I make unspoken promises to God to deserve her love and protect her until eternity. I find the virgin grail that will someday bear my children, and I drink from her cup. She rises abruptly, alarmed by the surging ascent of pleasure. I kiss her lips. "Trust me," I say, and she does. Her back curves with the arc of the rising sun and she tumbles, moaning, in my arms. Soldiers wrestle me from my memory of Fatima. They speak to one another and leave. Soon I am transferred to a clinic. I go where I am led and wherever I am, I return to the place in my mind where Fatima lives.

The swelling has lessened and the electric bulb seeps into my eyes. I find light for the first time in an eternity and it illuminates a scar from another life. The scar I drew with carelessness onto the face of my brother, Ismael. But Ismael is dead. A Jewish soldier, whose face is mine, has taken my brother's scar. I think I am dreaming. I reach my hand to touch. But he backs away. Later, not now, I am sure that it was not a dream. Ismael lives. My brother is a Jew. He is an Israeli soldier.

Oh, Father, where are you? We were separated and I wonder, have the Jews taken you, too? Are you somewhere in this prison? In this clinic?

I am still alive. I am returned to the peach orchard where I had discovered heaven in Fatima's skin. The camp is destroyed. The refugees have been made refugees again and I cannot bear the welcoming back. The graffiti of torture on my body is indignant and will have nothing to do with celebration. I see soldiers perched on lookout posts and my heart fills with hatred. Strangely, it is the first time I feel so. But I am certain it will not be the last.

There are too many people around me and I search their faces for Fatima. Um Jamal comes to me in search of her son and I cannot bear her anxiety, the pain of what she knows deep in her heart. I cannot look her in the eyes. I want her gone from my sight. I cannot tell her that Jamal's life was taken to give meaning to the word "example." A meaning to which it has no right. I cannot tell her that the child she carried, fed, and loved is buried inside a word, which takes its new form from Jamal's smile and big ears.

There is gunfire and people let us be. Mother is stoic, though I know she is crying. Her tears fall on the wrong side, into the bottomless well inside her. My little sister, Amal, is cowering in the corner. Something has crawled into her eyes and made them cavernous. Though I want nothing more than solitude, the force of Father's absence compels me to reach for Amal, and she comes in hurried need into my chest, squeezing my bruised body as if she will fasten herself to me for all time.

Father has not been seen since the war. The sky leans on my fractured ribs as I conceive the inconceivable. That Father, the man I thought could never die, is dead. I lean back, a pillow at last, and hear the words of Rumi, murmuring in the susurrus of Father's breath:

How does a part of the world leave the world?
How can wetness leave water? . . .
What hurts you, blesses you . . .
Darkness is your candle.
Your boundaries are your quest.

I can explain this, but it would break
the glass cover on your heart,
and there's no fixing that.

Are these enough words,
or shall I squeeze more juice from this?

And in my mind I tell Father what I have learned. Ismael is a Yahoodi, a Sahyouni who fights for Israel.

SIXTEEN

The Brothers Meet Again
1967

FIVE ISRAELI SOLDIERS, FOUR on the ground, one in the watchtower, were manning a checkpoint near the village of Bartaa. They rotated their duties in sets of two, shuffling and sitting back in the ennui of tedious cruelty. David was idling in the jeep when two Palestinians approached the checkpoint, IDs and permission slips extended for inspection. All was in order but the soldier at the gate ordered them to step aside, halting the long line of Palestinians waiting to cross. The soldier was a corpulent New Yorker whose family had immigrated to Israel.

"Hey!" The soldier stuck his head in the jeep, where David sat eating watermelon. "Come see this son-of-a-whore Arab. He looks like your fucking twin!" he said, laughing.

Dread washed away the boredom. Jolanta's butterfly wings fluttered in David's belly; Moshe's demon breathed down his neck. The secret he did not know, did not want to know, had followed him and he hesitated before getting out of the jeep.

Following the officer, David suppressed an impulse to kick his superior, to watch the fat New Yorker roll down the hill. He did not want to see that Palestinian again. The one who had his face without a scar.

Peering beneath the rim of his helmet, David approached the Palestinian and the two men became yoked in the same angles of their jaws, the same dimples on their chins, the same fullness in their lips.

Their stares bulged with questions—*Who the fuck are you, Arab?*—*How did you become a Jew, Ismael?*—and in the air hovered a secret David did not want to know.

With the sorrow of so much gone so wrong, Yousef asked using the few Hebrew words he knew, then in Arabic in case the soldier understood, "Is your name Ismael?"

The New Yorker–cum–Israeli soldier laughed.

Violent wing-flapping butterflies cluttered David's vision and demons blew in his ears.

David slapped the Arab. He struck him next with the butt of his rifle. He knew not why, but now he could not stop. He kicked the Arab's groin repeatedly. He did it again and again until *that* Arab—*that* face—was unconscious. The man's friend cried nearby. "Please, please stop. We are not terrorists. He has done nothing. Our permits are valid. Please," he begged.

"Okay. Okay," the New Yorker responded, pushing David aside. "I don't want to have to fill out all the paperwork for a checkpoint fatality," he said.

Yousef lay bleeding. "Okay. Take him where you came from. Now!" the fat soldier ordered.

David walked away breathless.

SEVENTEEN

Yousef, the Fighter
1968

I FEAR I MAY BE impotent. From when he beat my genitals, I think there is permanent damage.

Urinating hurts. But I hurt more when I see Fatima. She walks past the garage and I hide beneath a car hood, pretending not to notice her, when all my friends know she has no business in Jenin but me. And they all watch me hide, and they in turn hide from the sorrow on her face.

My little sister, Amal, searches for me, too. I see her with Huda, staring at me across the street. I know she is waiting for me to fill the void Baba left.

Soldiers search for me.

Mama is wasting away.

I am damaged, of no use to the people I love. I'll die if I stay here. But something in me remains afire. Something that refuses to break, insists on a fight.

EIGHTEEN

Beyond the First Row of Trees
1967–1968

As the conquest in 1948 did for Hasan, Israel's attack in 1967 and subsequent occupation of the West Bank left his son Yousef with a tentative destiny. The grip of Israeli occupation wrapped around his throat and would not let up. Soldiers ruled their lives arbitrarily. Who could and could not pass was up to them, and not according to any protocol. Who was slapped and who was not was decided on a whim. Who was forced to strip and who was not—the decision was made on the spot.

Yousef matured in the likeness of his father, his quiet temperament whispering Hasan's legacy. He found refuge in the belly of solitude and braced his air with deliberation and thought. Because the occupation curbed Palestinian movement, Yousef could no longer travel to his work and gave up his post at Bethlehem University, accepting a teaching position at the UNRWA boys' school, where his father had worked as a janitor.

For the same reason, Yousef was unable to escape to the hills at will. Instead, he tipped his after-hours energy into the garage he had inherited from his father. Before long, Yousef was away from Amal and his mother most waking hours. Occasionally, he could be found at the Beit Jawad coffeehouse, puffing on a hooka, idling with friends over backgammon or cards. But every Friday, after the Jomaa prayers, coerced by the call of solitude, the seduction of natural beauty, and the potent compulsion of habit, he would risk the humiliation and interminable delays at checkpoints to venture to the hills, as he and Hasan had done since before Yousef could remember. There, under the shelter of trees, Yousef read. It was a daring endeavor, each time a solitary incitement to honor his father's memory. Just as Amal continued to read at dawn, as she and her father had done, Yousef kept returning to the pastures with a book. These were the conditions of helplessness, grasping at continuity, salvaging what could be kept of their source of strength—Hasan, their baba.

Within six months, Yousef had endured torture and random beatings that had marked nearly every part of his body. He had been forced to strip before women and his students, had been made to kiss the feet of a soldier who had threatened to beat a small boy if Yousef did not kneel. Most men had endured such treatment. Most were broken. And most had returned from the humiliation with violent tempers aimed at their wives or sisters or children.

Yousef turned everything inward, as Dalia had done. He cloistered the pain, letting it tangle with powerlessness. Silence consumed their little shack in Jenin, and both Amal and Yousef would later recall those times with a thick taste of emptiness.

Toughness found fertile soil in the hearts of Palestinians, and the grains of resistance embedded themselves in their skin. Endurance evolved as a hallmark of refugee society. But the price they paid was the subduing of tender vulnerability. They learned to celebrate martyrdom. Only martyrdom offered freedom. Only in death were they at last invulnerable to Israel. Martyrdom became the ultimate defiance of Israeli occupation. "Never let them know they hurt you" was their creed.

But the heart must grieve. Sometimes pain emerged as joy. Sometimes it was difficult to tell the difference. For the generations born in the camps, grief found repose in a bed of necrophilia. Death came to resemble life and life, death, and there was a time in her youth when Amal aspired to martyrdom.

I can explain this, but it would break
the glass cover on your heart,
and there's no fixing that.

Yousef rarely joined the angry chanting of funeral marches. He
did not celebrate martyrdom, nor did he show grief. A deep
aching for life simmered inside him behind a shell of indifference.

Amal adored him so and longed to be in the folds of his every
day. Sometimes, she and Huda sat across the street from the
garage to watch her brother work, hoping that he would invite
her to look beneath the hoods. To share in his life. To reassure her
of family. To hug her as he had on that fortieth day after the war.

Yousef spotted her a few times but never asked her over.

They hardly spoke anymore, Yousef and Amal. After the
incident at Bartaa, when David had beat him to the ground,
Yousef closed the doors of his heart. Letters from Fatima came
and were not answered.

While Yousef encased himself in a simmering decision, their
mother roamed the crowded realms of her mind, embroiled in
discourse with shadows. Um Abdallah was Dalia's persistent
companion, the two of them knitting all day on the balcony
that leaned under their weight and shaded the front entrance
of their home. Amal and Huda often marveled at the two older
women, wondering if they were very brave or just unaware of
the balcony's rickety state. For it was essentially decorative,
barely wide enough to accommodate two people. Other than
that, Amal paid little attention to Um Abdallah then. But in
revisiting those times years later, she grew to love the woman
who had shown her mother such undaunted loyalty. Even when
Dalia was most confused, Um Abdallah listened to her gibberish
monologues and gently placed her back in the knitting chair if
she started to wander off.

Huda returned to live with her mother and brother soon

after the war. But she and Amal still spent their days together and that was the only sense of continuity they had.

As before, the girls mostly fended for themselves, but now Amal was bound by custom to ensure the proper running of the household. Before the war, the backdrop to Amal's life had been colored with Baba's love at dawn, Mama's stoic rearing, and Yousef's clandestine love affair with Fatima. Now, those hues were replaced by military green and the pale emanations of depletion. Neighbors looked at her with pity and whispered.

"What is the girl going to do?"

"She's almost marrying age. That's good."

"Yes. God willing she'll find a good man soon to take care of her."

Though her body had already begun to stretch and curve with new form, Amal was a child, twelve years old, on that cool January Friday when the citrons were ripe and the vines were being pruned and Yousef unexpectedly came home from the Jomaa prayers.

Amal was delighted by the surprise. She made lunch, their biggest meal, and was preparing the floor with a covering of old newspapers, where they would eat. The prospect of spending time with her elusive brother elated her and she was eager to flaunt her culinary skills. Dalia had also been coming up for air from the abyss of unreality and Amal thought it would be like old times. Something like the family they had been.

"Amal, can you deliver this to Fatima?" Yousef asked, holding out a sealed envelope.

Crestfallen, she asked, "Aren't you staying to eat lunch with us?"

Yousef felt Amal's dejection and pretended to follow the "intoxicating aroma" of her cooking, ending up next to his sister.

"When did you get so grown up, Amal?" he mumbled with a mouth full of the food she had prepared.

"I'm almost thirteen."

Surprised by the forward move of time, Yousef paused, sizing her up, seeing the physical evidence that time does indeed pass, irretrievably. He looked at his little sister and felt a lash of guilt for having paid her little mind since the war. "You're beautiful," he said.

Those perfect words, wonderful to her ears, resonated against Amal's chaotic, awkward sense of self. She beamed.

They shared the makloobeh—a pile of rice made golden in the syrup of lamb, eggplant, and ginger—and passed the cucumber yogurt sauce, the browned pine nuts, and the crisped onions. Amal was happy.

The meal was embellished with spurts of laughter from Mama, who found humor somewhere in the hive of her unseen world, while Yousef and Amal conspired purposelessly in risible peace and smiles, placing that time together in a box of good memories. The memory of their last meal together with Mama.

After lunch, Amal ran with Yousef's envelope to fetch Huda. Together they hurried on their familiar delivery mission of shuttling Yousef's and Fatima's love letters. "Just like the good old days," Huda said.

"Yeah. On our way back, let's see if the Warda house is still there."

Just like the good old days.

Fatima spotted Amal and Huda from her window and waited anxiously for a letter from her lover. Her dimpled smile brightened the house as she took the letter in a dramatic thrill.

"Help yourself to some cookies, girls. I have some hot tea on the stove," she said, tearing into the envelope as she walked to the back room.

They helped themselves and waited. A large mirror, its gaudy gold frame flashing with counterfeit gems along its border, leaned against the wall, projecting the fullness of Amal's form. She had never seen her entire body at once like that. They had only one mirror, small and insufficient, fixed above the bathroom sink in Jenin. In Fatima's home, she witnessed for the first time the buds on her chest, which had been sore for weeks. They rounded the cloth of her shirt in a bulge that summoned her hand to trace the signs of woman.

"What are you doing?" Huda, chomping on the sweets from Fatima's kitchen, looked at Amal's breast cupped in her guilty hand.

"My chest is sore," Amal said, trying but failing to capture a casual tone.

"Aunt Nadia says that's what happens when they start growing," Huda said indifferently. "I wish mine would start growing soon." She inspected herself with excited hope.

"Why?"

"Don't you like yours?"

"They hurt."

"I know you like them," Huda said accusingly.

"So?"

"Can I touch them?"

"No!!!"

The silence that followed was broken by Fatima's sobbing from the other room.

"Fatima's crying," said Huda.

"I can hear she's crying!"

"Fatima, are you okay?" Amal asked, pushing open the door.

Hunched beneath her oversized pale blue dishdashe, Fatima lifted her face from her hands. She looked terrible. She wiped her nose in vain, attempting to compose herself, but her hair clung to her wet cheeks and her eyes were red and swollen.

The letter was crumpled in her hand.

"Amal, dear, why don't you and Huda go on home now," she said very softly, achingly.

Amal and Huda walked the usual path, winding along the

hills of northern Palestine. They found the old Warda house intact, but Warda was not there.

Both felt the sting of losing their one-armed doll, their child, but neither mentioned it. They grieved privately in their young hearts, because it seemed infantile now to cry for a doll now that they had buried Aisha, a real baby who cried real tears and bled real blood. But the hurt of losing Warda was worse, and that was a secret each held from the other as they walked on from the Warda house.

The trees had lost their leaves to winter's chill and the silver wood of olive trees stood bare like colossal ancient hands, the gnarly and twisted guardians of time reaching from the earth, patiently resigned to wait for the ripe season. Homes, some centuries old, with dense vines hugging their masonry, dotted the hillsides, and shepherds moved about with their herds.

Many years later, Amal would recall that life-giving beauty she had taken for granted, never imagining something so breathtaking and ancient could be wiped away or that anyone would want to wipe it away.

At that time, most of the West Bank was still draped in green, the natural majesty that bows for the wind, sheds for the chill, and blossoms for the sun. But it changed. One home, one farm, one village at a time. Demolished, confiscated, razed—a ceaseless appropriation of Palestinian land. "Imperialism by the inch," Haj Salem called it. Today, the path where the girls carried Yousef and Fatima's love blends into barren wastelands, littered with the rubble of old homes, burned tires, spent bullet casings, and struggling olive saplings.

"I wonder what the letter said to make her cry." Huda was concerned for Fatima. Their walk back was brisk, at least until they reached the checkpoint.

There, a slender soldier asked, "Where are you going?"

"Jenin," Huda answered meekly.

"Jenin," Amal said, despising her own subservience.

On cue, they produced the papers and cards they had been instructed to carry since June 1967. These were the color-coded ID documents that identified Palestinians according to their religion and the area where they lived along with various permission papers for travel east, west, north, or south. Special permission was required for medical treatment, commercial movement, university passes, such that a single individual ended up carrying piles of pink, yellow, and green slips, crumpled and tattered from persistent fingers, sweat, and the constant unfolding, inspection, and refolding.

At the opposite side of the checkpoint, another soldier questioned Osama Jamal, a fourteen-year-old boy who lived in Jenin—not in the refugee camp but in the actual town where the camp was located. His father owned the local bakery that captured passersby with the aroma of fresh breads, manakeesh, and fatayer.

Osama was pushed to the ground and kicked by the soldier at the checkpoint. Another soldier helped him to his feet before turning angry Hebrew words on the first. While the soldiers quarreled, Osama limped away with a fractured rib and a crushed ego, praying that the two girls from Jenin had not noticed him.

Once out of the soldiers' view, Amal and Huda offered him help, but Osama refused until the pain conquered his pride and he relinquished his bags, leaning his body on their shoulders after they promised not to reveal that he had accepted assistance from girls.

"You're Yousef Abulheja's sister, aren't you?" he asked.

"Yes," Amal answered, thrilled that he had spoken to her. "Your nose is bleeding."

Huda produced a tissue from the constant stash she kept in her pockets because, as she repeatedly told Amal, "you never know when you'll need a handkerchief."

Amal had never been so close to a boy other than Yousef, her baba, or Ammo Darweesh. The proximity flushed her with modesty and timid excitement, and a rush of bashfulness lodged in her throat. She accepted the weight of his arm stretched across her shoulder, pushing her head forward and her gaze downward, while something fluttered in her belly. They walked in silence, paced by the labor of Osama's jagged breath, and Amal's gaze fastened itself to a wrinkle in his pants that disappeared and gathered with each stretch of the thigh beneath the cloth, while the ground moved beneath their steps.

"Do you get bread from my dad's store?" Osama asked, the pain truncating and elongating his words. Amal lifted her head. But he was not addressing her and she saw clearly that Huda was as oblivious to his interest as he was to Amal's.

"Don't talk, you'll make it worse," Huda responded with uncharacteristic assertiveness that was not quite confident but rather willful, and now Amal's shyness was rinsed away with envy.

At home, Amal found Yousef holding Mama's hand and talking into the stagnant air that hung over her forsaken eyes.

"Do we need bread? I can go get some," she interrupted, indifferent to the perceptible gravity in the room, wanting only an excuse to be in Osama's presence again.

"Amal, I need to talk to you," Yousef said. "But not now. Can you stay with Mama for a bit? I'll be right back." And off he went. Impatient to know what Yousef had to say and why Fatima had been crying, Amal looked uncharitably at Mama and sat in a rancorous mood next to her.

Dalia turned to her daughter. She surfaced tenderly above the fluid canopy of unawareness, touched Amal's hair with her lips, *maternal at last*, and said, "Yousef is leaving," seamlessly returning to her depths. *Come back, Mama!* Amal's heart called, but Mama had already retreated into her mind.

Amal knew what Mama said was true. Yousef was leaving. She feared he was being hunted by the Israelis. So many men had gone away in handcuffs and blindfolds, never to be seen again, siphoned into the place wherefrom emerge only the subjugated and broken. She felt the approach of something frightening. Something she could not yet view or grasp, like the foul breath of a hiding beast. It made her shudder and her legs erupted in a directionless stride. She ran, unsure where to go or even why she was running.

Huda. *Where is she?*

"Huuudaaa," Amal called beneath her friend's window.

Huda's head appeared in the window long enough to say, "Not now. I'll come over later. I can't talk now. Bye."

God, what is happening! Amal ran, unable to control the explosion in her legs, the tender buds on her chest tormented with every stride. Her eyes stung with tears, her lungs burned with the cold until she fell to her knees, exhausted, in the peach orchard, the place that had once bustled with activity during the spring harvest and had been a clandestine meeting place in the winter for young lovers to hide from the watchful eyes of their families. Now it was off-limits to Arabs, another domain she dared not trespass.

Yet there she was, just beyond the first row of trees ...

NINETEEN
Yousef Leaves
1968

Y ET THERE I WAS, just beyond the first row of trees in the peach orchard, and it was growing dark. It was cold and I was too lonely to be afraid. I folded my limbs, winding into exhaustion and making believe that I lay in the embrace of

Osama. I slept that way, melted into the darkness of a star-filled sky, and awoke before dawn above a thin layer of fog hovering low to the ground.

I don't recall how the sight to which I opened my eyes affected me then, but the memory of that morning's landscape takes my breath away now. It was the picturesque backdrop of my parents' lives—miles of pasture carpeting valleys nestled amid waves of olive groves. Trees like beckoning grandparents, hundreds of years old, wrinkled and stooped with heavy arms that stretched to every direction, as if in prayer. Those who took that glorious land, which had glistened green beside the blue Mediterranean waters since before Moses, claimed that it had been a "desert" that they had "made bloom." A magnificent sun poured its light over the hills like yellow paint and lit the old Arab homes that were enduring the perils of abandonment. No other soul was in sight and I thought then that I understood the formidable enticement of solitude.

Unthinkingly, I reached for my new breasts. Seduced by curiosity I caressed them with thoughts that roused shadows of guilt. Shame stirred, reminding me of scriptures, sin, and punishment. But I heeded nothing except the irresistible slip of my hand into my panties and there, under a tree in the forbidden peach orchard, I found the unspoken pleasures of womanhood.

My hand emerged guilty and bloody, evidencing the arrival of the mysterious and long-awaited menstrual cycle. I smelled my scent, even tasted my own blood, and believed that I had been transformed overnight into a woman, that my world had changed in a way that was magical. I got to my feet and started back to Jenin, confident that Yousef was not really leaving, that it had all been a misunderstanding.

A voice broke my fantasy in broken Arabic. "Stop!"

A soldier!

I lifted my pleading eyes toward the sun, but its indifferent and brilliant smile only blinded my sight with black spots as I was caught trespassing. First one, then two more soldiers were upon me like hyenas and I shook with fear. They asked me endless questions, passing the stack of identity papers between them. One soldier carefully refolded the papers and politely, compassionately, returned them to me. "Go home," he said.

Untrusting, I put a distance between them and me with reluctant, suspicious steps, until a primitive instinct discharged in my wobbling legs a sprint homeward. As I ran, a swoosh seemed to set my ear on fire as something terrible passed within an inch of my head. Then my abdomen cramped. My breathing frightfully quick and loud and my knees weak, I stopped at the edge of Jenin, not far from where Osama had asked to take a break from walking when Huda and I had helped him the previous day. I simultaneously looked and felt where my right leg was oddly wet and warm. In the inchoate realization that my own blood flowed, I entertained the notion of a colossal menstruation. My hand moved to the cramp in my side and as my fingers sank into a horrid slush, my knees buckled, my eyes bulged and rolled, and my last string of consciousness that day roiled from the depths of the earth, through my lungs, fleeing my breath as a wild scream.

I'd been shot.

I opened my eyes to light and an unfamiliar female voice speaking in Palestinian Arabic, "She's waking up." The light disappeared into a halo behind Huda's face. Fatima stood next to her and Lamya next to Fatima. I heard Fatima say that Haj Salem, Ammo Jack O'Malley, and Ammo Darweesh with his family and others from the camp were outside the hospital, smoking and waiting for news.

A familiar murmuring, that audible swirling of a broken

mind, caught my ear and I turned my head toward it, finding Mama and Um Abdallah, the two of them looking like immobile room décor. Mama was dressed in her beautifully embroidered thobe, delicate but steadfast. And I thought then not of the bullet or the pain, or of Yousef, of Osama, or Baba, but of Dalia. I could at last see through the gaunt shell of my mother to the colorful, daring, and vivacious Bedouin girl whose fire had been tamped with a hot iron and whose wits had been doused with the ashes of too much death and too many wars. Those were my meditations when I awoke from the surgery that removed the metal fragments from my abdomen. The bullet had come from the direction of a southern watchtower, not from the ground soldiers behind me who had checked my papers. Such was the conclusion of the physician who examined the trajectory through my body. The bullet had struck my right side just above the kidney and exploded, tearing chunks of flesh from my belly upon exit.

"It's burning," I said.

"Here. The doctor said you should take this for pain," Fatima said, handing me two orange pills.

"Bless your hands. Where is Yousef?" By their desolate expressions, I knew he wasn't coming.

"He looked for you . . . ," Huda began, and Fatima added that she was sure. "He would not have gone if he'd known you'd been shot."

Gone where?

"Here." Huda extended a letter Yousef had left for me.

Bismillah Arrahman Arraheem

My dear sister, Amal,

I have to go. Please understand. I've been writing this letter to you for weeks and I can't find the right words. Every time I sit down with a pen I remember a promise I made to Baba.

One Friday, while we sat in the west olive groves after the Jamaa prayers, Baba made me promise to take care of you if anything ever happened to him. He wanted you to get an education, to marry a good man. I was too naïve to believe the Jews would invade again, but I believe Baba sensed the war coming.

I thought Baba would be around forever. I don't know how to keep my promise to him. If I stay here, these Israelis will eventually kill me. They have all the power and they want all the land. So far, nothing is stopping them.

They've taken everything, Amal. And still they take more. I can't sit by and watch helplessly any longer. Please, little sis, forgive me for leaving. I'm going to fight. It's my only choice. They have scripted lives for us that are but extended death sentences, a living death. I won't live their script.

If I am martyred, then so be it. Be proud, pray for my soul, and celebrate my passing into Allah's kingdom, as all martyrs who die fighting for justice, freedom, and the land shall be there to let me in among them.

I am like a caged bird here. I know you are too. It breaks my heart that I cannot make for you the life Baba wanted us to have. It is unbearable to think of our future as nullified, condemned to an eternal refugee's life of subjugation and shackles.

The resistance is forming and eventually we will take back what is rightfully ours. You were born a refugee, but I promise I will die, if I must, so you do not die a refugee.

I must leave Mama in your care. It is a terrible burden for so young a girl. My share of the garage I gave to Ameen in exchange for his promise to look after you and Mama. I also left all my savings for you. I left it with Ammo Darweesh with instructions that it be used wisely, for your education if an opportunity arises. Please keep in touch with Fatima. She loves you.

Love always, Yousef

Yousef had started saving that money when he was sixteen years old, after he met Fatima, to pay for a nice wedding and a new home. I tried to understand, as he asked me to. But all I could feel was betrayed and abandoned. With Yousef's departure, I was now truly alone. It was January 20, 1968.

TWENTY

Heroes
1967–1968

JUST BEHIND THE GREENERY of the Jordanian town of Karameh, the earth ascends into stony hardscrabble hills, where a Palestinian refugee camp, another city of cold tents and muddy paths, was also the headquarters of Fateh, the Palestinian revolutionary fighters whom Yousef had joined under the leadership of a young engineer named Yasser Arafat.

In March 1968, a formidable Israeli invasion force marched through the morning fog over the Allenby Bridge into Karameh, intending to eliminate the guerrilla base of the Palestine Liberation Organization (PLO) in a matter of hours.

Israel miscalculated. The fedayeen fought with mad courage. Some fighters jumped with bomb belts around their waists, blowing themselves and Israeli tanks to pieces.

My brother Yousef was there, battling with incensed audacity in man-to-man combat that spread throughout Karameh. An enemy bullet took a chunk of his left thigh when he tried to rescue a wounded comrade. That story, witnessed by Yousef's subsequent limp, became legend in Jenin, where I was still recovering from my own bullet wound.

By noon that day, Karameh was destroyed, but the lightly armed band of fighters held their ground and Israel recoiled, abandoning vehicles and tanks in a hasty retreat. Thus, the myth of Israel's invincibility was shattered by my own brother and his comrades.

Within hours, news of the Battle of Karameh spread across the Arab world like a brushfire. Its glory reverberated in Europe and the Soviet Union, and foreign youth took to wearing the Palestinian checked kaffiyehs as a symbol of revolution and the power of the weak.

I could hear the radio blaring from the Beit Jawad coffeehouse down the lane.

"Come on, I'll help you. Let's go see," Huda said, putting my arm around her shoulder to stand me up.

Outside, I stopped to shield my eyes from the assault of daylight. Crowds were gathered, chanting, singing with the radio. Yousef's friend Ameen stood on a table at the coffeehouse, holding up the radio speaker. The crowd fell silent and we heard the voice of Yasser Arafat. "What we have done," the voice declared, "is to make the world realize that the Palestinian is no longer refugee number so and so, but the member of a people who hold the reins of their own destiny and are in a position to determine their own future." Goosebumps sprang up along my arms and back.

"Allaho akbar," the crowd roared. Jenin sang with self-worth and pride as people danced in the streets. Haj Salem made his way through the crowd when he saw me. Leaning to kiss my cheek, he said, "Your brother fought in Karameh. How about that! He's fine, I hear." Toothless smile in full beam, he walked away clapping with the people, fingers fully extended and spread apart in front of his old brown face. I saw him in the distance put his arm around Ammo Jack O'Malley, the chanting around them unceasing:

"Karameh, Karameh!"

"Yousef Abulheja! Jenin's own fedayee."

"Allaho akbar!"

*   *   *

Even when soldiers arrived to disperse the crowd, the concerto of a revolution in the making continued. From windows, music blared and the zaghareet of women filled the night. The aroma of baking goods suffused the darkness and made our night sweet when those treats were passed through windows and adjoining doors of neighbors to our home, in honor of my brother's heroism. *Karameh.*

Huda and I and other young girls had our own celebration. Too weak to participate, I watched my friends dance into the night.

"Since there's curfew, at least we won't have school tomorrow," Lamya said, and the others shared her thrill.

With hope kindled by our excitement plus a measure of naïveté, we mulled over the practical details of returning to our original villages, which we childishly took for granted as the inevitable outcome of the victory at Karameh. Our innocent deliberations that evening revealed the minutiae of our dreams. "A real bed.""No soldiers.""A playground.""A garden.""A bicycle." On went the list of our simple wants. We wrote them out, checked the top three, then compared our choices.

Huda wanted to sit by the ocean more than anything else in the world."Just to sit," she said, "since I can't swim."

I have never forgotten that. The simplicity of her innermost desire is now enough to make me cry.

The television channel broadcast footage of fedayeen parading through Amman, and adults packed around the few television sets in Jenin. Beit Jawad's coffeehouse had the most accessible screen and I could see Haj Salem and Ammo Jack O'Malley at their usual table trying to shoo others from their view. Vivid stories emerged and swirled. There were rallies everywhere in Jordan, where hundreds of thousands of ordinary people gathered in solidarity and praise. Women and children hurled flowers toward the revolutionaries. Grown men cried, breaking through the throngs to kiss their Palestinian brothers. The movement swelled overnight. Everywhere in Arab countries men lined up to join the PLO. Many from Jenin packed up the next day to join, only to be arrested by the Israelis, who had paid informers everywhere.

A month later, we were still under forbidding curfew. Our absurd lists of girlish dreams had soured with the accumulating garbage in the streets by the time an army jeep rode through to grant us permission to leave our homes. Even Lamya was eager to go back to school.

TWENTY-ONE
Tapered Endings
1969

WITHOUT BREAKING THE CONTINUITY of their dogged enterprise of knitting on the rickety balcony, Mama and Um Abdallah lifted their heads intermittently to glance at the world around them. By then Mama had plunged far into the abyss of her mind, defecting even from her own body, leaving it to the epidemic of misfortune, and it became necessary for her to wear a diaper. Um Abdallah, in her extraordinary loyalty, took charge of my mother's hygiene.

Mama's eyes were depleted and blank, her flesh shrank, and her respiration began to rattle. My family was gone and I was closing in on fourteen with a disfigured body. Life was mercurial and fickle, not to be trusted. One moment it had caressed me with the enchantment of a young girl's infatuation, my first crush on a boy, and seduced me with every girl's fantasy of finally becoming a woman. Then, cruelly and indifferently it had clothed me in maimed skin, spun from suspicion and the cotton of abandonment.

A portion of my smooth, soft flesh was torn from my waist. The sanctimonious angels who sit on people's shoulders to monitor and report sin to Allah tormented me with "I told you so," and I believed the horror that marked my body was punishment for the sin of masturbation. I bowed humbly before the smugness of those blabbermouth angels, submitting helplessly to everlasting purgatory.

There was nothing left for me but my father's dream, for which he had drudged for pathetic wages, to save enough that his refugee children might get an education. I plunged into that purpose, though I had no intellectual or scholastic appetite of my own. I had no dreams save the wish to be loved and free, as I had been during the dawns with my father.

To honor Baba, to make his dream reality, I devoured books of history, literature, mathematics, and science with ferocious purpose. At night, for self punishment and to sustain the momentum of my scholastic solitude, I fingered the rutted flesh of my abdomen, a reminder that I was damaged goods no boy would want. The loss of muscle made me limp for some time afterward, augmenting my sense of defectiveness.

Huda remained by my side during my recovery, but soon I pushed her away. I say now, with shame and self-reproach, that I begrudged the wholeness of her body and wished my misery on her, so that I might have a friend in the house of the cantankerous, wretched, and mutilated. But she was always there, sturdy in her loyalty, and she did not waver or resent my abandonment.

Despite the assault against it, my body persisted in the habit of waking before dawn, the daily commemoration of Baba, even though my memory had already dissolved the features of my father's face into a vaguely personified scent of honey apple tobacco. I read and reread the books he loved, and today, if I could make a wish list of material things, as we girls had done after the Battle of Karameh, I would covet only those tattered books.

I wrapped my new skin in a storm of paper and ink, unconcerned about my possessed mother wasting away kilo by kilo; about the crass incursions of imperious soldiers; or my best friend, Huda, and the love story unfolding between her and Osama.

I became known as a prodigious student and emerged from my self-banishment to the laudatory eyes of adults in the camp, who also approved of my indifference toward boys, which they mistook for piety. But I knew, and so did Huda, that it was just the anguish of deficiency. When I finally surfaced from the Siberia of my ornery determination, I found, once again, the enduring and solid ground of Huda's friendship, and we picked up where we had left off.

While I was submerged in shame, study, and repentance, Huda was falling in love. By then, it was known in the camp that Huda was Osama's girl, and it was only a matter of time before they would wed. In the physical transformations of adolescence, Huda's cheeks rose high under her streaked cat eyes and her lips ripened, flattening into a curvy stretch over her slightly crooked front teeth when she smiled. The "odd little girl with those rare eyes" had blossomed into a Cleopatra, with a silky river of black hair and fine olive skin. Osama was the envy of all the young men in town.

Huda and I were fourteen when we found Mama cold in her bed one hot June evening. We approached slowly, lighting the oil lantern on the wall. As we had always done in the face of uncertainty, each of us reached for the other's hand. Mama lay on her side, as usual when she slept, the shadow of her stiff form flickering against the wall. The murmur of conversation passing outside our window and the stale scent of an ending crept along the seams between the living and the dead. There, on the spongy foam and worn gaudy colors of her mat, on the floor, against the chipping bare wall of our little shack, in the makeshift nation of the forgotten, Mama had died alone.

My eyes vented quiet tears. I cried, not for this woman's death, but for my mother, who had departed that body years before. I cried with a bittersweet relief that she was finally and completely rid of the whorehouse world that had deflowered her spirit. I cried for the blunt impact of guilt that I could not, had not saved her somehow. I cried because, hard as I tried, I could not find in the small pale body the woman whose womb had given me life. And I cried for the imminence of a sad tomorrow on the barren, body-strewn soil of my days. Huda cried for me. Only Um Abdallah, who had left her constant companion to rest and returned to wake her, cried for Mama. She was the only soul who knew the person who had lived inside that emaciated corpse, over which the three of us wept.

Somewhere between me and the body of my mother hovered a memory of a time when Dalia had taught me to move an unborn baby inside its mother's womb. The baby was going to die, everyone was sure. The mother too, perhaps; people had their doubts. Dalia was finally there. "Um Yousef the midwife is here with her daughter, Amal," someone announced as we hurried inside where the woman had been straining, agonizing while we had waited for permission to leave our homes during curfew hours. None had been granted, so we had sneaked out, Mama's special scissors tucked in her thobe. The woman had exhausted herself trying to scream the pain away. To frighten death away from her child. The dim light and smell of childbirth had filled the small room where the woman moaned on the bed. Dalia had slowly put one hand on the woman's brow, the other on her belly, and begun reciting prayers.

"Breathe, child. Put it in Allah's hands. There's no better place for your fate than in his hands. Breathe, child." Mama's calmness was contagious. "Help me lift her." She motioned to me. The woman's aunt also stepped forward and together we inverted the woman, her legs high on pillows, her shoulders hanging from the rim of the bed. "The baby is tilted and could be tangled. We'll do what Allah wills." Mama's last words to those in the room: "Go out and pray for her and I'll yell if we need help."

We, she and I.

"Put your hands here," she instructed me, and put her own on the other side of the woman's abdomen. "Close your eyes, until you feel the movement, and let Allah guide your hands." I was frightened, but I understood well. *Whatever you feel, keep it inside*.

Humming, as if coaxing the baby, Mama rubbed the woman's skin for an eternity. Until there it was, the movement. "Now help me. Move your hands like this," she said, still calm, still humming. The woman was moaning but calm. *Breathe, child*. I breathed and my hands moved with the baby, opposite Mama's.

We were ready now. The women returned. "Your prayers helped," Mama told them, "but my daughter did the most difficult part." Peeking from the other side of the belly, she said to me, "*You* positioned the baby, Amal." She smiled broadly with pride, moved to her feet, and came to me with a kiss to my brow.

How had I forgotten that day and why had it come to me now, in Mama's death? Dalia had loved me. How could I ever have doubted that?

"Allaho akbar." The funeral procession ended in Mama's burial—the tapered end of my mother, the once-fiery Bedouin girl named Dalia, whose footsteps had jingled.

As is customary, women and men mourned in separate quarters. But Ammo Darweesh joined no one. I found him at the cemetery alone suffering a naked heartache, bound to his wheelchair.

Ammo Jack O'Malley mourned Mama's passing. "I met yer mum when she was just a young thing, all broken over her lost baby boy," he told me. "A good woman. Your father, too. I'm so sorry, Amal. El baeyeh fi hayatik."

Jack had a simple, spontaneous air that welcomed life as it came. His impromptu demeanor was not a manner of simplicity, for he was sharp witted and well educated. Rather, it was the legacy of experienced honesty and integrity that made him impervious to discord and invited the admiration of both Palestinians and our uniformed Israeli occupiers.

As far as we were concerned, Ammo Jack was an Irish Palestinian who visited his daughter in Dublin once a year and lived in squalor with us the rest of the time. He spoke Arabic as he did English, with that Irish inflection that curls the end of a sentence up into a question.

"Hello, dearie," he said to me in the days after Mama was buried. "Come over to yer ammo's house later on 'cause we need ta speak with ya, 'kay, love?" He spoke to me in English, something he had started doing to confirm the fluency that my teachers had reported to him, and later, to help me exercise the language.

"Yer Englizi is getting ahsan, eh?" He often mixed the two languages like that.

"Yes, my English is getting better."

"Good!" And he chuckled and coughed.

But what was going on at my uncle's house? Why did they want to talk to me? And who were "they," anyway? Whatever it was, I dreaded it. And for good reason. In their eyes, I was fourteen with no mother, father, brother, or sister, poor and pious. All together, I was ripe for marriage.

The next hours passed under an oppressive worry and I formulated schemes to avoid marriage, partly because I feared that as a married woman I would have to expose the extent of my disfigurement. I considered running away. But nothing could bring me to commit such a cultural wrongdoing. Besides, anywhere I went, I was bound to run into Israeli soldiers and settlers, for Israel had already begun massive land confiscations and construction of Jewish-only settlements around the centers of Palestinian life. I even contemplated faking mental illness or a host of other maladies.

By evening's arrival, I was spent, resigned with imagined defeat. Holding hands, Huda and I went together to Ammo Darweesh's home and she waited in the alley as I timidly approached the iron door and stepped into the roofless room where my uncle, Haj Salem, and Ammo Jack O'Malley sat on floor cushions, passing the hooka muzzle and sipping kahwe from tiny cups, unmindful of the chickens roaming next to them. As is the custom, sugar was declined out of respect for the dead. So the kahwe was bitter in deference to Mama's passing. I walked barefoot, a habit that coated my feet with stony skin and prompted people to greet me with, "Where are your shoes, child?"—sanction that was both compassionate and disdainful and reserved for those who lacked parental guidance.

"Take your shoes off, Amal, and come join us," someone said, before realizing that I wore none. I walked slowly toward them on the cobblestone. It was dark and the light from two lanterns was fluttering with moths and mosquitoes.

Appearing from the corner of my eye, a silhouette of outstretched arms hurried toward me. "Hello, darling!" said Khalto Bahiya, Mama's eldest sister. She lived in Tulkarem, where she worked as a maid in nearby settler homes; she had set out for Jenin as soon as she heard the news. Although she lived less than ten miles away, it took her three days to make the trip. Twice, she was turned away at the checkpoint. On the third try, soldiers allowed her through. But Mama had already been buried, and when Khalto Bahiya realized that she had not been able to kiss her little sister good-bye, she had hurled curses at the soldiers.

I hadn't expected Khalto Bahiya to be there, but I was

immensely glad to see her. She bore an uncanny resemblance to my mother, but the same beauty bloomed differently in each of them. My mother's fairness was exquisite and untouchable, roaming alone in an abandoned castle. Khalto Bahiya's beauty took you in immediately. Hers was easy and disclosed hordes of laughter stolen from wherever it could be found. Gravity, sun, and time had scrawled on their faces the travails of hard work, childbirth, and destitution. But even these lines disagreed on their faces. Khalto Bahiya's face incorporated them into her joy and her pain, so that lines appeared and hid according to her expressions and provided frames and curves to her tenderness. Gentle folds nestled her lips and made her face open when she smiled, like an orchid. On Mama, the lines had always seemed incongruous— as if her beauty could accept no change or outside interference. The wrinkles on Mama's face had carved her skin like prison bars, behind which one could discern the perpetual plaint of something grand and sad, still alive and wanting to get out.

"Come here, ya binti." Haj Salem motioned me to sit next to him with a raised arm, revealing a jagged oval of sweat that moistened his cotton dishdashe. I settled uneasily onto a cushion between him and my long-suffering Ammo Darweesh, who drooped in the disrepair of his wheelchair, fastened at one hinge by rope and tape. His youngest child, my cousin Fouad, was ill with a fever and slept in the communal room, the reason we endured the mosquitoes in the open courtyard.

Ammo Jack O'Malley rested comfortably on the other side of Haj Salem, the two of them playfully arguing like schoolboys over who was taking a longer turn with the hooka muzzle. "Damn Irishman." "Damn Palestinian." They laughed, one raspy and toothless, the other like a sputtering malfunction.

They had gathered to decide my fate. That much was clear.

"Amal, may the remaining years add to your life. We're all grieving with you for your loss," Ammo Darweesh started. After offering his condolences, he offered me a home: I could live with my uncle, who, for a living—minimal at best—made glass baubles that he peddled to tourists from the bag of curses and salvation of his wheelchair.

"You are family and I will do everything I can for you," my ammo said sincerely.

"Or you can live with me in Tulkarem," Khalto Bahiya interrupted with an inviolable sense of family. Even though she already had five mouths to feed, my khalto was prepared without question to assume responsibility for her sister's child.

My third option was to live in Jerusalem with Amto Sameeha, she whose parents had once saved Ari Perlstein's family.

Ammo Jack leaned forward, across Haj Salem, his small blue eyes prying their way through the fiasco of his hair. "There may be another choice, Amal," he said, capturing me in the intensity of his look. At that moment, the theater of chickens and hookas faded. Everything peripheral to the line of Ammo Jack's gaze held its breath. Ammo Darweesh cleared his throat. Haj Salem and Khalto Bahiya glanced at each other, then at the ground. It was Ammo Darweesh's place to say what came next.

"There is a school in Jerusalem that would like to have you," he said, half-convinced it was the right thing, half-ashamed he could not offer me something better himself.

"But the choice is yours," Khalto Bahiya interrupted, nervous that I might misunderstand their honest intentions. "Our homes are always open to you, anytime and for as long as you want."

Ammo Jack, still leaning forward but having unlocked his stare now, said, "It is a good place for girls like you, Amal, and the schooling is exceptional."

Like me?

It was an orphanage by night and a competitive academic institution by day. As a Palestinian orphan with impressive marks, I would be admitted without question or financial obligation. They had been discussing the subject even before Mama had passed away because Ammo Jack thought I would have a better chance at a merit scholarship to university if I graduated from that school.

But Haj Salem put it another way. "Your father would have wanted this for you," he said, challenging my most tender sympathies. "Everyone knows that you have inherited your father's love of books and it seems you are too far ahead to take more benefit from our schools."

Then he spilled his signature phrase, to which he had earned exclusive patent: "I've seen it all." He launched into a monologue to which I listened impatiently then, but which I would revisit many years later as the greatest wisdom ever imparted to me by another human being. "We're all born with the greatest treasures we'll ever have in life. One of those treasures is your mind, another is your heart. And the indispensable tools of those treasures are time and health. How you use the gifts of Allah to help yourself and humanity is ultimately how you honor him. I have tried to use my mind and my heart to keep our people linked to history, so we do not become amnesiac creatures living arbitrarily at the whim of injustice."

Now his stare stretched to the whole of my past and future. Some somber and deeply wise expedience deposited in his wrinkled brown face an unimpeachable promise that what he said was truth. "We don't like to see our own leave. This is hard on the hearts of your kin. But you have honored the gift of Allah with diligence and hard work, and all of us know that we should help you now to complete your journey, not to stifle Allah's gift."

I sat motionless, unbelieving, in the stupor of an accidental imposter. I had done nothing to earn the frightening credit they granted me. The diligence and hard work of which he spoke were merely cowardice and fear of purposelessness, of divine punishment, of rejection; fear of light and sound that seemed to turn up one notch into war, death, and the debasing surprises of lonely bullets that tumbled end over end in the flesh. Forthrightness scrambled to set the record straight that what they witnessed in me was pure fear, not a gift or its honoring. Honest language struggled on my lips to assemble the proper order of words.

"But . . . ," I said. "I don't . . . I mean . . . I'm not . . . God, I didn't . . . It isn't like that . . . You don't understand." Finally, my mangled thoughts came out in the honest-to-God simple truth of my existence since Baba had left: "I'm scared."

I vomited those words. My lips trembled and I almost cried. It was the unpredictability I feared and hated.

"Maalesh." Khalto Bahiya tried to comfort me, but I no longer needed reassurance; I needed food. My belly roiled a loud reminder that I hadn't eaten a thing all day. Khalto Bahiya had already prepared hummus, fried eggs, salata, and leftover koosa, bowls and platters of which she spread out on the ground over old newspapers. We all shared the food, arms reaching over and across to grab bites with strips of bread. The chickens pecked nearby at a handful of old bread thrown on the ground. We didn't use utensils, and we dipped into the same plates. Many years later, after I became accustomed to U.S. corporate luncheons, I amused myself by imagining the consequences of reaching and dipping my bread for a taste from another's plate.

I remained with Ammo Darweesh after everyone left and Khalto Bahiya went to bed next to my cousin Fouad, whose fever had broken and who was now wide awake drawing pictures on Khalto's sleeping face. "Where is his mother?" I asked, for the first time noticing her absence.

"She's visiting her parents," Ammo Darweesh answered, it being understood that he and his wife had quarreled and she had left him with the children, as she often did, to return a few days later.

It was that night that I learned the facts of Dalia's broken ankle so many years earlier in the small village of Ein Hod, before my time, before Israel, before refugee camps. My uncle showed me a picture of a dashing young man on a black Arabian horse peering from beneath a white turban. He told me how that handsome man had wanted to marry my mother. It was hard to believe my uncle and he were one and the same. The story he told resolved in my ears like a lyrical verse, settling into the poetry of Dalia and sinking into the quicksand of a Palestine that could never be the same.

"Is that Ganoosh?" I asked, happy to finally see a photograph of the fabled family horse.

"Yes! That's him," he answered, his face opening up to the fresh air of the past. He pulled himself closer to me, his useless legs, small and limp, dragging behind the force of his arms, and he let loose a string of tales about Ganoosh and Fatooma— about the goat that thought Fatooma was its mother and cried whenever the horse left its sight. The way my ammo had had to sleep in the stables when it thundered to ease the horses' fear. How they had carried him with great speed through the Galilee and along the Mediterranean coast. And how those magnificent animals were likely the greatest loves of his life.

The time I spent with my uncle that night is one of those occasions that increase in wonder with age. Ammo Darweesh filled the late hours with stories about Baba when they were young boys, about my jiddo and teta and great-grandparents. It was the nearest I would ever again come to the company of Baba, and I decided then that I wanted to live with my ammo rather than at the orphanage in Jerusalem or at Khalto Bahiya's home. When I spoke my thoughts, Ammo Darweesh's face closed, a web of lines gathering at the corners of his eyes.

"See this," he said, pointing to the photograph of himself. "This is you now, and if you stay here, you will undergo a similar transformation to what I am now." His face was now clear, revealing the truce he had made with his own fate to keep bitterness at bay.

"The future can't breathe in a refugee camp, Amal. The air here is too dense for hope. You are being offered a chance to liberate the life that lies dormant in all of us. Take it."

"But I don't want to leave Jenin."

"Then I have to convince you somehow. Because someday, when your father and I meet again, I will have to report to my older brother how I set his daughter on the right path, the one he would have wanted you to take."

That was all my uncle needed to say.

TWENTY-TWO
Leaving Jenin
1969

A CROWD OF FRIENDS AND family gathered at the little house where I was the only remaining resident, knotting the narrow alley just outside. They came to bid me farewell in a ceremony of kisses and hugs that lasted hours in the sweltering summer when Mama died. From the time people started arriving until I rode away with Ammo Jack in a yellow taxi, Huda and I kept our hands in a sure and sweaty lock. Osama was there, hovering around Huda with yearning and hurried glances that seemed to ladle into our palms the sap of some secret between them, something caught and oppressed by the strict ways of a religious culture that would not permit him even a gentle kiss on her cheek.

Ammo Darweesh's wife had returned from her retreat and the two of them, with their five children running about, were there with advice and gifts. "Study hard, and don't stray from your salat," my ammo whispered to me, laying a featherweight kiss on the lovely bond he and I had forged just days earlier. He wished they could take me in the taxi themselves, he said, but he reminded me that only foreigners were allowed to move freely.

Um Abdallah kissed my forehead with savage maternity that seemed to love indiscriminately. Haj Salem cautioned Ammo Jack to be sure to impress on "that orphanage" that they should take good care of me. "You remember now what I told you to tell them there at that orphanage," he said with as much sternness as his toothless mouth and wagging finger could muster.

"I forgot already, haj," Ammo Jack taunted him, and let loose a laugh.

"Damn Irishman!" Haj Salem said, turning away to hide his grin.

Khalto Bahiya had already returned to Tulkarem and we had said our good-byes the day she departed. Neighbors and friends made me promise to send word if there was anything I needed.

"Anything, Amal. Anything."

"May Allah extend your lives and expand your fortunes," I said, thanking them.

There were tearful embraces and "God be with you" and "Bless you" and "Oh, I can't believe they're sending away one of our own," and the like.

Lamya, her round face streaked with dry trails of earlier tears, took my free hand and deposited in it a pair of dice. "Here," she said with solemn penitence, closing my hand over the dice with her fingers, "I took these from your desk at school." She must have done it years before—or she had taken them from someone else's desk, because I had no recollection of it. But I thanked her, Huda and I both taking her in a threesome embrace, and I giggled silently at the petty torment Lamya must have inflicted on herself for having stolen from an orphan.

Osama stood at the front of the crowd gathered on the dusty

road leading to Jenin's refugee camp while Huda and I held each other in a long tearful embrace. She whispered in my ear that Osama's family had made an appointment to ask for her hand in marriage. She wanted more than anything to lunge into the safety of their love, and I was happy for the news.

"Congratulations." I squeezed my best friend tighter.

"I'm going to miss you, Amal. It's like half of me is leaving," Huda sobbed in my neck.

We stood crying, Huda with tears, I with my mother's silence and taut jaw. We were enfolded in each other like the last word of an epic poem we had never imagined would end. A childhood story we had lived together line by line, hand in hand, was ending and we knew it would close the moment we unraveled our arms.

"Don't you two worry, now. You'll see one another again," Ammo Jack called out from the taxi, waving me in.

It was time to leave.

Huda and I let go, and I got in the taxi.

I rode away in the sad wreckage of parting. Small children ran behind us in the taxi's dusty wake. The people I loved grew smaller in the rear window until they faded, then disappeared at the turn in the road. The dice from Lamya still clutched in my hand, I turned to face front. The car's vinyl burned the back of my thighs through my clothes and it seemed to burn through the grief of leaving as well. I was struck by that lack of grief and I tried to feel the sadness that had flowed moments earlier, but none came, as if jail bars had descended around my emotions.

"Hard to believe I've known you since you were born," Ammo Jack said, looking at me, searching my face. "You're as smart as Hasan and as tough as Dalia." He looked ahead now. "God rest their souls. Your parents were good people."

Their souls. *Their*.

I said nothing. My teeth were clamped together inside my

jaws, which I had unknowingly locked. A small band of tears leaked from my eyes—this time, and for the first time, because I missed my mother.

Whatever you feel, keep it inside.

More than an hour into our trip, Ammo Jack pointed from the window toward Jerusalem, its dome rising in the distance. "There it is."

The Dome of the Rock, where the prophet Mohammad ascended to heaven in the fabled Night's Journey, was the point where all of Jerusalem's stories met. I had a memory of standing inside al Aqsa, beside one of its twelve solid marble columns that surround the rock of the ascension. The image of that massive pillar, which reached higher than my five-year-old mind could fathom, was the impression I had taken away from a family trip to Jerusalem in 1960, before Israel had conquered it. Mama had kept a photograph taken that day of the four of us—of her and Baba, Yousef and me—standing in the tiled compound, the golden dome above us. It was our only family photograph. The camera caught me clutching my father's leg over his robe, as if I intended to go on photographic record as the sole proprietor of him. I looked small and serious and when I found that picture after Mama died, it hit me how little I smiled. Father's face, expansive and gentle, gave the impression of a smile, but his lips were relaxed. His smile was in his eyes. Mama stood next to him, upright in perfectly aligned symmetry, her natural posture, and unreachable depths clear in her eyes. Yousef gaily leaned on one leg with the heartwarming smile that always escaped from the right side of his mouth first, then spread across to the left. Of all of us, he appeared the happiest, the most tender, the most endearing.

After Israel conquered Palestine in 1967, we never went to Jerusalem again. It was too difficult at first and eventually we weren't allowed. On its first day of occupation, Israel bulldozed the entire Moroccan neighborhood of some two hundred ancient houses and several hundred residents, who were given less than two hours' notice to evacuate. Muslims and Christians alike, Greeks and Armenians saw most of their property confiscated, while they themselves were evicted to ghettos or exiled.

Ammo Jack asked the driver to take us to a place called Khilwa on the Mount of Olives.

"This place is a wee bit out of our way, but you'll like it. It's a good spot to see the city," he said to me. Moments later we were driving through narrow streets bounded by tall biblical stone walls, until we stopped along the edge of an old Jewish cemetery below the Seven Arches Hotel overlooking that eternal village.

I have always found it difficult not to be moved by Jerusalem, even when I hated it—and God knows I have hated it for the sheer human cost of it. But the sight of it, from afar or inside the labyrinth of its walls, softens me. Every inch of it holds the confidence of ancient civilizations, their deaths and their birthmarks pressed deep into the city's viscera and onto the rubble of its edges. The deified and the condemned have set their footprints in its sand. It has been conquered, razed, and rebuilt so many times that its stones seem to possess life, bestowed by the audit trail of prayer and blood. Yet somehow, it exhales humility. It sparks an inherent sense of familiarity in me—that doubtless, irrefutable Palestinian certainty that I belong to this land. It possesses me, no matter who conquers it, because its soil is the keeper of my roots, of the bones of my ancestors. Because it knows the private lust that flamed the beds of all my foremothers. Because I am the natural seed of its passionate, tempestuous past. I am a daughter of the land, and Jerusalem reassures me of this inalienable title, far more than the yellowed property deeds, the Ottoman land registries, the iron keys to our stolen homes, or UN resolutions and decrees of superpowers could ever do.

"Not a bad place ta be, eh, love?" Ammo Jack said.

I smiled shyly and got back into the car.

It was dark by the time we arrived at Dar el Tifl el Araby, Home of the Arab Child. The headmistress, Miss Haydar, greeted us at the gate with rehearsed poise and led us to her study, where she began laying out the history and rules. Under the electric light, Ammo Jack and I watched a clear comedown in Haydar's expression, as though we had somehow blighted her hopes. Over the next years I would realize that some elusive and ferocious romantic aspiration perked up in her whenever she knew a man was to enter the compound. Clearly, Ammo Jack was not what she'd hoped for, though neither of us understood then what was taking place in her face as she spoke to us.

"This institution was founded by Miss Hind Husseini," she said, "as in the Husseini family of Jerusalem," lending the emphasis of a raised brow. The Husseinis were Jerusalem notables with a well-documented history of leadership and prominence in the city through the centuries. Miss Hind had been a wealthy unmarried heiress when Israel had established itself on most of Palestine in 1948.

She had lived in a red-stone mansion adjacent to the hotel she owned where lords, diplomats, dignitaries, poets, and writers had lodged when they visited Jerusalem before Israel took the city. But in April 1948, three bloodied orphans had made their way to east Jerusalem, where they had wandered until someone had taken them to Miss Hind's doorstep. The children were from Deir Yassin, a village on the outskirts of Jerusalem, where more than two hundred Palestinian men, women, and children had been massacred by Jewish terrorists. Miss Hind had taken in the waifs. In the weeks that followed, as more atrocities were committed by Israelis, more children were taken to Miss Hind, until she closed the hotel and turned it into a shelter, then an orphanage, then a school.

Miss Haydar had been among those first orphans and she had been adopted by Miss Hind, who had remained unmarried. In the brief orientation with Ammo Jack and me, Miss Haydar did not share her own story. She merely, self-importantly, introduced herself as Miss Hind's daughter. The tragic circumstance of her adoption was disclosed by the girls during my first few days at the orphanage.

Miss Haydar was a hard-hearted woman. She compensated for her short stature with high-heeled shoes that she wore with more grace than her own bare feet. She moved in those awful things with natural ease as if she had never learned to walk but on her tiptoes. Her hair was henna dyed and the only thing about her that seemed soft. It framed a stucco face that suffered far too much makeup and limited eyes that had lived almost exclusively in the confines of the orphanage.

"You should feel privileged to have access to the education that will be provided for you," she said, her eyes burning into me. "Families pay a lot to send their daughters here." She was talking about the day students who came for school and went home afterward. I would learn to call them, as the other orphans did, the "outside girls," and I never befriended a single one in my four years there. We scrounged or bullied money and food from them, but meaningful friendships with them were difficult when we looked at their new shoes, nice uniforms, and other privileges that smacked of a "normal" we all coveted. Ultimately, however, their tuition, along with international donations, is what subsidized the existence of us orphans—the "inside girls" —in Jerusalem.

The main building was a five-story limestone beauty with the ornate arched doorways typical of Palestinian architecture. Its western wing served as a dormitory for girls aged ten to twenty-three. The remainder of the building housed classrooms, where I sat for biology, mathematics, Arabic, religion, geography, German, and English lessons. The balcony-hung back of the building looked on a large courtyard where a lonely basketball goal, well worn from use, stood at the far end, behind which a very old growth of ivy clung to the masonry wall enclosing the compound.

"Grab your things and follow me," Miss Haydar said, motioning imperiously toward my small bag of clothes. "Mr. Jack must go."

I wasn't prepared for another parting. My heart sank and my shoulders sagged. I fell to my knees and tears pooled behind my eyes, though I did not cry.

"Don't leave me, Ammo Jack," I begged.

He moved his colossal body to meet my eyes, shooing unruly hair from his brow with a trembling hand. In his other palm he held a small package, wrapped in newspaper and brown tape.

"I should not have kept this so long," he began softly. "I meant to give it to your brother Yousef. But I couldn't muster the grit to recount what I witnessed the day I saw this fall to the ground."

He handed the box to me awkwardly, in a painfully tender stroke.

"There was nothing I could do, Amal," he said, submitting to the questions he knew I would ask when I opened the box.

But Miss Haydar tore me away, impatiently pulling my arm. "No more of this. It's too dark to stay outside now."

She turned to Ammo Jack. "Thank you, sir. Please escort yourself to the gate."

Some thirty girls clamored to see the new arrival winding up the narrow, three-hundred-year-old stone staircase. I walked through their stares, my hard fists clutching the package from Ammo Jack and the dice from Lamya, the loose remnant of my former life. Miss Haydar showed me to my bed, a curious metal contraption she called a "bunk." Sixteen pairs of these bunks lined the rectangular room, eight along each of the long walls, and all thirty-one girls who lived in that room held me in their scrutiny. Sixty-two eyes, a silent tribunal etching into my flesh.

"Girls, show her around and make sure she knows the rules," Miss Haydar commanded, then pivoted away on her high heels. The girls came toward me and I cowered inwardly.

The closest one to me, a redhead with translucent skin and a soft smile, caressed my head. "Your hair is pretty. My name is Samra." I would soon learn her name was an unending joke in the orphanage because "Samra" in Arabic means "the dark-skinned one," and her carrot top stood out like an orange balloon in a dark ocean.

"What's your name?"

I didn't answer.

"Where are you from?" another asked. Then another and another.

"Why are you sad?"

"Will you be my friend?"

"Did Haydar give you her stupid dissertation?"

"Are you an orphan, too?"

Not getting answers from me, they started answering themselves.

"Of course she's an orphan, stupid!"

"Her name is Amal. I heard Haydar talking on the telephone."

"Why on earth would she want to befriend you, bucktooth?"

"Haydar is full of shit."

An admonition resonating with seniority came from a pretty dark-skinned girl with a silky blanket of black hair. "Get away from her!" she ordered. "Can't you see she's upset? Give her some space, you leeches." Everyone obeyed. That was my first encounter with Muna Jalayta, who became my dear friend.

Before she turned to leave, Muna assured me that it wasn't so bad here at the orphanage and that she would hold the girls off as long as she could. Then she smiled and left.

Alone and red eyed, bewildered and dizzied by life's turns, I opened the package that Ammo Jack had given me. Inside the crackle and hiss of tearing newspaper, inside a flimsy box, was an olive-wood smoking pipe. I lifted the pipe, holding the fragile memories of Baba, the two of us with his poetry and the rising sun. Near the mouthpiece, a line was worn in the pipe's shaft where Baba's mustache had rubbed against the wood over the years. The pipe still smelled of the honey apple tobacco that Baba had smoked, the scent of my father's labored breath and tired clothes when he unleashed his love through the pages he turned for me at dawn. I knew that smell so well that I had unknowingly come to think of it as the aroma of the sunrise. I curled up with Baba's love in my new bunk, letting that soothing waft of my father envelop my wounds and lull me to sleep on that first night in that Jerusalem refuge for Palestinian girls.

I never saw Ammo Jack again to ask him by what circumstance he had come to possess my father's pipe. In the summer of 1971, two years after he had escorted me to Jerusalem, I learned that Jack had died in his sleep. I could not return for the funeral because Jenin was under curfew. I also did not have money enough to make the trip, but news reached me that thousands of people had turned out to bid him farewell in a display reserved only for martyrs. Ammo Jack was deeply loved by everyone who knew him, especially the refugees in whose service he lived the last years of his life. Even some Israeli soldiers who frequently manned Jenin's checkpoints had gone to pay their respects to his daughter, his only relative, who had traveled from Ireland to bury him—for he had specified that he be buried in Palestine.

Haj Salem wept at Jack's funeral. After that he never returned to Beit Jawad's coffeehouse, where the two of them had shared countless hookas in the manufacturing of friendship—a dainty thing they had created from the playful grouchiness of men growing old in the tedium of a timeless battle to leave the world a better place for the young.

The Orphanage
1969–1973

MUNA JALAYTA WAS RIGHT: the orphanage wasn't so bad; and from the beginning she took me under her wing.

It was sometime during my second year, a hot summer night suffused with humidity and the sounds of vigilant bugs, that I could hear Muna tossing in the bunk above mine.

"You awake?" I whispered.

"Who the hell can sleep, besides the snoring dumbasses around us!" she huffed, dangling her head from the side of her bed. "Let's try the cool tile."

"Good idea," I said, getting out of bed and removing my night shirt.

"Even better idea. Naked on the tile." But the floor space was too cramped. "The balcony?"

"Sure, why not."

We stepped through the double doors into the open air and were instantly embraced by the moon.

"Wow! I've never seen the moon so close," she said, gripping the wrought-iron bars of the balcony. Her womanly form was outlined against the night's lantern sitting low in the sky.

"Full moons remind me of my father. Even though I can't really remember him. Isn't that silly?" she said, inhaling the night, eyes shut. "He told my sister that a full moon is a portal to God's ears. Silly."

"Let's complain to it about fat-ass Haydar. Maybe it'll suck her up into outer space," I said clumsily.

"And who says Abulheja doesn't have a sense of humor!"

"How did they die—your parents?"

A pause. "My father was a professor who lectured the truth about King Abdullah's dirty dealings with Golda Meir. The Arab leaders betrayed us just like the British. Sold us up the river. Sons of bitches. I'd kill every one of them if I could, from the Hashemites to the House of Saud." Another deep breath in the night. "Students loved my father and lined up for his classes. I suppose that made him a threat to the Hashemite monarchy.

"It was a February day and rain had started on our way home from my aunt's house. My mother, father, my sister Jamila, and I were hurrying under umbrellas. Mother was yelling at me to stop splashing in the puddles when an agent of the Hashemites of Jordan called out, 'Ahmed Jaber Jalayta.'"

When Muna's father reacted to the call of his name, the agent shot him once in the head. A second bullet tore through Muna's mother's lungs as she tried to shield her husband. Two quick gunshots and terror muffled by rain inaugurated Muna's first memory, at the age of four.

We lay on our backs, her head on my belly, mine on the ball of our nightshirts as the moon poured light on our dark skin. "I'm sorry, Muna," I said, stroking her hair and wiggling my sweaty toes against the metal balcony rail.

I remember that night clearly, the comfort between two friends. At the edge of Muna's memory, I felt an unstoppable evolution inside of me. No longer a girl, not yet a woman, I wondered which of us was better off—she who lived with the detailed terror of her father's death or I who lived without the knowledge of what had happened to mine. I leaned into Muna's hurt and kissed her forehead. We held each other on a carpet of moonlight and in quiet wonderment, I put my arms around her. She kissed my scar and we fell into sleep.

Muna took me into the folds of her clique, which was something akin to family. Among my new friends were the "Colombian Sisters," Yasmina, Layla, and Drina. They had been living at the orphanage for three years prior to my arrival. Following the 1948 war, their father had been able to emigrate to Colombia, where the three girls were born and had blossomed to the spicy beat of the salsa and merengue—which they taught me to dance. But their South American life had come to a halt when their father had died of cancer. Rather than use what little money he had on medical treatment, he had spent it to secure his family's return to Palestine, where an uncle had helped them find a small flat and sent the girls to the orphanage because it was the only route to continue their schooling. Their two oldest brothers, already out of school, had remained with their mother in Ramallah.

Whether the Colombian Sisters fought or got along, it was always drama. I could never get enough of Drina's laughter. It was a disorderly thing that tumbled off the walls like a drunken echo and always erupted from a wide-open mouth with head flung backward. She was the oldest of the three sisters and, with a strong athletic body, was also the toughest girl in school. Though I don't recall that she actually hurt anyone, her crass approach to everything often gave the impression that she was gearing up to maul the first person to annoy her. What I remember most about Drina was the quick snap of her head that positioned her eyes in a straight burning focus on the object of her scrutiny, demanding honesty and loyalty.

She snapped that look toward me once after I emerged from a grueling interrogation by Miss Haydar, who had held me for five hours in the dorm basement, the "dungeon," to persuade me to rat out my accomplices. The five of us, Muna, the Colombian

Sisters, and I, had broken into the art studio the previous night, as we had been doing every night of Ramadan. It was during the last week of that month of fasting that Miss Haydar had discovered us, and it was because of a pot of stuffed grape leaves brought to us by a French nun.

That nun was Sister Clairie, whose name I could never pronounce correctly. She had taken a special liking to Layla, the middle of the Colombian Sisters, during Christmas that year when a group from the convent had brought gifts to the world's less fortunate: us. Recognizing in Layla that spirit of giving, Sister Clairie had approached my friend with an extended hand. "My name is Clairie," she had said, uttering her own name as if water gurgled in the back of her throat.

"May I help?" she had asked, motioning to the nameless infant girl in Layla's arms.

"Thank you. She was left this morning at the front gate," Layla had said, carefully placing the baby into the nun's arms.

"Layla always takes the babies," Drina had said. "You'd think she'd given birth to them for all the fussing she does."

It was true. Layla's nurturing instincts were so pure and well-known to us that every wounded girl, physically or otherwise, was put into her care.

The same black hair, thick eyebrows, and full lips that fixed themselves around Drina's penetrating eyes were transformed on Layla's face by her sensitivity. The same features with distinct edges on Drina were soft and rounded on her little sister, Layla. The thick curls of hair, which all three had inherited from their mother, sprang from Drina's head in confused, reckless coils but fell as obedient tresses against Layla's back.

The good nun returned to the orphanage nearly every week after she had met Layla. Each time, Sister Clairie brought a box of goodies. Often, they were things to replenish Layla's medical supplies for the odd scrapes and cuts on girls who sought her out for mothering and bandages. But always there were chocolate treats and candy, which Layla shared with her sisters, Muna, and me.

To ease the hunger of Ramadan, Sister Clairie came each evening to the eastern wall of the orphanage and passed a warm pot to Layla through a small hole in the stones. Her charity was a delicious secret among the five of us friends. In Pavlovian fashion, we arrived at the hole at least half an hour before five, when the good nun was due to arrive. Already it was February, the crisp breeze chilling us on our reconnaissance mission as we gently shoved one another for a peek through the hole.

"She's coming!" I whispered when I spotted the fair skin and rosy cheeks in brown habit, a face that looked only for God and thrived in cloistered piety.

Drina pushed me out of the way. "I hope it's grape leaves and stuffed zucchini like yesterday," she said, peeking through the hole.

"Anything beats the crap Um Ahmed makes," Yasmina chimed in.

We all moved aside for Layla to receive the coveted pot of food, which she immediately passed back to us so she could speak with her Christian friend.

"I got it!" I assured everyone, hiding the pot in my blanket.

"Mmm, smells good," Drina mused, her nose in my blanket.

As we had been doing all month, we broke into the art studio to eat our meal. Yasmina, the youngest of the Colombian Sisters, the most practical and organized of us all, divvied up the food in five equal portions while we waited for the adan to beckon us with permission to break the fast. Muna fasted with us in solidarity even though she was Christian. We had no plates, so we used paint trays from the art supply closet and sat in a circle, our eyes tightly fastened to Sister Clairie's perfect gift and our ears keenly tuned to the first notes of the adan.

"Alllaaaaaaaho akbar ... alllaaaaaaaho akbar ..." poured in a musical lilt from the sky over us and we broke the fast "in the name of Allah the Most Merciful and Most Compassionate." We devoured the food in brief minutes, finishing together with the realization that we were all eyeing the pot for the last few drops of juice and flavor. Again, Yasmina stepped into her unofficial role as mediator. "Here's what we'll do," she said, rising to her feet, her black curls forced into a ponytail so tight it slanted her eyes and exploded behind her in a shaggy mop of wanton swirls.

"We'll play a game and the winner gets the pot," Yasmina announced. Looking around the room, she took her cue from a child's painting of balloons. "It's called the balloon game," she began, and assembled the rules, snatching ideas from the air. "To play the game," she explained, her bony form pacing, "you have to hop on one foot in a straight line and say the word 'ballooooon' in one breath until you run out of air. The one who hops the farthest wins."

I don't recall who won, except that it wasn't me. I do remember Drina's devilish look just before she sprayed paint on Yasmina, who fell out of the game as Drina erupted in her disorienting laughter. I jumped to Yasmina's aid with tubes of blue paint, which we squirted at Drina, while Layla threw paint randomly from behind the protection of her sister. Muna took no sides and hurled wads of papier-mâché at anyone in her line of fire. The images of that evening are paint-splattered and full of laughter that turned my voice hoarse for several days following. We stayed late that night, trying to clean up the remains of the paint fight, and many years later when I returned to visit the orphanage, I saw a group of young girls playing the balloon game in the courtyard outside the art studio.

Miss Haydar caught me returning to the scene of the crime the next morning to retrieve my blanket. She was waiting when I climbed through the art room window, which we kept unlocked on a rig. The pain of Miss Haydar's five-hour interrogation was finally eased by Drina's approval once she realized that I hadn't told on anyone. Earning Drina's respect was a prize.

Though we had so little and often went without food, my memories of those years are ultimately happy ones, rich in spirit and substance. Jerusalem's winters were white and bitter, and we fought off the frigid nights with one flimsy gray blanket each. It was against the rules to share beds or push them together and there was hell to pay if we were caught, but that was one rule we frequently broke, sharing blankets and body heat. A new girl came to the orphanage a year after me, and she peed all over us on one such night when we were massed together in warm sleep. Her name was Maha and she only stayed for a few months, but after that incident, we were more selective about who we let into our throng.

Um Ahmed, the cook, prepared three meals each day for some two hundred growing girls. Breakfast, for which I was often too late, consisted of one slice of bread and unlimited hot tea. Dinner was the same, with an added slice of mortadella. Rarely did the content of these meals change over my four years in residence. Lunch, on the other hand, was the time to really eat. It was always some kind of stew, cooked in a huge metal cauldron, served over rice. We could eat as much stew as we wanted until it ran out. Problem was, the only meat it ever contained was from the cockroaches that lived in great abundance in the kitchen.

I got used to that, too. In fact, we frequently held contests to see who could pick the most bugs from her stew. The dark menaces could be spotted easily in dishes like okra and tomato stew. But for mulukhiya, a dark vegetable stew, the task was infinitely harder. On those days, some hapless girl inevitably ate a roach by mistake.

Muna had that unfortunate distinction once. Satisfied that, having picked out three bugs, she had found them all, she ate her whole plate. To everyone's audible horror, she dislodged from her teeth a dark filament that turned out to be a hairy cockroach leg.

Someone yelled, "Muna Jalayta got one!" and the whole dining room erupted in laughter and jubilant chanting—"Muna! Muna!"—until Miss Haydar burst onto the scene ordering us "animals" to be quiet. It didn't last. As soon as Haydar was out of earshot, the ruckus resumed as girls came to our table, expressing condolences and paying homage to Muna, like a soldier wounded in battle.

Prior to meals, we had to line up single file in a tiny courtyard outside the dining hall. At Miss Haydar's insistence, we were required to stand in five equally spaced rows before she allowed us to enter. We accepted her bizarre behavior as some still unidentified form of dementia, for she actually took the time to measure the distances between girls in each row. This exercise was particularly painful in the wintertime for everyone except the three girls who made it to the courtyard in time to get the "pipe positions." These were the spots around a thirty-inch metal pipe that ran up the wall in the courtyard to vent hot steam from the kitchen. If you stood next to one of its three exposed sides, you had a source of warmth while Miss Haydar prattled about with her ridiculous yardstick. My tardiness did not afford me the luxury of a pipe position, and I could never get used to standing in the cold for half an hour like that.

Only once did I get the privilege of the pipe, but not because I made it to the courtyard in time. Drina took pity on me as I stood in line one particularly cold night when I was also suffering a fever. She ordered a young girl named Sonya from the best of the pipe positions to let me take her place. I gratefully accepted, shivering in that warm spot until we could enter the dining hall for our dinner of one piece of mortadella, a slice of bread, and as much tea as we liked.

Of course, I recovered under Layla's care, thanks to her herbal concoctions and cold compresses. None of us was surprised, or even disappointed, when Layla announced one evening that she was converting to Christianity to join the convent after graduation and live with Sister Clairie. Drina thought it was a phase but Layla did eventually join the Carmelite Order of nuns, devoting her life to God and to the girls who went to live at Darel Tifl orphanage, where we had come into young adulthood behind stone walls and beneath the hard watch of Haydar.

But for Layla's nurturing, I would have lived bald in the orphanage because my hair was frequently infested with lice. Lice inspection day was the first of the month. A few days before, we all got busy picking lice from one another's hair to avoid the dreaded shaver. We'd line up in trains, pulling lice and pushing the little pests into kerosene-filled cans. Layla looked after my hair. And thanks to Yasmina's "white comb," another of her ingenious inventions, which could pull out hundreds of the little buggers in one swipe, my long black hair never met the shaver.

A sad "shaver story" happened to a pretty young girl named Souad who was about to graduate and get married. Her beautiful chestnut hair had grown to her waist when Haydar claimed to have found lice in it. There was nothing anyone could do but listen to Souad's screams as her wavy locks fell to the floor. Drina believed that Haydar was jealous of Souad and made up the whole thing about finding lice in her hair. "She knew Souad was getting married," Drina said, "and the old hag couldn't bear it." We all agreed.

Among Yasmina's other great inventions was the Z-tongue. This was a language she devised, similar to pig Latin except with a "Z" sound inserted between consonants. To the great irritation of Miss Haydar, we became quite fluent in this speech, which we put to use poking fun at her corpulence and nostrils, which started at the human and ended just before the clown.

The friendships I forged in the orphanage are the substance of my fondest memories of adolescence. Of course, I could never replicate the bond between Huda and me. She and I were forever bound by our childhood, by six days of terror in the kitchen hole, and by a sisterhood that remained unmatched throughout my life. But fate had snipped a tear in our lives, setting us on divergent paths.

Huda was able to visit me once during my four years in the orphanage. Although travel to Jerusalem was difficult, she made it there with Osama in February 1973 to tell me that they were expecting their first child. Their togetherness had bloomed with a quiet splendor I could not understand then, and the life growing inside her cast a halo of promise and hope around them both.

At first, I could not find my best friend in the beauty who seemed so grown up, so much more of a woman than I. She looked alluring and exotic, her eyes part tiger, part human. But her steadfast and tender character hushed her beauty, and her face pulled you in. Even decades later, after time had scribbled lines on her cheeks and furrowed the tales of age in her brow, Huda's face could hold you spellbound, as you searched for the secret you knew was there, just behind the yellow streaks in her eyes. She didn't know the extent of her own beauty and that made it even greater.

"I've missed you," she said, tears at the rims of her eyes. I think it was at that moment in my life that I first felt the coolness of my own heart and found Mama's walls cementing inside me. It frightened me to think I could so easily do away with the pain of loss and separation. I leapt toward my childhood friend, muffling my discovery and our sobs on each other's shoulders. She cried because she loved me and had felt a great void in her life since I had left Jenin. I cried because although I loved her, too, I could not feel it with the same intensity as she.

In the process of trying to steady my gait in a life that shook with uncertainty, I learned to make peace with the present by unknowingly breaking love lines to the past. Growing up in a landscape of improvised dreams and abstract national longings, everything felt temporary to me. Nothing could be counted on to endure, neither parents nor siblings nor home. Not even one's body, vulnerable as it was to bullets. I had long since accepted that one day I would lose everything and everyone, even Huda. I understood that in my best friend's arms that day, and I cried selfishly for myself, and for the crystals freezing over my heart.

"You're the best friend I've ever had," Huda sobbed. "Jenin is not the same without you."

Huda learned to love what she had and to take what sweetness she could from life, her memories as pillars of strength. The refugee camp was good enough. She found solace in the bonds she forged by the strings of her own heart. With faith and prayer she could manufacture serenity, even after soldiers ransacked her house in their endless search for "terrorists." As long as she could return to the arms of love at the end of each day, that was all that mattered to her.

We spent Huda's visit on the school grounds, as I was not allowed to leave, while Osama went off to the Old City. I introduced Huda to the orphanage gang, all of whom embraced her with warm enthusiasm, and we spent the day in the fun world of young women. We listened intently to Huda's responses when Drina grilled her about sex, for Huda was the only one among us to have experienced the great mystery. We took turns listening to her belly, trying to wake the baby, begging for somersaults. It moved a few times, like a shadow behind a curtain, and we screamed with delight each time at the sense of magic and miracle that only babies can inspire by their mere movements. The six of us ate from a pot of lamb in yogurt stew that Huda had brought with her. Yasmina divvied up the meat, concentrating behind the lenses of her wire-rimmed glasses.

"Those are interesting glasses, Yasmina. I've never seen frames like that before," Huda said. We answered her almost in unison, "She made them herself."

"She's always making and inventing things, our Yasmina," Drina said with uncharacteristic pride.

"I can make you a pair, Huda, if you have the lenses," Yasmina offered, eyes wide, eager for the chance to construct something.

As much as we wanted to believe that nothing would change, that we would remain a family of five friends forever, graduation crept toward us. In 1973, Drina had been out of school for two years, but she had remained at the orphanage as a gym teacher while she took college courses at the Islamic University. Layla had already embarked on her journey in the Christian faith and moved into a convent, living behind other stone walls. Yasmina and I graduated together that year, both of us with high honors, and Muna had one more year to go.

Though Yasmina was the smartest and most studious among us, a scholarship came my way instead of hers. It was offered by a group of wealthy Arab-Americans for Palestinian refugees. Since Yasmina's family had fled to Latin America and never had lived in a refugee camp, she was not eligible. I think the opportunity for a college education abroad made her wish she had lived in a refugee camp.

I emerged confident and drained from the last of five arduous days of academic testing and waited for the verdict. I wanted desperately to win that scholarship, but only for the validation it offered. I couldn't imagine going anywhere but back to the familiarity of Jenin, or perhaps I would remain in the orphanage to teach, like Drina. Certainly, I was not prepared to go to the United States, where the scholarship would lead. The world at home frightened me enough. Why would I risk going into an unfamiliar world where no one spoke Arabic and where I knew no hiding places? Getting high marks was an end in itself. My father had wanted an education for me and I had obediently planted my life in the soil of his dream. I simply wasn't conditioned to plan for a distant future.

But Yasmina had a small genius of foresight and made plans and fallback plans. She slapped me hard across the face when I told her, rather casually, that I might not take the scholarship.

"Who do you think you are, refusing such a gift?" Her question tolled in my ear. Only by extraordinary odds and rare luck could someone like me find such an opportunity in the pitiable destiny that was my birthright. Who did I think I was, indeed.

"I'd give anything to have that damn scholarship!" Now she was screaming, not at me, but at something neither of us could see. She screamed at the cruelty of chance that would not notice her intellect and the hours she had spent in study. She had dreamed of college, and she dreamed even harder when there were rumors of scholarships.

I felt ashamed in the shadow of Yasmina's disappointment, and that evening, while I sat alone on the balcony, she flung open the doors of friendship with good advice. "Don't be stupid, Amal. Get past the fear," she said, and returned inside, leaving me to the indifference of a crescent moon cradled in a star-speckled black ether.

When I was a child, Haj Salem told me that answers can be found in the sky if you look long and hard enough. He told me that the arrangements of stars were divine hieroglyphics that could be deciphered by faithful hearts. To that tapestry of stars, I offered up my greatest wound. There was nothing left for me in Jenin but scraps of my childhood and the debris of the family lost forever, all of it packed beneath the boots and tank treads of patrolling Israeli soldiers. If I returned, unavoidable marriage awaited me in the traditional culture of Jenin's refugee camp. My awful scar, my disfigured body, made me dread marriage, which would surely bring a new flavor of rejection and abandonment.

Who was I, indeed! A pathetic orphan, stateless and poor, living off charity. The American scholarship was a gift I had no right to refuse. It sat mercifully in the path of my father's greatest longings for his children.

As the moon smiled in the sky, I begged the night to sweep me up by surprise with a dream that was my own. For in my life, I had not yet dreamed my own dream.

I could not leave without seeing Huda and Osama and their baby girl, whom they had named Amal.

As a going-away present, my friends at the orphanage pitched in with whatever they had, though it barely reached a fraction of the taxi fare. Amazingly, Miss Haydar made up the difference with one hundred shekels. More baffling still was the hug that accompanied her generous gift. I moved my eyes from the money to meet that talcum-faced woman who drew her eyebrows with a pencil and brought a grumpy temper to her commission of running an orphanage. Beneath her rutted exterior and slight insanity, I saw an insecurity and felt a sense of sisterhood when she put her arms around me.

"Thank you, Miss Haydar," I said sincerely.

"You're welcome. Make us proud."

Not wanting to be met by a crowd, I arrived in Jenin unannounced in the evening. I walked two miles from the Green Line, going through two Israeli checkpoints. Near the depopulated village of Allajune I found a Palestinian farmer who offered me a ride in his oxcart to Ziraain, on the perimeter of Jenin. He refused to take money—"I can't take money from a young Arab daughter"—so I thanked him and walked the rest of the way.

Three Israeli tanks were perched on the highlands overlooking the camp. Always there. Always watching.

It was dark when I started down the hill into the maze of slum homes and random alleyways, but I didn't need light to navigate. I could simply close my eyes and see the dirt paths carved between homes. There was Ammo Darweesh's chicken coop, my best hiding spot. One meter ahead was Lamya's window, hung at eye level with two metal bars that her father had welded there after he'd caught a boy looking in. Then the path broke into three and I took the middle, most narrow, toward Huda's home. The dwellings on either side were shoulder-width apart and I dragged my hands along their clay walls, just as Huda and I had always done. A few lights shone from windows silhouetted by tired souls shuffling about, but most of the camp was sleeping. The land was turned over to a choir of crickets, and the wild cats gathered on garbage piles looking for spoiled food or for the rats that foraged in the same territory. If I had not known the abiding generosity of the people in this camp, I'd have been afraid to be there after dark.

I stopped at a blue metal door, dented and scratched. I knocked lightly.

Osama peeked through a rusted-out hole before I heard the clangy whimpering of bolts coming undone in a hurry. Osama's grin made his eyebrows stand at attention beneath the commotion of his messy hair, and his familiar good nature greeted me with delighted eyes.

"Ahlan! Ahlan!" he exulted, motioning for me to enter their small courtyard. A solitary electric bulb buzzed in the far corner, beneath which I could discern the outlines of hens sleeping on a bed of hay. Vegetables were growing in a long rectangular pot, hand-painted, no doubt, by Huda. Osama stopped my approach to their living quarters, the shadows revealing a sweet mischievousness in his face.

"Shh," he said, finger to his lips. "Let's surprise her." He led me with exaggerated tiptoeing into their home. I followed, watching the young boy of my childhood, now a husband and father with a wispy mustache nesting on his boyish face and an irrepressible love for his family leaking from his pores. Later, watching Osama and Huda together gave me a sure sense that they were meant for one another. After three years of marriage they spoke to one another in a way that reminded me of two kittens at play.

Huda threw her arms around me when I poked my head into the kitchen. Predictably, she started to cry, and both Osama and I poked lighthearted fun at her sensitivity.

They took me to little Amal's crib. She was a chunky baby, olive skinned like her mother, downy black cotton for hair. I sized up each roll of fat on her legs, neck, and belly with gentle pinches and kisses while she slept, and I warned Huda and Osama that I was looking forward to revealing their past shenanigans to little Amal as soon as she was old enough to get into trouble herself.

"Do whatever you want," Osama begged, "but please don't wake her!" They exchanged a look that betrayed a romantic interlude that had been interrupted by my visit.

The three of us reminisced and got caught up on the camp gossip. Ammo Jack O'Malley's replacement was a kind but distant Englishwoman named Emma who rarely stayed overnight at the camp. Ammo Darweesh had been caught selling souvenirs to tourists in Jerusalem without a permit and was serving a three-month jail sentence for that offense. Huda had become good friends with Fatima.

"Silly girl," Huda said of Fatima, "she has refused every suitor." And it was understood, but left unsaid, that she would have no man but my brother.

Osama went to bed around two A.M., leaving us to "girl talk." Whatever he thought that to be, he wanted no part of it. Huda struggled to stay awake, but eventually she fell to the call of sleep and the lull of my hand stroking her hair. But something in me, apprehensive and expectant, kept me vigilant through the night and sleeplessness could not tame the foreboding, which grew as my future crept closer.

Anxious, I walked out into the darkness and climbed onto the roof of Huda's dwelling. In the hot summers of our childhood, she and I had spent countless nights sleeping on the cool roofs of our shacks, exchanging stories, giggles, and gossip. From that vantage point, the United Nations refugee camp stretched below me in one square kilometer, so many souls packed in for the long and stubborn wait to return to their Palestine. Soon, the adan beckoned its first call for Muslims to pray while the sun inched toward the sky from behind the hills. The melodic resonance of the adan wrapped itself around me as if it were Baba's strong arms and the dawn's breeze fluttered on my skin like Mama's silk scarf. The sun rose behind the Israeli tanks and lookout post and orange flooded the sky, illuminating the part of my life that was irretrievably gone. I felt an ache for my days in that refugee camp. But a usurped life was my inheritance and I claimed it then and there with all the force of my confusion and longing, while the cocks crowed the announcement of another day.

I left a letter for Huda by the coffee in her kitchen, knowing that would be the first place she'd go when she woke up. Inside the envelope, I placed a necklace with a gold charm bearing the inscription of the Kursi Surah that Muslims believe bequeaths divine protection. It was a gift I had brought for little Amal.

I started toward the nearest crossing into Israel, where I hoped to catch a taxi back to Jerusalem. I took in the aroma of fresh falafel hanging in the still air trapped in the alleyways of the cramped architecture. A cage of canaries sang from someone's balcony, and I could hear the faint cries of babies waking behind the thin walls. A few people shuffled about, beginning their day, and roosters pranced along wherever they could find space. I felt dizzied by the task of departure while my legs commanded me toward Haj Salem's door.

There he was, the marrow of my childhood's merriment, moving about at his front door. I stopped too far away to be seen, watching as he made futile attempts to sweep away the pervasive dust at his threshold. My back leaned against a wall and I let my body slide into a fold as Haj Salem pushed the broom with arthritic motions. Holding my knees close to my chest, I imagined approaching him with a touch to his leathery skin, to cadge just one more story from our stolen Palestine. Maybe the one about the hardheaded shepherd from Khalil who went all the way to Akka looking for his sheep.

"I've seen it all. Those Khalili folks are so hardheaded, I think that's how come Allah put so much granite in Khalil. Else they'd break the mountains with their heads," he'd say, and laugh his magnificent toothless laugh.

Tears welled in my eyes and I pulled my knees closer. "Damn dust," I heard him say in a tone of routine frustration as he turned back into his home. The constancy of his comical daily battle against the dust and daily defeat by it made me smile, and I pulled myself to my feet at the bang of his metal door closing.

Back in Jerusalem, I went to retrieve my bags from the orphanage and to say good-bye to that city and all it had come to mean to me. Reaching into my pocket, I found a sealed envelope and grinned, knowing it was a letter from Huda. I placed it in an old tin box given to me as an Eid present by a charity from one of the rich Gulf States many years earlier. It was scratched and dented and it held my most precious possessions—Baba's pipe, the chest piece of Mama's prized thobe, her faded silk scarf, the dice Lamya had guiltily returned, and a stack of letters from Muna Jalayta, accumulated over my four years at the orphanage.

Even though we lived in the same dormitory, Muna and I communicated the goings-on of the orphanage and our secrets through letters. It was a way to conquer the isolation and boredom of our lives. As it turned out, these letters would become the chronicles of times we shared extra food, picked bugs from our meals, and combed lice from each other's hair. They painted the colors of friendships born of mutual need for survival and kinship. They contained tales of the "white comb," silly games we invented, and our adventures breaking into the art studio and clinic to steal paints and nursing supplies to give to Layla. In those letters she also wrote often of the boy she loved. His name, ironically, was Osama. I used to joke that I felt pressure to marry someone by that name since both she and Huda, my two best friends, would be married to Osamas.

I think of those years with nostalgia. It is true we had no heat to warm our nights or our weekly bathing water, but we had much of the stuff that warmed our souls. We were friends who doubled as mothers, sisters, teachers, providers, and sometimes as blankets. We shared everything from clothes to heartaches. We laughed together and carved our names in the ancient stones of Jerusalem.

We all crawled from the pits of dispossession and tried to survive as best we could under Israeli occupation. Our greatest pleasures were moments of normalcy. A crush on a boy. A card game. Telling dirty jokes while we washed our clothes by hand on the roof of the five-story building. Words of encouragement from a teacher. The bond we forged was molded from an unspoken commitment to our collective survival. It reached through history, straddled continents, spanned wars, and held our collective and individual tragedies and triumphs. It was girlhood letters or a pot of stuffed grape leaves. Our bond was Palestine. It was a language we dismantled to construct a home.

IV.

EL GHURBA
(state of being a stranger)

TWENTY-FOUR

America
1973

FEELINGS OF INADEQUACY MARKED my first months in America. I floundered in that open-ended world, trying to fit in. But my foreignness showed in my brown skin and accent. Statelessness clung to me like bad perfume and the airplane hijackings of the seventies trailed my Arabic surname.

"It's okay. Haven't you ever seen an escalator before?" asked a pretty redhead at Philadelphia International Airport.

So, it was an "es-ka-lay-tor."

"You must be Amal." She extended a soft manicured hand. "I'm Lisa Haddad. My mom is just parking the car. We're your host family."

Lisa was younger than me but far more sophisticated and pretty.

"Hello," I said, looking at her with embarrassing envy.

"I decorated the guest room for you," Lisa said energetically on the short car ride from the airport to their home. It was easy to like her—difficult, in fact, not to. Her world was pastel colored, emotionally cushioned, financially solid, and politically inconsequential. I thought it odd and thrilling that she should seek my favor and approval.

"Thank you," I answered, unsure of the proper American response to her gracious enthusiasm. In the Arab world, gratitude is a language unto itself. "May Allah bless the hands that give me this gift"; "Beauty is in your eyes that find me pretty"; "May God extend your life"; "May Allah never deny your prayer"; "May the next meal you cook for us be in celebration of your son's wedding . . . of your daughter's graduation . . . your mother's recovery"; and so on, an infinite string of prayerful appreciation. Coming from such a culture, I have always found a mere "thank you" an insufficient expression that makes my voice sound miserly and ungrateful. I gazed at the cityscape. Ribbons of concrete and asphalt stretched and looped under more cars than I had ever seen. Row homes, factories, and warehouses overlooked the interstate, and smog blurred the clustered skyline of downtown Philadelphia. The scent of the city seeped into the car. Street vendor cheese-steak hoagies, greasy fries, diesel truck fumes, and car exhaust gave my nostrils a full-bodied welcome. It smelled like the irretrievable loss of white madonna lilies growing in the limesinks of Palestine, the bereavement of my country's camphires, which would burst forth each spring into fragrant flames of white and yellow clusters, delicate and fiery.

Lisa's mother, Angela Haddad, spoke softly, pointing out the Museum of Art, the William Penn statue, City Hall, Independence Hall, and other monuments that meant nothing to me. She kept her neck perfectly straight and her long fingers wound tightly on the steering wheel of her Mercedes as she drove through the city. She had an impenetrable elegance, and though she was extremely generous and kind to me, I found it difficult to relax in her presence.

"Mom, is Dad coming home this week?" Lisa asked her mother.

Lisa's father lived with his girlfriend and came to visit his family occasionally. I thought it was an odd arrangement until I met him. He was a tall, swashbuckling parvenu who had married an heiress, Angela, and used her money to subsidize expensive womanizing, a cause he championed in Philadelphia's finest gentlemen's clubs. "She your mom's new project, sugar?" he asked Lisa, nodding his head toward me on the one occasion that he arrived to take his daughter "out."

"This is Amal, Dad," she answered uncomfortably.

"Hello, 'Omar.' Name's Milton Dobbs." He extended his hand and I shook it. "That's what I love about your mother, sugar, she's always trying to save the world. It's why I married her in the first place," he said, raising his voice to reach Angela, who stood ignoring him behind the kitchen counter.

"No, you married me for my money," Angela retorted in classy, unaffected dryness.

"I'm not sure if he's coming this week or not, darling," Angela answered as she continued to point out notable Philadelphia sights. "And this, Amal, is your home for the next three weeks, or longer if you wish," she concluded, slowing her car into the long circular driveway.

At the door, my eyes widened to take in the enormity of their home, the likes of which I had never imagined. Money flaked off the air of its oversized, immaculate rooms, and I could barely comprehend that Lisa and her mother lived alone, with part-time domestic help, in that expanse.

What I recall most vividly of my first night in the United States was sleeping for the first time in a real bed. Not a mat or a bunk. I stretched my limbs in a large, soft sea of white linen and down soaking up the fatigue from my jet-lagged body. Over the bed, Lisa had hung a poster of a man with leather hair and a leather jacket unzipped in a comically seductive pose. Lisa loved him, she informed me, calling him "the Fonz." Leaning against the wall was a gift for me: a 1973 baby-blue Schwinn bicycle, which Angela taught me to ride in the coming days. As if to brace myself with context in that big bed, I reached to the past, moving my hand over the mangled skin of my belly. Snuggled in luxury on the threshold of a world that brimmed with as much promise as uncertainty, I was starting a new life. But like the scar beneath my hand, the past was still with me.

In Philadelphia I wandered among the contrasts of wealth

and poverty, a desperate smile plastered on my face. I found no commonality with the men and women who walked with purpose and self-possession, nor with the human beings asleep on the city sidewalks. I marveled as these self-assured Americans went about their daily business. They bought groceries, walked to work, ate dainty foods, and chatted in outdoor restaurants. I felt diminished, out of place, and eager to belong.

Angela helped me with the daunting paperwork that had to be understood and completed before I could commence my first year of study at Temple University. I had never dealt with so many papers and forms for health insurance, library registration, school ID—and on went the list. But I was ready before classes started and with Angela's help, I moved into the dorm.

Elana Rivers, a wisecracker with a massive bosom, asked our dorm mother if there was a form to register her boobs. Within the first months of classes she was well established among the upperclassmen as easy prey, a distinction that earned her invitations to the "right" fraternity parties. She often staggered loudly back into our dorm in the wee hours. She made no attempt to speak to me, though she referred to me not infrequently as "the Arab," pronounced "ay-rab," or as "the rag head."

One evening, I watched her taunt a drooling pizza delivery boy in the foyer of our dorm. Dumbstruck by Elana's lasciviousness, he ogled her with a comical hang-jawed expression that made me chuckle in passing. At that, she turned sharply toward me. "Oh my God!" She burst into laughter. "The ayrab thinks this is funny." Swift fear flushed my face, draining away my amusement as Elana came toward me. "Have you ever had sex?" she asked unctuously.

I froze. I had never even kissed a boy. Thankfully, a disgusted voice behind me intervened, "God, Elana! Do you ever stop?"

It was Kelly Mason, a pre-med student whom I knew from

science classes. "What? I'm just making conversation," said Elana. But Kelly whisked me away, pushing herself daringly in front of Elana, who did not bother me again.

Save the occasional lunch with Kelly, my first year in college was friendless. It was an isolated and busy year. My accent was a social handicap, or at least I regarded it as such. So I did little more than study and ride my bicycle all over town. Whatever attempts I made to participate in the social arena were clumsy and unsurprisingly ignored or snubbed. I was left with books, and the payoff was a perfect 4.0 average for both the fall and spring semesters.

I found my place eventually and settled comfortably among a small group of friends with whom I shared a house until graduation. It was a run-down three-story brick row home that became known in our junior year as "the Outhouse," after sewage backflowed onto the floors.

I remained on solid academic ground throughout college, but the Palestinian girl of pitiable beginnings was trampled in my rush to belong and find relevance in the West. I dampened my senses to the world, tucking myself into an American niche with no past. For the first time I lived without threats and the sediments of war. I lived free of soldiers, free of inherited dreams and martyrs tugging at my hands.

But every house has its demons.

I metamorphosed into an unclassified Arab-Western hybrid, unrooted and unknown. I drank alcohol and dated several men—acts that would have earned me repudiation in Jenin. I spun in cultural vicissitude, wandering in and out of the American ethos until I lost my way. I fell in love with Americans and even felt that love reciprocated. I lived in the present, keeping the past hidden away. I did not write to Huda, nor to Muna or the Colombian Sisters. Nor to Ammo Darweesh, Lamya, Khalto

Bahiya, or Haj Salem. But sometimes the blink of my eye was a twitch of contrition that brought me face-to-face with the past.

Walking downtown once, I thought I saw my mother, the gust of a ghost breezing through my reflection in a store window. I paused, starring at my mother's daughter. Dalia, Um Yousef, had bequeathed to me the constitution that could not breathe while holding hands with the past. She could isolate each present moment while existing in an eternal past, but I needed physical distance to remove myself. I thought at that moment that no other soul could understand me as she might.

The undercurrent of my life in America was a sense of shame that I had betrayed my family—or worse, myself. But I consigned myself to American mores and subscribed to their liberties.

There were, however, moments that prodded me to look into the abyss separating me from those around me. During the sewage incident that gave our college house its nickname, the commotion provoked memories of Jenin, where the open sewers sometimes overflowed and we would scramble, gathering old clothes and towels to plug the joints of our dwellings. Vile as the experience and subsequent cleanup were, Huda and I could not contain our excitement and anticipation at being allowed to sleep on the roof to escape the foul odor. Other children did the same, and we filled the air with calls, jokes, and giggles of young refugee souls. We were naïvely full of dreams and hope then, blessedly unaware that we were the world's rubbish, left to tread in its own misery and excrement. There, on the flat rooftops, we offered up our wishes and secrets to the starry Mediterranean sky. There were no soldiers then, before the war of 1967. Our wants were simple, but they could not have been more complicated. Always we thought about returning to Ein Hod. We thought it was paradise. Those untroubled nights on the rooftop hang in innocence. The evening call to prayer was our blanket and we slept in a little-girl embrace, Huda and I, until the dawn came with whatever book Baba chose to read to me. The foul slosh that glistened in the alleyways was, as far as we were concerned, a temporary inconvenience that offered a delightful escape.

So, in Philadelphia, while my housemates made frantic calls to their parents, the landlord, the health department, and insurance companies, I was unperturbed. While they acted as if their world had come to a shitty end, I felt a sweet nostalgia and longing for old friends.

The divide could not have been greater, nor could it be bridged. That's how it was. Palestine would just rise up from my bones into the center of my new life, unannounced. In class, at a bar, strolling through the city. Without warning, the weeping willows of Rittenhouse Square would turn into Jenin's fig trees reaching down to offer me their fruit. It was a persistent pull, living in the cells of my body, calling me to myself. Then it would slouch back into latency.

I worked two jobs through most of college. The university hired me as a peer tutor and I worked "under the table" on weekends at a twenty-four-hour convenience store in West Philly, a "bad neighborhood" where white people ordinarily did not go, especially after dark.

"You've got a death wish," my housemates said to me. "You're pressing your luck working in that area." They were sure I would turn up a rape victim, or at least get mugged. "You don't know this country well enough yet. I'm not being racist. It's just a bad place."

But each Friday, I set out on my bicycle through the hurried energy of Broad Street, turned right to the fine homes on Spruce, all the way to the dilapidation of West Philly. *Opportunity* took a detour around Thirtieth Street, and *Liberty for All* slouched in its chair like a lazy student. In West Philly, nature and architecture hunkered down with the ghost of slavery, letting litter and urine move in the place of flower bushes. Young men loitered in bell-bottomed jeans and Afros. In the beginning they whistled, called me "mama," and made references to my backside. But as my face became a constant part of the weekend landscape, they called out my name in a rhythm that whistled, acknowledged my backside, and welcomed me, all in one word. Old women, imposing matriarchs, gossiped on their porches and kept watch over the neighborhood as best they could. They too eventually turned their mistrusting expressions into generous smiles when they saw me coming. Little girls, their hair chained in obedient cornrows, played double dutch in spectacular displays of coordination. It seemed to me that black folk brought a beat to every task. In a day, they restored a church by the coincidence of their song. Their enslaved culture had given birth to rock and roll, I learned—a kidnapped race that came to define the entire culture with its music.

Sometimes there were killings and muggings. Drug pushers and pimps. Perhaps foolishly, I felt no fear in the darkness of West Philly. The soldiers in my life had raised the bar for bad guys. So the frightened teenagers with a gun, who once held up the store for forty dollars, weren't scary at all.

There were three of them at half past midnight one Saturday. They walked in together, their hasty plan still written on their faces with marks of apprehension. Three customers were already in the store and Bo Bo, the owner, had left only an hour earlier. Two of the boys went to opposite corners of the store and the third waited in line at the register where I stood behind the counter. I knew something was wrong, and as I collected money from the paying customer, I replayed Bo Bo's instructions in my head. "If you ever get held up, just give them all the money and don't hold back," he had said when I had first started working a year earlier. At the counter, the young robber laid down two packs of spearmint gum and a bottle of Coca-Cola and added a 9 mm. Then, he demanded money. His eyes were flooded with fear and his dark skin was pulled smooth by his youth. The other boys busied themselves collecting loot from the shelves and covered the door. I was struck by the irony of that boy's fear and my calm. As I emptied the cash register of its contents into a brown paper bag, I thought how I should be more frightened. The boy's gun was a toy compared to M-16 assault rifles. "You. Stop!" An M-16 in my face. "You. Go this way." An M-16 at my chest. "Everybody, turn back. This is now a closed military area." An M-16 swinging across the crowd, maybe fired a few times in the air if we didn't move fast enough.

After I gave the boy all the money, I showed him a hidden change box where his friends could find an extra thirty dollars. Then I gave him a carton of cigarettes. "I don't smoke," he remarked, stunned.

They left. I called Bo Bo, not the police. The following weekend, also on Saturday, Bo Bo came to the store dragging a boy by the collar. "Is this the one?" he asked. It was that same frightened young man who had threatened me with a 9 mm. I nodded and Bo Bo, whose real name was Bernard, turned his brawny black body on the boy, knocking him and the contents of the candy aisle shelf to the floor. "You either pay me now what you stole or you show up here every day to work it off," he growled with authority only a fool would dare disobey. The young man—Jimmy was his name—kept working for Bo Bo even after he had paid his debt. The police never knew about it. "He just got caught in the dragnet, is all. It's an old web that squeezes black folk until they got no more juice," Bo Bo told me.

What I knew for sure was that people in West Philly thought I was beautiful, not different, and my accent was not a call for mistrust. The very things that made me suspect to the white world were backstage passes in the black neighborhoods.

The Telephone Call from Yousef
1978–1981

T HE SUMMER OF 1978, before I started graduate study at the University of South Carolina, I gave in to the egging of my housemates to go to Myrtle Beach.

I had, for the previous five years, selfishly tuned the world out. The Yom Kippur War came and went in 1973, as did further turbulence in Palestine, and Jimmy Carter's Camp David Accords were soon to be signed—all without response from me. I deliberately avoided political discussions, did not write to the people who loved me, and let myself be known as "Amy"—Amal without the hope. I was a word drained of its meaning. A woman emptied of her past. The truth is that I wanted to be someone else. And that summer at Myrtle Beach, I was Amy in a bathing suit, lounging on the sand as far away from myself as I had ever been.

It took me days to find a suitable swimming suit. A bikini was out of the question.

"Wow. Were you in an accident or something?" Kelly asked in the changing room when she saw my belly.

"Something," I answered.

I chose a conservative black suit because it had a cluster of plastic daisies, a rather silly-looking thing, on the fabric that fell over the most obvious indentation in my abdomen.

I had assumed the Mediterranean shores of Haifa would be the dominant beaches of my life. But at age twenty-three, I swam in ocean water for the first time, and I wormed my toes in the Atlantic sand of a South Carolina beach.

I stretched my body to receive the sun, the same one that had risen over Jenin since the dawn of my life and had brought me purple skies and poetry in the asthmatic baritone coming through Baba's chest.

No soldiers here. No barbed wire or zones off-limits to Palestinians. No one to judge me. No resistance or cries or chants. I was anonymous. Unloved. Wearing my first bathing suit, I remembered Huda's great yearning after the Battle of Karameh, when we thought we would return to our Palestine. "To sit by the ocean. Just to sit, since I can't swim," was her wish, at the top of that naïve list we had made in our youth. *Huda*.

One year into graduate studies in South Carolina, I received my green card and adopted the United States as my new country.

Amy. Amal of the steadfast refugees and tragic beginnings was now Amy in the land of privilege and plenitude. The country that flowed on the surface of life, supine beneath unwavering skies. But no matter what facade I bought, I forever belonged to that Palestinian nation of the banished to no place, no man, no honor. My Arabness and Palestine's primal cries were my anchors to the world. And I found myself searching books of history for accounts that matched the stories Haj Salem had told.

Another year passed. *Whatever you feel . . .* I kept it all in. Until one day when the telephone rang at five A.M. Half-sleeping, I picked up the receiver.

"Hello."

"Aloo," answered an accented male voice. "Amal?"

"Aywa," I said, suspecting his identity and fully awake now. He chuckled, a sound I could recognize anywhere. It was the muffled laughter that first escaped from the right side of Yousef's mouth, then stretched a smile across his handsome face. A lifetime ago, Fatima had told me that my brother's smile had melted her heart the first time she ever saw him, when he was sixteen and she fourteen.

"Finally, little sister! We've been trying for months to find you."

Someone took the phone. "Amal! Habibti, darling! We found you." It was Fatima.

Amal. I cried at the sound of my Arabic name. The telephone was an inadequate connection to transmit the warm longing and surprise as we tried to speak through sobs and static.

"We're pregnant." Their first child. "Where are you in the U.S.? We're in Lebanon now. You know what they did to the PLO in Jordan, the bastards."

I heard Yousef interrupt. "Not now, habibti," he said to his wife.

"Okay, darling." And she continued.

It was a long story of endless fighting—"Yousef will tell you all about it"—through which ran a river of endless love—"but you already know that."

My brother had risen through the ranks of the PLO in the decade following the Battle of Karameh. The movement gained so much popular support in Jordan that the Hashemite monarchy feared for its own survival and crushed the Palestinian guerrillas and civilians in terrible massacres that marked the ninth month as Black September. The PLO was thus pushed into Lebanon in 1971, under the leadership of Yasser Arafat, and my brother took up a teaching position at an UNRWA school that served the Sabra and Shatila refugee camps, where he also continued to operate within the ranks of the Palestinian fighters.

"I never gave up waiting for him, you know . . . I'll tell you all the details when we meet again. Yousef misses you terribly. So do I, darling," Fatima said.

Despite the long years of absence and the uncertainty of Yousef's whereabouts and Fatima's fate, each had held fast to their love, resisting the pressures of tradition to marry any other. Finally, in 1977, after difficult probing, Yousef learned that his love had not married, and he immediately sent Fatima a letter that took almost a full year to travel less than fifty miles south through underground channels to Bartaa village, where Fatima still lived with her mother.

"It was as if Allah opened the heavens and dropped that letter for my heart," Fatima said. The heart that longed for my brother as much as life longed for breath. Within three months, they were united and married in Beirut. To make that journey, Fatima said a final farewell to her family and country, because once she left, Israel would not allow her to return to the land it occupied. She gave up everything she knew to marry my brother and never regretted it. He was thirty-four and she was thirty-two.

"Little sister, you better get here before Fatima makes you an aunt!"

"When is she due?"

"Sometime in the middle of June."

"It's December now. That gives me a few months to save up for a ticket and finish my master's."

"A master's degree? . . . Baba sure would be proud."

Even after so many years, I longed to make my father proud. Wherever he was. I looked out the window and saw that the sun was making its ascent, and I got choked up for the force of light, Baba's smile, coming into the room.

"Hurry up and get here, sis. We miss you."

"I miss you more. I'll be there soon."

Yousef left a number where I could leave a message for him to call me at a specified time. Reluctantly, I hung up the phone.

I graduated in June with no plans but to go to Lebanon. Ever since Yousef's call, I had thought of little else but to return to my family, to myself. But I had also forged real ties in America and in many ways, the place I had called home for the past years had become part of me. I was sad to leave my friends, but I was happy in the face of what awaited me as I boarded a plane to Beirut, hoping to arrive before Fatima made me an aunt.

V.

ALBI FI BEIRUT
(my heart in Beirut)

TWENTY-SIX

Majid
1981

A GUST OF WARM, DRY wind greeted me as I stepped off the plane onto Lebanon's soil. Beirut International Airport was an ominous place, made so by too many rifles strapped to too many uniformed soldiers. But the guttural silk tones of Arabic rippled through me as I heard the melodic calls and responses of my language. It's a dance, really. A man at a desk was offered tea as I walked through the metal detectors. He said, "Bless your hands" to the one making the offer, who responded, "And your hands, and may Allah keep you always in Grace." Calls and responses that dance in the air.

Emerging from tense immigration lines, I found a tall, haggard man standing impassively behind a sign that bore my name. His dark eyes were set deep beneath straggled eyebrows. Sparse hairs sprang haphazardly at his jawline in a vain struggle to become a beard, and a meticulously symmetrical mustache could not conceal the fullness of his lips. When our eyes met, recognition pulled his face into a smile.

"Al hamdulillah ala salama," he said, extending a hand. "My name is Majid. Your brother sent me to pick you up."

"And God keep you in safety, too," I replied. *Calls and responses.*

"I knew you right away. You look like Yousef."

"We take after our mother."

He smiled, taking my luggage.

Beirut's traffic moved in jolts amid a bedlam of honking horns. Bicycles darted between cars as Majid drove patiently through the uproar, apologizing for the "foul lexicon" of the street as mustached drivers, irate and sweaty, hurled colorful insults at one another. Arabic profanities are often nothing more than a gratuitous reference to the anatomy of a female relative. Simply the mention of it. "Go, fool! Your mother's pussy." Another, "Are you waiting for the red carpet to move your damn car? Your sister's pussy!" And there's always "Curses upon your father and your father's father!"

Dispersed in the pandemonium, peddlers sold newspapers, flowers, and Chiclets while the aroma of freshly baked bread—the streetside displays of sesame kaak with crushed thyme and cheese—crawled through my senses into memories of Palestine.

"It's good to be on Arab soil again," I thought aloud.

"I hear you've been gone quite a while," Majid said after a brief pause.

"Yes, quite a while."

"Sorry. I didn't mean to pry."

"No, it's okay. I went on a scholarship and couldn't go back to Jenin. You know how it is when you're gone for a while. The Israelis don't let you come back . . ." *Furthermore, I had nothing, no one, to go back to. And to be honest, I wanted to be an American. I wanted to pack away my baggage of past and tragedy and try on Amy for size.*

I turned my head to the open window to end the subject and inhale more of the hot jibneh and zaatar on sesame kaak from the sidewalk carts.

Majid called out the window and a vendor, a slender, kindly old man, approached with two large kaaks wrapped in newspaper.

"May God give you a long life, haj," Majid said to thank the old man, and paid him.

"And may he grant you and your family happiness, son," the old man replied.

"I'll bet you haven't had one of these in a while." Majid turned to me with a jibneh kaak. *That smile again.*

Thrilled, I thanked him: "Bless your hands. They're made of kindness and chivalry."

"I knew something could make you smile."

Majid's shy, fine manner contradicted the gruff exterior I had first noted. "My mother and I often took long walks together when I was a boy and I'd always make her stop to buy me one of these tasty things," he said, gently parting the silence. I listened, not wanting to spoil his memory with conversation or interrupt the smooth equanimity of his voice.

The dented small Fiat barely accommodated Majid's long body, pushing his head slightly down from the roof and his knees up near the steering wheel. We ate in the sun-dusted quiet of the car, windows up and occasional horns barking at our slow pace, and his color reddened when the hand shifting gear accidentally brushed against my leg.

"Excuse me. I'm very sorry."

"It's okay."

Farther on, traffic dwindled on the potholed, partially paved roads.

"Why didn't Yousef come himself to pick me up?"

"I can't believe I forgot to tell you," he exclaimed, lightly smacking his forehead. "Fatima had her baby. You have a niece!" His eyes widened as those of bearers of good news do. "Yousef was hoping for a boy, but he melted just the same when he saw his daughter," Majid said.

I'm an aunt!

"Don't all Arab men want a son first?" I joked, feeling more comfort with this man. We laughed.

"Actually, I imagine a little girl. Sara, after my mother, mercy on her soul. But truly, whatever Allah grants is a blessing," Majid replied. His voice was like velvet, his profile an embodiment of certainty, and his presence assuring. *He looks like Che Guevara.*

Shatila was one of three Beirut-area refugee camps. Next to it,

Sabra, and both were similar to Jenin's camp, densely packed mazes of concrete and clay shacks that had risen from the indignity of handout tents for Palestinians who had fled the war in 1948. Culverts carried raw sewage in the alleyways, where children played and floated paper boats downstream.

I knew we had arrived when children began to swarm around the Fiat. We had done the same when I was a child. In particular, we had badgered visitors and UN investigators to no end, desperate to pose for their clicking cameras. Though we never saw the photos, we nonetheless had fought one another for positions in front of their lenses. Seeing the children at Shatila now gave me a look at myself as I must have appeared to those visitors—bedraggled and needy. But in truth, we had been excited when they visited and we had happily basked in their Western grace. We had wanted only their approval, expressed in the passing attention of a camera shutter, a smile, a question, and sometimes, candy treats, which Huda and I had always shared.

Majid reached into the glove compartment, pulling out a handful of candy. "I did this once and now they expect it. I get in big trouble if I come empty-handed."

Majid at the center, giddy children around, the sweetness of candy. How Huda and I would have loved such a man in our youth. "Doktor Majid! Doktor Majid!" the children called out, and he caught the surprise in my face. I had not taken him for an educated man. I had viewed him with Amy's eyes. This he saw. And I lowered my eyes, embarrassed by the judgment he knew I had made in our initial contact.

A white sun followed us through the trash-strewn town to Fatima's and Yousef's house. It was a single-story structure with two crumbling steps leading to the front door. Its roof, like others, was mostly corrugated metal and asbestos held in place with rocks, old tires, and anything else to lend weight against the wind. Outside, a crowd of some twenty men was gathered, improvising chairs, laughing, smoking, and passing a tray of knafe, a cheese delicacy soaked in sweet syrup. No doubt in celebration of my niece's birth.

There he was.

Yousef! My brother, dear God!

Now, after thirteen years of separation, only a small distance remained. Twenty footsteps at most. Easily traversed. A short walk along a dirt path where a canary cage and potted flowers tried to defy poverty.

"Amal!" He saw me and rose at once among his PLO comrades, the waxed tips of his mustache curled at the corners of his smile.

I dropped my small handbag and ran to him. Safe in his embrace, I remained there as long as I could, trying to siphon the lost years from his massive chest, which felt so much like our father's. For a moment, my brother's arms dulled the aloneness of my life.

In the courtyard, a group of women, wives of the men outside, were keeping watch over mother and infant. They leapt with hugs and kisses when we entered.

"It is nice to finally meet you," said several at once.

"Fatima has told us so much about you," said others. A woman in a dotted red scarf pursed her lips and said, "Fatima told us you were shot when you were little, may Allah shoot them all."

"Amen to that," said another. "Here, have some tea. And knafe."

The eldest among them, in a traditional embroidered thobe and white headscarf, rose with some labor, interrupting the others. "You think she's here to see you? Or her kinfolk and the baby?" She led us into the communal space of my brother's three-room home. A kitchen and bathroom off the courtyard made up the rest of the house.

Fatima appeared comatose, depleted from twenty-one hours of labor, and my baby niece lay swaddled next to her mother in angelic sleep. They had named her Falasteen, the Arabic word for Palestine.

"How original," I joked to Yousef, who reached for his baby girl.

Broad-shouldered Yousef, his vast tenderness cradling tiny Falasteen, was a sight to behold. When I think of him now, that sublime moment of unspoiled, unconditional devotion to his family is what I see. I still hear his words. "I am holding the most perfect of all God's creations. Like a turn, little sister?"

"Ismallah, ismallah!" I took my baby niece with great care, my heart tiptoeing in that house of love. Her small mouth opened in a delicate yawn and I moved closer to drink her scent. There is nothing quite so pure, as if pieces of God live in the faint breaths of babes. In Falasteen's yawn, I caught a whiff of divine promise, bequeathed even to us.

I placed my niece at her sleeping mother's breast and watched my brother, turgid with affection, look back and forth from his wife and to his newborn daughter. In that refugee camp, which Israel would label a "breeding ground of terrorists" and a "festering den of terror," I bore witness to a love that dwarfed immensity itself.

Later, alone with my brother in the courtyard, it was time. "I have something for you," I said, removing Baba's pipe from my pocket. I handed the package to him slowly, as Ammo Jack O'Malley, mercy on his soul, had given it to me years before when he took me to the orphanage in Jerusalem.

The heavy, turtle-paced creep of gravity prodded Yousef to rise on his legs. And the frail waft of honey apple tobacco, as he uncovered our father's smoking pipe, turned those legs to clay. Yousef's shoulders drooped and I saw my brother cry for the first time in my life.

"How did you get this?" he asked, composing himself and wiping tears.

The constant, background-humming craving for just one more moment with our father moved to the forefront of our yearnings, crowning the next hours between brother and sister getting to know one another as adults. He was sorry for having left me in Jenin. He'd have taken us with him, if he could have. "I'm sorry I wasn't there for you when Mama died." He hadn't heard about my being shot until a year after. Life hadn't been easy. *Nor for me.* But we were a family again and now there was a baby, a promise that we could live on.

"I didn't know what else to do, Amal. But I want to make it up to you. I want to be here for you now."

"You did the best you could, brother. I know that," I said.

"There are some things I never told you," Yousef began. He looked down at his hands, as if placing the words in his palm first before uttering them. "Our brother Ismael, the baby we lost in forty-eight, is alive," Yousef said, looking intently at my face.

He was surprised when I told him that I already knew, or at least I had always suspected ever since Huda and I had overheard him talking so many years earlier about the *Yahoodi they call David.*

"Does Huda also know?"

"I don't think your conversation that day left the same impression on her as it did on me. Anyway, we never spoke of it."

My brother and I served Fatima in bed when she awoke and the three of us feasted together on reunion and family, nibbling from the side dishes of Nablus jibneh and watermelon. I can replay the details of that day in my mind now, only they come to me strangely without sound. The rhapsody of mother and child is metered in the shallow bobs of Falasteen's little head as she breastfeeds. Fatima is beautiful, overjoyed, in love. Something funny is said and I notice a silver filling in Yousef's back teeth as his laughter opens his mouth wide. The bread—the large, thin Iranian khobz that I love—is torn and passed.

Later, Yousef saunters proudly around the camp holding his baby girl. I take her for a while, and Yousef leans back in his seat, lighting our father's pipe with fresh tobacco. He inhales the smoke and his eyelids fall, moving my brother to some memory that makes him grin. He opens his eyes and we are secure in the scent of our father. My memory can read the movement of his lips but cannot hear the words now: "Baba and Mama would have danced today," Yousef says. Since he was a boy, he had wanted to watch them dance again as they had the day Jiddo Yehya returned with his forbidden fruits from Ein Hod, and all the refugees had rejoiced.

I snapped many photographs that evening in Shatila, but there is one in particular that I treasure, that I framed and placed on the mantel. It evokes the details of that day's happiness. It is the photo that would one day leave my Pennsylvania home in a CIA evidence box, after which I would frantically search for the negative to print another copy. My big brother is frozen in a silly, toothy grin holding his firstborn child, Falasteen, while Fatima, the love of his life, sweetly leans on his shoulder, smiling, in their tiny dwelling in that shanty refugee town.

Fatima and I bonded as women that summer in Lebanon. I was no longer the little girl who delivered their letters and played barefoot in the camp, but a young woman she could take under her wing. We shared domestic responsibilities, marking time with Falasteen's development, and Fatima embarked on a matchmaking mission to pair me with a husband.

She had only one man in mind, a physician by circumstances similar to mine. He was a refugee and an orphan who had earned a scholarship through the United Nations and spent eleven years at Oxford, specializing in vascular surgery.

I faked disinterest, of course. But she goaded me, joking about how frustrated I must be at my age without a man.

"Well, you should know, since you did not have sex until you were thirty-two!" I retorted.

"Yes. And it was surely worth it!"

"Please. I don't want to hear about my brother's sexual competence," I yelled, hands pressed over my ears.

She laughed. But when I confessed to a string of disappointing relationships in the United States, her voice deepened, pulling words from a wisdom at her core.

"Amal, I believe that most Americans do not love as we do. It is not for any inherent deficiency or superiority in them. They live in the safe, shallow parts that rarely push human emotions into the depths where we dwell. I see your confusion. Consider fear. For us, fear comes where terror comes to others because we are anesthetized to the guns constantly pointed at us. And the terror we have known is something few Westerners ever will. Israeli occupation exposes us very young to the extremes of our own emotions, until we cannot feel except in the extreme.

"The roots of our grief coil so deeply into loss that death has come to live with us like a family member who makes you happy by avoiding you, but who is still one of the family. Our anger is a rage that Westerners cannot understand. Our sadness can make the stones weep. And the way we love is no exception, Amal.

"It is the kind of love you can know only if you have felt the intense hunger that makes your body eat itself at night. The kind you know only after life shields you from falling bombs or bullets passing through your body. It is the love that dives naked toward infinity's reach. I think it is where God lives."

In the long wait for one another and in the sacred love nestled in war, Yousef and Fatima had discovered this secret.

*   *   *

Majid came to visit my brother one Friday after Jomaa prayer. The day marked the end of my second week at the UN girls' school where I had taken a summer teaching post. It was also a milestone day, when baby Falasteen first smiled.

Walking past me with a tray of nuts and coffee for her guest, Fatima whispered in my ear, "This is the doctor I've been telling you about."

The man she hoped to pair me with was the man who had picked me up at the airport.

In the glory of her matchmaking, Fatima suggested that Majid show me around the city since I hadn't left the camp in a month of being there. He hesitated and I was embarrassed. Fatima's scheme was obvious and it made for an uncomfortable situation. Yousef frowned at the impropriety of his unmarried sister being seen about with a man. He trusted Majid, of course. But there was an order to things. There was rectitude.

"I just mean that Amal can help you with deliveries," Fatima added, undeterred.

Majid volunteered regularly in the camp, which meant he attended a fair number of childbirths.

Fatima continued, "Um Yousef, mercy on her soul, was a midwife and she taught Amal. The two of them delivered a lot of babies in Jenin."

Dalia and I had been a team.

Majid turned to Yousef in deference to his authority in the household. My brother made no protest and Majid in turn welcomed my help. "Um Laith is expecting next week," he said. He'd be honored and relieved to share the responsibility. If, of course, I was interested.

I turned to Yousef, out of love, to affirm that matters in his house were subject to his judgment. He understood the gestures and loved us all. "It's fine by me. Allah give you strength." His sister and dearest friend together would complete his joy. He wanted to make things right. To honor his promise to Baba and to me.

Yousef smiled his goofy grin, privately now in cahoots with Fatima.

Wudu, then salat. Ready, I held new scissors over a flame "in the name of Allah, Most Merciful and Compassionate." Majid was running late and I was to go ahead to Um Laith's house.

Walking there, Fatima remarked that I was too quiet. "Don't be nervous; you've done this a million times."

Unthinkingly, I responded as Mama once answered me. "Don't talk. Now is not the time for it." I immediately reproached myself. *I'll explain to Fatima later*.

The baby was all wrong inside. I sensed the trouble immediately. "Help me invert her!" I cried, and recalled that I needed to be calmer. *Whatever you feel . . .*

I paused, mumbled a prayer. *Breathe, child*. I breathed, *Dalia, help me*, and pressed my palms to feel for the baby. "Put your faith in Allah's hands," I whispered to the distraught woman. *Let Allah work through your hands*, Dalia whispered to me.

Majid arrived and beckoned for an ambulance. I heard "cesarean," "That's enough," and Fatima said, "Wait."

The baby rolled in time to not die or kill its mother. The umbilical cord was out of the way; the head was where it was supposed to be. Majid took over, delivered a boy, and sent mother and baby to recover in the clinic.

"Where's Amal?"

I had washed and left, pursued by the labor of hours past, the gnawing memories of years past. Pursued by Dalia. How it hurt, ever sweetly, satisfyingly, to be Amal again—not anonymous Amy.

I kept walking and there he was. "I've never seen that done before. I didn't know it could be done." Majid had cut his hair. Months later, he would tell me that he had done so for me, to make a better impression. "They didn't teach us that in medical school . . . You look a little white. Are you okay?"

"I'm tired." I looked down. *I miss my mother.*

"Can I walk you back?"

I nodded, *Yes.*

"Hungry?"

Starved. Where is this going?

"I just . . . I can smell shawerma from Abu Nayif's restaurant," he said, his words tripping over themselves. "I think it might be fine since word will spread by tomorrow that you're my medical assistant." He was trying out the sound of random thoughts, hoping something would fit, fill an awkwardness he didn't realize was charm. "But if you think it too forward, I can just pick up food and bring it to the house."

We had helped a woman and her baby win a round over death, Dalia had helped me find another piece of myself, and now Majid was stumbling through our intricate culture for a route to a simple meal with me.

Of their own accord, my lips stretched and curled into a smile. Devilishly I suggested, "We could eat downtown." He straightened, grinning the awkwardness off, relieved not to have offended. A dimple that I hadn't noticed before appeared on his left cheek, a small shadow made deeper by late-day stubble and by his smile that I loved.

It was growing dark by the time we walked back to leave a note for Fatima. Yousef would be late, but Majid and I both wanted to be home before he returned. So we settled for shawerma by the ocean.

"Finally, the 'Bride of Palestine,'" I said, face-to-face at last with the Mediterranean, smoldering with moonlight. "My father used to call her that. Jiddo Yehya—I never met him—used to take him and Ammo Darweesh to its shores when Palestine was still Palestine."

"She'll always be Palestine," Majid spoke softly, as if reluctant. He leaned back, exhaling. "You know," he added, his voice lighter and quicker, "the Lebanese call her the 'Bride of Lebanon.' I think Greece and Italy claim her as their bride also."

"She gets around."

"A regular tramp."

He laughed and I imagined his dimple. The comfort was strange and pleasing, the darkness vast and punctuated with stars, the moon halved, pouring on the water.

"See there," Majid said, motioning to a studded sky.

"See what?"

"Do you know what Leo looks like?"

"Yes, that's my zodiac sign," I said.

"I know," he answered. "Can you see the outline? Follow my fingers." Tracing the hook of the lion's head, he said, "That's Algieba, there's Ras Elased, Alterf . . ."

"Those are Arabic words. Are they actual names?"

"Yes. The stars were named by Arabs. The names they gave them are still used. But the constellations have Greek names. Can you see where I'm pointing?"

I moved behind him, the better to find the stars. Instead I saw that his shoulders spanned from one end of the ocean to the other.

"How do you know so much about the sky? Or that Leo is my sign?" I asked, backing away.

"*Al-Sufi's Suwarul Kawakib*," he said, looking intently above. It was Majid's most prized material possession—one of the first comprehensive descriptions of the constellations, written in the first century. "I'll bring it with me on my next visit with Yousef."

"And," he added, "your brother and I are close. We've spoken about you." He looked directly into my eyes. "Mostly recently . . . because I asked." A small, moon-shadowed smile stretched from his lips all the way to my heart.

Fatima was waiting when I returned.

"Well?" she asked.

"He's nice," I said, not wanting to give her the satisfaction but dying to tell her every detail.

"Aha! You like him. I can tell. But you don't want to admit I'm the master matchmaker around here," she boasted, patting herself on the back.

"Okay, smarty pants. But what if I didn't? You tried to push me off on some strange man! What kind of an Arab are you?" I joked.

"He's hardly a stranger. He's been your brother's best friend since the Battle of Karameh. Majid is the man Yousef saved when he took the bullet in his leg in sixty-eight," Fatima said.

It surprised me that Majid had ever been involved in fighting. "How did a PLO fighter get a scholarship to study in England?"

"Yousef found out that Majid had been a perfect student in the camps and had tried but failed to get a scholarship to study. So your brother set out to make sure his friend got one. He had connections with UN staff because of his work at the school, and he was able to get Majid's application to the right people."

"He didn't tell me that," I said.

"I'm sure he will. Just tell me first, who is the master matchmaker around here?"

"My silly sister-in-law."

"Good to hear you admit it. That look you gave me on your way out was scary," she laughed.

TWENTY-SEVEN

The Letter

1981

MAJID PERSISTED IN AMAL'S thoughts. He filled her daydreams, where she replayed their time together, searching for hidden meanings to his words. She began to grow agitated when a full week had passed without word from him. And for another two weeks, Amal tossed in the anxiety of waiting for Majid's next visit to her brother's home.

She continually surveyed her surroundings for the dented little white Fiat, hoping—no, praying—to find him visiting a patient in the camp or training physicians there. She listened vigilantly for news of his whereabouts, impending house calls, or plans to visit his comrade. Her condition was easily discerned among the women of Shatila, and they whispered in private when they saw the young schoolteacher looking about for—they were sure—signs of el doktor Majid. Though gossip it was, the women did not talk out of malice, but rather, out of habit and nostalgia for their younger days when love had been the grandest of possibilities. It is also true that in a refugee camp, where so many people live in so small a space, not even secrets can find a place to hide.

As was their routine by now, a band of girls caught up to their teacher on her walk to school one morning. "Good morning, Abla Amal!" Amal turned to her students, each in her blue uniform, white hair ribbons, books strapped to her back. Raja, a slight girl with mischievous eyes, came running. "Abla Amal," she panted, "el doktor Majid is coming to Mirvat's house tomorrow to check on her father."

The mere mention of Majid's name stirred in Amal a thrill she attempted to hide from her students. "That's good. How is

Abu Jalal doing after his surgery?" she inquired with labored casualness.

"El doktor is coming in the evening, abla," Raja reiterated, ignoring her teacher's question.

"El abla asked you about Abu Jalal!" another girl growled at Raja, then lowered her voice, adding firmly with a gratuitous light shove, "Not about el doktor!"

"Okay, girls." Amal gave them a sideways glance, endeavoring to fill the title of "abla" with the authority it merited. "Go on to your classes."

And along they went, giggling, tickled to have had a part in a subject of gossip overheard from their mothers.

Amal remained late at the school, preparing for the next week's lessons and passing time until evening's approach, hoping for an encounter on her way back. Finally she left, walking slowly the long way past Abu Jalal's house, looking in all the alleyways wide enough to accommodate a parked car, but she saw no white Fiat.

Dejection was on her face when she entered her brother's house.

"Where were you?" Fatima hurried toward Amal, helping her unload her books.

"I had to prepare some lesson plans for the next three weeks," Amal answered quietly.

"I sent some kids to fetch you. Majid was here. He left not fifteen minutes ago," Fatima said. Again, the mention of his name stirred Amal's depths.

"Salamat yakhti." Yousef approached his sister with a kiss on her forehead "Majid left this book for you. Said to take good care of it."

She took the book slowly. Majid's prized copy of *Al-Sufi's Suwarul Kawakib*. She looked up at her brother, inspecting his eyes for remnants of a conversation with Majid. Surely Yousef would not have taken the book without questions, nor would Majid have given it without explanation. An exchange between them would not occur with deception or hidden liberties. Honesty is a matter of honor. And honor is paramount.

Still, Yousef said no more and his face betrayed no useful hints. Amal found nothing in her brother's expression but an annoying artlessness.

Yousef yawned. He stretched his bulky limbs, rolled his head toward his wife. "Fatooma, habibti"—as he addressed Fatima when he wanted something—"I'm going to bed early, are you?"

"Your brother is wearing me out," Fatima whispered happily in Amal's ear.

"Agh"—the sister covered her ears—"I don't want to hear about my brother in that way."

Fatima kissed Amal's cheek, laughed her way into the sleeping room, and closed the door behind her. Amal walked out into the courtyard, the old book secure in her grip. She brought it close to her nose and fancied that she could sense Majid's cologne mixed with the antiquity of the leather book cover. She opened it, staleness coming off the parchment pages. Inside, tucked in between the cover and the first page, lay a small white envelope: *To Amal.*

She took it. *Yousef knows.* Majid would not have made him an unwitting messenger. *Fatima knows, too.* Going to sleep early was part of their conspiracy.

Now, Amal would also know.

Bismillah Arrahman Arraheem
  Dearest Amal,
  I am not sure how to start this letter, except to tell you that since that day I picked you up from the airport, I have thought of little else but you. And since that evening on the beach, you have

been in my dreams. I have avoided coming to Shatila with the hope of making sense of what I feel. But every thought comes to this: I am in love with you.

I have given my life to the resistance and sworn many an oath to the struggle. I thought my heart was too full with pledges and responsibilities to make another promise. But you have touched my heart in places I had not known were there. And I am compelled to one more promise, and it is this: If you will have me, I will love you and protect you for all my days.

Yours,
Majid

Amal read it again. And again. *Ba-boom, ba-boom.* Her heart beat as vigorously with love as it once had beaten with fear.

"I wish I could see the look on her face when she reads it," Fatima said to Yousef, annoyed that he would not reveal to her the contents of the letter, which Majid had been obliged to share with Yousef.

Fatima pouted, playfully vexed to be the last to know. She narrowed her eyes to focus a thought. "If you don't tell me, I'm going to join Amal in the courtyard," she warned her husband, unable to contain a smile despite her best effort to give a serious ultimatum.

"Habibti, please stay with me," Yousef whined like a little boy, lying on their bed with Falasteen asleep in his arms.

She kept her eyes narrowed and crinkled her nose, and Yousef delighted to watch her face surrender to a willing smile. In a last attempt to hold her ground, she bit her lip, and the sight of her thus was more beauty than Yousef could bear.

"I suppose I can wait until morning," she said, turning to retrieve her nightshirt from a drawer.

The baby had put extra flesh on Fatima's body and stretched

her belly, and now she hid herself self-consciously behind the dresser to change her clothes.

"Go back with the baby," she ordered Yousef when he rose toward her.

"Why? Falasteen is sleeping."

"Well, I'm just changing. Go back." She held her nightgown to hide her body. The light switch was out of reach. Yousef understood and lowered himself before her.

"Let me see," he whispered at her knees. She stopped, trembling as if he would see her, touch her for the first time. As she loosened her hold on the gown, her husband rested his head against her waist. He kissed the body that had borne his child, moving along her curves, swallowing life from the marks of motherhood on this woman who held his heart, dreams, and aches inside of her. The gown fell completely and love rose from them over their small dwelling in the Shatila refugee camp. From a man making love to his wife and from his sister in the courtyard, reading and rereading a promise of love.

TWENTY-EIGHT
"Yes"
1981

WE MET IN SECRET two days later. Majid wanted my answer in private, away from voices and expectations. So it was, at our favorite spot just outside the quaint seaside village of Tabarja, that Majid and I held each other for the first time. The blue Mediterranean lapped at our bare feet and stretched at its far edges into a cloudless sky. You could not discern where the ocean ended or the sky began, and somewhere in all that blue the startling enchantment of love found me.

Majid turned to me, his penetrating eyes black in the blue light.

"I talked to your brother. You know I had to do that first . . . ," he said, breaking into the tension. "Will you marry me, Amal?" he asked in sincere, committed blue, the ocean and the sky his comrades and conspirators in the question.

I had been waiting to answer. I had practiced in the mirror saying "Yes." A surprised, happy "Yes." A matter-of-fact "Yes, of course, I will." So much preparation just to utter that little word.

But all I could do was nod my head in assent, and my body took him in its arms, absorbed the lovely blue crackling with love.

He brushed his lips against mine, pulled me closer, and I felt as if I had lived all my life for that kiss.

"I love you," he said.

The most perfect words.

Whatever you feel, keep it inside. Mama was wrong. "I love you, too," I whispered at his ear, willingly falling into my words.

I listened to the breath entering and leaving me in Majid's arms. Never had I been so aware of life or so grateful to live. To have a sense of blue.

We returned together, to give the news. Some of my students caught up to us as we walked through the alleyways. They greeted us, giggled, ran away and returned, blurted out "el doktor Majid and Abla Amal are going to get maaarrriieeed," then ran away again.

The span of Majid's shoulders moving next to me, the music of his steps, the clearing of this throat provoked a dream that rearranged my life, putting him at its center forevermore.

TWENTY-NINE

Love
1981

They met daily during their monthlong engagement. Majid came in the very early morning that had been so magical in Amal's childhood. She waited eagerly each time, her heart suspended in the mist of daybreak, until she heard his steps approaching. He walked briskly, impatient to see passion expand her bottomless black eyes when they set upon him. Though when they beheld each other, their desire to hold and feel one another was tempered by rectitude, by loyalty and respect for Yousef's and Fatima's good names, and by their approaching wedding.

They talked, less for meaning than to hear the other's voice. Majid learned the nuances of an earnest love, the lines it drew from the eyes of the woman who loved him truly, the fullness of his own breath in her presence, the way time passed too quickly when they were together and too slowly when they were apart.

Their affection seemed to take on a life of its own during these times together, such that Majid and Amal had a sense that words were intruders. So they spoke in whispers. Time thus passed over these soft exchanges, the occasional laugh or smile offering each something upon which to hang his and her heart, until the sun started its ascent, and they prayed together the first salat.

Low to the earth, the sun found the two praying and cast long shadows that stretched their forms far behind them. Then they left one another, contented.

"Are you coming after work?" she inquired each time.

His answer was always the same. "Inshalla," God willing.

*   *   *

The evenings were lovely, always seeming full, hopeful, and clear when Majid was near. I can see them now as if I were an outsider looking through someone's window. The five of us, Fatima, Yousef, Majid, baby Falasteen, and I, sit around the plates of fried tomatoes, hummus, fuul, olives, zaatar, eggs, yogurt, and cucumber. A starry black sky is our roof in the courtyard where we all talk and laugh, as if we had been together all our lives. Falasteen plunges her hand into the hummus and Fatima licks it off her baby's fingers. The baby loves this and continues to stretch her little fingers to her mother's mouth. I feel then that I can't wait to have a baby of my own.

Some nights Majid brought his telescope and taught me secrets of the night's sky. Once, on a Thursday at the beach nearing sunset, Majid saw my maimed belly. He put his hand there, untroubled by the rutted skin. His hand moved lovingly over my abdomen and he kissed its waves of scar tissue. He gave my body the acceptance I had been unable to give it myself. It was an act so tender that it banished the shame. A scar of hatred soothed by Majid's kiss.

The day quickly approached, and never had I been at the center of so much joy and attention. The zaghareet of women resound in my memories of that time. Fatima's friends, who were now my friends as well, waxed and plucked my skin and rubbed oils and balms all over my body. They burned frankincense to perfume my hair and blessed me with their murmured prayers and incantations. One woman, bless her, gravely took Fatima aside to ask if she had instructed me on what to expect and do on my wedding night.

THIRTY

A Story of Forever
1981–1982

ADORNED IN GOLDEN JEWELRY far more humble than her mother's had been, Amal delighted in her wedding. She wore a virgin's white silk and danced with the women of Shatila, who charged the air with their songs and thrilled the evening with their dancing bodies. In their secret world apart from men, the women removed their hijab. Heads of dark and henna-dyed hair unraveled beneath, and each tied her scarf around the arches of her womanhood. They moved their hips, tracing curves of Middle Eastern rhythms, seduction and feminine pride. They danced to honor the bride and bless her marriage with their joy, celebrating centuries of Arab women who have danced together in a private world to which no man is privy.

"Aaaaaahh eeee aaaaaahh," one elderly matriarch began at the top of her voice, and the crowd fell silent. "May Allah touch this bride's womb with fertility."

Amal's elder female relatives should have been the ones to hurl those ancient calls for blessings. But Fatima was her only female kin in Lebanon, and she was not yet old enough.

"Aaaaaahh eeee aaaaaahh," the old woman continued, heaving prayers into the air. At the end, excitement erupted in the women's zaghareet, ululations pulled from their Arab foremothers to shake merriment from the air.

The spectacle reminded Amal of a time at the Warda house when the girls had played aroosa, one pretending to be the bride and the others wrapping their scarves around the bones that would someday flare into hips. They acted out wedding scenes and tried to oscillate their tongues rapidly to produce zaghareet.

Only Huda, shyly at first, knew how to make that thrilling sound. From then on, she was their designated "zaghareet coach," and Amal had secretly asked her not to teach Lamya, since Lamya could already do a somersault.

If only Huda were here now. Amal silently longed for her best friend at her wedding. And that wish led her to others. To her mother, the beautiful iron-willed Dalia. To all the girls of the Warda house, and to Muna Jalayta and the Colombian Sisters. To the dawn and her father's soothing voice. To the calls and responses of her country and days of el ghurba. She smiled throughout her wedding without once tightening her jaws. Watching the celebration, Amal wandered nostalgically in and out of her memories.

As the hours passed, the women replaced their scarves and veils to join the men, merging the two celebrations into one. Someone then placed Amal's hand into Majid's. The groom was dressed in white, a sword belt around his waist, the hems of his kaffiyeh threaded with silken red. Amal turned to face her husband, the coin-studded veil framing her vision, and the wedding party danced, arms linked in a circle around the couple.

A gale of love brewed in them both. A want so heavy it made their knees weak and their palms sweaty inside the grip of their hands. They turned to smile at the crowd, for the sake of what's proper, the way newlyweds should conduct themselves at their wedding. But Majid never let go of her hand. From the moment he felt his bride's small fingers slip into his, he did not release them until he carried Amal to his Fiat, and they rode away into marriage.

Majid carried his wife again to their apartment in the al-Tamaria building in Beirut. In time, the sword belt fell and the silk pushed against their skin, until flesh found flesh. He rose over her, drinking her nakedness. He had had many women during his ghurba days in England, but no body had enchanted him with such love. It was the body of Amal, long vowel, his yearnings and hopes. He leaned into her, kissed her lips, closing his eyes to take in their softness. She felt his breath fall softly on her face and opened her legs, like wings, taking her lover, her husband, into her body. There, they surrendered to a tempest that tore into the best-hidden parts of their hearts and Amal awoke the next day to a dream floating low on a landscape of love.

At last, fate had surprised her with a dream of her own. A dream of love, family, children. Not of country, justice, or education. Amal would have gone anywhere, as long as Majid was by her side. He became her roots, her country.

Their lives merged, and she cherished the smallest details of marriage to him. They brushed their teeth at the same sink; they ate and prayed together. They wrote their names in the sand like young lovers, holding hands all the while. He shaved her legs while she nibbled on his neck. She trimmed his hair and he washed hers. They took nothing for granted. Theirs was a raw intimacy, unabashed, the kind of love of which Fatima had spoken, that dove naked into itself, toward infinity's reach, where the things of God live.

*　　*　　*

"What are you reading, habibti?" my husband asked.

I showed him the cover. "It's a collection of American poems about roses."

"The English are in love with the rose, too."

"My grandmother Basima used to cross them. Here's one by Robert Frost, the rhyming poet: 'The rose is a rose, and was always a rose, but the theory now goes, that the apple's a rose.'"

Majid replied, "What's so special about a rose? Have you ever really inspected one? They have thorns. They aren't particularly fragrant. They're difficult to grow and are frail when you do get them to bloom. I'll take a dandelion any day over a rose. Now that's a flower. It's humble, hearty, keeps coming back no matter what you do to it. And it always blooms a brilliant yellow smile."

"Spoken like a true communist," I teased him. "So what am I? A rose or a dandelion?"

"Agh! I should have seen that trap coming. You, my dear . . . are not a flower, something that blooms one day and wilts the next. You are the beat in my heart."

"Great answer! Go on . . . ," I teased.

"Do I get a prize for great answers?"

"Maybe." I smiled.

". . . the light in my eyes," he said.

"You're good. A prize is in order, sir."

"Oh, madame, you are too kind." Majid arched his brow mischievously. "I'll collect my prize now."

We found a small house near Shatila so that I could continue my teaching job in the camp and be closer to Fatima and the baby. But we kept our apartment in Beirut for nights when Majid worked late.

We were as happy as anyone can hope to be. Even as rumblings of war sounded from radio reports and coffeehouse conversations, Majid and I spoke of making children and growing old to the pitter-patter refrain of grandchildren.

When my menstrual period did not arrive on time, my elation was as vast and diaphanous as the morning sky and it was multiplied twofold that afternoon, when the UN clinic confirmed both my and Fatima's pregnancies. We calculated that our babies had been conceived during the same week.

"The doctor thinks I'm due sometime in the middle of September," Fatima said.

"Me too."

"You think Yousef and Majid planned it?" She was almost serious.

"I wouldn't put anything past those two."

* * *

Majid's thrill pulled him to his knees, face-to-face with my maimed belly, suddenly charmed with new life. The fine components of that perfect evening have long been pilfered from my memory by age. But I can invoke its purity, that sense of unmitigated contentment that leaves you without a right to ask for more.

He kissed my belly. "Hello in there!" he said, then looked disbelievingly at me. "We're going to be parents, Amal!" He was excited as a schoolboy.

We talked for a long while, but I no longer recall the words, only the joy.

A month later, naked in our bed, Majid and I were making plans as expectant parents do. Our limbs laced and wrapped in each other, we spoke of our future and the future of our baby.

"If the situation becomes more heated, habibti, Yousef and I agree that you, Fatima, and the children should leave until things settle down," Majid said solemnly, tightening his body around mine.

Israel had been striking Lebanon to provoke the PLO into retaliation. In July 1981, Israeli jets killed two hundred civilians in a single raid on Beirut, and Ariel Sharon, Israel's defense minister at the time, issued a public vow to wipe out the resistance once and for all. The rhetoric was weighing heavily on Yousef and he was concerned for us should Israeli attacks intensify. Protecting the refugee camps was the priority. Toward that end, the PLO leadership ultimately struck a devil's deal to keep the women and children safe.

But by April 1982, the United Nations had recorded 2,125 Israeli violations of Lebanese airspace and 652 violations of Lebanese territorial waters. Israel amassed twenty-five thousand soldiers on the border and continued to illegally deploy provocative maneuvers to the south of Lebanon. The PLO resisted retaliation and so did the Lebanese government.

But Yousef correctly surmised that Israel would find a reason to invade, regardless of whether the PLO took action.

Yousef and Majid, even Fatima, convinced me it was for the best. I was to return to the United States, renew my green card, and begin immigration proceedings for my husband, Fatima, and Falasteen, who was by then nearly one year old. Yousef's fate was bound with the PLO, but he needed the peace of knowing his family would be safe.

"Amal, do not think you are abandoning us," Yousef said, soberly reading my mind. "You very well could save their lives."

* * *

My pupils conspired to prepare a farewell party on my last day at school. Ranging in age from ten to fifteen, in identical navy blue uniforms, they brought sweets and hot tea to class and moved their desks together to make a table. Two girls, Wafa and Dana, synchronized their tablas and the others linked arms to perform a dabke, pulling me in to dance with them. Before I left, each handed me a letter, a drawing, or a handmade going-away gift. One little girl, Mirvat, had stitched for me a small pillowcase with the words "I Love You" in English.

I promised that I would return, sure that I would, that my departure was a temporary and ultimately unnecessary precaution. That is what I said to my students before leaving them in Shatila.

Leaving Majid was infinitely harder.

"Please, Majid. Please, habibi, come with me," I begged him.

"Habibti, you know I can't just leave. Soon people are going to need doctors more than anything. I can't turn my back on them."

I wished then that my husband was a coward.

"If anything happens, I promise to live at the hospital. Even Israel will not bomb a hospital," he reassured me, and pulled me close. "Before you know it we'll be together, raising our baby and maybe expecting another. I love you eternally. What we have is made of forever."

Love. Eternally. Forever.

Those were my husband's words at the airport the day I left Beirut. I hung on to each one. Each syllable.

I promised my brother, as he asked me to promise, that my first order of business upon arrival in the United States would be to apply for asylum for Fatima, who stood behind him holding a well of tears in her eyes and little Falasteen in her arms. She and I comically maneuvered a side-winding embrace around our swollen bellies, already in the second trimester, and we kissed good-bye in that ribbon of humor. On cue, Falasteen pressed her open mouth against my cheek. "Ammah," is how she uttered my name.

I kissed my husband once more and spent the next hours of travel trying to shoo away dark premonitions, circling like buzzards in my head.

THIRTY-ONE
Philadelphia, Again
1982

The earth is closing on us,
pushing us through the last passage,
and we tear off our limbs to pass through . . .
Where should we go after the last frontiers?
Where should the birds fly after the last sky?
> —Mahmoud Darweesh, "The Earth Is
> Closing on Us," written in the aftermath
> of the PLO's exit from Lebanon

NINE O'CLOCK, ON THE morning of May 16, 1982, twenty-six hours after I left Beirut, I was in Philadelphia, with the cheerless void of not wanting to be there. It seemed a lifetime had passed since I had first come to that city, unsure of my step, frightened that an escalator would drag me under, jealous of Lisa Haddad's hair.

Immediate tasks in hand, I called Dr. Mohammad Maher, Majid's former mentor in England, settled now in a Philadelphia professorship.

"Amal, I have been expecting your call," he said in a voice husky with age and cheer. "Please. Wait for me in the baggage claim. I'll be there in less than thirty minutes."

Unknown to me, Majid had been corresponding with Dr. Maher for months, making arrangements. Already I had employment. I was to prepare clinical trial reports for federal audits.

"The pay is good. I'll just need to show them proof of your degree. If you decide for something else, I'll help you."

Majid was like a son to him. "So please, I would love it if you called me ammo, or just Mohammad if you'd rather. But none of this *doktor* business."

Touched and without adequate words—"thank you" conveying a dearth of gratitude—in Arabic I said, "Allah keep you in Grace and a bounty of goodness upon you. This kindness of yours, doctor . . . Ammo Mohammad . . . is humbling."

Life was quickened here. I had forgotten that. Within two weeks I had been trained on the job, visited an obstetrician, and gone five times to the immigration office. My husband was cleared to come to the United States, but a response for Fatima's visa would require at least another month.

With rows of taut African braids and a kind smile, the INS lady said, "I know it's a mess over there. I'll do all I can to push it through."

"Thank you." *May Allah smile on you with plenitude and love.*

The city seemed to have changed while I was away. West Philadelphia had become a miasma of drug-infused poverty. I saw despair now where authority had been in the faces of the heavy matriarchs, still passing the days in the shade of habit on their porches.

Old friends—Angela Haddad, Bo Bo, and Jimmy. "It's nice to see you again, Amal." An apartment in the northeastern part of the city, wanting to avoid becoming a burden on the Mahers.

While I waited to receive my family, biding time with hope and sporadic telephone conversations with my husband or Fatima, Ammo Mohammad and his wife, Elizabeth, fashioned themselves into a surrogate family. Ammo and Elizabeth had been married nearly fifty years. They had served as healers, he a physician and she a nurse, living on the small salaries of aid organizations in the plains of Africa after leaving Oxford. Now in the United States, with the grand compensation of North Americans, their lives had an air of restlessness, of want for children. Though their bodies carried their seventy-odd years well, age had eroded bones and carried off vigor, forcing them to slow their pace where they could recruit young medical skill to carry on the legacy of their work. Medicine Without Borders. A labor of love, but not enough. My arrival, with life swelling my abdomen, stirred the sediments of their advanced years. Latent and undeniable, the instinctive affinity of the old for babies and children delighted them now and they protected my swollen state.

Elizabeth saw to it that I ate well, consumed vitamins, and went to regular checkups. She sat nearby each day as I dialed and redialed numbers to Lebanon and the INS, there to share the disappointment of no answers or busy circuits.

Her fading blond hair, short above her neck, curved behind her ears in a way that dismissed vanity. She moved through days tall and erect, and her long, slightly arthritic fingers took little rest from her determination to save the world while simultaneously keeping her husband's life in order. Her mornings started with coffee, which she had been giving up for the past forty years. She would fix Ammo's red bow tie, as much a part of him as his hazel eyes. They'd part with a brown-bag lunch and a kiss, a rite that had not wavered in all their years of marriage.

Elizabeth had retired when Ammo took a faculty position at the University of Pennsylvania. Her time was spent in the service of their medical charity, her newfound indulgence of spa treatments, and water aerobics three times a week. My arrival changed her patterns and, as the delivery date approached, she invested her time in me and our mother-daughter assembly. I still spent more nights in Elizabeth's guest room than in my apartment.

The accretion of days without word from Majid, Yousef, Fatima, or the INS amassed around me. A sum total of void and portents of the evening news. Then it all crumbled on June 6, 1982.

Israel attacked Lebanon.

I wasn't paying attention to the small screen on the kitchen counter, but Ammo was, and I noted the change in his face before hearing the news. We had all been holding our breath for weeks and now what we had feared moved languidly, like a cloud, across Ammo's expression, pulling the color from his face and causing it to droop.

I heard the shrill broadcast as I met his sad eyes.

"A massive invasion." "Intense aerial bombardment." "Ninety-thousand-strong invasion force moving up the coast of Lebanon." The television headlined "Operation Peace in the Galilee." Such was history's name.

Operation; how words are violated. Majid performed operations to save lives.

For five interminable hours, I dialed and redialed, but Lebanon's telephone lines convulsed with relatives trying to reach one another as Israel began systematic destruction of communications in the country. At last, the heavens parted. A ray of sweet mercy touched my world with the sound of my husband's voice at the other end.

"Habibti. Oh God, your voice is all I need to get me through this hell," he said, as if reading lines of my own heart. I had reached him at the hospital, war tearing all around it. I could hear the thunder of bombs muffled by distance, the blaring of ambulance sirens. The squeal of terror far away, where I wanted to be.

"Majid, please come now," I begged.

"Habibti, the injured are pouring in by the hundreds and the hospital is already short of staff. They need me. So many doctors have abandoned them already. Please stay put and take care of our baby. I will come . . . I promise we will be together soon."

Not knowing when we could speak again, we held on, filling every second with the love we vowed would never die. He promised to remain in the hospital.

"I dreamed you gave birth to a baby girl, little Sara, and we were picnicking on the shore of Sidon. Remember when we wrote our names in the sand?"

I could barely speak. "Of course I remember." I sobbed, "I saw her, in the sonogram."

"Her?"

"Yes. We're having a girl. We're going to have Sara."

A long pause followed. "In the end, you're all that matters. It is you that I owe, more than anyone here. Isn't that right, darling? I love you more than you imagine. Perhaps I've done all I can here."

Little Sara.

In a while it was time to hang up, a task that felt like turning a valve to expel the air from my lungs. But Majid was coming to me now and it would be a matter of only days, a week at most.

I turned to God with the immediacy of every woman's faithful vow. *Keep my family safe through this and I'll live to deserve your mercy.* I prayed and prayed. As Dalia had prayed in another time and another place. In another war.

Their telephone lines remained severed.

Each day, I cleared the cobwebs of my nights' dark premonitions and shuffled through my days, my mind always tuned to the news. I dialed and redialed, infected with dread. Ariel Sharon marched his military into Lebanon—known as "the Oasis of the Middle East" for its splendor—and laid siege to Beirut for two grueling months, during which Israel deprived its people of water, electricity, and medical care.

My heart became metallic, leaded with the ink of newspapers and the tinny tone of broadcasters. In the office lounge, a television reporter: "Humanitarian organizations are warning of . . ." I couldn't listen.

"Management needs to do something about the food in this place," one of my co-workers said. Others went on about the dire parking situation: "It's too damn far, especially when it's raining."

I had lost contact with Majid and felt as if I would also lose contact with life itself.

Bombs and more bodies to receive them. I prayed and called the Red Cross. Called the INS. Please. They were doing the best they could, and no, I couldn't go there. All flights had been suspended. *How will my family get here?* The BBC showed high-rise buildings crumble like dried cracked clay, whoever had been inside also broken.

"Israel is striking back against the PLO, a terrorist organization whose aim is to slaughter Jews like they did the Munich athletes." Israel's stated aim was self-defense. To dislodge the PLO, a six-thousand-member resistance.

By August, the results were 17,500 civilians killed, 40,000 wounded, 400,000 homeless, and 100,000 without shelter. Prostrate, Lebanon lay devastated and raped, with no infrastructure for food or water. Israel claimed it had been forced to invade for peace. "We are here for peace. This is a peacekeeping mission."

Decades later, still searching for the fate that forgot me, I sifted through the accounts of peace. In his epic memoir, *Pity the Nation: The Abduction of Lebanon*, British correspondent Robert Fisk described phosphorous Israeli shells:

> Dr. Shammaa's story was a dreadful one and her voice broke as she told it. "I had to take the babies and put them in buckets of water to put out the flames," she said. "When I took them out half an hour later, they were still burning. Even in the mortuary, they smouldered for hours." Next morning, Amal Shammaa took the tiny corpses out of the mortuary for burial. To her horror, they again burst into flames.

Ronald Reagan dispatched Philip Habib, who brokered a cease-fire deal in which the PLO evacuated Lebanon. Yousef had to leave or die. He left because it was the only way to keep Fatima and the babies safe. So they said.

The PLO withdrew from Lebanon only after an explicit guarantee from U.S. envoy Philip Habib and Alexander Haig that the United States of America, with the authority and promise of its president, Ronald Reagan, would ensure the safety of the women and children left defenseless in the refugee camps. Philip Habib personally signed the document.

Thus the PLO was exiled to Tunisia carrying the written promise of the United States. The fate of those I loved lay in the folds of that Ronald Reagan promise.

THIRTY-TWO

A Story of Forever, Forever Untold
1982

O N SEPTEMBER 10, I awoke in a terrible fright, trying to discriminate night from nightmare. The clock read 3:02 A.M. as the telephone rang in the corner of my mind.

It was Yousef.

He had arrived at his place of exile with the PLO. Tunis was their destination at the end of an agonizing departure from Lebanon, whereby Yousef and his comrades had been forced to leave their wives, children, and parents behind. These sacrifices were the small parts of Yasser Arafat's ragtag deals on behalf of his people.

Now Yousef suffered the surreal and oppressive responsibility of delivering news he wished he did not have to utter to his only sister.

Majid had kept his promise to me, living in the shelter of his hospital, which was clearly marked on every side and on its roof with the universal symbol of medicine, a red cross. But at the urging of his co-workers, he had returned to our apartment for a respite from the constant blare of sirens. He had slept deeply and soundly in our bed, the place where we once had found deliverance in love and where we had conceived our child; and when he had returned to his duties, he had found an inferno where the hospital had been. My brother was there, searching for Majid, and together they had helped rescue as many people as they could.

"Only by the Grace of Allah were you spared, brother," Yousef had said, relieved to see Majid alive.

Yousef did not know what surged through my husband then, only that it filled him with determination enough to spend the next twenty-six hours tilling the destruction in that garden of dismembered corpses and perished souls. Carnal ash materialized in thin air and thickened, clotting their windpipes as they trudged through puddles of blood toward screams for help. They pulled out Majid's patients, dead under the rubble. His colleagues who had urged him to go home and get some rest were found in crimson pieces.

Exhaustion dulled their senses and weighted down their bodies until Yousef and Majid finally left, spent.

They were dragging themselves on borrowed strength when they came upon a dead woman whose stiff body clutched the body of her child, a small girl with a ribbon in her hair—whose body in turn was gripping her mother. They had seen worse, but the sight of that mother and her child summoned a small reserve of energy in them both, enough for them to throw their arms around one another. And sob.

Majid turned to Yousef and asked, "Have you been able to reach Amal?" Yousef had not. "Amal is having a little girl. I'm going to be a father, brother," Majid said calmly, as if everything around his words was paralyzed. "I'm going back to London in the morning, and from there I will join Amal or she will come to England. Look at what these pigs do. I can't risk making a widow of Amal and an orphan of my Sara."

"Allah be with you, brother." Yousef embraced his comrade again and they parted in silence, Majid heading to our apartment on the fifth floor of al-Tamaria apartment building, and Yousef returning to the refugee camp of Shatila.

Five hours later, an Israeli bomb leveled the al-Tamaria, and another leveled the adjacent building.

"I looked everywhere, Amal. But I'm sure he was inside. No one survived it," my brother sobbed through the telephone, his speech torn and mangled by love and by the general impotence of perpetual victims.

"I'm sorry, Amal." My brother was somber, his voice so terribly heavy in my ears. So full of sadness. "I should have insisted he come with me. I've been trying to reach you since then but I couldn't get through until we reached Tunis . . ."

I listened . . . the heavy syllables pounding my sense of what was real. Rocking on the floor in my own two arms, I pressed the telephone receiver to my ear. I was not filled with grief, anger, or even love. Nothing came over me. But everything rushed out. Yousef's words now traveled through me like a stream, pulling life from the cells of my body and gathering it beneath me. Memories of rain beating on the windshield of Majid's Fiat; the calluses on his feet when they rubbed against my bare legs; the hair on his chest when I lay my head there; the lines around his mouth when he laughed; the arch in his brow that was a smile of its own; the small wrinkles beneath his ears; the smooth skin on his back when he sat up in bed; his touch, his kiss, his integrity, his love . . .

All of it pooled on the floor around me like a tenebrous underbelly. Until at last, I sat captive in a vacuum of thought, numb and rocking on the floor, still holding the receiver as my brother's voice, with its unbearable sadness, faded in that emptiness.

Majid. My love.

The dreams he and I had dreamed circled around this new reality. The children we would have, the places we would go, the home we would build, the laughter we'd share and the songs we'd sing, the life we'd live, the love . . . oh the love we would love, danced like ring-around-the-rosy, around the reality that Majid was dead. Killed. Ashes, ashes, all fall down.

I confronted the weather outside my apartment, walking in a daze along the leaf-strewn sidewalk. A fiery display of fall's orange, green, yellow, and red lined both sides of my Philadelphia street. An old woman walking her dog nodded hello. I passed young lovers on a park bench as I continued through the cool wind, entranced and numbed to fate, until I reached Elizabeth's door, ten miles later. Startled from his sleep, Mohammad cracked the door suspiciously, then opened it wide for my enormous body.

"They killed Majid," I said, matter-of-fact.

I love you eternally. What we have is made of forever.

Majid. My forever story of love, forever untold.

Love. Eternally. Forever.

My husband's words at the airport the day I had left Beirut.

They remain in my mind, like ashes in an urn. The glory of love, like life, quite simply reduced to dust.

"Oh dear God!" Mohammad helped me inside. Just then, I felt the intimate kick of the baby inside me, and I noticed that the sun had also risen.

THIRTY-THREE

Pity the Nation
1982

THAT WEEK IN SEPTEMBER, starting with Yousef's telephone call, is the mantelpiece of my life. It is my center of gravity. It is the point on which all of my life's turning points hinge at once. It is the deafening crescendo of a two-thousand-year-old lineage. It is the seat of a demonic God.

On September 16, in defiance of the cease-fire, Ariel Sharon's army circled the refugee camps of Sabra and Shatila, where Fatima and Falasteen slept defenselessly without Yousef. Israeli soldiers set up checkpoints, barring the exit of refugees, and allowed their Lebanese Phalange allies into the camp. Israeli soldiers, perched on rooftops, watched through their binoculars during the day and at night lit the sky with flares to guide the path of the Phalange, who went from shelter to shelter in the refugee camps. Two days later, the first western journalists entered the camp and bore witness. Robert Fisk wrote of it in *Pity the Nation*:

They were everywhere, in the road, the laneways, in the back yards and broken rooms, beneath crumpled masonry and across the top of garbage tips. When we had seen a hundred bodies, we stopped counting. Down every alleyway, there were corpses—women, young men, babies and grandparents—lying together in lazy and terrible profusion where they had been knifed or machine-gunned to death. Each corridor through the rubble produced more bodies. The patients at the Palestinian hospital had disappeared after gunmen ordered the doctors to leave. Everywhere, we found signs of hastily dug mass graves. Even while we were there, amid the evidence of such savagery, we could see the Israelis watching us. From the top of the tower block to the west, we could see them staring at us through field-glasses, scanning back and forth across the streets of corpses, the lenses of the binoculars sometimes flashing in the sun as their gaze ranged through the camp. Loren Jenkins [of the *Washington Post*] cursed a lot. Jenkins immediately realized that the Israeli defense minister would have to bear some responsibility for this horror. "Sharon!" he shouted. "That fucker [Ariel] Sharon! This is Deir Yassin all over again."

What we found inside the Palestinian Shatila camp at ten o'clock on the morning of 18 September 1982 did not quite beggar description, although it would have been easier to re-tell in the cold prose of a medical examination. There had been massacres before in Lebanon, but rarely on this scale and never overlooked by a regular, supposedly disciplined army. In the panic and hatred of battle, tens of thousands had been killed in this country. But these people, hundreds of them, had been shot down unarmed. This was a mass killing, an incident—how easily we used the word "incident" in Lebanon—that was also an atrocity. It went beyond even what the Israelis would have in other circumstances called a terrorist atrocity. It was a war crime.

Jenkins and I were so overwhelmed by what we found in Shatila that at first we were unable to register our own shock. We might have accepted evidence of a few murders; even dozens of bodies, killed in the heat of combat. But there were women lying in houses with their skirts torn up to their waists and their legs wide apart, children with their throats cut, rows of young men shot in the back after being lined up at an execution wall. There were babies—blackened babies because they had been slaughtered more than 24 hours earlier and their small bodies were already in a state of decomposition—tossed into rubbish heaps alongside discarded U.S. Army ration tins, Israeli army medical equipment, and empty bottles of whisky.

Did I know those women, or those babies? How many of the children had been my students? For forty-eight hours, Israeli soldiers, sodas and chips handy, watched that malignant rush. *How does an Israeli soldier, a Jewish man, watch a refugee camp being transformed into an abattoir? Fatima. Falasteen.*

Down a laneway to our right, no more than 50 yards from the entrance, there lay a pile of corpses. There were more than a dozen of them, young men whose arms and legs had been wrapped around each other in the agony of death. All had been shot at point-blank range through the cheek, the bullet tearing away a line of flesh up to the ear and entering the brain. Some had vivid crimson or black scars down the left side of their throats. One had been castrated, his trousers torn open and a settlement of flies throbbing over his torn intestines. The eyes of these young men were all open. The youngest was only 12 or 13 years old.

In the next passage, I found the fate of Fatima and her friends—those friends who had been at her side the day she gave birth to Falasteen. The women who had kissed me because Fatima had told them so much about me. The women who had gossiped about me when I fell in love with Majid, and who had sung, danced, and cried at my wedding.

On the other side of the main road, up a track through the debris, we found the bodies of five women and several children. The women were middle-aged and their corpses lay draped over a pile of rubble. One lay on her back, her dress torn open and the head of a little girl emerging from behind her. The girl had short, dark curly hair, her eyes were staring at us and there was a frown on her face. She was dead. Someone had slit open the woman's stomach, cutting sideways and then upwards, perhaps trying to kill her unborn child. Her eyes were wide open, her dark face frozen in horror.

An Associated Press photographer pressed his finger and sent the scarlet darkness of that scene around the world. I saw the photo in the Arab press and first recognized the woman's pale blue dress. *Fatima's favorite dishdashe, worn thin in nearly two decades of use.* The curly-haired little girl behind her was my niece. *Falasteen.*

Yousef called me, screaming. *Screaming.*

Even through the telephone wires, there was enough agony in his voice to break the sky. I can still hear it shatter the wind when I walk.

"How much must we endure and how much must we give?" he wailed like a child. "Fatima! My darling, Fatima! Did you see what they did?" he asked, *screamed*, and he answered himself, "They ripped her belly, Amal!"

I had no words.

"They ripped my Fatima's belly with a knife! . . . They killed my babies!" He screamed more. "They killed my babies, Amal. Oh God! Oh God . . ."

His sobs shook the ground beneath my feet and I thought the force of his grief would tear the sun to pieces. He hurled objects within his reach and I stood in Pennsylvania, mesmerized by the sound of breaking glass at the other end of the world. He cried with no measure of control, gripped in a seizure of pain. Tetanus. Thunder.

He cursed Israel, the Americans, Ronald Reagan, Arafat, and the world, sparing no leader and no god or devil. "Damn them to hell. Damn them to this hell they made for us."

At the base of his voice I heard the silent howl of wrath burgeoning in him, the raw substance of despair and rage concentrating into resolve. He vowed vengeance, swore to cut their throats like pigs. He beat his head against the wall with no mercy for himself, still holding the telephone to his ear, still cursing. Still crying—the cries of a soul dying.

That frenzy of pain dismantled him. Yousef was irreparably undone. They killed my sweet brother in absentia when they murdered Fatima. And his heart now beat with the force of his rage.

"THEY SLAUGHTERED MY WIFE AND MY CHILDREN LIKE LAMBS!"

The line went dead. And I stood, besieged by the trickery of destiny. By stolen futures and the unbearable sorrow of extinguished love.

Again, I walked outside, freshly fallen leaves crackling under the weight of my steps. I overpowered my tears with a tight clench of my jaw. I was afraid to cry, lest I feel the storm inside my brother.

Whatever you feel, keep it inside. Oh, Dalia, Mother! I understand!

I removed my shoes, took off my socks and sweater.

The better to freeze my heart.

And I imagined myself screaming at Philadelphians, who went about their daily American lives.

Ten blocks later, I collapsed at Rittenhouse Square and, I was told, did indeed grab a woman, begging her to tell me what she found so funny in the world that she could laugh at that moment, with her friend, on a bench in the park?

My water broke and an ambulance carried my wet, pregnant, and barefoot body away from the crowd of onlookers, who stared in pity at the deranged little woman about to give birth.

My obstetrician, who was called by the hospital at the behest of the medics, alerted Mohammad, who immediately summoned Elizabeth. The two of them heard the news and needed only one look at my face to know that Fatima and Falasteen had not survived. But I looked away from their eyes, afraid their sorrow might free the tears I labored to contain.

For ten hours, my body convulsed with contractions. I wanted the labor to go on until eternity. My eyes turned to glass, my heart to ice, and no breath left my body without first being stripped of its sound. I held it all in, gripped it with my fingernails. Imprisoned it all in an inexpressible clench of my jaws.

Whatever you feel, keep it inside.

I wanted the pain to last longer, to become more intense, to kill me, too. The need to hurt was far greater than the need to push and I saw the confusion, even fright—or terror—of the nurses who came in one after the other "to check on me."

The aging elegance of Elizabeth's face was damp with compassion and a discernible desire to lift me out of my own fate. But in her wisdom, she said nothing, merely holding my hand without once letting go, as I gazed into space clinching my jaw tight on its trembling hinges, lamenting the few tears that escaped in a silent journey from my eyes.

At last, my baby's instinct for life conquered me and I let go. I pushed, drenching the cloth beneath me with the pulp of childbirth and tears, freed at last.

The head began to emerge, tearing my flesh, and I thought of Fatima's belly ripping at a murderer's blade. I yelled her name like a battle cry—"Fatima!"—pushing harder and harder to rip my body as hers had been ripped. I wanted to bleed for the penance and torment of purgatory. Why should I live while Fatima lay rotting in an unmarked mass grave? Why should my baby be born while hers was torn from her womb? I pushed with a heart that loved and longed for Majid. I pushed again, with the determined force of self-punishment, of contrition and apology for living.

At last, my child lay wrapped in my arms, like a flower bud. I settled my being in the rhythm of her jaw suckling at my breast, while she spooned life over my hardened heart, like moss cushioning a stone. But I kept my distance, going only through the mechanics of caring for a newborn. This fragile infant had forced upon me the will to live, and I resented her for that, for all I really wanted then was to die.

THIRTY-FOUR

Helpless

1982–1983

But you do not see, nor do you hear, and it is well.
The veil that clouds your eyes shall be lifted by the hands
    that wove it,

And the clay that fills your ears shall be pierced by those
 fingers that kneaded it.
And you shall see.
And you shall hear.
Yet you shall not deplore having known blindness, nor
 regret having been deaf.
For in that day you shall know the hidden purposes in all
 things,
And you shall bless darkness as you would bless light.

—Khalil Gibran, "The Farewell"

I EMBARKED ON MOTHERHOOD WITHOUT Majid and
with only a thread of will. Elizabeth and Mohammad were
there, steady and compassionate. I moved in with them, at their
insistence. In many ways, they saved us, Sara and me.

I watched my child with curiosity, nourished her body for the
sake of duty. I held my emotions in a tight fist and hard jaw. But
Sara's scent was irresistible, an intoxicating, wordless promise
that weakened me. So, at times, I sneaked over my heart's
fortress to inhale her baby smell into the deep parts of myself
that still craved love. And I would lose myself in the rhythm of
her suckling jaw, the warmth of her helplessness, the insistence
of her endless needs.

A week after the massacre at Sabra and Shatila, *Newsweek*
magazine determined that the most important story of the
previous seven days had been the death of Princess Grace.

The following week, the cover story was "Israel in Torment."
Israel, a victim.

American press "reports" agitated the ghosts crowding my
mind. Aisha's sweet face would smile before my eyes, annoyed.
Fatima and Falasteen, too, would come knocking at my visions
in search of a decent grave, for an honest reckoning of what
had happened to them. Thoughts of Mama, Baba, and Yousef,

and a deluge of longing for Majid's touch, would build up an oppressive weight that then would crumble over my heart, like the concrete of our building that had crushed my husband in his sleep. The only way to stop the emotional storm from gathering was to splash cold water over me. Literally, I needed physical coldness to mute it all. Otherwise, I'd have gone mad, I'm sure of it. But the storm was always there, latent, lurking in the vast clench of my iron jaw. So I stopped reading or watching the news and I feared touching Sara, lest I infect her with my destiny. Lest she warm my heart and unthaw the wrath and the ghosts and madness I feared lived inside me.

I shut down. My defenses pricked anyone who dared to come near me, including Sara, though I secretly continued to consume her scent at night while she slept, to fill my lungs with the reason I needed to breathe. I loved her in spite of myself. I loved her immeasurably. Infinitely. And I feared that love as much as I feared my own fury at the world.

Ariel Sharon remained free to pursue the politics of violence, until eventually he rose to the highest office of power in Israel, becoming prime minister of the Jewish state. The citizens of Israel elected him on February 6, 2001, more than a year into the second Palestinian uprising, and the American press described him as "a portly old warrior" and a "tough veteran of Israel's many wars." The forty-third president of the United States of America, George W. Bush, referred to him as a "man of peace."

How the memory and horrors of Sabra and Shatila were vanquished.

The last time Yousef and I spoke was in January 1983, though he said he would try to call again before "this was over."

"Before what's over?" I asked.

"Yasser Arafat is a coward who leads his people to slaughter with the rope of American lies," he said.

"Brother, you sound ill. Are you okay? Where are you?"

"I left the PLO," he said. He had done so shortly after they had been exiled to Tunis and now he spoke to me from Lebanon.

"Lebanon?" I gasped. "How did you get back there?" I was sure the Americans did not know. He must have sneaked in. But how? Who was he working with? And, my God! Why was he there?

He answered nothing and I began to feel the frost in his voice. "Don't ask questions, Amal . . . I just called to be sure you were fine and secure," he said, each word emerging stiff, isolated, chilling.

"Yousef. I love you. Please leave Lebanon. Please, my sweet brother. We can come together again and find a life, maybe in France . . ."

He didn't answer.

"I named my daughter Sara. You should see her. She looks like Majid. Are you there? Hello! Yousef! Please . . . Yousef. Yousef? Please answer me, I can hear your breathing."

Silence.

"Yousef, please. You aren't alone. There are thousands of fighters who lost as you did. As we all did. You and I still have each other. I know your pain, Yousef. You know I know it. I have hateful thoughts just like you. But please just . . . brother. Don't get yourself killed. I couldn't bear it. I need you, Yousef."

The telephone connection was severed. My brother was irretrievably gone. He had traversed the burning abyss, before which I still cowered, and landed on the calm, detached shore of vengeance. He had left his soul to rummage through Sabra and Shatila, where his wife and daughter lay in a mass grave beneath a garbage dump, under the impunity of their killers, under the broken promises of superpowers and under the world's indifference to spilled Arab blood.

THIRTY-FIVE

The Month of Flowers
1983

APRIL ARRIVED IN 1983. On its eighteenth day, the month of flowers saw the harvesting of the bile that had been sown in Lebanon. Fire was vomited from the bowels of revenge, injustice, and yes, history, sending plumes of smoke onto every turned-on television screen.

My dreams the night before had forced me out of bed at three a.m., but I cannot recall those dreams now. I took coffee before taking in the sunrise, while Sara took my breast in her hungry sleep. I rocked her in my lap, her rapacious little lips suckling my nipple, and I reached for *The Prophet*, strewn on the floor among the chaotic piles of my books. I read these words, last read to me by my father when I was too innocent to understand:

> A little while, and my longing shall gather dust and foam
> for another body.
> A little while, a moment of rest upon the wind, and another
> woman shall bear me.
> Farewell to you and the youth I have spent with you.
> It was but yesterday we met in a dream.
> You have sung to me in my aloneness, and I of your
> longings have built a tower in the sky.
> But now our sleep has fled and our dream is over, and it is
> no longer dawn.
> The noontide is upon us and our half waking has turned
> to fuller day, and we must part.
> If in the twilight of memory we should meet once more,

        we shall speak again together and you shall sing
            to me a deeper song.
    And if our hands should meet in another dream, we shal
            build another tower in the sky.

I did not read the newspapers that day. Always, there was an excuse to avoid the news, and always, I took it. But it came to me anyway on that eighteenth day of the month of flowers.

A man had driven a truck loaded with explosives into the U.S. embassy in Lebanon, killing sixty-three people and wounding scores more. The triangular compound was a horrid place, littered with body parts. Footage showed survivors dazed by the blast, walking aimlessly in what could have been hell. A man, overwhelmed by the bloodbath, sobbed against a wall. Another man and a woman, each having thought the other had not survived, threw their arms around each other. Towers of black smoke rose from the ruins, paling in the sky, as the ABC reporter choked on the mist of death. He excused himself and I knew the smell he was breathing at that moment. "Terrorists hit the U.S. embassy here . . . ," he said.

Elizabeth and I sat red eyed in front of the television for hours, transfixed. Tearful family members of the victims gave emotional interviews and the stillness of my heart reached through space to commune with their pain.

A while later, the day found me burrowed in the sofa cushions, watching Elizabeth lovingly feed my daughter the soft baby food from a jar. The television was off. A persistent breeze lifted the thin curtains, fluttering a few moments of tranquility into that turbulent day. The neighbor's rose vines had grown high and pretty outside the window. Across the room, Elizabeth cajoled baby laughter with a flying spoon and airplane sounds and I thought, as I always did, that I should be the one feeding my child. So, I tightened my jaw to keep her baby laughter from unearthing love in the gray stillness inside me. But I smiled anyway at the spectacle, discreetly filling my inner quietude with an irresistible, but secret, joy, and at that moment, the FBI, the CIA, and local police were surrounding our home.

I answered the doorbell, hoping to find Yousef standing there. But my heart dropped at the sight of their badges.

"Are you Amal Abulheja?"

"Yes, can I help you?"

"We'd like to have a word with you," said a handsome blue-eyed man in a spotless dark suit. "If you don't mind," he added politely, professionally. They were all polite and professional, in fact. All six of them suddenly inside my house.

"My name is Jack O'Malley," the agent began, but I interrupted him as that name smiled in my mind.

"I knew a Jack O'Malley once. He was from Dublin. Worked for the UN in a Palestinian refugee camp."

"We need you to come with us," he said dryly, a tone unbefitting his name.

I left Sara in Elizabeth's care, voluntarily submitting to go with O'Malley for further questioning.

There, on a folding metal chair centered in a small bare police room, I sat subdued by curiosity and foreboding.

"My name is Jackson. Tom Jackson, ma'am. I have some questions," said a corpulent man with an angry face. "Do you know this man?" he asked, sliding a photograph toward me on the table separating us.

I took the photo of Yousef with trembling hands. It showed only his face, in harsh details I had never before seen. The deep lines around his eyes held the pitiless resolve I had heard in his voice the last time we spoke. The upward-curling waxed tips of Yousef's mustache, where he had carried the memory of Jiddo Yehya, were cut off.

It was Yousef's face, but nowhere in his features could I find the brother I had known all my life.

"This is my brother," I said, and I feared the answer to the question I could not utter: *Why do you ask?*

O'Malley, who had been standing silently against the bare white wall, stepped forward, slowly leaning his weight on the table to meet my eyes with the fire in his. "We think he's the terrorist who bombed the embassy in Beirut. What can you tell us?" He enunciated each jagged word with profound contempt.

I locked my jaw and threw away the keys. I didn't believe them and my heart retreated to its inner tundra. But my senses exploded with awareness, heightening the experience of disjointed details in the room. The slight, almost imperceptible sway of the hanging light, the cheap smell of a man's aftershave, the sniffle of someone with a cold, the shift of another's weight, and the dirt particles grinding on the tile beneath his shoes. A wrinkled note, torn from a school notebook, landed before me. Yousef had written it and it had passed through the hands of many, including a CIA informant, making its way to me, for whom it was intended.

Forgive me, Amal. It is time they taste a small dose of the heaps they have fed us all our lives—Yousef.

For the next ten hours I answered their questions and their accusations. They may have been as drained as I was, but they remained unsatisfied with my answers. "Yes, I know he left the PLO . . . I don't know why . . . Because he called me and told me . . . That's all he told me . . . I don't know anything about the Islamic Jihad group . . . I swear."

He had done it all, they thought, the planning, the recruiting, and the bombing. "I don't believe you," I said.

"We don't believe you, either."

Ammo Mohammad arrived with his lawyer and I was, a day later, at last free to go.

I remained in the absolution of my inner darkness, but demons followed me there too, crowding the back alley of my days with a past too dense. I let Mohammad go on without me while I roamed the streets of Philadelphia, trailed by government agents who made no secret of their presence and thenceforth for many years rarely left me.

Rain fell and I welcomed the distraction of the splash of my boots on the pavement. The agents behind took cover beneath black umbrellas, maintaining only a few steps away from me until I stopped at a bar. It was a musty red-lit rectangular chamber with brick walls hoisting life-size photographs of Humphrey Bogart and Marilyn Monroe. It was the bar on South Street where I had first tasted alcohol during my college years at Temple. Drenched, I found an empty stool at the far end of the bar and settled in. My hair was soaked with rain and my yellow T-shirt clung to my skin, revealing fine feminine contours on one side and the unsightly legacy of one Israeli soldier on the other. A string of Long Island iced teas cocooned me in a fog, where the only sound was the sermon of colliding ice cubes in my fat glass of liquor, which I raised once in recognition of the two trench-coated agents drinking tonic at the other end of the bar. Somewhere in my befogged state, I heard a voice ask in surprise: "Hey . . . Aren't you that girl that used to live with Angela? What's your name . . . Omar or something. Amy? No, Omar, right?"

It was Milton Dobbs. I recognized him immediately. Angela Haddad's ex-husband. Without a word, I returned to the solace of my drink. He mumbled something to his friends and they all laughed.

Suddenly a clarity shattered my oblivion. Attention in the bar turned to the television screen. The music was turned down.

Everything seemed to give way to the voice of a reporter standing amid the wreckage of the U.S. embassy. "Rescue teams are still finding body parts," said the broadcaster, and I watched the wretched scene, frightened that the FBI could be right. That the brother I loved with every part of me had done it. But then I thought about the brother I knew and was sure it could not have been him.

The two poker-faced agents watched me, not the reporter.

"Fucking terrorists!" Milton declared, puncturing an abscessed resentment inside me. From the corner of my eye I saw him turn in my direction as he shouted, "I think we ought to carpet-bomb the whole fucking place. Get rid of every last sand-nigger."

Rage nominated me to hell.

I rose, blind with anger. The truth I knew swarmed over me like locusts, and fire screamed in my veins. No crevice of my being did not sting as I watched my arms pound fists into Milton, who floundered beneath me in shock, blood running from his nose and the flying white dress of Marilyn Monroe winging on the mural above us.

I was a small woman, with a frame bearing no more than 105 pounds, and in no time I was handcuffed, hearing the testimony of a bystander, and I stood there panting.

". . . she flew like a . . . I mean it, officer. She literally flew off that-there barstool and knocked him clear off. Shit, I never seen a woman do that," he told a police officer, pausing between thoughts to laugh and marvel at what he had witnessed.

A crowd gathered, but the men who had been trailing me all night still sat at the bar. Behind the faces circling Milton and me, I saw Jack O'Malley.

A humiliated Milton refused to press charges, dismissing me as "a psycho bitch."

The police removed the handcuffs and left. The crowd thinned. And I don't know why, but I walked up to Jack O'Malley and rested my head on his shoulder.

Looking at my swollen hand, he called to the bartender, "Can we get a bag of ice for the lady?"

My brother was a boy who walked the hills of Tulkarem and drank from the water springs in Qalquilia. He played soccer with the abandon of youth on the plains of Haifa and fed from the bosom of an ancient lineage in the land of his forefathers. We played backgammon, he and I. He was a man with a smile that melted many a Mediterranean heart. Truly, it was the most beautiful smile I have ever seen. He was denied, imprisoned, tortured, humiliated, and exiled for the wish to possess himself and inherit the heritage bequeathed to him by history. His own heart he devoted to one woman only, for whom his grief shook the earth and spilled the blood of those who stood on it.

The picture from O'Malley's pocket made its way to television screens across the country and my brother Yousef became the poster boy of all things vile and evil in the world.

Once, when I was four, Yousef tickled me so hard that I peed in my pants. When I was six, he spent days upon days teaching me how to blow a bubble with chewing gum. With the same patience, he taught me to whistle. In the sweetness of my youth, he and I walked together endless miles to the markets. We are captured in a photograph—the two of us digging into an orange in front of the Damascus Gate in the Old City before Israel conquered it. We ate figs, olives, and peaches straight from their trees. I spied on him while he read dirty magazines with his friends in our pitiful refugee camp. I read his love letters to Fatima and in his absence, mocked his sentimentality, like any bratty little sister would do.

While his unforgiving face peered out at the world from television screens, I found the picture I had taken the day Fatima gave birth in the Shatila refugee camp, now forgotten killing fields and mass graves. The lines around Yousef's eyes were all made of love. His expansive smile hung by the tips of his mustache, the meticulous legacy of Jiddo Yehya's love, which my brother had waxed daily into his appearance. Yousef looked silly in that picture, frozen in his toothy grin with newly born Falasteen cradled in one arm and Fatima, the love of his life, sweetly leaning on his other shoulder.

THIRTY-SIX
Yousef, the Avenger
1983

I SEE HER FACE IN everything I do. Everything I touch. Her tired blue dishdashe. I buy her many others, but she loves the blue one. I see her take it off so many times. Many times, I remove it for her. And I see her put it back on in the mornings. She doesn't even know I watch her. My beautiful wife. Mother of my Falasteen and another from my loins; I'll never know its name.

She pulls it down from the top to feed our daughter at her breast and I pull it up from the bottom to kiss her legs. "The Americans signed the paper," she reminds me. "We'll be safe. The Jews will not risk making a liar of their only supporter."

I kiss her thigh and look upon our second child growing inside her. I can say I love her, but those careless, overused words would demean the immensity of what I feel. Fatima is the air I breathe. She is the reason for all promises. The embodiment of tenderness. She is love.

She holds me for a long time after I am called to go. "No matter how long it takes for us to be reunited, I'll wait. I'll wait for you until the end of time," she says, her brown eyes filling with tears.

"Baba." Falasteen kisses me.

I see Fatima standing there, waving good-bye. Falasteen holding on to her mother's blue dishdashe.

I leave.

In a photo, that dishdashe is ripped and stained with blood. God, I beg of you, put me inside that photograph! At least to bury her with honor, with our children.

I no longer possess myself. I drown in a sorrow you cannot fathom, and a rage you cannot imagine presses upon my heart.

I am an Arab son. Born of Dalia and Hasan. My grandfather is Yehya Abulheja and my grandmother is Basima. I am the husband of Fatima, father of two. I am a haunted man, possessed now by their corpses. A storm brews inside me. I do not sleep and I cannot see the sun. Demonic wrath bubbles in my veins. May it lurk after I am gone. May you taste its vinegar.

I seek vengeance, nothing more. Nothing less. And I shall have it. And you shall see no mercy.

VI.

ELLY BAYNA
(what there is between us)

THIRTY-SEVEN

A Woman of Walls
1983–1987

CONSTANT MOTION OF BOTH body and mind kept my life at a steady murmur. I rejoined the working society, stepping unobtrusively into the steady American flow. I returned to work in the pharmaceutical industry, leaving Sara in the care of Elizabeth most of the time.

I spent long hours there, expertly producing whatever the company asked of me. Strangely, the details of capitalism came easily to me. I felt no pressure when others scrambled at deadlines. Behind my icy eyes was a scorn at the utter unimportance of their bottom lines, the damaging rush to the next material benefit. I performed my job meticulously and easily.

I was a woman of few words and no friends. I was Amy. A name drained of meaning. Amal, long or short vowel, emptied of hope. Only practical language could pass the lump in my throat, formed there from love that meanders in the soot of a story that almost was. And anyway, what words can redeem a future disinherited of its time?

My life savored of ash and I lived with the perpetual silence of a song that has no voice. In my bitterness and fear, I felt as alone as loneliness dares to be.

Few of my co-workers liked me. They mistook my coldness for arrogance. These were the people who had seemed so self-assured and grand when I had first stepped foot in America many years earlier. I judged them harshly now, as they called me names behind my back, "ice queen" and "super bitch." I ignored them, but I envied them the bliss of their small fears and the ease of their security.

I faced the world behind a thin layer of contempt. Only Sara was a threat to my hardness. She was the hearty vine, lovingly creeping along the stone of my character. The warm ember, forever aglow deep within. From the shadows of a heart more afraid of love than of death, I watched time stretch her bones and unfold her lovely skin over a young woman's body. She was the brilliant color in the middle of the gray desolation of my world, the point where all my love, my history, and my pain met in a perfect blossom, like a flower growing from barren soil. God forgive me, the more she grew, the more I feared to be near her, to touch her. I was afraid to transmit my jaded frost to her, that my touch would be callused, the wrong complement to her soft, unconditional tenderness. So, I tended to the demands of motherhood, containing that burning love behind the cold walls of fear and long work hours.

Until she was four or so, Sara still came to me dripping with affectionate need. She would squiggle her little body in my lap, clinging to me for a story or a song, and from my clenched jaw I obliged. Her scent would seep through my skin to fan the flames of motherhood. By the end of the story or song, I'd feel tired of the fight to contain the heart that wanted nothing more in the world than to surround that perfect creature born of my body with its affection. I dreamed of it, imagining how I would sweep her up in my arms in loving play. How I would tickle her mercilessly, the way Elizabeth did, for the heart-filling pleasure of her laughter. I imagined the endless kisses I craved to plant in her memories. I never did, and eventually she stopped coming to me, constructing walls of her own to keep me out as well. Thus we lived behind our solid barriers, each craving the other's love.

I had already been dismantled by the loss of everyone my heart had ever embraced and I would not allow the vulgar breath of my fate to spoil her promising life.

>   I can explain this, but it would break
>   the glass cover on your heart,
>   and there's no fixing that.

So I watched her with a chronic ache as her wits and beauty unfurled in untouchable loveliness with each step she took through time.

I was a better mother during my daughter's first few years, and as I look back, I think our house had something to do with that.

When Sara was still small, I bought a dilapidated old Victorian home in a northern Philadelphia suburb. I restored the house myself over the span of three years, filling every potentially idle moment with labor and motion.

There was something soothing, perhaps merely numbing, in the mindless strokes of painting the walls and the repetitive motions of sanding the wooden floors. I stripped the deposits of neglect from the doors and railings, uncovering the glory of oak's raw grain and the love poured into it by some long-departed master carpenter. I picked crud from crevices, revealing the ornate details of someone's architectural vision. I cleaned and I scrubbed and I mopped. I laid new tile and polished old floors. I hung new curtains and replaced broken glass, added light and recommissioned four fireplaces. In the frenzy of restoration, I unintentionally loosened the crusted layers of loss, clearing fear from a small patch of my heart. There, I held Sara, my small child, and rocked her at my breast, reading to her at dawn as my father had read to me in the long-ago days of love.

Each morning, I settled into a rocking chair that I had salvaged from someone's garbage and read by the east-facing French doors as the sun made its way through the orange sky, rising behind a hundred-year-old maple tree in our backyard. I am not sure that Sara was ever aware of me carrying her out of bed every dawn while she was still deep in sleep because after I had read to her and finished my coffee, I'd return her to the warmth of her bed and head for work, leaving Elizabeth to Sara's waking hours. I remember clearly the last time that I read to her at dawn.

It was the middle of her third year. She lay in a blanket on my lap as I reached into a pile of books, randomly retrieving Khalil Gibran's *The Prophet*. Randomly again, I opened the book to this passage, which Majid and I had read the night we learned that our child grew in my womb.

> Your children are not your children.
> They are the sons and daughters of Life's longing for itself.
> They come through you but not from you, and though
> they are with you yet they belong not to you.
> You may give them your love but not your thoughts,
> For they have their own thoughts.
> You may house their bodies but not their souls,
> For their souls dwell in the house of tomorrow, which you
> cannot visit, not even in your dreams.
> You may strive to be like them, but seek not to make them
> like you.
> For life goes not backward nor tarries with yesterday.
> You are the bows from which your children as living
> arrows are sent forth.
> The archer sees the mark upon the path of the infinite, and
> he bends you with his might that his arrows may go
> swift and far.
> Let your bending in the archer's hand be for gladness;
> For even as he loves the arrow that flies, so he loves also the
> bow that is stable.

In the rise of the sun, as I read those words to my sleeping child, I heard her father's voice in mine and felt his fingers run through my hair the night we read Gibran together. He leaned and kissed my lips, the apparitions of an expired love story. Majid was still here, running beneath my surface like an enchanted river from which I may never again drink, in which I may never again swim. Majid is the dream that never left me. The country they took away. The home in sight but always beyond reach.

The moment imbued me with yearning and I was defeated by the want to reverse time to the days of plenty. I held my breath and clenched my jaw to keep from remembering love or wanting it ever again, and I laid Sara in her bed with care now, turning to dress myself in the chill of *Amy* and a fine black suit before leaving for my job.

THIRTY-EIGHT
Here, There, and Yon
1987–1994

SOON, AN UPRISING CLIMBED from the ground to Palestinian hands, and the rocks they threw cracked the morbid glory of imperial victory. It was an intifada, a spontaneous combustion after twenty years of Israeli occupation. It was a shaking off of oppression and it spread through the hearts of Palestinians everywhere. They took to the streets hurling sticks and stones. Israel responded by breaking their bones with "might, force and beatings," following the command of Yitzak Rabin, prime minister of Israel.

Here, Amal read. From Norman Finkelstein's *The Rise and Fall of Palestine*.

Israeli press and human rights reports put flesh and blood on the data. The 1 April 1988 issue of *Hotam* reported the case of a ten-year-old beaten so black and blue during an army interrogation that he was left "looking like a steak." The soldiers "weren't bothered" even when they later learned that the boy was deaf, mute, and mentally retarded. The 13 July 1988 issue of *Koteret Rashit* reported the "disappearance of 25 children" and jail threats to their parents for "annoying" the army about the children's whereabouts. The 19 August 1988 issue of *Hadashot* featured three photos of a blindfolded six-year-old in an army jeep. The caption reported that many children his age would be held in detention until "ransoms" of several hundred dollars were paid, and that, as they were carted away, the children often urinated in their pants "from fear." Under the heading "Deliberate Murder," the August 1989 bulletin for the Israeli League for Human and Civil Rights reported that the Israeli army (apparently sharpshooters from "special units") had targeted an "increasing" number of Palestinian children in leadership roles. "Carefully chosen," the victim was usually shot in the head or heart and died almost instantaneously. Dr. Haim Gordon of the Israeli Association for Human Rights reported the case of an eight-year-old tortured by soldiers after refusing to reveal which of his friends had thrown stones. Stripped naked, hung by his legs and brutally beaten, the boy was then pushed to the edge of a rooftop before being released (cited in the January 1990 bulletin of the Israeli League). The 15 January 1990 issue of *Hadashot* reported the case of a thirteen-year-old who was thrown into detention after his fingers were deliberately broken and who was then left without any medical treatment or food because his father was unable to pay the ransom of 750 dollars. The 26 January 1990 issue of *Davar* reported the case of a sixteen-year-old girl who was beaten by a club-wielding policeman ("he even tried to push the club between my legs") and then thrashed in prison for refusing to sign a confession. The 29 June 1990 issue of *Hotam* reported the case of a thirteen-year-old detainee who, refusing to supply incriminating evidence against his brother, was "smashed" in the face, had "bruise marks on his entire body," was not allowed to drink or eat "for hours," and was forced to "urinate and defecate in his pants."

Reporting on the grisly fate of Palestinians as young as fourteen arrested on "suspicion of stone-throwing," the 24 February 1992 issue of *Hadashot* quoted an inside source at the Hebron detention center:

"What happened there . . . was plain horror: They would break their clubs on the prisoners' bodies, hit them in the genitals, tie a prisoner up on the cold floor and play soccer with him—literally kick and roll him around. Then they'd give him electric shocks, using the generator of a field telephone, and then push him out to stand for hours in the cold and rain . . . They would crush the prisoners . . . turning them into lumps of meat."

Amal read these accounts, never knowing that the blindfolded six-year-old boy was Mansour, the youngest child of her friends Huda and Osama.

Mansour had been rambunctious and wide-eyed. His brothers had frequently teased him for being a mama's boy and he had accepted the label with unabashed delight in Huda's smiling arms. When a photographer took his photo, as he sobbed beneath the blindfold in the back of an army jeep, Mansour was praying for his mother to rescue him, and she, Huda, was going wild without her baby boy. The army held him for one week, the time it took Huda and Osama to raise the five hundred dollars' ransom and determine Mansour's location. No one ever knew what exactly happened to little Mansour over the course of that week, but when he was finally returned to his family, he looked no one in the eye. And he had lost the ability to speak.

*   *   *

There, Huda and son cloaked themselves in a habit of song at the doorstep of sleep, coaxing the night with melodies to open the doors of pleasant dreams. In the same family room, Osama, Amal—their firstborn—and the twins, Jamil and Jamal, would listen, allowing the lure of Huda's voice to entice them too into slumber. These were the folk ballads of Palestine through which Huda came to lull her entire family to sleep during the years of that first intifada and for a time beyond that.

> Oh, you who passed by and waved with the hand
> You marked the secrets of love in my heart
>
> I heard your voice when you talked
> Like a bird singing on top of an olive tree
>
> Oh, flying bird in the high sky
> Say "hello" to the dear sweet one
>
> Your name, my soul, will stay in my mind
> Written on my forehead between the eyes

Though they lived with the indignities of dispossession and military occupation, Huda sang with an unassailable freedom that comes only to those with unwavering faith. Huda and Osama still loved each other with the cravings of youth and the mercies of kittens. Their Amal was her father's princess and her mother's friend. She eventually married a Syrian and moved to Damascus with him. The twins, who came along in 1978, were strong, stubborn, inseparable, and protective of each other and their family.

At the other side of the world, Amal cradled her anguish like she should have her own child. She lived in a prison of her own making, a jail of ice to keep the world away. She gritted her teeth through much of her life, holding her breath as she moved through a cloud of silence. She prowled the trenches of that silence, that fear. She lost her way, lost some fundamental part of her makeup, but she knew not what it was, nor where or how to reclaim it. After a time of avoiding all news of Palestine, she now found herself reading everything there was to read about her homeland and her people, but she did not lift a pen to write a letter to Huda, nor to anyone else. She read as if each book were the piece of an elusive puzzle she needed to solve. She read to remember. But mostly, she read to punish herself with the intense guilt of having been spared.

And Huda sang. And she prayed.

"Please don't throw rocks, yumma," Huda begged Jamal and Jamil, her ten-year-old twins. "Don't break my heart. Don't break your father's heart while he waits in their jails. They took him just like that. I don't want them to take you too."

But they threw rocks at Israeli tanks anyway, because boys will be boys and the young shall never respect the fragile breath holding them to life. They did it not for the sake of freedom, for such a concept was too precarious. They did it out of peer pressure, for the nature of small boys that attracts them to the adventures and trials of men. They threw rocks under an umbrella of abstract politics, which they did not understand, because they were bored with nothing left to do after Israel closed their schools.

Their hearts pounded with excitement, with the rush they felt when they whisked their own lives from the jaws of death chasing them so closely. Real-life cowboys and Indians. Some of their friends had already fallen by Israeli bullets. The stakes were great, making each day's narrow escape a near-orgasmic high. This went on for two years during the intifada, ending when Jamal was shot at the age of twelve.

Jamil watched his twin brother fade from life as the other boys ran for cover. He was struck by death's lack of drama. Its matter-of-factness. Its quiet authority. Jamal just closed his young eyes, expressionlessly, simply as if he were falling asleep, and never opened them again.

For Jamil, the loss of his twin came to define him. It pressurized into a temper that closed in on every tender spot, fossilizing his heart and squeezing bile from it. Anger drenched his vision. It coated his thoughts. It banished laughter, even lust, from his adolescence.

Huda still sang at night, tapering her melodies into a humming as she checked on each remaining member of her family: her children, Amal, Mansour, and Jamil. When she was sure they were sleeping, she prayed one more rukaa, a bonus for the day to curry favor with Allah, that he might protect her children, touch them with steadfastness, grace, and wisdom.

It was during these hours that Huda thought of Amal, wondering what had become of her lost friend.

Amal moved through time in the United States, each day like the one before, all of it forced and unreal. She hovered in the narrow junctions between madness, depression, love, and fury. Her life stood still in a room of fear, with whispering walls that laughed with Dalia's delusions. That burned with Yousef's fury. *Or is it my fury?* That cried with Yousef's pain and shook with her own. Walls she wouldn't look beyond, wherein swirled those angry and anguished voices. She disliked herself, emptied her world as much as possible and encrusted that emptiness with fear, on the lookout for pain, anger, or love that might break her fortress and fill the emptiness. She avoided her daughter, trying to douse that burning love, that dancing tenderness with its spangled promises. That sweet voice calling her, "Mommy, will you read to me like you did when I was a baby?" That heart-melting first-grade fantasy, "Mommy, it's true. I heard it on the news. The tooth fairy is raising her prices." She took all that in, unable to resist sweet indulgence. But she rarely gave back. Not for selfishness, but for the fear that the soot of her life might smudge the purity of her child. So it was for a perverted selflessness that she denied her daughter, and herself, the rhapsody of that magnificent love she felt to her core. Only at night, when Sara was sleeping, did she mercifully permit herself a whiff of love. Under the cover of night, she folded her arms over Sara, inhaling the soft fragrance of maternal love until the world seemed bearable again.

> I can explain this, but it would break
> the glass cover on your heart,
> and there's no fixing that.

When Amal thought of Palestine, she thought of Huda. She thought of her uncle Darweesh, of Aunt Bahiya, Haj Salem, her cousins, and Jack O'Malley. And frequently she thought of that other possibility, Ismael, the brother that Yousef had sworn was still alive. A Jew named David.

More and more, David's thoughts were of Amal, all that remained of his phantom family. Moshe had been the one who finally had told him, a dying man's confession. Learning the truth of his origins so late in his life had indicted every thought, every love, every conviction that had built David into himself. The truth that put Moshe to rest at last was David's undoing. To learn that his very existence was the fruit of Arab love; that his first breath had awaited him at the arch of an Arab woman's womb; that his first milk had come from her breasts; and that the first to love him had been Arabs. This knowledge cast David into a gaping chasm between truth and lies, Arab and Israeli, Muslim and Jew.

"You were wrapped in a clean white blanket, close to your mother's chest, when I first saw you," Moshe had recalled. "The Arab woman served us food that day and I caught her eyes, briefly, before she hurriedly looked away. She hated me. Hated all of us. We were suddenly masters of her land, masters of her family's fate, and we both knew it."

"What did she look like?" David had asked his father.

"She was beautiful. I didn't see that then because I despised the Arabs. But my mind could never let go of that glance when our eyes had met. Her face has tormented me all my life, son."

Moshe's confession had left David wondering if he had killed his own relatives in the wars he had fought for Israel. The truth encroached on his every day and spilled over into David's embedded mistrust, even hatred, of Arabs. The two truths of one man, each as true as the other, opposite the other, repelling the other in an infinite struggle for David's soul. The confession shook David to the core, unhinging his deepest beliefs.

The truth took another toll when he told his wife. The tug of his roots, nagging him to learn more, changed David. His wife could not bear his secret. That her husband had not been born a real Jew did not suit her upbringing nor her family's sense of propriety.

They eventually divorced, splitting down the middle with ideological cleavers: their eldest son, Uri, a zealous Zionist, wanted nothing more to do with his father, standing squarely with his mother, while Jacob asked to live with his father. He was not prone to demagoguery or conflict and found David's secret palatable, even interesting.

Jolanta gave her blessing for David to do whatever his heart commanded. Be he Jew or Gentile, Jolanta loved that boy. God only knows how much. That love had saved her once upon a time. Jolanta had done what neither Dalia nor Amal could do: she had transformed the energy of her pain into expressions of love, and David was the sole beneficiary.

Jolanta had been remorseful, prepared to help David find the family of his birth. She had always found excuses where guilt arose, but the truth always returned, daring her to face it. Now she could and wanted to set the record straight. To embrace the woman who had given birth to her David and find reconciliation in the truth. For if life had taught her anything, it was that healing and peace can begin only with acknowledgment of wrongs committed. And only then was Jolanta truly sure that David was, indeed, her son. The truth set her free and she found the urgent path of peace, where religion and history bowed before the sympathies of two mothers forever joined by their love for one boy.

"I want to meet them too. Let me help you search for your Palestinian family," she asked her son, her eyes shimmering with remorse, resignation, and freedom.

Of course, by then Dalia had already passed away. Yousef had gone off to fight with the PLO and Amal was living in Pennsylvania. David and Jolanta searched together, but there was no one left to find. But David pressed on quietly, making telephone calls that led him from Huda to the orphanage to the Colombian Sisters to Muna Jalayta and others, until he was able to locate Amal Abulheja in a Philadelphia suburb.

Amal knew of the possibility of David's existence. Yousef had been sure that Jewish soldier was Ismael, and Amal wondered if they would ever meet. Two decades later, when David at last contacted her, she felt that she had been waiting all those years for him to call.

THIRTY-NINE

The Telephone Call from David

2001

AMAL WAS PREPARING THE salad, cutting vegetables and looking up occasionally to check the clock as she waited for her daughter, Sara, to return home for dinner. Sara had only a few days left before she would be returning to school from winter break, and this would be their first night together since she got back. She had been busy volunteering for the local Amnesty International chapter and an activist group called Students for Justice in Palestine while catching up with old friends over her break. But in her heart, Amal understood the painful truth that her daughter wanted to avoid the still and quiet company of her rigid mother, even after having been away for nearly five months at college.

This evening, however, was theirs to share with only each other and Amal wondered if her daughter was feeling anxiety, dread, or, perchance, the same happiness that filled her own heart as she prepared dinner for the two of them. She had made Sara's favorite dish, makloobeh, the Palestinian dish that never failed to remind her of Yousef. She pushed those thoughts aside and marveled instead at how the call of Palestine had come to live inside her American daughter.

Then, the telephone rang. Amal put the knife on the cutting board, wiped her hands, and checked the clock. It was six P.M. She picked up the telephone receiver, sure it must be Sara calling to tell her she was on her way.

"Hi, Sara," she said, but by the silence on the other end she quickly realized it was not her daughter. "Hello?" she added.

"Hello. Is this Amal?" replied a male voice in accented English.

"Yes. Who is this?"

"I am David Avaram," said the voice.

She did not recognize the name, but by the surname, Amal suspected this stranger was Israeli. "Do I know you?" she asked.

"No . . . I mean yes. Well, no, you don't know me, but . . ."

She was about to hang up the phone, annoyed by the interruption since Sara was due home any minute now.

"Wait, please don't hang up," he said, perhaps sensing Amal's intention to end the call. "I guess I wasn't as prepared for this call as I thought."

A memory rushed up in Amal's mind from a buried past. *"He's a Yahoodi they call David."*

Could it be? Her hands began to shake and she nearly dropped the phone.

"I think you might know me as Ismael," he said, but Amal could form no words for the storm of a past rising in her mind. "I am sorry to call like this. It's just that . . . I have been looking for you for a long time. And I . . . now, I mean, I will . . . ," he stammered, trying to find the words he had practiced for days before finally calling her.

Amal could not yet form words.

"This is unfair to you. Maybe it was a mistake to call like this. I'm sorry, Amal. I will go now," he said, and Amal panicked.

"No!" she said, louder than she meant to. "Don't go."

"Thank you," he said. "I know this is a shock, but I will be in the United States in two days and I was wondering . . ."

Amal heard the loud engine of Sara's 1970 VW Beetle pull into the driveway and found herself quickly making plans to meet her long-lost brother, as if making plans to have lunch with a neighbor. They were both struck by the awkward practicality of those last moments on the phone. Flight information, date, time, her address, his cell phone number, her cell phone number.

"Thank you, Amal. Bye for now," he said.

"Bye," she answered, unsure what to call him.

She kept the phone to her ear, listened to the click ending the call, heard the front door of her house open, and watched the slender form of Sara walk in, reading something from her cell phone that was making her smile.

"Mom, sorry I'm late!" Sara called into the kitchen from the doorway where she stood sending a text message. She stopped to look toward the living room when she heard the phone fall, and she put her cell phone away upon seeing Amal.

"Mom, are you okay? Your face is really pale," she said, hurrying into the living room. When she got close enough to see the tears on her mother's face, Sara realized that she couldn't remember ever having seen her mother cry before.

"Mom. What's wrong?"

Amal looked at her daughter, smiled with so much love, and took Sara's hand, gently pulling her to sit. "There's something I have to tell you," she said.

Although Sara was stunned to learn about David and hurt that her mother had kept so much from her for so many years, she was mostly intrigued. She was grateful to know, however belated. To know of her own family. To be invited, in a way, into the mysteries of her mother. She felt, above all, a rare closeness with her mother, the iron-willed woman who suddenly appeared vulnerable, almost fragile, to her.

"I have an Israeli uncle that you've never even met. He's coming here. Wow. And I'm nearly nineteen years old and just finding out," Sara stated, not accusingly.

"I'm sorry, Sara. I thought I could keep the past behind us. I knew, or at least suspected, that he was alive. When I was young, I overheard Yousef talking about Ismael and a man named David. But I never thought to learn more or to look for him."

"Uncle Yousef also knew? Maybe he was trying to find him before he died in the car accident."

The car accident. How Amal had lied to her daughter. *God, how will she forgive me if I tell her everything I've held back?*

"Mom? You okay? Where'd you go?"

"Habibti. There's so much I have to tell you." But Sara only heard the word *habibti*. When had her mother stopped calling her that? "When Yousef saw Ismael, he was a prisoner being tortured," Amal said.

"Did Ismael torture him?" Sara asked.

"I don't know. And I think we should call him David." The thought that Ismael had tortured Yousef was harder to bear than if David had done it. "There was another incident when Yousef was badly beaten at a checkpoint not long before he left me in Jenin. I think it was David who beat him."

Sara was silent for a moment, trying to process her mother's words. *Ismael was David and David had beaten and maybe tortured Yousef. And at some point, Yousef left my mother in Jenin. Who did he leave her with? Was she alone?*

"Mom, we don't know this man. If he hurt Uncle Yousef then who knows what he could do."

Amal turned to her daughter, put her hand to Sara's head, and stroked her hair. "I have to meet him, habibti. I can't not."

FORTY

David and Me

2001

I HAD ONE HOUR TO clean the house before David arrived. After some discussion, Sara decided she didn't want to be home when he got there. "I think the two of you should have some time alone the first time you meet," she said.

"So you're satisfied now that he's not going to kidnap and torture me?" I joked.

"Not entirely. That's why I told our favorite nosy neighbor that you have a hot date tonight," she said, winking at me. "That way I can be sure someone will keep a constant eye on you through the window."

I smiled, absorbing something new and precious between us.

"I do want to meet him, though. So, I'll be home around five-ish," she said, pulling the door closed as she left.

Moments later, as I turned to tackle the cleaning, she burst back through the door. "Mom, please, can you give me a ride?" Her Beetle would not start.

When I got home, David was already there. He was early. The house was still a mess. My heart pounded and I heard myself exhale before stepping from the car into the chill of winter. David stood next to "Little Maple," the tree I had planted in our front yard some eighteen years earlier to accompany "Old Maple," the graceful giant that grew in the back.

We stared at one another before I approached him, both of us uneasy and unsure. He looked older than I had imagined. He looked like Yousef.

"Hello, Amal."

"Hello . . . David." He had not been Ismael for fifty-three years.

In the house now, I moved the vacuum cleaner out of the way, apologizing for the mess, as I always did with guests, even if I had spent hours cleaning the house.

He smiled slightly. "It's okay. I don't have much time. A car will arrive in a few hours to take me."

"I didn't realize you'd be leaving so early," I answered, detesting my casual tone of voice but not sure of how to be or act, or what to say. We chatted in that awkwardness, empty conversation to patch up what felt like holes and unraveling expectations. His flight here had been uneventful except for the man next to him who had snored. That had been "a little uncomfortable," and the directions I had given had been detailed enough. "Good." He said he had been to New York a few times for work but that this was his first trip to Philadelphia. He liked what he had seen so far. I asked what he did for a living. "An engineer. Boring stuff." Where did I work? "Drug company. Boring stuff." We both had kids. *How about that?* "One daughter, Sara." He had two boys, Uri and

Jacob. Divorced. "Sorry to hear that." He asked, "What about you?" *What about me?* "That's for another time. Do you like Philadelphia?" *Damn, I already asked him that.*

He ran his hand slowly over his hair as if to wipe away the blasé front we were both putting on. This sort of perfunctory exchange wasn't what he had expected. *Nor I.*

Looking around my house, David's eyes rested on a restored drawing of the founders of Ein Hod, who had first settled there during the Byzantine empire. Legend had it that Saladin el Ayoub himself had granted the land to one of his generals as a reward for valor in battle. That general was my great-grandfather many times over, who had married three women and fathered most of the town.

"That's our great-grandmother," I said, pointing to a sepia photograph of a young woman wearing a shy smile and an embroidered thobe with a white scarf loosely framing her stunning face. "Her name was Salma Abulheja. Her beauty was legendary in Ein Hod, so girls in the village were often named after her," I told him.

He looked on in silence at the proof of what Israelis already know, that their history is contrived from the bones and traditions of Palestinians. The Europeans who came knew neither hummus nor falafel but later proclaimed them "authentic Jewish cuisine." They claimed the villas of Qatamon as "old Jewish homes." They had no old photographs or ancient drawings of their ancestry living on the land, loving it, and planting it. They arrived from foreign nations and uncovered coins in Palestine's earth from the Canaanites, the Romans, the Ottomans, then sold them as their own "ancient Jewish artifacts." They came to Jaffa and found oranges the size of watermelons and said, "Behold! The Jews are known for their oranges." But those oranges were the culmination of centuries of Palestinian farmers perfecting the art of citrus growing.

David straightened the sag in his shoulders and cleared his throat. He knew the improvised history of modern Israel was not really his. The heritage that ran through his blood was vintage, yet somehow that, too, was not his. Fate had placed him somewhere between, where he belonged to neither.

"Can I get you something to drink?" I offered. "Do you like kahwe?"

"Ah . . . Arabic coffee. Yes, I would love some."

Grateful for something to do, I darted into the kitchen.

There, I laid my hands gently on the counter, slowly pushed my weight on them. My jaw was taut. *Ismael, the helpless baby who got lost and haunted us, is here, all grown up.* I hadn't made kahwe in a while. *Where are those demitasse silver cups?* I found everything. *What's he doing?* I stood over the frothing kahwe, mixing it until it was the right viscosity. *Dalia taught me how to make it just right.* I poured a little of the light brown foam of kahwe into the traditional silver cups, then filled them with the darker coffee beneath.

"Here you are." I served him kahwe by the fireplace, where he stood staring at the photograph I had snapped in Shatila in 1981. In the frame, Yousef is grinning. You can see his teeth. Fatima's shy smile is formed from the deepest love. And Falasteen is swathed and nestled in her father's arm.

David turned from that picture, eyes moist. A quiet spread before us, like a glass pane, beyond which you could see the air swirling with fifty-three displaced years. *Dalia gave all her children dark, round eyes that could fill endlessly with sadness.*

"I look just like him," he said, shattering the glassy silence.

The scar snaked in a sinuous path down and around David's eye. I imagined him a baby, scar healing but still red, held closely to Dalia's chest.

"That is what your brother did when he first saw me. He just stared at my scar," David said.

"His name was Yousef," I said softly, indignantly. "Did you hurt him?"

My question riled ghosts of a nation, their torment unmitigated by justice or remembrance, coming to my side in flickering black and white movie reels. Images of my father holding me and reading from Khalil Gibran's poetry in his deep voice, the soldier's boots, the wheelbarrow, and the ethereal face of little Aisha; Sister Marianne and all the orphans; the explosions and the cries, the restless woe and howls of finished people. I submitted to the memories of a dense past and it filled me with a sadness that I wished were anger instead.

His head fell, as if he understood the aches of habitual injustice and chronic derelictions of exile. "Yes," he said, his chin quivering.

I wanted to hate him, because I loved Yousef. But in David's melancholy face, I could see the shadows of Mama's eyes, Baba's nose, and David's own mistaken identity.

"Amal, do you have something stronger than kahwe? Liquor?"

"Beer."

"That'll be fine."

I watched him drink. His manner resonated with profound loneliness. A solitude abetted by "something stronger than kahwe." He had the sad dignity of a man resigned to eating alone at a table set for five. Not pitiful, not strong, just a man I hardly knew, with the incalculable capacity for error, goodness, love, hatred. *This, my brother.*

I sank into my sofa and, leaning back, noticed the sheet of dust over the coffee table. And with daring desperation, I longed to see Yousef, just once more. *What would he do here with Ismael and me?* Three siblings, emerged from the cradle of boundless tragedy. Each separated from the others but forever pursued by whispers torn from the consciousness of the others.

David was my brother and he was an Israeli who had fought for Israel's wars. The contradiction could only be reconciled in his regret. But what I wanted revealed to me could have changed everything.

I pressed my palm over my own scar, felt the callus ruts and harsh furrows, and remembered the whoosh of the bullet that had plowed my abdomen. I needed to be in the belly of my memories, to hear what David would reveal.

*　　*　　*

"Was it you who tortured him when he was in prison?" Amal asked.

"No," he answered quickly, as if surprised she would suspect such a thing.

"Then, it was you who beat him at the Bartaa checkpoint, wasn't it?"

"Yes," he whispered.

"Why?"

David lowered his eyes and tried to explain the urge of power to impose itself for the sake of imposition. The elixir of unopposed force and the daredevil thrill of impunity.

"There is no reason or logic. I was twenty years old and they gave me total power over other human beings, Amal. I was angry. Somehow I knew he was connected to the secret I knew my parents harbored. And somewhere inside, I feared I might be an Arab. Rage and the impunity I knew I had throbbed in my arms when I was holding the rifle." He looked at his empty glass. "May I have another?"

She poured, watching the beer stream into the glass, and she remembered the water she had poured that day for Yousef when he had returned bloody, carried by his friend Ameen.

"I was one of only a few people who knew why Yousef was at the checkpoint that day, when ordinarily he would have been working," Amal began.

David looked up.

"He was on a lover's errand. I know because I was the courier who shuttled Yousef's and Fatima's love letters between Jenin and Bartaa."

Yousef's and Fatima's affair had grown years old, far beyond the ordinary courtship. Their initial infatuation succumbed to the warm tedium of Yousef's insistence on becoming a man worthy of Fatima. He delayed marriage until he could afford to provide adequately for her. When his studies were completed and he had accumulated a small hoard from his work as a teacher, Yousef asked his uncle Darweesh to stand in place of his father for the time-honored traditions of marriage. The day he faced David at the Bartaa checkpoint, Yousef had set out to prepare Fatima for the convoy that was to follow to ask for her hand.

"Huda always accompanied me on the letter deliveries to Fatima's house and we split the profits. Yousef paid us quirshean, one quirsh each per delivery, and Fatima always sent us home with candy and homemade sweets," Amal went on.

Their route to Bartaa was a tree-lined footpath of untamed sabr plants, intoxicating jasmine, and wild areej wafting along the path. It was on one of these trips that Amal and Huda found Warda, the one-armed doll of the Warda house.

The girls would gambol along, pausing to pluck fruit and dates from their vines, tuck flowers in their belts, and gossip and argue as young girls do. Nearly halfway, they rested under "the twins," a pair of cedar trees with enormous trunks, the only survivors of a family of saplings imported from Lebanon some three hundred years earlier.

Under "the twins" or the olive trees behind the Warda house, Amal violated her brother's and Fatima's trust by reading their letters.

She and Huda acted out love scenes, as they imagined them to be.

Amal: Oh, Fatima, I love you.
Huda: Oh, Yousef, I love you more.
Amal: No, Fatima, I worship you.

Such sentimentality made them laugh, until the letters became heavy with indecipherable want and an intimacy they dared not fathom. Once, saturated with curiosity, Amal and Huda ventured to act out the content of a particular letter. Startled by the scene, they pulled themselves apart quicker than they had plunged their tongues into each other's mouths.

"Karaf!" Amal and Huda wallowed in mutual repulsion. "Gross!"

They stopped reading the letters after that, believing that they had been fooled, that the letter they had acted out had been written to pay them back for their nosiness. Thus, Amal and Huda turned their attention to more urgent matters, putting details of the ever-popular Warda house in order and collecting their letter-delivery fees.

After carrying a beaten and battered Yousef home from the checkpoint, Ameen had remained with Yousef until very late in the evening. Dalia had sat nearby, meandering the unseen labyrinths of a deconstructed reality and embroidering with Um Abdallah on the balcony that leaned under their weight and shaded the front entrance of their home.

Though their world had become restricted by soldiers, Amal and Huda had retained the habits of girlhood—playing hopscotch in the alleyways, indulging in the card games they invented during the claustrophobic curfews, and attempting that elusive somersault. Their inclination for snooping also had returned, and the day Yousef lay recovering from the beating at the checkpoint, Amal and Huda paused their play intermittently to spy on him and Ameen from the south window. They could see clearly the lewd magazine inside the covers of a benign hardback in Ameen's hands.

Amal and Huda feigned repulsion, each knowing full well the other's interest, and took turns at the window, pretending to check up on Yousef, who slept in the stupor of pain.

Huda returned wide-eyed from her turn at the window to report a new development. "Your brother is awake. I think they're talking about the bad magazine."

Back in spying position, they struggled to hear the exchange between Yousef and Ameen, but they could decipher only bits. There was talk of "that Yahoodi" and she heard Yousef say, to the disbelief and consternation of Ameen, "He's my brother, Ismael."

Huda heard it all and she cried when Amal warned her, sternly, not to reveal Yousef's secret, even though neither was entirely sure what the secret was. But they kept it to themselves, not for loyalty, but rather because they would not have known what to repeat. *Ismael was dead. Everybody knew that!*

David listened, longing to go back in time. He would have done things differently. He would have taken Yousef in his arms and called him "brother." *Would that have made the difference? Would Yousef have married Fatima and remained in Palestine? Would history not have happened?* So many questions. At the end of each was where David lingered. Now he turned his sorrow, as big as his life, to his sister, Amal. "Was that the first time you learned of my existence, when you overheard Yousef and Ameen?" he asked.

"Yes and no." She attempted to explain that, for her, he had lived in the mist of other people's memories. "I was born years after you disappeared. To me, you never seemed real, even after I learned of Yousef's discovery."

David inhaled, swallowing words he was too vulnerable to utter, and freed a sigh instead. Then, with a soft intensity, he asked, "And now?"

"Now, what?"

"Am I still an abstraction?"

No, she thought. *Of course not. You and I are the remains of an unfulfilled legacy, heirs to a kingdom of stolen identities and ragged confusion.* In the complicity of siblinghood, of aloneness and unrootedness, Amal loved David instinctively, despite herself and despite what he had done or who he had become. She ached to gather him in an embrace and absolve the pangs of conscience that tormented him. She wanted to fill a seat at his table and share in his loneliness. But all that left on her lips was an arid, "I don't know."

FORTY-ONE

David's Gift

2001

ON JANUARY 20, 2001, a disbelieving and fascinated David locked his attention on the letter that I had not unfolded since Huda had handed it to me thirty-three years earlier in the hospital bed where I lay recovering from the bullet. I never showed that letter to anyone until now. Even in 1983, when FBI and CIA agents swarmed into my life demanding information, I did not divulge the letter's existence. Not because it concealed relevant evidence, except of my brother's humanity—but simply because it was mine.

Now I produced it for my brother David, who seemed to eye it as a historic document, an academic thing for study, for forensic science, or for museums and private collectors. At David's impersonal gaze on my bundle of family relics, I almost returned the letter to its box. But the first fold revealed the date; it was an impossible coincidence that I would meet David and open Yousef's letter on the exact day of the year that Yousef had written it thirty-three years earlier.

In that moment of implausibility, I heard my father's voice:

> Thus the tears flowed down on my breast,
> Remembering days of love;
> The tears wetted even my sword-belt,
> So tender was my love.

A longing crystallized in the still air of my Pennsylvania home where I sat across from the brother who had grown up in a different world only a few geographical miles from Jenin. I watched my arm extend the letter toward David and saw the physical evidence of time intersecting itself in that gesture, as Huda had extended her reluctant arm thirty-three years ago, with that same piece of paper, folded along the same tragic lines.

As David read the words of Yousef, his initial intrigue changed to something personal and he began to cry. In his tears I glimpsed, but did not fully understand, the grim spirits of a mistaken identity.

"Did you ever suspect? I mean before Moshe told you?" I asked.

"I always knew something was not quite kosher." He paused, grinning at the accidental humor. His lip raised on the right side only, as Yousef's had. Old Maple swayed outside, her leaves brushing at the window to the sibilant rush of winds.

"I guess it started when I was twelve, sometime before my bar mitzvah when my cousin Ilan told me in the heat of a fight that I was 'not a real Jew,' that he'd overheard his parents remark in private that I was a goy who could never be of the People."

Shaken by the incident, David had taken the matter to his mother, who had reacted with characteristic tenderness, enfolding his worries in the vast warmth of her protection, and adding, in an acerbic footnote, "Ilan is stupid and always has been." That had been the end of it for a while, but David had learned many years later that his mother had gone to Ilan's parents that day and had unleashed her wrath at their doorstep in a string of invectives and curses, leaving David's aunt and uncle struck dumb.

David smiled, imagining the look on their faces as his mother exhaled fire at them. "She must have made quite an impression because my uncle practically paid for my entire bar mitzvah," he chuckled.

"What was her name? Your mother."

"Jolanta. It means violet in Polish"—he smiled—"and that was her favorite color."

David painted a portrait of Jolanta as a warm, engaging woman whose wardrobe could have been mistaken for a field of wildflowers. She was short and grew round with age and had "the thickest eyelashes you've ever seen." Always, she wore her dresses to mid-knee, short sleeves in the summer, long sleeves in the winter, with matching shoes and purse, and if a dress had no purple or pink hues in its flowery pattern, she pinned to it a small bundle of fresh violets, which she grew indoors.

"She loved to cook and feed anyone who walked into our home. As cliché as it sounds, cookies were always ready on the table when I came with friends from school. On holidays she used to prepare huge spreads and invite as many people as our home could seat, plus a few extra. She arranged those gatherings and cooked with much enthusiasm and love."

David spoke of Jolanta with palpable devotion. In my mind, she was everything I had wanted Mama to be—loving, attentive, and affectionate. She had been a young girl of seventeen, frightened and weak, when Allied soldiers had liberated her camp. Her entire family had been murdered during the holocaust of World War Two. The irony, which sank its bitter fangs into my mind, was that Mama, the mother who gave birth to David, also survived a slaughter that claimed nearly her entire family. Only the latter occurred because of the former, underscoring for me the inescapable truth that Palestinians paid the price for the Jewish holocaust. Jews killed my mother's family because Germans had killed Jolanta's.

"What about your mother? What was she like?" David asked.

A sunless spirit arose from within and draped itself over me like an emaciated coat of armor, ready to battle any ill scrutiny of Mama's memory. The incessant motion of Mama's hand, which had lived independently of her will, the taut clench of her jaw, her impervious solitude, efficient midwifery, and stoic character would not compare favorably to the flowery nurturing of Jolanta, complete with matching accessories and cookies after school.

David's question was a call to arms. It was Dalia and me against Jolanta and David. Dalia and me against the world. And I laid bare the fundamental truth of Mama's heart, which I had found in the endless early-morning reflections of exile, peeling back the layers, the personal fortress that she and destiny had conspired to construct.

"She loved beyond measure," I said.

That declaration rolled from my lips of its own volition, as truth gushes forth once it is acknowledged, as the air erupts from a drowning man's lungs once he is rescued.

"When I was young I thought her cold. But in time I came to understand that she was too tender for the world she'd been born into," I said. Sorrow gave Dalia an iron gift. Behind that hard shelter, she loved boundlessly in the distance and privacy of her solitude, safe from the tragic rains of her fate.

David listened attentively, grateful for a sketch of the woman who had given him birth.

"She lost something fundamental the day in 1967 when she thought I had been killed in the explosion that tore away the kitchen where I was cowering in a hole with my friend Huda and baby cousin Aisha," I continued. "I suppose that was the last straw. Over the years I've often wondered with enormous guilt if I could have saved her." If I had not gone off with Sister Marianne to Bethlehem, leaving her in that tent hospital alone with the demons that had surely begun to feast on her. *Had I remained, embraced her, would that have made the difference?*

From the tin box where I kept Yousef's letter, I removed Mama's silk scarf and the embroidered breast portion of her favorite thobe, the inanimate remains of her brief years on earth. I had wrapped them in plastic covering, which had preserved her scent over the decades. David held Mama's clothes to his face and inhaled.

"She didn't bathe much." I smiled, suddenly and for the first time overcome by what seemed like the exquisite charm of Mama's less than desirable personal habits. In that lighthearted interstice, I understood that Dalia, Um Yousef, the untiring mother who gave far more than she ever received, was the tranquil, quietly toiling well from which I have drawn strength all my life. I had to travel to the other end of the earth, improvise like a dog, and bathe in my own grief and inadequacy to understand how her persevering spirit had bestowed on me determined will.

"What happened to her?" David asked.

"She sank into dementia not long after the war in sixty-seven."

But I could not explain to David that her condition had been nothing short of a merciful kiss from God.

Dalia matured in her youth, searching the darkness of her nights for the son she had lost, reproaching herself for not knowing where to find him. She did not love for the pleasure of fulfillment or gratitude. She loved against her will. She took little sleep from the night, lying awake on her foam mat until Baba returned and she, hiding behind feigned sleep, could be sure he ate the food she had left for him. She poured fantastic energy into her daily industry of cleaning, cooking, embroidering, washing, folding, birthing, planting—and she prayed five times each day, religiously. When Ammo Darweesh needed a wheelchair, she secretly sold the second of her twin ankle bracelets and laid the money on my uncle's doorstep. She let me share in that secret. She watched over us all, carefully and unobtrusively from the shadows, hardening or recoiling into her mystery if anyone approached her with tender thanks. Alas, her heart was not of ice at all, but of a roiling lava contained by her own will, held back with her iron jaw and tireless fluttering hand, and the contents of that heart were seldom betrayed. Perhaps what made reality fade from her mind was not the unending string of tragedies that befell Palestinians, but rather, an immeasurable love that could not find repose.

"I used to wish Mama was different. More like Jolanta, perhaps," I said, remembering Dalia, remembering how I had once thought her a selfish, hard, efficient mother who reared me from a cool remove.

"I loved Jolanta. She was the only mother I ever knew. But she allowed me to live a profound lie that came to much personal harm, for the sake of uncontested motherhood," David admitted, as if to protect Dalia from an unfavorable comparison. He paused and took a drink. "Jolanta loved me, too. I have no doubts. But love cannot reconcile with deception."

He gathered hurt from his distant stare and focused it in a grip around his glass, placing it on the table as if to mark the spot wherein lay the betrayal.

Love cannot reconcile with deception. And it cannot become inured to an existence paid for with the currency of another's misery—my mother's misery.

"When you were talking about Jolanta, her demonstrative adoration, I felt envious of you," I confessed. "But I think now, contrary to what I believed in the stupidity of youth, no other woman than Dalia could have been a finer mother to me."

FORTY-TWO

My Brother, David

"AT LEAST YOU KNEW who you were and where you came from," David said, motioning for another beer.

"I have to run to the store for more," I said. "Want to come?"

"Of course."

The car ride was difficult, a new environment to conquer together before we could reach the same level of comfort we had attained in my home. But it was a short ride, so we filled it with niceties. "Beautiful town," David said.

"That's the Delaware River."

"Snow doesn't accumulate like this in Israel." *Israel.*

"It does in Lebanon." *Lebanon.*

Back at home, another beer and my long-lost brother was enough at ease to recall the difficult trip he had made with Jolanta to her hometown in Poland.

"Other than the day she died, seeing the death camp where she lost everything was the saddest time of my life," he said.

"I'm going to have another cup of coffee. Like another beer?" I offered.

"Please." He looked at me, and I looked back without judgment.

He told me about Moshe's confession. How it had unraveled him.

Here he was now, decades later, holding it together with *something stronger than kahwe.*

"I tried to pretend my father had taken his secret to the grave," David said, swallowing more from the glass. "But his words flooded every moment of silence, every hour of insomnia."

"And Jolanta?"

"I felt she had betrayed me," he said. An unsettled score in the lap of the deep affection he held for her. With Moshe, it was different. "My father and I weren't as close," he said, "and also, because he did tell me, I could let it go. He told me everything. Even things he didn't have to tell. The day he confessed, I felt closer to my father than I had in all my life."

Moshe had used his last breaths to reveal the past and to beg his son's forgiveness. He had spoken of his dreams, the aspirations of the Jewish people for a homeland. He had unveiled the secrets of the Irgun, the atrocities they had committed to run Palestinians out of their homes. "Mercy was a luxury we could not afford," Moshe had said. He had described the faces that haunted him. "Too many, my son." The Arab woman whose ankle bracelets had chimed when she served him lamb. How he had learned to love her Arab child and had turned to drink to hush her cries of "Ibni, ibni," that remained as clear to him as on the day he had seized her son from her arms. "I heard her and kept walking," he had whispered to David. Moshe had spared no memory, sweet or horrid, before he passed away finally into the night.

*   *   *

At last, the full story of that fateful time during the Nakbe, when my family lost their baby boy and the land was swept away, unfolded there in my Pennsylvania living room, some fifty-three years later. But I was the only survivor to live that moment with

Ismael, our missing link, and I felt depleted by the wounds of others.

I leaned back into the sofa, closing my eyes as I close a book after the last page has been read. But David had one more thing to say.

"I know the things my father did make him a terrorist, to you and others," David said. "He did some evil things, but he was not evil. He was good to me. He was my father, Amal."

I did not reply. I held David's words, felt their weight in my palms, and felt my eyes well with tears.

"Do you understand, Amal, what I am saying?"

I understand. "There are things I will tell you. In time," I said.

"If it's about Yousef, I already know," he said.

Just then a horn blared in my driveway. It was the taxicab arriving to take David to the airport.

"Don't go," I pleaded instinctively.

"I don't want to go," he answered immediately.

We caught each other in a desperate stare, each looking into the other's eyes for evidence of a mutual imperative to refasten a destiny torn. And something formed between us in that reflexive moment. Something soft.

David changed his flight to the next morning.

"Here's to new beginnings," he said.

Before I could raise my glass to meet his, Sara walked through the door. I could see from the anticipation on her face that she had been waiting to return home since the moment she had left, and I felt immensely happy to see her at that moment.

"Habibti, I want you to meet my brother, David."

VII.

BALADI
(my country)

FORTY-THREE

Dr. Ari Perlstein

T HE PAST SEEMED LIKE a dream now. I do not know when its ghosts stopped haunting me or when my baby girl became a woman. Or when I grew into Dalia's legacy as a distant mother.

Some months earlier I had discovered that I had aged irreversibly. My naked reflection stared back at me in the mirror, the graceless specter of a body reshaped by the pitiless hands of age. The years had thickened my waist and loosened my skin. My breasts hung like wilted flowers and my hair had turned into winter.

Only the scar on my abdomen had not aged. The webbed skin was as young and tight as it had always been, embalmed by cruelty, that indelible ink of memory and preservative of time. I ran my hand over my patch of pickled youth as I had done countless times in my life. But I did it now with a stale, vestigial nostalgia, with Sara's words hovering at my thoughts like dragonflies over water: "Mom, I'm going to Palestine. I want you to come too." And there were the other voices too. *Breathe, child.* I'd breathe them away but they'd return.

"It isn't just because of these filthy politics and injustice, Mom," Sara said, the rims of her eyes darkening into red and tears pooling over them. "I want to know who I am."

There it was, her life's sorrow at having so little family. So little sense of belonging. So little of a mother. A great big "so little" throbbed under her decision to go to Palestine, behind her eyes. But she was her mother's daughter, and I watched her yank it all back inside, cover it with resolve, and concentrate it all in the burning challenge of her gaze. *Whatever you feel, keep it inside.*

"I'll think about it," I said, turning away from the urge to take her in my arms.

I did think about it. In fact, I thought of little else, until I stood before myself in that mirror and made the decision to return to Jenin, after three decades of exile.

After four hours of questioning and unmentionable searching at the Lod airport, Sara and I were cleared to proceed.

"Sara!" shouted a male voice.

My daughter rushed past me, landing in the arms of a handsome young man. I realized who the boy was when I saw David standing behind him. She and her cousin Jacob had been corresponding since David had come into our lives.

Jacob was twenty-three years old, the younger of David's two sons and most like his father. "Shalom, Aunt Amal," he said, revealing a welcoming youthful smile, for which I was not prepared. *Aunt Amal. Shalom.*

"Hello, Jacob," I responded, turning from the awkwardness toward David, who took me in his enormous embrace. Standing there, my smallness in his bigness, in what felt, what *smelled* even, like Yousef's arms, I was twelve years old again, motionless in Yousef's embrace after he returned naked from the dead in 1967, the green ruffle of his borrowed clothing irritating my skin—much as the Nike logo on David's shirt now rubbed against my cheek.

"It is good to see you, sister," he said.

"You too, David. You too."

I wanted to see Jerusalem before going to David's home in Netanya. To stop by the orphanage and to find Ari Perlstein's office.

"But Jerusalem is in the opposite direction," David insisted, and I let that be that. He had the same *so little* sorrow in his face. That ache of not belonging and the shakiness of an inverted identity.

Ari Perlstein will have to wait, I thought, even though Ari had no inkling of my pending visit. Before leaving Philadelphia, I had tracked him down over the Internet but had shied away from calling him. After all, what would I have said? *I'm Hasan's daughter, remember him?* Or, *Hi, guess who? I'll give you a hint: Go back fifty, sixty, seventy years or more. Another hint: Ein Hod, ring a bell? Ha ha. No, really.*

*   *   *

"Dr. Perlstein?"

"Yes." A small head lifted itself from the sea of books pushing at the seams of the professor's small office.

"I wonder if I might have a moment of your time. I've traveled a long way to meet you."

"Forgive me, at my age, my mind fails sometimes. Do I know you?" he asked, his benevolent demeanor just as I had imagined.

"No. But I believe you knew my father, Hasan. Hasan Abulheja."

The wholeness of the room—its walls of books, pounds of dust, and absent-minded old professor—gasped and held its breath for a long moment, until Ari's eyes, spread large behind the bifocals on his nose, leapt beneath the bush of his brow. He maneuvered his small body fitfully around the messy wooden desk, coming toward me, his limp now accompanied by a shuffle.

"Ya ellahi!" he whispered in Arabic until he was upon me, his trembling, age-spotted hands impatiently brushing away tears from his magnified eyes. "Is Hasan here?" he asked, his voice breathless, exhausted by the sudden desperation of the stolen past, by the great urge to know, to see his old friend.

"No. We believe he was killed in 1967."

We believe he was killed in 1967. I had never uttered those words before, nor had I known that I believed he had been killed in 1967.

After an interminable silence, he offered, "You look like Dalia," and he smiled a gentle, grandfatherly smile. "Sit. Sit."

"There are others outside who would also like to meet you, sir. My daughter, Sara, my brother, David Avaram, and his—"

"David Avaram . . . Abulheja?" he interrupted, clearly confused by the Jewish name.

"No, just David Avaram. It is a long story . . . If you have time."

"As of now, my schedule is clear," he declared triumphantly. He grinned, shifting the ill-fitted dentures in his mouth as he dialed his assistant.

Ari had never married, devoting himself to study, and a graceful loneliness emerged as he spun the yarn of his life with the wisdom of a man who had read far more books than the hundreds crowding us into the center of his office.

Ari was a splendid storyteller, reminding me so much of Haj Salem, whom I was sure must have passed away by now. We all sat spellbound by the tales of his youthful adventures with Baba, from the first day they met at the Damascus Gate to the day my father helped them escape to the western portion of Jerusalem, shortly after it had been taken by Israel. He spoke of Dalia's click-clacking ankle bracelets, of Jiddo Yehya's perfectly symmetrical upward-curled mustache that climbed nearly to his eyes when he smiled, of Teta Basima's cooking and gardening, of Ein Hod's trees and orchards, of war's unforgiving savagery, of fury and a friendship that had saved his life. And where his memory trailed off, I picked up with mine.

In Ari's office, we were three generations hauled together by the willful drag of a foreclosed story swindled by fate but gathered in that moment to demand to be told. The story of one family in an obscure village, visited one day by a history that was not its own, and forever trapped by longing between roots and soil. It was a tale of war, its chilling, burning, and chilling-again fire. Of furious love and a suicide bomber. Of a girl who escaped her destiny to become a word, drained of its meaning. Of grown children sifting through the madness to find their relevance. Of a truth that pushed its way through lies, emerging from a crack, a scar, in a man's face.

Emotion overwhelmed us all in that tiny office, where daylight falling through a solitary, small window high on the wall was the single hint of an outside world. The softening light was the only evidence that time had not stood still as I imagined young Ari and young Hasan sharing a tomato behind the market cart, that gesture laying the foundation of an eternal friendship. I had told David many stories of Baba, and this was one more lovely part of Baba to know.

"Your father was so happy when Yousef was born. I think I had never seen him happier or more proud," Ari said, clearly conjuring an image of my father that only he could summon.

I was suddenly a child again, wondering if Baba had been as happy at my birth—maybe happier? Not happy at all, perhaps, for another mouth to feed in a refugee camp?

Ari brought me back from time. "Where is he now, your brother Yousef?" he asked.

Just then, the adan began to pour itself into the air. Into my skin.

"Allaaaaaaho akbar, Allaho akbar . . ." The adan sang from several minarets at once. That melody, which I had not heard for far too long, flowed unhindered to the moth-eaten corners of me, running through me like a river, like baptismal water.

"Ashhado an la ellaha Allaaaah, Ashhado an Mohammadun rasool Allah . . ." I sat there, eyes closed, opening the gates to a wounding nostalgia and longing for my lost family, for my lost self, and I let the song of a people swell the pause that climbed onto the end of Ari's question. *Where is your brother? Yousef?*

"Hayo ala salaaaaat. Hayo alal falah . . ." And the church bells of the Holy Sepulcher rang, lilting to the cadence of my sweetest and bitterest memories. I stood on my legs as the rhythm of Islam resurrected Fatima's dimpled smile in her sky-blue dishdashe dress, taunting a thousand uncried tears.

"I don't know," I answered Ari, surprised by the softness of my voice. So there would be no misunderstandings, nor more questions, I continued, "They say he was the man who drove the truck bomb into the U.S. embassy in 1983."

Sara gasped. She had never known.

Jacob's face fell, in the way that rocks fall off the side of mountains. He had never imagined.

David silently held himself under the weight of my words, not wanting them to fall so close to his son, whose eyes turned into a pleading exclamation: *But they're supposed to be good. GOOD Arabs. Our peaceful Palestinian relatives. Not TERRORISTS!*

Sara's face opened like a wound. Disbelieving, intrigued, hungry for the full story of her life, hurt by the mother who had held so much back from her.

I was too tired and drained to meet her reaction.

The sky-blue dishdashe dress, ripped in the middle, levitated from the corners of my mind where I had long ago turned out the lights and spread above me like a cloud. I turned and saw Majid in my daughter's features and closed my eyes at once, too weak to feel anything more. Afraid that I might find my brother's fury lurking in my depths. Afraid his fury might also be mine. Afraid, always afraid.

But this time my defenses were no match for the oppressed memories and loves, rising up behind my ice with torches, blazing and demanding. Demanding that I cry for them, at last pay them with the tears they deserve. Release their dues in fury and sadness. Give them their long-overdue acknowledgment with remembrance and pain.

"Laaa ellaaaha ella Allah," concluded the adan, and I saw the quiet comprehension facing me behind Ari's eyes.

Ari, the boy whose childhood and even whose right leg had been damaged beyond repair by Nazi bigotry. The limping boy with only one friend, taken to an Arab village to breathe fresh air, unpolluted by the awful memories of his parents, forever damaged by concentration camps no matter how much they tried to pick up the pieces of their lives. Ari, the hunted boy, suffocating and cramping in a taboon while Arabs sought Jews, any Jews, to exact vengeance after 1948. Ari, the young man who watched his parents fade like ghosts into the mortal anguish of their memories, leaving him with relics of their lives, an eighteen-pearled brooch and shelves of books.

"Here is her brooch." He showed it to me. *One, two, three, four, five, six . . . eighteen delicate old pearls.*

Ari, the man who could not marry because, like me, he feared love more than he feared death. Because, for the hated and pursued, the reverse side of love is unbearable loss.

Ari—the "self-hating Jew," as he was called by his countrymen; "my friend" as Baba had called him—understood. And he pulled a blanket of compassion over my words. *He drove the truck bomb into the U.S. embassy in 1983.* To shield my words, to shield me and Yousef's memory from the chill of the fact of those words. I saw it in his face. Our eyes met and interlaced, until two heavy tears fell like anchors, their weight yanking me to my seat as they disappeared on the red Jerusalem stone floor.

Ari, the young Jewish man in my parents' wedding photo, walked me through his last memories of my father, taking me on an ox-drawn cart that my father had borrowed to hide the Perlsteins on their wobbly journey to the other side of Jerusalem's divide, when East Jerusalem was yet unconquered. The hand-drawn Star of David flag, which my father had made from a bedsheet for the Perlsteins to wave on the Israeli side when they crossed over, so they would not be mistaken for Arabs and shot, was hidden beneath Baba's clothes as he navigated the dangerous path. They traveled through night's darkness, where resolute men patrolled with anger's purpose, guarding the year's remains against the Jews, who in turn patrolled in the uniforms of a sudden nation on the other side, complete with a resolve and anger of their own.

"My parents were too frightened to move, to open their eyes," Ari began, "but I kept watch through a crack in the side of the cart. When a Jordanian soldier called out, waving at your father, I thought for a fleeting moment that Hasan had set a trap to betray us at the last moment. Fear turned to suspicion inside that cart, not unlike the one where so much of our boyhood was stored in the wooden planks and uneven wheels. A plan came to me, a betrayal before being betrayed. I started to reach for the dagger, the one Hasan had concealed beneath a blanket atop the cart—'just in case we need it,' he had said."

Ari paused. Inhaled the stinging memory before exhaling it in words, as David's trembling hands reached into his satchel for the drink he kept close at all times.

"But before I could get out of the cart, we were moving again. And I sank into such shame for having thought what I did."

Ari faced me squarely, in a facing-up way, his eyes stretched large behind his thick glasses, and continued. "For the rest of the journey I trembled in my mistake, my private betrayal of the friend risking his life to save mine. My betrayal before being betrayed.

"I don't remember the next hours, or if they were minutes. But soon Hasan stopped and showed us a crawling path to the other side, handing me the flag that he had painstakingly painted himself with the Jewish star, the same blue star that fluttered over the demise of his country.

"He put his arms around me. 'May we meet again, brother,'

were the last words I heard him say. 'Forgive me,' I replied, and crawled on my way with my parents."

Ari paused, as if to say *That's it*. In the hollow of that cavernous pause, I was a child in Baba's arms asking about Ari Perlstein and watching the sad silence of Baba's hands close the book, closing that particular dawn with it. *No. That's not it*.

"After having lost his home, his land, his son, his identity to the Jewish state, your father risked his life to save mine and my family's."

That was it.

From the corner of my eye, I could see Jacob's face repositioned in relief, as he measured the acceptability of his Arab relatives by their deeds toward Jews. I found the boy irritating, though Sara seemed to take a sincere liking to him.

We were tired when we left Ari. I was tired of the story. Tired of the past.

On the ride to Natanya, I asked David to take a slight detour. "It's a wee bit out of our way," I said in an Irish accent, imitating Jack O'Malley, who had said those exact words to me when he had taken me to the orphanage so long ago. No one understood the significance of the accent and I did not bother explaining. *Later, I will tell Sara all about O'Malley, the orphanage, the Colombian Sisters, and Haydar, the headmistress. Huda and I will tell her about the Warda house behind the third olive tree past the twin cedars on the path to Bartaa and we will sleep a night on the rooftop with our children as we did in our girlhood.* I felt giddy and sure. The land seemed to welcome my return.

Despite the turmoil, it felt right to be there. I could feel meaning coming back into that word that had been drained of hope and left as dumbfounded letters. I was Amal there, not Amy. "I like hearing people call you Amal, Mom," Sara said to me when we were in Jenin the following day.

And in Khilwa, the detour "a wee bit out of our way," where a biblical stone wall parted like a curtain on the Mount of Olives, I stood on fabled ground overlooking Jerusalem, just as I did with Jack O'Malley the day I said good-bye to Jenin. Now I was going back to Jenin. Time was looping backward.

Now that ancient village with walls made of secrets and trees planted in blood looked inanimate. Around Jerusalem and in the West Bank, settlements on every hilltop—with their manicured green lawns and red roofs metastasizing into the valleys like an earth rash—contrasted cruelly with the crumbling Arab homes below, where sewage from these settlements drained and where settlers often dumped their garbage.

Tall, much too tall, buildings towered over the city. Apartment buildings for Jews only, fortified settlements, angular hotels, and imported shrubbery watched like prison guards over the native arched windows and doors of masonic buildings, the arches from which the word "architecture" derives.

But regardless of the frantic "Judaising of Jerusalem," the Old City seemed cold. Cruel, even. And, eventually, undeserving.

How could this have happened?

"Wow!" Sara said. "It's beautiful."

No it isn't, I wanted to say. *It's only stone.*

Why do dignity and honor hinge on stone and soil? Generation upon generation disembowel the earth, building monuments from her entrails to mark their time, to mold the dream of some relevance in an immense universe, to manufacture a significance from utter randomness, to attain immortality by seizing, stamping, gouging an immortal earth.

"It is only stone, Sara." My thoughts escaped.

"Stones that represent history, Mom," she said, turning to me in disbelief that I would belittle what seemed so grand. "It's magnificent."

"I'll show you an olive tree in Jenin—Old Lady, she's called—that has more history than the Old City walls. It's more beautiful, humble, and authentic than the chiseled stone here," I said, believing my words only as they emerged. "And," I continued, wounded by love for this perfect creature born of my body, "it is you who is magnificent."

FORTY-FOUR

Hold Me, Jenin

2002

JENIN HAD BEEN IN the news lately: "DEN OF TERROR." "NESTING GROUND OF TERRORISTS." "TERRORISM BREEDING GROUND."

It was a taller Jenin than the one I had left nearly thirty years earlier.

Shack built over shack. Stone instead of adobe. "Vertical growth" is the technical term. One square kilometer of United Nations subsidies where forty-five thousand residents, four generations of refugees, lived, vertically packed.

The air was busy when I arrived. Everything seemed to move and scurry. Even children played nervously. There were no old men sitting on upturned buckets in lazy games of backgammon, a constant scene from my youth here. Young men, washed clean of dreams, ran in the alleyways with rifles strapped to their bodies. They were preparing for the inevitable, stocking up on food, setting up defenses, booby traps, and sandbags against the coming storm. Anger and defiance had their arms linked, marching in a military left, left-right-left step with no place to go but the boundaries of that one-square-mile patch of a taller refugee camp. Suicide bombers locking their belts, lovers locking their arms, little girls locking their knees, and mothers packing their children into the innermost, lowermost rooms.

It was March 31, 2002.

On March 20, a suicide bomber had killed seven Israelis in the Galilee, which was in retaliation for Israel's killing of thirty-one Palestinians on March 12, which was in retaliation for the killing of eleven Israelis on March 11, which was in retaliation for Israel's killing of forty Palestinians on March 8, and on and on.

While we were revisiting the past in Ari's office, Israeli tanks were hammering at Yasser Arafat's Ramallah headquarters in the present. And while Yasser Arafat was holed up in a room inside the rubble of his former headquarters, where the view outside his window was of the barrel of an Israeli tank, Mr. President George W. Bush announced that Arafat ought to "stop the terror."

Later at David's house, Sara asked her uncle to silence the television broadcasting "that enormous ego with such a little brain to go with," as she put it. "You would think the logistics of 'stopping terror,' i.e., an intact building and a police force, might occur to the president of the United States. But nooo. Not our Dubya. He says 'terror' so much I'm beginning to think it's a medical condition. Some kind of incurable verbal tic. Terrorterrorterrorterrorterror!" she said in overwrought frustration.

My daughter.

The next day, we were entering the much-taller-than-before Jenin. The much more crowded Jenin. The busy, resolute, angry Jenin. Not the passive, waiting, putting-it-in-the-hands-of-Allah Jenin of my youth. My daughter and I held hands as we walked up the snaking alleyways, the sun trembling on sewage rivulets. Music, playing inside homes, spilled onto our path and I heard Fayruz, her voice climbing like freedom toward and into the sky.

> For your sake, oh city of prayer, I pray.
> Ya bahiyat el masakin. Oh rose of all cities.
> Our eyes travel to you each day . . . to ease the pain of your
> churches and to wipe the sadness from your mosques . . .

I stopped, spread my arms to my sides to touch both walls of the alley, and ran my palms along the stone of those taller, closer-together homes. "This is how Huda and I always walked through these corridors," I said to my daughter.

"You have no idea how moving it is for me to be here, where you grew up. I can't wait to meet Huda and hear stories of you two." Sara was visibly excited.

Another song now. This one reached into the heart, first with the wail of its nye, then with its words.

Unadeekum. I'm calling your help, tugging at your hands and
     I kiss the ground beneath your shoes . . .
I give you the light in my eyes . . .
And I take my share of what pains you.
I have held nothing back for my country . . .
And I scoffed in the face of my oppressors, an orphan, I,
     bare and without shoes.
Unadeekum. I'm calling your help, holding my blood in
          my palm . . .

Ahead, some children giggled at two grown women running their palms on the walls as they walked. A rush of squawking chickens batted their useless wings in an attempt to flee from the small children chasing them. Some things had not changed.

The old had died, the young had aged, homes had grown taller and alleyways more narrow, babies had been born, children had gone to school and chased chickens, and the olives had twisted with fruit. Still, the refugee camp of Jenin remained as it had been, a one-square-mile patch of earth, excised from time and imprisoned in that endless year of 1948.

A voice from my past crept behind me. "You're in Jenin." It made my heart explode with the memory of love. With the memory of life. "Must you always state the obvious?" I said, turning to the tiger eyes of Huda. We flung ourselves around each other, laughing through tears.

"You got fat," she said.

"So did you," I said.

"Must you state the obvious?" she said, imitating me.

She pulled Sara into our hug and the three of us, jolly, made our way to her home.

"It's only me and my youngest, Mansour, in the house now," she said, panting as we trudged up the sloping alley toward the small shack not far from the dwelling where we had spent our youth. "The Jews took Osama last month. Jamil, one of my twins, comes often to check on us, but most of the time we don't know where he is." She stopped, stored up a breath, and went on. "He's with the resistance," she said, opening the metal door of her home. "The Jews killed his twin, Jamal, when he was twelve years old. Jamil never got over his brother dying in his arms like that. Sit down, I'll make us some tea."

Huda's beautiful eyes shone from a face engraved by decades of weather and by the loss of her child. In her eyes, our shared yesterdays tarried with the taller, denser Jenin of the present. The continuity of our friendship was stored in those eyes, and I searched them to find the sense of home, which I had expected to feel in Jenin but did not. Had I changed that much? How unnatural it felt to pick up strands of a past I had abandoned long ago.

"Mansoooooour!" Huda called to her youngest. Within minutes, a tall, languid young man bent his back to enter the house. He acknowledged our presence with a passing look, not rude and not polite. His arms dangled, as if they were weighed down by his hands, which were splattered and brushed with paint of all colors.

"Habibi, this is Amto Amal. She's finally back. And this is her daughter, Sara," she said. He shook our hands, looking through us, and he left as he had entered, in matter-of-fact silence, bending his body to clear the doorway.

"That was my baby, Mansour. He's an artist!" Huda said, emerging from her tiny kitchen with a tray holding three glasses of hot tea and some biscuits. "But don't be offended. Mansour doesn't talk. He stopped speaking when he was six."

Later that day, Sara and I watched Mansour paint a mural portrait of a recent shaheed, the one who had blown up the Jerusalem café. He moved his arms in large fluid brushstrokes along a wall that would greet the looming Israeli invasion. Soon an implacable face emerged from the paint, its larger-than-life eyes peering beneath a tightly swathed kaffiyeh into the futureless 1948, into the freedom of a defiant death exploding in a shit-pile of glory.

Though he spoke to no one and gave few more than a passing glance, Mansour was much loved in the camp. It seemed everyone knew his name. Passersby stopped to admire his work, pat him on the back, and mumble private thanks and prayers for the boy and his talent.

"He's very talented, isn't he?" Sara said.

But it was more than artistic ability. It was his silence. A quiet so dense and thick that it seemed to exist on the verge of materializing. He painted from the depths of its hush, and it hovered around him like an invisible force.

"It makes me angry knowing what they did to him. How they got away with it," Sara said. Over tea, Huda had given us the abbreviated version of his kidnapping at the age of six, when he had been taken blindfolded in the back of an Israeli army jeep and returned a week later for a ransom of five hundred dollars. "Of all my children, he was always the most sensitive. The one who needed me the most," Huda had said.

Ammo Darweesh had become a beloved patriarch in the camp. I could see that by the number of people at his home, most of whom recognized me when I stepped through his door. "Are you who I think you are?" one of my cousins exclaimed, coming to embrace me.

"Praise be to Him who brings our loved ones home from el ghurba," another said. "Praise to Him." And they all rose excitedly to greet me but waited respectfully for my uncle to see me first.

I made my way to Ammo Darweesh, leaning on his wheelchair to meet his outstretched arms. "Ya habibti, ya Amal." My ammo began to cry. "You bring the winds of Hasan and Dalia into this house, darling. You bring me joy, beautiful daughter." I kissed his hand three times, touching it to my forehead between each kiss.

My heart swelled with love and memories, more and more so as Sara and I spent the evening there. Ammo Darweesh had grown old and frail, but he was spirited during those hours with us. My cousin whispered to me, "I haven't seen my father this happy in a long time, Amal."

Not until our third night in Jenin, on April 2, did I learn that Haj Salem was still alive.

"We take turns taking food to him every day, just like our mothers used to. The children here do not know him the way we did. I am not sure when he stopped the storytelling. It was gradual, I think. Mostly he just chips away at wood sticks now with a small pocket knife, which we intentionally keep dull," Huda said.

I would visit him first thing the next day.

We were in for the night. Lights all over town were out or locked inside by blackened windows. Israel had launched a bombing campaign against nearby Bethlehem, the little town of, and moved hundreds of troops to towns around Jenin.

Nestled in candlelight and sandbags, Huda and I reminisced, unpacking the burdens and delights of memory for our children and finding gems we had almost forgotten. We made Huda's home that night into a shack of small happiness in a one-square-mile mute sea of anxiety.

Slouched against a stack of sandbags, Mansour sketched on a pad across from us, smiling occasionally. Sara's vocabulary narrowed to three basic words, "Tell me more," while Huda and I tossed back our shared life, tasting it now through our grown children. The Warda house, home of our one-armed doll, climbing trees, hopscotch, Yousef's dirty magazines, Baba's solitude, the dawn, Mama, Haj Salem, spit-string contests, war. The latent instinct of sisterhood moved us to clasp hands, as we had done since we had awareness, and we walked hand in hand to the end of our memories. Sara lay her head in the nook of my shoulder, wrapping her arms around me, as she had not done since she was too young to remember. And while the air outside was foreboding and pulsed with coming death, I burned with the love I had denied myself and this perfect child resting in my arms. It occurred to me then that I had found home. She had always been there.

"Let's put the night in the hands of Allah and try to get some rest. May Allah protect us and protect my boy Jamil wherever he is right now," Huda said, and we closed our eyes where we sat, reclining on the floor cushions and on each other. Hours passed, but it seemed like we had only just closed our eyes when a volley of voices shouted throughout the darkened camp, "The Jews are coming! The Jews are coming!"

The Jews are coming.

In a moment, an exquisite creature hurriedly entered, bending his shirtless body to clear the doorway. A lantern in his hand illuminated the outlines of hard muscles beneath his brown skin. He whispered to Huda, "Yumma, are you awake? Mansour, brother, where are you?" He flicked the light switch. "It's okay. The Jews will not be here for another hour."

An hour.

Swollen with tears, my dearest friend wrapped her body around her son. She kissed him with frantic love, making sure that no space on his handsome face was left unkissed, no inch unloved by his mother. Huda knew that Jamil might never return after that hour. The spectacle of that good-bye moved me to grip my daughter, both of us pulling ourselves and our tears away from a moment where we had no right to be.

"Mansour, brother. If anything happens, it's up to you to take care of Mother," Jamil said, understanding the silent response of Mansour.

When Jamil went to leave, something extraordinary happened. It lasted for less than an eternal thirty seconds and I believe that only I witnessed it. As he turned—a black-and-white checkered headband tied behind him, communist red armbands marking two violently perfect limbs—his untamed round black eyes fell accidentally onto Sara, and a stare held them both in place. An unexpected urgency, a plea. A sudden love wanting to be. Some fantastic desire, which neither of them could afford. A familiar oasis between two strangers, calling to them both.

"Jews! Jews!" we heard, and the moment was banished by that call to find refuge in that refugee camp. Mansour turned out the lights, lit another lantern, and hugged his brother. Jamil kissed Huda on her forehead. "Allah yihmeek ya ibni," she cried, praying for his protection.

"Khalto Amal," Jamil said flatly, "after whom my sister was named," stating the obvious. He did not allow his eyes another glimpse of that oasis standing next to me.

Instead, I watched his presence pass over my daughter's skin, like a caress. Like an apology, a regret before the end. A rite of the dead.

Jamil reached to the only wall hanging, brought the frame

close to his face, kissed its glass, and returned the photograph of Jamal, his twin, forever twelve years old.

Then, Jamil was gone.

At two A.M. came the roar of rolling tanks, like the purr of a beastly cat. We held each other. The metal teapot, cooled by the night, sat where it was left. Mansour pulled close into the arms of his silence. He kept drawing. Huda faced her mat toward Mecca and prayed quietly.

In time, other sounds came. The raspy shelling of tanks. The shrill of helicopter missiles. The thunder of airplane bombs. The clap of explosions. The cacophony of military power was parceled amid a devious quiet, where the *ti-ti-ti-ti* of critters leaving their holes and cries of small children could be heard as soldiers went from home to home. The sounds of death and destruction rose and fell, lasting nine days, which we spent in the innermost, lowermost room. A bigger kitchen hole.

"Remember?" Huda turned to me.

"I remember."

We knew homes and buildings were being leveled nearby. The scream of bulldozers, like an orgy of dragons, made the earth quake beneath us, and we devised an exit plan for if and when they came toward us. Huda wrapped a small package of family photos along with her family UN identification cards, tucking the small bundle into the chest pocket of her thobe. Sara and I kept our American passports in our respective brassieres. All of us kept our shoes on.

Through it all, I held my daughter close in a private dream, falling in love with her as if I had just given birth to her once more. We talked for nine days, dismantling the unuttered words of a lifetime. As death rained from the sky and bullets sprayed the outer walls of Huda's home, Sara and I peeled back the pain and bitterness we each had held so dear and found our shared longing for Majid despite, or perhaps because of, the terror we felt.

"I wanted so much to know. To talk about him with you, you know. Why wouldn't you even talk about him?" Tears quivered in the rims of her eyes. Majid's eyes. Infinite black spheres; a lazy arch in the corners and one brow that could lift itself away, like a smile. The feminine version of Majid in our daughter's face. In the dust of memory I could find nothing whole, only pieces of him. A particular wrinkle. A scar. Cowlick at the base of his neck. The sky and the Mediterranean blending into a single hue. But I could conjure his scent, indeed. The dew of his sweat after labor and after love. After so many years, Majid was the scent of blue.

"I'm sorry, Sara." I opened my hands and unhinged my jaw. "I was afraid . . . so afraid of what I might feel." I put my heart in my open hands. "Do you remember what it was like when the Twin Towers fell on September eleventh?"

Her brow lifted. "Yes. I remember you stayed in your room all day the next day and didn't go into work. I thought you took it pretty hard and I'll admit I didn't understand. What does that have to do with my father?"

And there was Yousef's voice, oppressed and sad and angry and impotent coming through telephone wires of twenty years ago. "Your father was killed the same way. Israel bombed our apartment building the night before he was going to leave Beirut to join us." There, it came through my heart and my lips. There was no fury or rage or despair. Just a sweet pain. A sadness I could drape over my heart, in my open hands, to keep it warm.

"Oh, God!" She held me dear, tightly so.

"I grieved three thousand times. Then I grieved for myself, a lonely woman without the honor given to the wives of the fallen. The reverence for their loss, for their children's loss. It was eloquent and grand. So moving and charged with solidarity. And there was me, in the mirror with the disparate worth of my husband's life. The disdain for my loss. FBI always there, somewhere. The past always loomed. But on September eleventh, I faced the last moments of your father's life. I saw him in every person who tried to jump and every body they pulled from the rubble. And I saw myself as I was never allowed to be, consoled, understood, and loved."

Sara was crying. Guilt, because my behavior then had irritated her. "Oh, Mom. I'm so sorry. I had no idea. I was so insensitive. I didn't understand."

I looked at my daughter and knew, as I know the sun will set and rise again, that I loved her with a longing and depth more profound than time, more profound than God.

"Shhhh, habibti. You don't need to explain anything. I wasn't a very good mother. I should have told you. We should have talked like this years ago. I'm the one who's sorry."

Activity outside made us all jump, Huda from her sleep. I was eleven again in the kitchen hole. Huddling again, praying, Mansour drawing. We held on, checked our papers, passports. Shoes tied, ready to run. Stretched our legs; a cramp could be fatal. But we didn't stand up; bullets could come through the windows. Huddle, huddle in the innermost lowerermost rooms. Fear flying from hearts like little birdies in the air. *Chirp, chirp.*

Sara was frightened beyond anything I'd ever seen in her face. Even the color of her face retreated and hid. I rubbed back the hair from her forehead, kissed it. I kissed her face. Kissed away the fear. Until it was calm again.

Bullets and tanks and helicopters went back to their bullet and tank and helicopter world. Quiet, and so were we. An occasional scream or a cry. Soldiers inspecting their work, perhaps. Quiet, but for the chirping of invisible birdies.

Now it had been quiet long enough. We exhaled, blowing the birdies into a corner, and began to whisper. Then talk.

"Was it love at first sight? When did you fall in love with my father?" Sara asked, but I could not define a moment. I had a sense that I had always loved Majid. How can one find the first moment of love? When, in what instant, does the night's dark sky become blue?

"I don't know, habibti," I answered honestly, but her expression demanded something else. A story.

"Well, on that ride from the airport. After we got to the camp, your father got out of his Fiat with candy falling from his grip for the dozens of children gathering around him. It was such an endearing sight . . ." And the memory of my husband, of blue and love and loss, settled gently in my throat. Tears fell from my eyes. Mercifully, they fell.

"Tell me more, Mom."

The quiet didn't last. We heard more explosions now followed by intermittent fire.

The terror raging around the walls of Huda's small shack pushed us together into the wonderful bonds of mother and daughter and friendship.

"You know," Huda began, "Fatima wrote to me about you and Majid. She seemed so happy." Then Huda let her eyes fall to the floor. "But I didn't get the letter until many months later, until . . . after . . ."

"Do you still have the letter?"

"Of course. It's right here, with all my important papers," Huda said, pulling the bundle from the chest pocket of her thobe. She removed a folded piece of orange paper and I remembered the pad of orange stationery that Fatima had kept in her kitchen pantry, a detail tucked in my memories of Lebanon.

I unfolded it and began to read how Falasteen was getting so big. That Yousef worked and worried too much and how happy they were to have me with them in Lebanon. The letter spoke of Majid and me, and Fatima praised her own matchmaking skills, taking full credit in her letter for our marriage. She had just received the news of her second pregnancy and she had written, "You're not going to believe this, but Amal is pregnant also. She's due in September, too!" She wrote how much she missed Huda and missed her family in Palestine. "Someday," she said, closing her letter.

Inshalla. Ya Rabby, we will be together someday. All of us. Yousef, me and the kids, Amal and Majid with their kids, you and Osama with your kids. I dream of this day.
   Love,
   Fatima

On the seventh day, Mansour was taken away. Soldiers blew open the lock on the metal door, hemorrhaging through. While two soldiers ransacked the house, another demanded Mansour strip to his underwear. We looked away in a futile attempt to save him some dignity. They blindfolded and handcuffed him. And Mansour's silence draped itself over him like an overcoat as they took him, leaving his drawings littering his home.

"Allah be with you, son," Huda said. Not crying. She had run out of tears, I think. "Mansour will come back. They will beat him up. They always do. He always comes back," she said, mostly to herself.

Always is a good word to believe in.

We collected Mansour's art in a small pile of papers. It was the world as he saw it. Huda praying, Sara resting in my arms, Jamil victorious in battle, Sara's profile, all of us bent over a small meal with the angel of death standing guard over us.

Precious little water remained and we were nearly out of bread. *What had happened?* We dared not remove the sandbags over the window to look out and were too afraid to move near the mangled metal door, which offered a lookout hole.

But it was calm now. It had been calm for a while. *Soon, they will ride with loudspeakers allowing us to leave our homes.* But they did not and we ran out of water and finished the bread. We

303

thought surely someone would come soon to clear the dead, whose unseen bodies forced us to breathe through cloth soaked in rosewater.

The odor became unbearable. The markings we made on the wall indicated that two days had passed since the bombing had stopped, but we could see nothing through the hole in the metal door. An infinite cloud of dust and debris of demolished homes hovered in the air.

We licked the last drops of rosewater, breaking the bottle to get at the last bit, and we slept. "The world cannot possibly let this go on," I said to Huda.

"The world?" Huda asked sarcastically, rhetorically, and uncharacteristically, deeply bitter. "Since when does 'the world' give a goddamn about us? You have been away too long, Amal. Go to sleep. You sound too much like an Amreekiyya." With that, she and her wisdom pulled up the cloth over her nose and closed her eyes. The next dawn, the sun rose over the haze of a decimated refugee camp. I heard the sound of a large vehicle. *A Red Crescent ambulance.* I left a note that I would return with supplies from the aid truck, and I stepped out, covering my face from the assault of light and dust. I walked on into an eerie stillness, like the quiet of a graveyard where the imperceptible sounds of vanished souls and banished little histories crawled up my feet from the earth like ants.

I thought it was over. I thought the Israelis were gone. It had been quiet. I thought the car I heard was a rescue vehicle, an aid truck.

I was wrong.

It was an Israeli military truck. I saw it stopped ahead in a prairie of rubble where hundreds of homes had stood only days before. The bed of the truck was weighed down with lifeless bodies stacked on top of one another, like lumber. The truck had stopped to remove the mangled body of a Palestinian hanging dead on a protruding metal stake on the side of a partially demolished building. Its head was hugged around by a black-and-white checkered headband, and around its arms by two communist red armbands. Symbols made hollow by death in that truck of lumber.

The weight of my mistake fell on me. Cautiously, moving only my eyes, I looked upward and saw the snipers. *The Jews are still here. Click. Click.*

I turned in horror toward the shrill of metal switching on itself and felt the muzzle of a rifle at my forehead before I saw the young face of the soldier standing before me.

The moment made a space for us, pushing the dust away, and fixed us together.

Here we are now. I see his contact lenses swimming in his eyes and sweat bubbling on his forehead.

I feel an inexplicable serenity. Death, in its certainty, is exacting its due respect and repose before it takes my hand.

But he does not shoot.

He blinks hard. And a solitary drop of sweat travels from his brow. Down the side of his face. I watch it fall and note his smooth skin, still too young to need a regular shave.

The power he holds over life is a staggering burden for so young a man. He knows it and wants it lifted. He is too handsome not to have a girlfriend nervously waiting for his return. He would rather be with her than with his conscience. With his burden or with me.

I know he has killed before. He knows I know. But he has never seen his victim's face. My eyes, soft with a mother's love and a dead woman's calm, weigh him down with his own power and I think he will cry. Not now. Later. When he is face-to-face with his dreams and his future.

I feel sad for him. Sad for the boy bound to the killer. I am sad for the youth betrayed by their leaders for symbols and flags and war and power. For an instant, I think he could be my nephew. But no. Uri has no doubts of his duty to kill for Israel. This soldier is not my nephew.

Strange, strange, he is handsome and I, loving.

Is this how Yousef saw David? With inexplicable love?

Oh, David! *Brother.* I see you so clearly now. You have lived a stranger in your own skin. You searched for years to find me, never giving up when each lead to your family sent you to a grave or a morbid headline. Nowhere but in the temporary release of alcohol could your heart find repose. You searched for the one last hope that I, your sister, might traverse the abyss of your loneliness with the peculiar will of those who can find no place to belong. And when you found me, I did not come near enough. You confessed your shame and your sins, but I only perched myself on my own pain and sat in silence. Oh, brother! I feel a newness, the coming of rebirth. It will begin with your forgiveness. I will come to you when this is over. This will end soon. *The world cannot possibly let this go on.* The devastation here is beyond comprehension. Israel cannot possibly cover this up. It will not happen. The world will know at last. Things will change. I will come to you soon and beg your forgiveness. You're my flesh and blood. You are the son of Hasan and Dalia. The grandchild of Yehya and Basima. Father of two. I want to speak to this soldier whose gun still points at me. But what is there to say? And would words shatter the immensity of life and death so close to one another?

I close my eyes, the wholeness of my life flickering, flashing, and taking form. I have made so many mistakes. I have not loved enough. I have not loved enough.

A voice screams, "Laaa aaaahh," and I know it is Huda as I feel my eyes bulge in horror at the sight of my wandering daughter, exposed to snipers.

I forget about the soldier and rifle at my head.

I can fly. I swear it. I fly to her.

I throw myself on top of her, happy to be fat because my weight has pushed her down.

I am unbelievably happy. Euphoric because the snipers did not see her and we are safe on the ground. Low beneath the clouds of dust.

Somewhere in the distance, the muezzin begins to call the faithful to prayer. The adan comes from the sky like a bouquet of sad lilies. "Allaho akbar" reverberates over and into the putrid smell of this destruction. In its echo I can hear the shackled song of the Orient. I look into my daughter's frightened eyes beneath me and am overcome with warmth. I am delirious with love for my daughter. My precious little girl.

Sara.

My life's loveliest song.

My home.

I am too exhausted to move. I whisper to her, "I love you."

I dream of growing old to the pitter-patter refrain of Majid's and my grandchildren she might bear someday.

VIII.

NIHAYA O BIDAYA
(an end and a beginning)

FORTY-FIVE

For the Love of Daughters
2002

A MAL WAS SHOT.

Even as she spilled from her own body and her eyes were emptied of her, Amal died without knowing death. She died with the joy of having saved her daughter's life. With contented thoughts and with love. She died in a whisper, as if death itself was humbled by the unfolding of a wounded heart and did not want to spoil that tenderness by announcing its presence. As if death had sung for her a lullaby.

That day is whereupon Sara's twenty years converge and rummage through its minutes in search of answers, of purpose, or of the will to fortify the memory of it. Or to fortify the mind from the memory of it.

The lazy haze of that day.

The abyss of their thirst.

The apocalyptic dust floating in the air like algae.

Sara did not know why her mother had gone out that day. *Had there really been a Red Crescent ambulance?*

Sara's eyes had just opened from inside a dream when she stepped through the door to reach her mother. She was dreaming of her violin recital, just before her tenth birthday, when she looked into the audience and saw her mother's face soft in a mist of pride. *Do you remember, Mom?*

But in her dream she played for an audience of only two, Amal and Majid, from whom came a resounding applause, swelling the theater of her dream. Majid's face was hers. Sara had tried throughout her life to reconstruct her father's features from her own reflection. "You look so much like him," Amal once told her daughter. *Do you remember when you told me that, Mommy? I do. I was five.*

In her dream she bowed to them both. Suddenly, her grandparents Dalia and Hasan, her uncle Yousef, Fatima, cousin Falasteen, Great-Grandfather Yehya and Great-Grandmother Basima, Ein Hod and her great-uncle Darweesh's horses, and all the faces and stories that had saturated Sara's time with her mother in those days in Jenin. Her ancestors joined in the applause for her, the fruit of their seed. The auditorium rumbled with their laudation, dropping the lush landscape of Ein Hod into the background. The applause stepped up into thunder— *Was that the Red Crescent ambulance?*—cracking the center of her dream, wherein she saw her mother's profile standing outside, in the reality seeping closer. So, she kept walking off the stage, toward Amal and Majid, whose face was no longer hers but that of an Israeli beneath a soldier's helmet. She walked to her mother between the languid daintiness of her violin recital and the shocking devastation of Jenin. She was coming to Amal in the unsteadiness of a waking dream.

Then came the scream, and she was awake beneath her mother's weight.

You are the prettiest of mothers.

Sara can never forget those last minutes of her mother's life. At least ten minutes, maybe an hour, an eternity not long enough. It repeats in her mind and she records it in the letters she writes to her departed mother on a Web site for the world to see:

> *Your face is looking down at me. The words "I love you" are formed inside your half-parted lips, cracked from thirst. But no sound leaves you. I want to tell you then that I know you used to come into my room at night, when you thought I was sleeping, to put your arms around me. I know you loved me. I*

want to tell you this. Your breath was always full of love and it was full of sorrow. I want to tell you this, but I am terrified, because now I have the ultimate proof that you love me more than you love life. I wonder what you are thinking. I need your forgiveness. I need you, and I beg God not to take you. Not now. Not like this.

The sniper's bullet, intended for Sara, burrowed in Amal's flesh and drained her entrails of life in a pool of warm brown. It coated Sara's dream, and every dream she had thereafter. Until the siege ended a week later, Sara was covered in her mother's blood. The soldier who had held his gun to Amal pulled Sara from her mother's lifeless arms. She fought him to stay. She asked him to shoot her. In her shock, she saw him surprised that she spoke English. As the soldier dragged Sara back to Huda's home, he said to no one in shaking, broken English that he "cannot shoot anymore."

The soldier gave Sara and Huda his thermos of water and two days later brought another and instructed them where to find "the woman's" body when the camp "opens." He had hidden Amal's corpse beneath an uprooted olive sapling. He gave them food and enough to drink while the siege continued, but not enough to wash a mother's blood from her daughter's skin.

When the siege was lifted, reporters swarmed into the camp. Food and water followed and survivors set about their searches for each other, for their dead, their possessions, their will. Schoolbooks, unpaired shoes, utensils, the things of living scattered amid destroyed homes. Haj Salem did not survive. Fleeing neighbors had tried to get him out, but the advancing bulldozer would not stop and its tonnage decimated the old man's house while he was still inside. When she heard this, Sara wept and wrote to her departed mother:

313

Do you know, Mother, that Haj Salem was buried alive in his home? Does he tell you stories in heaven now? I wish I had had a chance to meet him. To see his toothless grin and touch his leathery skin. To beg him, as you did in your youth, for a story from our Palestine. He was over one hundred years old, Mother. To have lived so long, only to be crushed to death by a bulldozer. Is this what it means to be Palestinian?

April, the month of flowers, forever holds Sara in her mother's arms. It is the month when mother and daughter fell in love again and stayed up all night talking while a fury swirled outside the walls protecting them. It is the month when Amal at last found home in her daughter's eyes. Her Web site, www.aprilblossoms.com, is where Sara records her memories of that month, the month from which all things come and to which all return. The month from which Sara loves and hates.

Sara will go back to Pennsylvania. This is certain, for she has already written too much and her name is on an Israeli list of "security threats." There is no place to hide in this land, where even shadows are uprooted. But Sara's heart will never leave Jenin.

Huda roamed the camp in a daze. That place where she was born, where she had been abused and terrorized, loved and cherished, had once again been destroyed. The remains of people's lives protruded from the waves of ruin. Huda wandered, looking for something to find. A woman's bathrobe still hanging on a bathroom wall, still standing amid the rubble. It was the bathrobe of her friend and neighbor. That was a find. But she left it there. A human hand, only fingers visible, jutted from the ground. Someone buried alive. She gingerly walked around the hand, murmuring the Fatiha for that person's soul. A little girl's shoe. Schoolbooks everywhere, torn and imprinted with tank treads. A doll. She picked it up. It had but one arm. Huda sat slowly on the ground, the one-armed doll in her hands. She looked at it. Looked hard. She felt the circular motion of time breeze through her heart and saw herself a girl again. It made her smile, ever so sadly. She ran her hand over the doll's head, smoothing its matted hair in a stroke that replenished her tears. She cried with a small whimper, something like the sound of a heart that keeps breaking. And with grace, Huda closed her eyes in prayer: *Oh, Allah, help us all get through this life.*

Only at the burial did Huda scream. She wailed over the body of her childhood friend. It was the only body she could bury. Jamil was never found. She knew, as mothers know, that her son would be killed. But what mother's heart can truly prepare for that? She just screamed. A primitive call into the ether. The love and death of children creasing and contorting her face. Huda dug her fingers into the earth over the graves, kneading the dirt as if she were fondling fate itself, grabbing fistfuls of her pain and heaving it into the air and onto her face. She sat there sprinkled with dirt, crying.

David was there too. He stood quietly next to Huda over the seven long rows of graves. They knew one another well, for it was Huda who had given David the names and rumors when he came looking for his family. But now they did not talk. No one spoke.

The few remaining men in Jenin dug the graves. Children looked on in curiosity as the shrouded bodies were lowered into the ground. Women heaved dirt from the graveside and slapped it on their own faces. They mourned with a primal trilling that the world did not witness.

David cried silently. He stood over his sister's body, inside the torment of sobriety, smelling of the want of liquor. Though he made no sound, the force of his grief was strong, hovering over the graves like rain that cannot fall. His tears welled inside a loneliness that could not be drowned, rocked, or touched.

Ari did not stand. He crouched over Amal's grave, sorrow on his back, and spoke to her softly. "Take this," he whispered to her body, "I owe your father my life. Tell him I never had a better friend." And Sara watched Ari drop the eighteen-pearled brooch over her mother's shrouded form.

Mrs. Perlstein's brooch was buried with you, Mother.

When the hours had accumulated on them exhaustion and thirst, the wailing gave way to the plaintive silence of tired grief. Ari limped into the crowd of mourners and prayed the Muslim prayer for the dead. They recited the Fatiha, dousing their faces in amen, cupped in their hands.

"Your grandfather is the one who taught me to pray," Ari told Sara later.

"I wish I'd known him," she said.

"I will tell you everything I remember. I knew your grandfather since he was a boy and was by his side when he married your grandmother Dalia. I can even tell you about your great-grandparents, Haj Yehya and Haje Basima. If you like, I can take you to Ein Hod and give you a tour of your origins. I have not been back there since I was a boy. It will be poetic to return there now with Hasan's granddaughter. Indeed it will. You will do me a great favor to come. It will please your grandfather Hasan, wherever he is. I am indebted to him."

Stories from Jenin trickled out into neighboring towns. The sight of a boy dangling from a metal post, headband and armbands marking him as a fighter. The story of an old man, a centenarian haj, who was crushed to death inside his bulldozed home. The one about the Palestinian-Amreekiyya who was killed protecting her daughter. This woman had survived an Israeli bullet in her youth and died by the one intended for her child. Her story reached far and wide. Her tale sent Muna

Jalayta calling the Colombian Sisters, crying, "Amal was killed in Jenin." That tale traveled abroad and put an ache in the heart of Elizabeth, who cried on her husband's shoulders for the woman and her daughter whom they had helped and loved. It made Angela Haddad and Bo Bo mourn the passing of an old friend. But that story, too, quietly passed.

When Israel finally opened the camp, the UN never came. The American congressmen who tour suicide-bombing sites and express eternal allegiance to Israel never came. Jenin buried fifty-three bodies in a communal grave, Amal among them, but hundreds remained missing.

The official report of the United Nations, prepared by men who never visited Jenin and spoke to neither victim nor victimizer, concluded that no massacre had taken place. The conclusion was echoed in U.S. headlines: "NO MASSACRE IN JENIN." "ONLY MILITANTS KILLED IN JENIN, SAYS ISRAEL."

They murdered you and buried you in their headlines, Mother.

How do I forgive, Mother? How does Jenin forget? How does one carry this burden? How does one live in a world that turns away from such injustice for so long? Is this what it means to be Palestinian, Mother?

Just around Sara's heart, a silent scream has formed like a fog. It bears no words or definition. At times she thinks it is a political or humanitarian urgency to set the record straight. Other times it feels like anger. But in the shade of solitude, it is a wordless whisper from the depths of her, an unmistakable longing for just one more moment with Amal to answer her mother's last words and say "I love you, too."

FORTY-SIX

Pieces of God
2002–2003

A RI MADE GOOD ON his offer a few weeks later, taking
Sara to Ein Hod. The two of them asked David to go along
and all three walked through the village. Modern sculptures
dotted the terrain. A few artists, mostly French Jews, worked
outdoors on landscape paintings and residents walked about
in shorts and summer dresses. "This is your family's home," Ari
said, pointing to a splendid stone house with beautiful gardens
and fruiting trees.

"Can we go inside?" Sara asked.

"Let us ask." Ari knocked on the door.

A pretty Jewish woman in her early thirties appeared.
Realizing that the strangers at her door were there on an errand
of Palestinian nostalgia, she refused them entry.

"I know what this is about. You must understand this is our
home now." She emphasized the word *our*. "Besides, my baby
is sleeping." With that she closed the door and the would-be
guests left.

Sara took photographs of the stables, where Ganoosh
and Fatooma once lived. She had promised her great-ammo
Darweesh to visit that stone building of his fondest memories.
Three of his sons, Amal's cousins, had been part of the resistance
and lost their lives in the fighting. The others were imprisoned,
and Darweesh had wished for death to come to him during
that time. But he survived in his wheelchair—in an innermost,
lowermost space.

David and Ari found Basima's grave where the cemetery had
been, just above the village. Most of the headstones had been

removed. But a group of white-streaked red roses peeked over the tall grass.

"This is approximately the spot where we buried her," Ari said. "Dalia planted these roses."

Sara caught up with Ari and David. In their last days together, Amal had told her daughter about the grave and the roses. The story still fresh in her mind, she knew right away what the men were looking at.

"Should we say the Fatiha for my great-teta Basima?"

"Of course," Ari said.

"Will you teach it to me? The Fatiha?" David finally asked.

"Of course."

Before the day was over, Sara drove a bit farther to Haifa's shore. She had promised her amto Huda to take pictures of the sea. In all her life, Huda had not been able to fulfill her girlhood wish of going to the ocean "just to sit, since I can't swim."

In Jenin, Sara at last found the extended family she longed for. Huda became a maternal friend. Her great-ammo Darweesh had produced quite a large contingency of cousins—first, second, and third. But most of all, she loved Mansour.

A year after her mother died, Sara was still in Jenin, still helping in the slow rebuilding effort with occasional funds from wealthy gulf states. She took a job with a French nongovernmental organization and lived with Huda. Her uncle David came around often and so did Jacob. All very different people, they found one another in the memory of loss and the hope of rest, becoming something of a family.

Following his sister's death, David stopped drinking. This is what he wrote on Sara's www.aprilblossoms.com Web site:

I do not drink anymore, sister. Somehow you gave me this gift. I'll never be wholly Jew nor Muslim. Never wholly Palestinian nor

Israeli. Your acceptance made me content to be merely human.
You understood that though I was capable of great cruelty, so am
I of great love.

Sara was eventually deported back to the United States, where she took a job with al-Jazeera news agency. Her cousin Jacob went with her to study at Amal's alma mater, Temple University. It seems he was predisposed to mathematics, like his uncle Yousef.

During Sara's stay in Jenin, she was able to sponsor a visa for Mansour, whom she grew to love as the brother she had never had. Osama was released from Israeli detention and both he and Huda encouraged their son to go. Thus, shortly after Sara returned to her home in Pennsylvania, she sent him a ticket to join her and Jacob, to live in the old Victorian house that her mother had restored and where Sara had grown up.

David wrote of this on www.aprilblossoms.com:

Huda and Osama tell me that Mansour is studying art and working part-time with Sara. "He's doing well," Huda said. "I get letters all the time. Look." She showed me a pile of them. "Look what he wrote here," she said, reading a passage that described his awe at a world without military occupation. He had never imagined how thrilling to the spirit it is to live by one's own terms and move freely about.

I visit Huda and Osama often. She makes such sumptuous food and they are very good about keeping me in line when I crave the drink. "Have a hooka instead," Osama insists, and we smoke together muaasal. The honey apple tobacco is by far the tastiest.

Yesterday I was there, and Osama remarked how our children live like siblings together in your Pennsylvania home. One

American, one Israeli, and one Palestinian. "How nice that is,"
Huda said, her tiger eyes the prettiest I have ever seen.
   "Yes, indeed," I said, inhaling the smoke of honey apple tobacco.
   Love, David

. . . Love, Ismael

FORTY-SEVEN
Yousef, the Cost of Palestine
2002

I PLAN IT. I LIVE it. I see it. I'll make it happen. I'll kill. I will. But I can't. I know I can't. Love came to me in a dream and placed her lips upon my brow.

"Love is what we are about, my darling," she says. "Not even in death has our love faded, for I live in your veins."

My darling wife. Beautiful Fatima.

And I struggle to fall back into my dream to find her once more.

I know I cannot desecrate Fatima's love with vengeance. Much as I want them to bleed, I'll not besmirch my father's name with the lies they will tell. I can't leave Amal alone in the world. I haven't kept my promises. I tried. To protect my wife and children. To set my sister's life toward family and love. I tried, Baba.

Now I've gone so far. Can I turn back? The wheels have been put in motion.

"I'm not going to go through with it," I say.

"He'll not go through with it. The coward. But it will go through him," they say.

It will go through me.

I'll live this pain but I'll not cause it. I'll eat my fury and let it burn my entrails, but death shall not be my legacy.

321

"I understand, brother," another tells me.

Someone else drives the bomb into the American building. It goes through me.

And I see on television what I saw in my darkness. It lives in me with the necrotic years that will not end. And my face is broadcast and printed around the globe.

"The world knows your face, Yousef," they say, and a bullet is handed to me. "Do the honorable thing if you're found."

My gun and solitary bullet are in my pocket. I carry my death, the honorable thing, in my clothes as I, their terrorist, search for work in the dank realms of life. In Basra I am a laborer. In Kuwait, I haul stone. In Jordan I am nearly a beggar. Then, I am a school janitor. *How fate is stubborn and holds to habit.* I lay my head in a room beneath the library. *How fate is merciful.* And everywhere, I am alone with my father's books, my bullet, Love and the memory of her, the past, and memories of a future.

I write so many letters to Amal. Stacks of them line my dirty walls. But what new hell will come to her if we are in contact and I am discovered. And oh, Ismael. I've carried your scar on my shoulders for so long that it has sunk into my own skin. Here it is.

I read April's news and weep tears. I weep darkness and love. Here it is, at the library where I live: www.aprilblossoms.com.

Dearest Amal, with a long vowel of hope.

> *Sometimes the air is redolent with the sighs of memory. A waft of olive wind or the jasmine of Love's hair. Sometimes it bears the silence of dead dreams. Sometimes time is immobile like a corpse and I lie with it in my bed.*

> *And there I sleep, waiting for the honorable thing to come of its own accord.*

> *For I'll keep my humanity, though I did not keep my promises.*

> *. . . and Love shall not be wrested from my veins.*

AUTHOR'S NOTE

Although the characters in this book are fictitious, Palestine is not, nor are the historical events and figures in this story. To accurately render the settings and history, I relied on many written sources, which are cited as references and, in some instances, quoted in the text. I am grateful to these historians who have set and continue to set the record straight, often at high personal and professional costs.

Writing this story and getting it published has been a long journey that started in 2002. It was first published under the title *The Scar of David* by a small press that went out of business shortly thereafter. But in the meantime, it was translated into French and published by Éditions Buchet/Chastel under the title *Les matins de Jénine*. And it was through Marc Parent, my wonderful editor at Buchet/Chastel, that Anna Soler-Pont, of Pontas Literary and Film Agency, became my agent two years after the original publication. From there, Anna began breathing new life into this novel. As a result of her efforts, the story was translated into twenty languages and Bloomsbury offered to release it again in English. I am immensely grateful to Anna and to Bloomsbury for this second chance. In particular, I wish to thank Alexandra Pringle, who believed in this story enough to take it on under such unusual circumstances. And I wish to thank Anton Mueller, my editor, for the literary insight and expertise (and patience with me) that made this novel so much better. I wish to also thank Janet McDonald for her excellent copyediting.

The seed for this book came from Ghassan Kanafani's short story about a Palestinian boy who was raised by the Jewish family that found him in the home they took over in 1948. In 2001, Dr. Hanan Ashrawi sent an e-mail to me after reading an essay that I had written about my childhood memories in Jerusalem. The e-mail read: "A very moving article—personal, Palestinian, and human. It sounds like you can write a first-rate biography. We need such a narrative. Have you thought about it?" So, to Dr. Ashrawi, I owe the initial confidence to write. A year later, I traveled to Jenin when I heard reports that a massacre was taking place in that refugee camp, which had been sealed off to the world, including reporters and aid workers, as a closed military zone. The horrors I witnessed there gave me the urgency to tell this story. The steadfastness, courage, and humanity of the people of Jenin were my inspiration.

An award from the Leeway Foundation gave me a cushion to absorb the financial difficulties that I encountered while writing. I'm thankful to this wonderful organization and to all similar institutions that value and seek to support artistic expression. The love and encouragement of friends assuaged my many episodes of self-doubt, particularly when debt and publishing rejection letters began to mount. I will always be indebted to Mark Miller for his friendship and support that never wavered, not even in my grumpiest hours. I am also grateful for the love and editorial help of many, especially Mame Lambeth, who read this manuscript three times at different stages of its development, and David Mowrey, for being the best friend I've ever had, and for all the Saturdays when he graciously accepted my arrival at obscenely early hours of the morning for breakfast.

A warm thank-you to the following individuals, whose generous spirits, advice, and encouragement had an impact on the creation or direction of this novel (whether they know it or not): Dr. Evalyn Segal, Gloria Delvecchio, Karen Kovalcik,

Peter Ciampa, Yasmin Adib, Beverly Palucis, Martha Hughes, Nader Pakdaman, Anne Parrish, William Kowalski, Dr. Craig Miller, and Anan Zahr.

Although I met him only once in person, and briefly so, the late Dr. Edward Said influenced the making of this book in no small way. He lamented once that the Palestinian narrative was lacking in literature, and I incorporated his disappointment into my resolve. He championed the cause of Palestine with great intellect, moral fortitude, and a contagious passion that touched so many of us in many ways. To me, he was larger than life, and though we all knew he was sick, I also thought him larger than death. Alas, I was wrong. The sad loss of him, felt by many thousands of us, is echoed in the pages of this story.

My most profound gratitude is to Natalie. Being her mother has been my greatest joy, and the miracle of unconditional love that she gives and accepts is my heart's sustenance.

Abla: teacher

Abu: father; father of

Adan: Muslim call to prayer

Aeeda: cooked sugar used as a depilatory

Ahlan: welcome

Ahsan: better

Ammo: paternal uncle

Al hamdulillah ala salama: Thanks to Him for your safe return

Allaho Akbar: God is bigger. Western press explains this phrase as meaning "God is great," which is an erroneous translation that strips it of spirit and context. "Allaho akbar" is used in nearly every conceivable context among Arabs, and always as a humbling reminder that God is bigger than any event or circumstance and therefore faith in Him is the answer.

Ammoora: adorable

Amto: paternal aunt

Ana ismi: My name is

Areej: fragrance

Aroosa: bride

Ashhado an la ellaha ella Allah, Ashhado an Mohammadun rasool Allah: The shehadeh—the Muslim declaration of faith proclaiming the oneness of Allah and that Mohammad is his prophet

Aywa: yes

Baba: dad

Babboor: an open flame used for heating and cooking

Babel Amoud: Damascus Gate

Binti: my daughter

Bismillah: in the name of Allah

Bismillah arrahman arraheem: in the name of Allah, most Merciful, most Compassionate

Dabke: folkloric dance unique to Palestine, Syria, Lebanon, and Jordan

Dal'Ouna: famous folk song and dance

Dinar: a Middle Eastern currency

Dishdashe: traditional long robe, worn by both men and women

Egal: a rope-style tie, usually black, used to hold a hatta in place on the head

El baeyeh fi hayatik: a phrase of condolence that means "May your life be extended"

Ellahi: my Lord

Fadeeha: scandal

Fatayer: a type of baked bread with either cheese or zaatar and olive oil

Fatiha: the opening surah of the Quran

Fedayeen: resistance fighters

Fellaha: peasant woman

Fellaheen: peasants

Fils: coin currency

Fuul: a bean paste, typically eaten with bread

Habibi: my beloved (masculine)

Habibti: my beloved (feminine)

Haj: pilgrimage to Mecca; title of someone who made the pilgrimage to Mecca (masculine)

Haje: title of someone who made the pilgrimage to Mecca (feminine)

Halaw: sweets

Hatikva: Israel's national anthem

Hatta: male headdress

Hayo ala salat: flock to prayer (part of the adan)

Hayo alal falah: flock to your well-being (part of the adan)

Hijab: female head covering

Hisbiya Allah wa niamal wakeel: a phrase equivalent to putting a situation in the capable hands of Allah

Hummus: a traditional Arab snack made of chickpeas and tahini

Ibn: son

Ibni: my son

Inshalla: God willing

Intifada: a rising up or uprising; a shaking off of oppression

IsmAllah: God's name; used as praise and to ward away evil

Jibneh: cheese

Jiddo: grandfather

Jomaa: Friday

Kaak: a type of bread baked in long rolls with sesame

Kaffiyeh: Palestinian headdress, usually checkered black and white or red and white

Kahwe: coffee

Karaf: gross

Khalo: maternal uncle

Khalto: maternal aunt

Khan el Zeit: a street name in the Old City of Jerusalem

Khobz: bread

Kitab: book

Knafe: a cheese and pastry delicacy in syrup

Koosa: zucchini, usually stuffed

La ellaha ella Allah: There is but one God

La hawla wala quwatta ella billah: There is neither might nor power but with Allah. It is a saying to express one's powerlessness to reverse tragedy.

Maalesh: It's okay

Makloobeh: Palestinian dish with lamb, rice, and eggplant in a cinnamon and cumin spice mixture

Manakeesh: bread baked with olive oil and zaatar

Muaasal: molasses tobacco

Mulukhiya: a stew of mulukhiya plant in chicken broth and garlic

Nye: ancient Middle Eastern flute

Oud: Middle Eastern instrument similar to the lute

Quirsh: a coin currency

Quirshean: two quirsh

Quran: Muslim holy book

Rahma: mercy

Rukaa: a unit of prayer

Sabr: patience; also the name of a tenacious cactus plant

Sahyouni: Zionist man

Salam alaykom: Peace be upon you—a common greeting

Salamat yakhti: Greetings, sister

Salat: prayer

Salata: salad

Sanasil: stone barriers that spiral up hills in Palestine to halt erosion

Shaheed: martyr

Shawerma: a sandwich of shredded rotisserie meat rolled into bread with salad and sauce toppings

Shehadeh: Muslim declaration of faith

Sheikh: a man of distinction in tribal traditions, usually by religious accomplishments

Sitti: my grandmother

Surah: chapter from the Quran
Tabla: small hand-held Middle Eastern drum
Taboon: large oven used for baking bread
Teta: grandma
Thobe: caftan
Thohr: noon
Um: mother of
UNRWA: United Nations Relief and Works Agency
Wahhid Allah: Proclaim the oneness of Allah
Wleidi: my son
Wudu: ablution before prayer
Ya: oh
Yaba: dad
Yahood: Jews
Yahoodi: Jewish man
Yihmeek: protect you
Yumma: mom
Zaatar: crushed thyme, turmeric, and sesame
Zaghareet: ululations

REFERENCES

Benvenisti, Meron. *Sacred Landscape: The Buried History of the Holy Land Since 1948*. Berkeley: University of California Press, 2002.

Chomsky, Noam. *Fateful Triangle: The United States, Israel, and the Palestinians*. Updated edition. Cambridge, MA: South End Press, 1999.

Finkelstein, Norman G. *Image and Reality of the Israel-Palestine Conflict*. New and revised edition. London: Verso, 2003.

———. *The Rise and Fall of Palestine: A Personal Account of the Intifada Years*. Minneapolis, MN: University of Minnesota Press, 1996.

Fisk, Robert. *Pity the Nation: The Abduction of Lebanon*. New York: Nation Books, 2002.

Gibran, Khalil, *The Prophet*. New York: Alfred A. Knopf, 1923.

Imulkais of Kinda. *The Sacred Books and Early Literature of the East*. Vol. 5, *Ancient Arabia*. Edited by Charles Horne, trans. F. E. Johnson with revisions by Sheikh Faizullah-bhai. New York and London: Parke, Austin and Lipscomb, 1917.

Karmi, Ghada. *In Search of Fatima: A Palestinian Story*. London: Verso, 2002.

Khalidi, Walid. *All That Remains: The Palestinian Villages Occupied and Depopulated by Israel in 1948*. Washington D.C.: Institute for Palestine Studies, 2006.

———. *Before Their Diaspora: A Photographic History of the Palestinians, 1876–1948*. Washington D.C.: Institute for Palestine Studies, 1991.

Palumbo, Michael. *The Palestinian Catastrophe: The 1948 Expulsion of a People from Their Homeland*. New York: Olive Branch Press, 1991.

Rumi, Jalal al-Din. *The Essential Rumi*. New York: HarperCollins, 1996.

Said, Edward W. *The Politics of Dispossession: The Struggle for Palestinian Self-Determination, 1969–1994*. New York: Vintage, 1994.

Slyomovics, Susan. *The Object of Memory: Arab and Jew Narrate the Palestinian Village*. Philadelphia: University of Pennsylvania Press, 1998.

Reading Group Guide

These discussion questions are designed to enhance your group's conversation about *Mornings in Jenin*, a powerful story of one family's endurance through sixty years of the Palestinian-Israeli conflict.

About this book

Mornings in Jenin follows four generations of the Abulheja family through upheaval and violence in their homeland. The family has deep roots in Ein Hod, a tranquil village of olive farmers. When Israel declares statehood in 1948, the peace of Ein Hod is shattered forever: The entire community is forced to move to a refugee camp in Jenin. As the young mother Dalia Abulheja guides her sons through the caravan of chaos, an Israeli soldier snatches her baby, Ismael, from her arms. The soldier brings the Palestinian child home to his wife, a Holocaust survivor, founding a family based on a lie: Baby Ismael grows up as David, an Israeli who will unwittingly fight against his own people in wars to come.

In Jenin, the Abulheja family welcomes a daughter, Amal, who loves nothing more than listening to her doting father, Hasan, read Arabic verses. But in the war of 1967, Hasan disappears, Dalia loses her wits, and young Amal barely survives a week hiding in a bomb shelter. Amal must leave Jenin behind in order to fulfill her lost father's wishes for her education. As Israeli-Palestinian tensions reach a crescendo in 1982, Amal loses almost everyone she loves in the Lebanon War. She must raise her newborn daughter, Sara, by herself in America, forever scarred by the loss of her homeland, her family, and her love. Only a visit from an Israeli named David—Amal's long-lost brother, on a quest for his true identity—can shake Amal from her stoicism, inspiring a return trip to the Middle East with her daughter. Together, Amal and Sara rediscover a shattered homeland that may never be the same.

Mornings in Jenin unveils the humanity behind one of the most intractable political conflicts of our time, revealing the universal desire for a homeland, community, and safety.

For discussion

1 *Mornings in Jenin* opens with a prelude set in Jenin in 2002, as Amal faces an Israeli soldier's gun. How does this prelude set the scene for the novel to come? Why does the novel open here, in contemporary Jenin, rather than at the beginning of the Abulheja family's story? Why do you think the author wanted the reader to know in the prelude that the main character was "an American citizen"?

2 Discuss the dual traditions of land and learning in the Abulheja family. Which members of the family seem to value land over education, and vice versa? In which family members do these two traditions come together? What common values do all members of this family share? How do these values compare to the values of farmers or of those who in another way live "close to the earth" in other countries?

3 The boyhood friendship between Hasan and Ari Perlstein is "consolidated in the innocence of their twelve years, the poetic solitude of books, and their disinterest in politics" (9). What do Hasan and Ari learn from each other? Considering that Palestine had historically been a country where people of all three monotheistic religions lived in relative harmony, do you think such friendships between children like Ari and Hasan were unusual then? Could two children like Hasan and Ari have become friends in a later time period? Why or why not?

4 In Jenin, the early morning "was a time and place where the hope of returning home could be renewed" (41). What rituals take place in the early morning hours? What is the significance of the title *Mornings in Jenin*?

5 Find scenes in the novel when family strife and political strife intersect. What are some problems that the Abulheja family faces day-to-day? Which family conflicts are caused by the political situation, and which seem common to families in all parts of the world?

6 Discuss the series of events that lead to Ismael's new life as David. What connections can be drawn between Moshe's kidnapping and Israel's actions toward the Palestinian people? What wounds are healed when David discovers his real identity?

7 Hasan tells his daughter, "Amal, with the long vowel, means hopes, dreams, lots of them" (72). What hopes and dreams does Amal's name suggest for the Abulheja family, and to what degree is she able to fulfill them? How do her hopes and dreams change when she calls herself "Amy" in America?

8 After surviving a week underground during the 1967 conflict, Amal denies knowing Dalia. Why does she renounce her mother? What are the consequences of Amal's "disgraceful lie" (74)?

9 Haj Salem tells Amal, "We're all born with the greatest treasures we'll ever have in life. One of those treasures is your mind, another is your heart" (133). How does Haj Salem's speech influence Amal's decision to go to school in Jerusalem? Explain why Amal considers his words "the greatest wisdom ever imparted to me by another human being" (133).

10 Amal and Yousef both lose the people they love most in the attacks on Lebanon in 1982. How do brother and sister react differently to their tragedies, and why? How does this tragedy drive them further apart, instead of closer in their grief? How do you think Amal's reaction might have been different had she not been pregnant?

11 Amal associates Dalia's stoic behavior with a line of her mother's advice: "Whatever you feel, keep it inside" (204). When does Amal follow Dalia's example, and when does she break from it? How does Amal's behavior with her daughter, Sara, resemble Dalia's mothering? Discuss how Amal comes to the following realization: "Dalia, Um Yousef, the untiring mother who gave far more than

she ever received, was the tranquil, quietly toiling well from which I have drawn strength all my life" (274).

12 Consider the Israeli characters within *Mornings in Jenin*: Ari Perlstein, Moshe, Jolanta, and David's sons. How do their experiences compare to the experiences of the Abulheja family? What do these Israeli voices add to the novel?

13 What layers of meaning can you find in the title of part III, "The Scar of David," which was the original title of the book?

14 On page 270, when David asks if Amal still sees him as an abstraction, she thinks, "No . . . You and I are the remains of an unfulfilled legacy, heirs to a kingdom of stolen identities and ragged confusion." What do you think Amal means by this? How do you see this statement in the context of the Palestinian struggle?

15 In their final conversations, as tanks roll through Jenin, Amal explains many of her hardships to her daughter, Sara. Why did Amal grieve "three thousand times" on September 11th (300)? How was Amal's experience similar and different from the widows' of 9/11? How did Sara misinterpret her mother's grief at the time?

16 Nearly all of the characters in this book are transformed in one way or another by personal and international events. How are the transformations of Moshe, Dalia, Amal, and Yousef similar and how are they different? Of them, who undergoes the most dramatic change?

17 Why does the novel end with words from Yousef, who lives in exile? What mood does Yousef's perspective create at the end of the book? Is it a surprise to learn that Yousef had not driven the bomb truck into the U.S. embassy in 1983? Considering that the PLO fighters who were exiled to Tunis in 1982 lost their families in the Sabra and Shatila carnage and none chose to respond with violence, why do you think the author chose this ending? What is the significance of the chapter title "The Cost of Palestine"?

18 If at all, how has this story changed how you view the Palestinian-Israeli conflict? Did you learn things that surprised you?

19 In the chapter where the story comes full circle to the prelude, how do you think Amal can face this soldier holding a rifle to her

head with "a mother's love and a dead woman's calm" (305)? In this same chapter, consider the following passage in the context of how you think of soldiers and war, whether in your own country or elsewhere:

The power he holds over life is a staggering burden for so young a man. He knows it and wants it lifted. He is too handsome not to have a girlfriend nervously waiting for his return. He would rather be with her than with his conscience . . . But he has never seen his victim's face. My eyes, soft with a mother's love and a dead woman's calm, weigh him down with his own power and I think he will cry. Not now. Later. When he is face-to-face with his dreams and his future. I feel sad for him. Sad for the boy bound to the killer. I am sad for the youth betrayed by their leaders for symbols and flags and war and power.

Suggested reading

Khaled Hosseini, *The Kite Runner* and *A Thousand Splendid Suns*; Sandy Tolan, *The Lemon Tree*; Jean Said Makdisi, *Teta, Mother, and Me: Three Generations of Arab Women*; Edward Said, *Out of Place: A Memoir*; Ibtisam Barakat, *Tasting the Sky: A Palestinian Childhood*; Sari Nusseibeh, *Once Upon a Country: A Palestinian Life*; Rajah Shehadeh, *Palestinian Walks: Forays into a Vanishing Landscape*; Ghada Karmi, *In Search of Fatima: A Palestinian Story*; Mourid Barghouti, *I Saw Ramallah*; Elizabeth Laird, *A Little Piece of Ground*.